TRIO OF SEDUCTION

Also by Cassie Ryan:

VISION OF SEDUCTION

CEREMONY OF SEDUCTION

Published by Kensington Publishing Corporation

TRIO OF SEDUCTION

CASSIE RYAN

APHRODISIA

KENSINGTON BOOKS
http://www.kensingtonbooks.com

APHRODISIA BOOKS are published by

Kensington Publishing Corp.
119 West 40th Street
New York, NY 10018

All Kensington Titles, Imprints, and Distributed Lines are available at special quantity discounts for bulk purchases for sales promotions, premiums, fund-raising, and educational or institutional use.

Special book excerpts or customized printings can also be created to fit specific needs. For details, write or phone the office of the Kensington special sales manager: Kensington Publishing Corp., 119 West 40th Street, New York, NY 10018, attn: Special Sales Department, Phone: 1-800-221-2647.

Aphrodisia and the A logo Reg. U.S. Pat. & TM Off.

ISBN-13: 978-0-7582-2067-7
ISBN-10: 0-7582-2067-7

First Kensington Trade Paperback Printing: August 2009

10 9 8 7 6 5 4 3 2 1

Printed in the United States of America

To Phillip, for reminding me that the young, vivacious girl I used to be is still alive and well twenty-five years later . . .

Acknowledgments

Thanks must first and foremost go to Darian, my biggest fan, even though he isn't allowed to read these books until he moves out. ☺

Also, thanks to Jon—anyone who can live with a writer without losing their sanity deserves all the appreciation they can get. You encouraged me to follow my dreams and write, and I'm thankful for that every single day.

Thanks also to my critique group, the Butterscotch Martini Girls (www.butterscotchmartinigirls.com). Without all your love, support, and sometimes more-honest-than-I-want feedback, ladies, none of this would be possible. ☺

To my amazing agent, Paige Wheeler, for all that you do.

To Audrey LaFehr, my editor, and the entire team at Kensington for all their hard work and support.

To all my readers and fans. I LOVE all the emails and letters and appreciate all of you who have fallen in love with these characters. Long live Tador!!

1

I'm smiling. That should scare the hell out of you.

Kiera Matthews took a deep breath and prayed for patience. She knew her temper was already on full simmer when she started thinking in sarcastic quotes.

"It's only because of your past assistance to our people that I don't report you to the council at once." Council Member Danen stood before her, all five feet nothing of impotent arrogance.

Simmer flashed to near boil, and Kiera resisted the urge to scream. But she couldn't quite stop her eyes from narrowing at the rail-thin man with the dour expression who stood before her. She supposed she should be thankful he had agreed to meet with her at all—even in the middle of a deserted parking lot at midnight.

The council was not only arrogant, but they also had a tendency toward drama.

"Bullshit, Danen." Kiera took a step forward, invading his personal space. "The only reason any of you put up with me is because I'm the only doctor willing to treat you—regardless of insurance or circumstances that would be best left undiscovered by the human community."

Danen's already knobby chin jutted out farther as he pursed his lips in obvious distaste. "Let's cut through all the preliminaries, Kiera. What exactly do you want?"

"I want the council to listen to reason before it's too late." She fisted her hands at her sides to keep from giving in to the urge to shake the little man. "The civil war happened a quarter of a century ago, Danen. My mother would still be alive if not for the fallout from that." Kiera's temper fed fuel to her rant, and she couldn't seem to stop the flow of words that spilled from her lips. "The Cunts used to be a proud people with a rich heritage before they let Sela put her wishes above the well-being of the entire race. In fact, before she started spreading dissension, the Klatch and the Cunts lived in peace as one people—as it was meant to be. Long before the name of our race became synonymous with traitor in the human dialect."

She tucked a wisp of blond hair, which had come loose from her ponytail and fallen across her eyes, behind her ear. "Now you can't even say 'cunt' without it being construed as a serious insult. Don't you think it's time to reevaluate what's best for our species as a whole?"

Danen's gaunt features stiffened, and his already pale skin glistened in the light of the full moon. "You aren't yet twenty-four. Not even old enough for a coming-of-age—even if you were pure blood."

The snub about her split heritage hit hard, and she winced. No matter that she was now a grown woman, the taunts that rang in her ears as she grew up still haunted her.

Danen stared down his sticklike nose at her, while his bloodless lips thinned into nonexistence. "As it is, you are in no position at all to question the council. You've lived on the fringes of our law since you were a teenager—and only because you've been useful as a doctor. You're more human than Cunt. Your mother made that choice for you when she openly married that useless human."

Kiera's anger exploded, and a vivid picture of throttling the little man sprang into her mind. "My mother was a full-blooded Cunt, you little bastard—"

Shouts broke through the still air of the stifling Phoenix night, cutting off her words and rechanneling her anger into self-preservation.

Blue and pink bolts of electricity—the weapons of choice for the Cunts and Klatch, respectively—snaked through the moon-lit sky, raising the small hairs on Kiera's arms.

The stench of sulfur hung heavy in the air, and she tasted the tang of ozone on the back of her tongue.

Skin tingled as adrenaline flooded her system, and she crouched into a fighting stance.

Her gaze scanned her surroundings in search of the enemy as training and instinct kicked in.

Thank God for a human marine colonel father who taught his baby girl to kick some ass when needed.

A pink sizzling bolt arced straight for her, and she rolled to the left. A tingling sensation crackled up her right side, nearly stealing her breath. A rush of pure power—no doubt fueled by adrenaline—surged through her as she completed the roll and landed lightly back on the balls of her feet.

"You did this!" Danen screamed behind her, too intent on his own self-righteous fury to duck.

She shifted her balance and, with one leg extended, swept the man's feet out from under him, catching his frail form in her outstretched arms before his head hit the blacktop. "Get down, you arrogant ass! I didn't bring anyone."

Danen shoved out of her embrace, thumping hard on his ass against the blacktop, and then crab walked away from her. "You're a traitor, Kiera Matthews!" He pushed up onto his knees and raised his hands, blue energy already sparking from his fingertips.

Without thinking, Kiera straightened, took two running steps and then snapped her right heel forward into a front kick.

The blow caught Danen square in the chest.

The gangly man flew backward to land hard on the rough blacktop. His body bounced once, his skinny limbs akimbo, before he came to rest and lay still.

"Danen!" came a voice from off to her left.

Kiera had no time to check on the old man or even to try to explain. The council guards had a reputation for killing and maiming now and sorting out the truth later.

A pink energy bolt zoomed toward her face before she could do more than close her eyes against the impact.

She held her breath, but other than a surge of power through her entire body, she felt nothing.

Angry shouts and cursing filled her ears, but no searing pain like she had expected.

What the fuck?

Kiera snapped her eyes open in time to see two burly blond guards lunge for her.

She feinted left.

Both guards changed the direction of their attack to follow.

She brought her elbow around, and aided by the first guard's forward motion, smashed him in the nose.

Hot blood spurted, coating her forearm as she allowed the momentum to bring her full circle.

The injured guard howled in pain and cradled his mangled nose.

With her right foot still planted firmly, she struck out with her left, hitting the second guard just above the kneecap.

A sickening crunch filled the air as his knee dislocated. His ashen features contorted with pain before he crumpled.

She spun around, alert for more attackers, and found only one.

A Klatch—the sworn enemy of her mother's people. Or at least they had been for the past twenty-four years.

Her fleeting thought of attack was interrupted by his easy, arrogant stance—not to mention he was the most beautiful man she had ever seen.

Lucky for him, unlike most of the Cunts, she attacked only those who threatened her. So she stayed alert and studied the dark stranger.

Mercy, not lust. Yeah, that's it.

She had seen several half-breed Klatch in her clinic over the years, but had never met a full blood that she knew of—or at least one with this much presence. Power radiated off this man in nearly visible waves, and she had the sudden urge to trace the muscles she saw through his tight black T-shirt.

She knew she should be terrified. After all, this man was an enemy to Cunts everywhere, and yet, all she felt was . . . safe.

Kiera shoved the disturbing thought aside to study later.

The stranger stood a good six inches taller than her own five-feet-six, with a stocky compact build that reminded her of a boxer. Even when he remained still, he exuded a contained physical energy she somehow knew would be formidable when unleashed.

Thick dark hair fell to his shoulders and shadowed the right side of his face. The left side, which was illuminated by moonlight, was chiseled, rugged and handsome.

His sensual mouth curved into an amused grin, which matched the laughter shining in his dark eyes.

Great. Caught staring like an open-mouthed idiot!

Her mouth went dry and her heart pounded so loud she was surprised he couldn't hear it. She closed her mouth and moved her balance to the balls of her feet for lack of anything better to do.

"Nice moves." He held his arms wide as if to show he was no threat. But the sudden wave of heat zinging through her body said differently. "I saw that energy beam hit you in the face." His voice was rich and dark like decadent chocolate, and she could tell he would have a beautiful tenor singing voice. Hell, just his speaking voice was enough to melt her into a puddle. Kiera wasn't sure she could handle his singing without experiencing spontaneous combustion—or orgasm.

The thought sent a wave of shivers through her body.

"I have never seen a human survive that," he continued, thankfully unaware of her thoughts. "Are you all right?"

The word "human" hung in the air between them like an accusation, and the familiar shame of being a half-breed burned inside her chest.

Bastard.

Shame morphed into anger in an instant, and she wrapped it around her like a shield. "No thanks to you, I'm all right." She stalked forward until she stood just outside his reach. "I spent months getting them to agree to meet, and now the Cunt Council thinks I set them up!"

His dark brow furrowed. "For what—" His gaze snapped to somewhere over her shoulder.

"Look out!" He lunged forward, knocking her over just as a searing wave of heat sizzled past.

Kiera landed on her back, hard. All the air whooshed out of her lungs in a painful rush.

The hot blacktop dug into her skin through her cotton T-shirt, but she barely noticed.

Instead, it was the hard muscles of the very warm male pressing down on her that filled her senses. She raised her gaze and gasped as she nearly drowned in the deep purple—almost black—eyes staring down at her.

A surreal sense of déjà vu and destiny flowed over her, and she frowned against the intense sensation.

His gaze burned into hers for another moment, and then he blinked, breaking the strange spell that held her. He took a deep breath, which only served to press their chests more tightly together, and said, "Hold off, Gavin! I'm fine."

His loud words made her jump, and she nearly laughed as she realized the reason for his deep breath had nothing to do with tormenting her with his hard body.

When he had lifted his head to shout, both halves of his face were bathed in moonlight, giving her an up close view of the angry red scar that ran from his temple to the right side of his mouth. It gave him a rakish, dangerous air, and her fingers itched to trace the puckered red line and sample its texture.

He dropped his chin, and his warm breath feathered against her face. "Are you all right?"

"Prince Ryan!"

She jumped again as the new male voice startled her out of her reverie. *Shit! I'm under a Klatch prince?*

Panic and mortification flowed over her, quickly followed by a large dose of protective anger. Since when did she let her guard down in such an unknown situation?

Kiera braced her legs, and in a quick maneuver her father taught her, she reversed their positions.

He struggled against her move, and when she put all her weight on her right knee to catch her balance, instead of blacktop, her knee met flesh. Hard.

"Urgh!" The prince curled up, his body instinctively protecting itself as he clutched his crotch.

Heat seared her cheeks as she realized she'd landed all her weight on his groin.

Damn it. He shouldn't have moved!

Kiera pushed to her feet and fled into the night.

Ryan de Klatch, the Tenth Prince of Klatch, rolled onto his side as he concentrated on sucking air into his lungs to cool the throbbing pain in his balls. The smell of burnt oil, tar and exhaust filled his senses, and he coughed—then winced as the spasms reached his aching groin.

Footsteps pounded closer until Gavin, the captain of the Klatch royal guard, filled his vision. "Prince Ryan, are you hurt?"

Ryan swallowed hard. "Only my pride." *And possibly my ability to add to the Klatch bloodline.*

Gavin's serious expression never changed. "My apologies for being late, my lord. There were a dozen more Cunts around the side of the building we had to neutralize. The other guards are keeping the perimeter clear."

"Good thing you have confidence in my ability to defend myself." Ryan rolled onto his back and sat up. Nausea roiled inside his stomach, and he widened his thighs to give his tender balls some room to recover.

"If I thought you couldn't, I would've brought more men and not let you out of our sight. I figured you could hold your own against one old man, a few guards and a tiny wisp of a woman— until you tackled her, that is." The guard stood and held out a hand to help Ryan up. "My lord," Gavin added as an obvious sarcastic afterthought.

Ryan shook his head and laughed. He accepted the hand and stood, adjusting his jeans so they wouldn't pinch his injured manhood. "Bastard," he said with affection. Gavin had taught Ryan much of what he knew about fighting and spell casting— at least those portions that weren't considered acceptable for a royal prince to learn. The rest he had learned from a royal tutor. Over the years, Ryan had forged a close bond with the guard, which he still appreciated today.

There had been many times over the course of his life that those "not acceptable for a prince" skills had kept him alive or unharmed.

Except for that once.

He traced his fingers over the bottom edge of his scar where it met the side of his mouth as he shoved the painful memories away.

He glanced back at Gavin and smiled, bringing himself back to the present. "If you were so sure I could handle it, why did you aim an energy beam at her?"

Gavin's lavender eyes narrowed. "None of my guards sent that beam. Are you sure it was a Klatch beam?"

"Very sure. It was pink and came from your direction." Unease tightened Ryan's stomach. Perhaps there were even more Klatch traitors they hadn't discovered when the Seer was found. If so, he had to settle things with the Healer quickly. The sooner the Triangle was instituted, the better.

"I'll get to the bottom of it, my prince; you have my word."

Of that, Ryan had no doubt. Gavin was an excellent captain of the guard and had held that position for the past forty years—although thanks to the regenerative powers of their home planet of Tador, the man still looked to be a very fit midthirties.

Ryan nodded in response and then grinned as he thought about the little blond ball of fire who had nearly emasculated him. "If that 'wisp' of a woman is the Healer, I'm in for a long, bumpy ride." In his mind's eye, he replayed the scene, enjoying both the passion in her eyes when she'd defended herself from the guards and the sensual wonder in those same blue orbs when he lay on top of her with their gazes locked.

Gavin grunted. "I think perhaps before we return to Tador, we should stop by the store and buy you an athletic supporter with a sturdy cup."

"I don't intend to give her another chance to rack me, but thanks." Ryan brushed blacktop debris off his shirt and jeans.

"You did notice she's part Cunt?" The guard's voice was sharp as his gaze swept the parking lot, never landing on Ryan. "Or did that escape your notice while you were pressing against her softer parts?"

Surprise had Ryan turning to look at the guard. He had assumed she was human, and since she used no magic to defend herself, he hadn't bothered to expand his senses to check.

The guard chuckled. "I didn't think you'd noticed. You always have been a sucker for a pair of nice eyes and a shapely . . . form . . . my lord."

Gavin had fought in Tador's planetary civil war against the Cunts and still held some resentment—like most Klatch. After all, hundreds of Klatch died, unaware, the day Sela and the Cunt Council decided to try to overthrow the throne.

Ryan bit back a sigh. He and his generation had fought and even killed a few Cunt warriors over the years, as well. However, those were all in self-defense, as far as he knew. He wasn't naive enough to think most Klatch would be content to wait until their lives were threatened to kill their old enemies.

As it was, he had a few Cunt resentments of his own. His fingers traced the roughened scar that ran from his temple to the right side of his mouth. Painful memories threatened to flood back, and he shoved them aside again. Lately, those memories had ridden much closer to the surface than was comfortable.

Grappling with the little Cunt spitfire definitely hadn't helped.

If the Seer was right, and this blond beauty was the Healer for the Triangle, then he had much bigger problems than dealing with the past. The entire planet was in for an uphill battle. "Did you also notice she didn't attack me and that the other Cunts didn't seem too friendly toward her?" He thought back over their brief conversation. "She said the Cunt Council now thought she was a traitor."

"Doesn't mean we know where her loyalties lie," Gavin said matter-of-factly, although he didn't sound like he believed his own words, which surprised Ryan. "She's the doctor who treats both Cunts and Klatch with no questions asked. Her mother was a Cunt, but the daughter has never allied herself with either side beyond that." Even as he spoke, his gaze scanned their surroundings in a constant state of alert. Ryan had grown used to it over the years and took no offense.

"If she has been declared a traitor, she's no longer safe here on Earth," Ryan said softly as his mind filtered through all the ramifications of such a statement.

The old man, who still lay in a heap on the asphalt, groaned, cutting off their discussion.

Ryan motioned for Gavin to follow him and then headed toward the shadows before the man came to. The whole purpose in coming here tonight was to find the Healer, so there was no reason to stay longer. "Call nine-one-one for the old man, Gav. It looks like the Cunts aren't coming back for him."

"As you say, my lord."

Ryan ignored the proper words, since Gavin's tone showed he would've been more than happy to leave the man lying on the ground indefinitely. But Ryan also knew Gavin's personal feelings on the subject wouldn't affect his judgment or his job—or at least it never had. "For now, we have to get back to Tador. I think I need to have another discussion with the Seer."

2

Kiera slammed the front door of her house behind her and turned the deadbolt so hard, she was surprised the doorframe didn't crack.

Emotions swirled through her in a rush that made her head swim. "Months of careful planning wasted!" She leaned back against the door and allowed herself a few deep breaths to calm the coursing adrenaline.

The entire Cunt council would think she was a traitor by now, which meant she wasn't safe here. The days of them tolerating her for her medical skills were long gone if they thought she tried to hand over a council member to the Klatch.

Not that they would waste magical resources to terminate her. They would send their half-breed or outright human contingents to do their dirty work. But at least those two groups were susceptible to human weapons.

"Damn him!" The dark eyes of the Klatch prince burned through her mind's eye, bringing with it each sensual memory of how his hard body had felt on top of hers. Angry with herself for noticing, she shrugged the sensation away. "Why did he have to show up?"

She glanced around the living room still decorated as her father had left it—an eclectic mix of United States Marine Corps military medals, sports memorabilia and old west collectibles.

Her heart ached at the thought of leaving this all behind.

Despite all the evidence to the contrary, she had held out hope that some day she would come home and find her father sitting in his favorite ratty recliner, laughing and joking like he used to. But it had been five long years since she had found him unconscious on the floor with all the indications of multiple energy-beam hits to the chest.

Which meant witches of one race or the other.

Of course, the military doctors didn't recognize the symptoms, and she couldn't very well enlighten them. She knew better than most that humans didn't like what they didn't understand. In her small clinic, she had treated many Cunts, as well as Klatch and Cunt half-breeds, who had been injured at the hands of humans. Then again, there were also many cases where they had injured each other.

A heavy weariness threatened to settle over her as it always did when she thought about the past. She shoved it aside and banged her head back against the door a few times, hoping to break herself away from the emotions those memories brought.

She had never found out who or why her father had been attacked, and he hadn't woken since.

However, she was enough her father's daughter to know he would want her to put her own life above sentimentality. He was as safe as he could be in the Phoenix VA hospital; now she just had to get herself to safety.

Kiera closed her eyes and carefully walled off her emotions, just as she had so many other times over the years. She pictured pouring all her pain and fear into a large shoebox and then closing the lid before stacking it on top of the growing pile of closed boxes inside her mind.

Her eyes snapped open, and the familiar calm of knowing what to do and carrying it out enveloped her. "Get your butt in gear, woman!" She smiled as she said the words aloud, since she could almost hear her father's deep voice booming those same words.

She jogged down the hallway and into the kitchen until she came to the pantry just under the stairs. The door swung open at her touch, and rather than stepping in, she reached inside and up above the doorframe. Her fingers traced the seam of the wall where it met the ceiling until she found the latch, which to anyone else would feel like a rough spot on the sloping ceiling of the pantry. She pressed the latch for exactly four seconds and then let go and stepped back.

A large cubby as wide as the pantry door slid open from the ceiling to reveal a black backpack full of everything she would need to get away or even start a new life, if it came to that. She hefted the backpack over one shoulder and then dug a quarter out of her pocket and tossed it inside the cubby, where it landed with a quiet *thunk*.

The quarter was a signal between her and her father, which would let him know which safe house she planned to go to first.

Kiera swallowed hard as she realized her dad would probably never see it, and she was totally and completely on her own. She clenched her jaw and closed the cubby with the quarter still inside. After she closed the pantry door, she walked down the short hallway to the garage.

Her father's Humvee sat next to her purple PT Cruiser, and she huffed out a breath as she realized she would have to leave her car behind, too. That was the price of having such a distinctive car in a closed community—not to mention the "WTCHDR" license plate. It had been somewhat of a joke at the time, but over the years since she had opened her clinic, it had made her easy for her target clientele to find.

Her gaze swept the inside of the garage to make sure nothing had been disturbed.

Floor-to-ceiling cabinets ran along each side of the garage, and at the back, where normal people would put a washer and dryer, her father had installed a heavy-duty fireproof gun safe, which ran the width of the space and stood six feet high. Her father had it specially made and equipped with state-of-the-art security measures.

Marine colonel's liked their firearms and other goodies protected.

Kiera pressed her thumb to the entry pad of the gun safe. After scanning her thumbprint and matching it to the approved users—only she and her father—a small black panel popped open to reveal the combination lock.

Her fingers reached for the dial.

A blur of dark orange fell from above, knocking her arm away.

Kiera whirled to face her attacker, and a loud "mrowwr" sounded near her feet.

"Damn it, Shiloh!"

Her father's orange tabby cat swiveled his head, and she found herself on the receiving end of an unblinking orange-eyed glare. The effect was made more intense by the fact that a perfect line of white ringed both eyes like fur eyeliner. The rest of Shiloh was alternating stripes of dark and lighter orange, with white only around his eyes, on his toes and at the tip of his tail.

"Sorry, Shi," she mumbled as she reached for the safe's dial again. "It's been a rough day."

In one fluid motion, the cat jumped up on top of the gun safe, curled his paws over the top edge and rested his chin lightly between them.

Kiera sighed. She had forgotten all about Shiloh. Her escape plan hadn't included a cat. However, since Shiloh and her father had basically adopted each other a few months before he was attacked, she couldn't very well leave Shiloh here to fend for himself.

Though she would pity the person who broke in here with the moody tabby on the loose.

Kiera and Shiloh had developed somewhat of an uneasy co-existence since her father had gone to the hospital. Kiera didn't particularly like cats, and Shiloh loved to annoy her. She'd actually grown used to having the feisty feline around and even held an odd fondness for him—something she would never admit openly.

The combination dial slid toward the last number, and the safe made a loud click as bars disengaged and allowed her to pull the heavy door open.

The strong scent of chocolate-covered cherries filled her senses, and the familiar sting of unshed tears burned the backs of her eyes. Her father never smoked his signature cigars inside the house, but whenever he cleaned his weapons or rearranged items in his safe, there was always a fat stogie clamped between his teeth.

Damn, I miss him.

She mentally shook herself and steeled her resolve. After all, her father would kick her ass if he found out sentimentality had gotten her captured.

Inside the safe, she found all her father's weapons just as he had left them, along with extra ammunition and enough knives and other tools of combat to supply a small rebel army.

She pulled a large black gun duffel from the bottom cabinet and loaded an assortment of guns, ammunition, knives and other goodies into the bag. Guns weren't always very effective against either race of witches, but there were enough humans and even half-breeds who were sympathetic with the Cunt Council that the assorted hardware would probably come in very handy.

The Humvee opened when she pressed in the code just under the door handle, and she tossed the gun duffel into the hidden panel under the back hatch and then set her backpack on the backseat.

A quick trip to the kitchen provided a bag full of cat food, basic nonperishable human food and medicinal supplies, which she placed next to her backpack.

"Shiloh," she called to the cat still perched on top of the gun safe.

The cat stretched and then yawned before he jumped down and ambled forward as if he had all the time in the world.

"I wish Dad had gotten you used to a cat carrier. Then I could just toss your kitty ass in and get moving!"

Shiloh ignored her angry words and finally made his way to the Humvee, where he jumped in and curled into the front passenger seat where he had always ridden when her dad had taken him on trips.

Kiera slammed the door to the Humvee and walked back through the house, arming security sensors and testing locks. She knew nowhere was impenetrable, especially for the Cunts, but she refused to make it easy for them.

Finally, she slipped inside her room and pulled a large shoebox from under her bed. It held the last remnants she had of her mother, and she couldn't bear the thought of them being taken or destroyed. Her mother had risked her life and her place in Cunt society to marry her father and try to give Kiera a normal life—and she had paid for it, dearly.

Kiera would always respect that, even though the decision had taken her mother from her.

With a last look around at the top floor of the house, she took the stairs two at a time, and almost as an afterthought, grabbed her father's framed military medals off the wall and tucked them under her other arm.

She pulled the garage door shut behind her and set the house perimeter alarms before she turned back to the gun safe. The shoebox and the framed military medals fit snugly in the bottom drawer after she rearranged the Japanese throwing stars and the nunchucks. The drawer slid easily closed, which allowed her to close the heavy safe door and click the entry pad back in place over the combination dial.

With a last wistful look at her PT Cruiser, she slid into the Humvee and fastened her seatbelt. "Hold on tight, Shiloh. This may be a bumpy ride."

Kiera drove until her eyes stung with fatigue. Shiloh purred softly on the passenger seat beside her, where he had curled, dozing through four changes of license plates, three stops for gas and one indulgent stop at a drive-through Starbucks for an iced venti caffe latte with a quad shot of espresso.

"Damn cat. A lot of help you are." She scowled at the peaceful feline, who seemed to only purr louder at her words.

Her headlights cut a dim path through the darkened haze of predawn, and she almost missed the slightly obscured gravel driveway to the safe house she and her father had set up in case of emergency. There were actually seven of them in different locales, but she chose this one since it was the closest to home.

The Humvee barely fit down the small gravel road to the cabin, and the screech of low hanging branches brushing the side of the vehicle made her jump until her tired brain made sense of the noise. After a few winding curves, the headlights shone on a small log cabin with a tiny attached garage.

Adrenaline surged back into Kiera's veins as her gaze swept the perimeter for any sign of something out of place. When nothing jumped out of the shadows at her, she stopped the Humvee and slid out of the driver's side with the Ruger her father had given her cradled in her palm. She disengaged the safety and started forward with the muzzle of the gun pointed down and to the side.

The strong scent of pine and rich earth filled each breath,

and she breathed deep since the smell brought back cherished memories of time spent camping with her father.

Something brushed her right ankle and she bit back a scream.

Then her mind processed the identity of the orange streak that raced toward the front door of the cabin.

Shiloh.

"Fucking cat," she muttered under her breath. *My own fault for not shutting the car door.* He would have to fend for himself if he wasn't careful.

Her gaze swept over everything, cataloging distances, possible hiding places and escape routes as she went.

The attached garage was manually operated with a handle that had a keyhole in it. It marred the rustic simplicity of the log cabin next to it, but since a garage would make it easier to conceal the Humvee, she really couldn't complain. The windows of the two-story cabin were dark, and large thick trees and foliage enclosed the sides of the structure, casting it in further shadow, since only slivers of moonlight peeked through the thick cloud cover.

With the Ruger a comforting weight in her hand, she carefully made her way around the side of the cabin where Shiloh had disappeared. She slid in between the side of the cabin and close-growing trees, thankful for the generous cover the forest provided.

Her tennis shoes crunched softly against the pine needles that padded the forest floor, but she detected nothing out of place.

When she reached the back corner of the house, she approached the porch that ran the full length of the cabin and overlooked the lake.

Soft sounds of the water lapping against the shore blended with the crickets and the lone hoot of an owl in the distance.

She peered across the lake, but even in the weak moonlight, she could see there were no boats breaking the glossy surface.

Kiera turned her attention back toward the porch, which was supported by large round beams of thick wood since the ground veered sharply down toward the lake. This would be a great place to watch the sunrise and sunset—after she made sure there was no one here who wanted to kill her.

Details . . .

She crouched, her gaze sweeping under the porch to make sure nothing hid between the large wood supports. She found nothing but overgrown vegetation and rocks.

The hair on the back of Kiera's neck prickled along with a strong sense of being watched.

She straightened, her Ruger coming up to firing position.

Two wide orange eyes stared back at her from the porch, over the barrel of her gun.

"Mrowwr."

Kiera's hands shook as she slowly lowered her arm and briefly considered strangling the cat. "I should fucking shoot you," she whispered to Shiloh through clenched teeth.

The cat stretched and padded to the back door, where he promptly sat and began to clean his paws.

A few deep breaths calmed her heart enough to allow her to finish her perimeter check. When she found nothing out of place, she unlocked the front door and systematically checked each room of the small cabin.

Only a few dust bunnies greeted her, so she pulled the Humvee into the garage, unloaded half her cache of weapons and closed and locked the door behind her before venturing back inside the cabin. After a last quick look around, she set the alarms and stumbled upstairs to the master bedroom.

Her eyes burned and her limbs felt as if they weighed a thousand pounds each. She collapsed on the bed, not even bothering to kick off her shoes. Shiloh jumped up beside her, curling against her stomach, and she closed her eyes, sighing as the soft purrs soothed her to sleep.

Ryan stepped through the portal back onto his home planet of Tador and winced as bright sunlight surrounded him. Goose-flesh marched down his arms at the sudden temperature change, and he stepped off to the side to leave room for the Klatch guards who followed him. It took a few minutes for his eyes to adjust to the bright clear day after the inky blackness of the *between*.

For some reason, he always forgot Phoenix and Tador were on opposite schedules. Most likely because the bone-chilling cold of the *between*—the portal between the two worlds—took all his energy and attention just to traverse.

Fatigue weighted his limbs, and he briefly considered stopping by his rooms for food and sexual sustenance. As a Klatch witch, he needed sexual energy to survive and thrive just as much as he needed food and rest. However, whereas before tonight his fantasies had always been filled with soft willing women with dark hair and lavender eyes, they now featured a hellion with blond hair, deep blue eyes and sensual full lips.

"Here." Gavin handed Ryan a small leather bag. "There's some cheese, bread, fruit and a small skin of wine. That should hold you until you return from your discussion with the Seer. She is out at the waterfall looking for the hidden alcove mentioned in her childhood journals."

No one had been more surprised than Ryan to find out the imaginary friend he had played with as a child had actually grown into a flesh and blood Earth woman—not to mention a powerful seer. Before the Seer and Prince Grayson were married a few weeks ago, Katelyn had found mention in her child-hood journals of a hidden alcove with a statue that related to the Triangle that could save Tador.

Apparently, the Seer was finally getting around to searching for it.

Everyone hoped whatever lay in that alcove would help them unravel some of the mystery behind the Triangle and all it entailed.

Queen Alyssandra had taken a big chance reinstituting the Triangle she had only read about in some of the ancient queen's journals. But the planet of Tador was too far gone for her to fully heal it on her own. She knew she needed Ryan and Grayson's help to institute the Triangle and heal Tador.

And it couldn't happen soon enough, if Ryan had finally found the Healer.

A sensual memory filled his mind of how the Healer's lithe body had felt under him while her defiant gaze blazed into his. His cock surged to life inside his already tight jeans, and he widened his stance, trying in vain for a more comfortable position—especially since his balls were still tender from their earlier mistreatment.

Gavin cleared his throat, startling him from his musings. Ryan glanced around and realized the remaining guards had gone on their way, leaving just him, Gavin and the portal sentry. "Sorry, I was just taking a moment to—"

"Don't bother to make up an excuse." Amusement danced in Gavin's lavender eyes. "I know you well enough to know you were thinking about your Healer—even though you should be replenishing your energy between some willing Klatch maid's thighs." The guard shook his head. "I must report to the king and queen. I'll catch up with you later to see if the alcove has been found. I want to get out of these uncomfortable Earth clothes as soon as possible." Without waiting for an answer, Gavin walked down the path toward the castle.

Ryan watched Gavin as he disappeared down the path without a backward glance. He had to admit Gavin had a point. A pair of breeches was much less restricting than the pair of tight jeans he wore—especially when even the smallest thought of the fiery blond made his cock hard. He shook his head and laughed at himself.

A gentle breeze tousled Ryan's hair and brought the rich scents of roses, jasmine, gardenias and fertile soil. He inhaled, enjoying the lush clean air after the thick stench of car exhaust and heat-baked asphalt in Phoenix.

Phoenix was one of the cleaner cities he had visited on Earth, but it couldn't compare with the paradise that was his home world. *At least for now . . .*

His thoughts turned dark as he started down the opposite path that would take him to the waterfall.

The destruction of Tador edged closer and closer to the populated areas with each passing day. If the Triangle wasn't instituted soon, the utopian landscape before him would end up as nothing but a desolate wasteland like the outlying areas.

His chest tightened at the thought of such a fate, and he shoved it away. He and the rest of the royal family would fight until their last breath to save Tador and their way of life. There was nothing he wouldn't do to save the planet.

Leaves and twigs crunched softly under his boots, and the sound of rushing water grew louder as he neared the waterfall. As always, the rhythmic music of the falls mellowed his mood and filled him with hope.

He skirted around the maze, which was made of thick green vines and shrubs meticulously groomed to keep the inner paths clear. The faint sound of female giggling reached him from just beyond the nearest maze wall, and he smiled.

Apparently there were some Klatch currently enjoying one of the many intimate dead ends within the maze. He hoped someday soon to show the Healer—

"Ryan!" The Seer's voice reached him a moment before she jogged into view. Her long red hair streamed behind her, and her green eyes flashed with agitation. "Hurry, the Healer needs you." She grabbed his hand and pulled him forward toward the waterfall.

Urgency sliced through him as he followed her. His guards had told him no one followed the Healer as she left. What if they were wrong and he had left her in danger?

Katelyn pulled him down to sit across from her on the sandy shore of the pool at the base of the waterfall. Her normally pale cheeks were flushed with color, making her freckles stand out, and a small crease furrowed between her red brows.

"Katie-cat," he said, using a nickname he'd given her when they were children and he thought her nothing more than an imaginary friend. "Calm down and tell me what's going on."

She sat cross-legged across from him, adjusting her flowing skirt around her legs before taking the bag Gavin had given Ryan and setting it aside to take both of his hands in hers. "I had a vision about the Healer, and I think she's in danger."

Anger and a sudden urge to protect the Healer rushed through him. He started to push to his feet, but Katelyn tightened her grip on his hands.

"Sit," she ordered. "I need to see if I can induce a vision, and I need you to help me focus it since I assume you saw the Healer." Katelyn's intense gaze burned into his as the question hung in the air between them.

Ryan knew Katelyn didn't often try to induce visions. Visions usually came when she least expected them, and those she tried to force cost her dearly. She must be truly concerned to attempt this.

"Yes," he answered before her impatient glare burned straight through his skull. He remembered the hard knee to the groin the Healer had left him with and winced.

Katelyn's laugh startled him. "From the look on your face, I'd say I like her already."

He opened his mouth to retort, but she didn't give him a chance.

"Close your eyes. Picture her as clearly as you can—eyes, hair, expressions, smell—everything you can think of will help."

Resigned, he closed his eyes and focused all his energy on picturing the Healer as he had last seen her.

When the Healer had neatly reversed their positions right before all her weight had settled squarely on his bollocks, he'd been surprised and more than a little impressed. Not only did he outweigh her, but she'd caught him by surprise since he had been too intent on her innocent blue gaze.

He smiled to himself; he would have to remember not to be fooled in the future. Innocent in some ways she may be, but he'd seen her fight, and she definitely knew how to take care of herself. The scene where she fought off the two Cunt guards replayed inside his mind and then dissolved like mist on the wind. Ryan stiffened as he fought to retain control, but then Katelyn's gentle pressure against his hands reminded him why they were there.

In his mind's eye, the scene reformed, and he saw a small log cabin with a dirty off-white attached garage. His senses expanded and refocused until he saw four humans dressed in black. They slipped silently through the woods, and he knew instinctively they were after the Healer.

"No!"

Katelyn's tight grip on his hands reminded him to stay focused, and he let her lead the way as their line of sight slipped easily through the front wall of the cabin and into each room until they found the Healer.

She lay face down, fully clothed, on top of a small twin bed with a large orange cat curled beside her. Some of her golden blond hair had come loose from her ponytail and wisped around her face in silky tendrils. Her left hand was curled under her chin, while her right was hidden from view under the pillow.

Lavender smudges sat just under her closed eyes, nearly

eclipsed by the thick fringe of golden lashes that rested lightly against her cheek. Her full lips were parted slightly in sleep.

The cat's head snapped up as if he sensed their scrutiny. He blinked large orange eyes and stared straight at them in accusation.

His fuzzy head swiveled toward the window over the bed, and he stood and hissed, his tail bottle-brushing as his back arched.

The Healer bolted to a sitting position, and her right hand emerged from under the pillow gripping a gun that looked almost too large for her hand. She scanned her surroundings, and when she seemed to find nothing amiss, she stood and ran from the room.

The sting of a hard slap across Ryan's jaw pulled him from the vision, and he opened his eyes to see Katie-cat's face nearly nose to nose with his.

It took a few minutes for the rushing sounds of the waterfall nearby and the smell of the plants to fill his senses again. Once they finally did, he noticed the strain etched across Katelyn's face and the dullness of her eyes.

"Are you all right?" Her voice was raspy and weak, and he blinked to clear the remaining lethargy left from the vision.

"I could ask you the same thing."

Ryan nodded and immediately dug into the bag Gavin had given him to find the bread. Carbs would help Katelyn recover faster. "Here. Eat this and then you can tell me if that's future, past or present we saw." He bit back all the other questions that flowed through his mind. Adrenaline still raced through his veins, and he had to concentrate on calming his galloping pulse. Ryan struggled against the urge to run off in search of the Healer.

Katelyn broke off a piece of bread and took a bite.

He didn't rush her, even though his mind screamed at him that action was needed now. Silence flowed between them as she ate half the bread and drank some of the wine. Color slowly seeped back into her cheeks, and her green eyes sparked once more with intelligence. She broke off a small piece of cheese and then sighed.

"You look like you're feeling better," he observed. "Are you ready to talk, or do you need another minute?"

She cocked her head to one side and considered him—a familiar gesture she'd done even as a child. "I'm well enough to answer you intelligently before you explode from practicing too much patience."

"So much for subtlety," he snapped then instantly regretted lashing out. Katie-cat was tying to help, and at great physical cost to herself. There was no reason to take out his frustration on her.

He tipped his chin toward his chest and allowed his hair to slip forward and hide the scar he carried since the day he'd turned twenty. At night, he still relived the searing pain of the metal cutting his flesh, along with the deep sense of betrayal and anger that inevitably went with such dreams. He resisted the urge to trace with his thumb the lower edge of the puckered skin where it met the side of his mouth, and he opened his mouth to apologize to Katelyn.

"No need to apologize or to cover your scar around me. Although, one of these days when you feel comfortable, I hope you'll trust me with the story of how you got it."

He glanced up into her intense green gaze, which held only fond affection, and knew he couldn't tell her. Even as much as he cared for her, the memories were too raw and painful.

"You forget. I know you too well." She grinned and handed him a piece of cheese. "You always were a moody bastard. The Healer will have her hands full." She nodded toward the cheese he held in his hand. "Your turn to eat while I talk. And, anyway, I think that scar makes you look dark and dashing, like a pirate."

Ryan bristled against her description of him and then nearly laughed as he realized Katelyn probably knew him better than anyone besides his two boyhood friends—Grayson and Stone.

Both of his male friends were now happily married to women Ryan adored. He hoped he was as lucky when his time came. His Healer had captured his lust and intrigue already, but he hoped she would also capture his mind and his heart. As a full-blooded prince of Klatch, he had always known it was his responsibility to carry on the line, which meant he would marry most likely for duty rather than love. Seeing his two friends so lucky in their matches had made him afraid to hope that lightning would strike a third time.

He took a bite of cheese then washed it down with some wine. The fruity flavor of the wine burst over his tongue and then spread warmth down his throat as he swallowed.

The gentle breeze tousled her unruly mane of red hair, and Katelyn brushed a few strands out of her eyes, tucking them behind her ear. "That vision felt like the future, but I can't be sure. You know I'm not as accurate with visions I try to call, rather than those that just come to me."

A tightness in Ryan's chest that he couldn't quite name made him long for more action and less discussion. "Is there any way to know where to find her or how much time we've got?"

"You don't think she can take care of herself?" Katelyn pierced him with her questioning green gaze. "I don't know anything about guns, but I would think sleeping with one under her pillow would tell me she knows enough about them not to blow off her own head."

"I know she can take care of herself," he said, remembering her fight with the two Cunt guards. "But—"

"But, you would feel better in all your maleness to go rushing in and kick some ass even if she doesn't need it, and even if it makes the situation worse."

Irritation at Katelyn's sharp tongue snapped through him,

and he clenched his fists as he searched for a suitable reply. When he found none, he bit back a sigh. "Damn," he finally muttered under his breath. He raised his gaze to hers, careful to keep his scar covered with his hair. "Okay, yes. I would feel much better being able to do something rather than sit around here and wait."

Her expression turned to one of tender pity. "Do you want some advice you're going to hate but probably need?"

"No, but I have a feeling you're going to offer it anyway."

Katelyn shrugged, and a small smile played at the corners of her lips. "I think it's going to be quite a challenge to bring a woman of half Cunt heritage to Tador. But no matter what, you need to remember that she is a woman first and a Cunt second. She has survived perfectly well without you this long, and probably won't welcome the Klatch male tendency toward being overbearing."

She took one of Ryan's hands in hers, and despite himself, he enjoyed the cool comfort her gentle touch gave. "Regardless of the Triangle or anything else, you need to treat her like a person with her own strengths and personality rather than just as a warm body who will help us with the Triangle ceremony." A small crease formed between her brows, and her voice lowered with intensity. "Everyone wants to feel special in their own right. Remember that."

Ryan's brow furrowed. He had the distinct impression that Katelyn offered something from personal experience, but he would be surprised if Grayson had been that daft in courting her. However, if that had been the case, his Katie-cat wouldn't have let anyone get away with mistreating her, and Grayson had probably paid dearly. He smiled grimly. "I'll keep that in mind. Thanks."

"Make sure you do," she said, her voice full of playful challenge. "Or I'll help her kick your ass, and I'm sure the queen would help, too."

He gave into his habit and traced his thumb over the roughened skin at the bottom of his scar where it met the right side of his mouth. "Don't worry, I have no desire to go up against you three. Any man who does, deserves all the pain and humiliation he gets."

3

"We just retrieved Danen from the human hospital, my lord."
The barrel-chested guard dipped his chin in an approximation
of a bow and then winced and gingerly touched his fingers to
his broken nose.

"Fine. Keep him comfortable and away from any of the
other council members for a few days." *Until I can decide what
to do with him.* Marco, head of the Cunt Council, waved the
guard away. Danen was an arrogant fool, and Marco was sorry
the man hadn't been left for dead. That would've been one less
ego-inflated councilman to deal with.

Marco sighed as he turned the situation over inside his mind.
He used to believe the Cunt cause was just, and that purely coexisting with the Klatch as they always had wasn't enough.
They had convinced themselves they were the superior race
and should hold the throne and the symbiosis of their home
world.

It hadn't taken long after the failed civil war to see that Sela,
the self-named Queen of the Cunts, was after power only for
herself and not any advancement for the Cunts in general. But

by then, it was too late. Marco had continued on, rising through the ranks of the council in hopes he could once again bring true meaning back to their cause.

A short, bitter laugh escaped him. Even that self-delusion wasn't enough to salve his regrets anymore. And now his inaction had hit very close to home.

Why the hell did Kiera meet with Danen and not me?

Even as the words trailed off inside his mind, he knew the answer. She knew Marco agreed with her cause so, therefore, had arranged a meeting in an attempt to sway others to her way of thinking.

Foolish woman.

He had known Kiera Matthews all her life, and had, in fact, been in love with her mother, Cecily, in his much-younger days. However, it hadn't lasted, and they had parted as friends, although Marco admitted his pride had smarted when she had fallen in love first with a Klatch and then with a human.

It had nearly killed him to watch Kiera as she grew up, knowing she could have been his child had circumstances been different. But his position on the council and his loyalties to Sela's increasing demands wouldn't have left much room for a wife and a daughter—something he sorely missed now that he was older and wiser. Not to mention, they could've been used as pawns against him at any given moment.

He sighed and turned to look out the second-story office window into the nearly surreal predawn.

Hints of a rainbow of colors peeked over the horizon along with the first rays of sunlight. Phoenix had both beautiful sunrises and sunsets due to all the different minerals in the mountains and rocks, and each one was more amazing than the last.

Almost as breathtaking as on his home world of Tador.

His chest tightened with longing. It had been nearly a quarter of a century since he'd seen the magnificent waterfalls and the densely grown maze near the gardens, not to mention the hot baths where he used to go with his friends.

The same hot baths where he'd met Cecily.

Weariness and old memories weighted his limbs, and he scrubbed his hands over his face in a vain attempt to chase away both. Rough stubble on his jaw reminded him that he hadn't shaved in the last two days.

"My lord?"

He nearly jumped at the guard's voice, and then he chided himself for not being more careful. Being a Cunt became more and more dangerous with each passing day. If he showed any weakness, he would find himself knifed in the back and bleeding to death on the marble floor.

He narrowed his eyes as he turned back toward the guard. "I distinctly remember dismissing you." His voice was pitched low with twin notes of irritation and boredom—something he had learned out of necessity after twenty-four long years of serving Sela, the Queen of the Cunts.

Fear flashed through the guard's watery blue eyes. "Yes, my lord. But . . ."

"But what?" Marco's voice was soft but distinct, and he nearly smiled when the guard's already pasty face whitened a few more shades.

"I thought you should be apprised of Danen's new orders regarding the doctor."

Marco's brow furrowed. "Danen is not the council head. He has no authority to give orders without approval of myself or the majority of the council."

The guard swallowed hard, and a bead of sweat trickled from his hairline to carve a path over his temple and down onto his cheek. "Yes, my lord. Danen gained approval from one other council member and Aedan, the Queen's consort."

Marco's jaw clenched along with his fists as a spurt of fear shot through him. Not for himself, but for the fiery little doctor.

Kiera wasn't his flesh and blood, but he had worked hard to ensure she had a place in Cunt society if she wanted it, even if it was on the periphery.

That was the least he could do for Cecily, since he had gotten her killed. "What were the orders?"

"That Dr. Matthews is a traitor to the Cunts and must be killed immediately."

Marco nodded once but was careful to keep his face a blank mask. "Thank you for informing me. Keep Danen confined on my orders, and tell no one his whereabouts or that you've even seen him. Dismissed." This time he watched until the guard closed the door behind him.

For a long moment, his mind sifted through possibilities, discarding them one after another until he was left with only one.

One he swore he would never take.

He smiled grimly. How arrogant he had been to think himself invincible and his cause so clearly in the right. No matter how readily he now admitted his mistake, sacrificing his pride to correct it would be one of the hardest things he had ever done.

His gaze fixed on the exploding sunrise—possibly the last he would ever see if he took this path. Sela wasn't very forgiving, especially of those like himself who were harder to replace. Not impossible—no one was irreplaceable. Just more difficult.

For the first time in many years he felt . . . peace. He shrugged his shoulders, not used to the sensation and not sure if he could become used to it again.

It was time to contact an old friend. And if his old friend didn't kill Marco on sight, maybe something could be done to help Kiera out of her current situation.

* * *

Gavin scowled as he pushed through the bone-chilling cold of the *between*—the pathway between Tador and Earth. With a wave of his hand, the portal opened in front of him, slowly expanding until it was an oval big enough for him to step through.

He winced as the bright morning Phoenix sunlight nearly blinded him after the inky blackness of the *between*. Heat prickled against his skin in thick waves, and he shivered.

It was probably eighty degrees outside, which would rise to well over one hundred later in the day, but after the numbing cold of the *between*, he felt as if he'd been plunged into a sauna.

He scanned the area as his body adjusted, alert for any treachery.

It had been nearly twenty-four years since he or anyone else had used this portal, and for good reason. The Cunts had used this particular portal to transport en masse behind the castle on Tador the day they tried to overthrow the current queen's parents, King Darius and Queen Annalecia.

The screams of pain, betrayal and anger from that day still haunted his nightmares, along with the stench of charred flesh and death.

His jaw clenched as those vivid images replayed themselves inside his mind's eye.

Guilt still lay heavy on his shoulders. He hadn't been at fault. However, his best friend had not only sided with the enemy but had planned the attack using his knowledge of Gavin's defense tactics. If it hadn't been for his unlikely friendship, many might still be alive today.

He shook his head to clear the disturbing memories.

As soon as the uprising had been contained and all the Cunts banished to live on Earth with the humans, Gavin had sealed this portal along with several others that led to areas not easily protected or patrolled in the long-term.

In fact, that was one of the few times Gavin had actually appreciated his special talent.

Every Klatch—and every Cunt, for that matter—had one special skill beyond normal witch's abilities which was uniquely theirs. Gavin could create portals between Tador and Earth, although they weren't always stable, and he could seal and unseal them.

He had been surprised to receive a request to meet here, but the location told him instantly who requested the meeting, even though the note had held no signature.

The very same man who had betrayed not only Gavin, but his entire race that day.

Long-held pain and anger burned in Gavin's chest, and he swallowed it back. Logic, not emotion, was needed when dealing with the Cunt Council. It was his job to be aware of anything that might pose a threat to his royal charges, so this meeting couldn't go unacknowledged.

Due to his past history, he had thought about having another guard go in his stead. However, there was none other he trusted to cross wits with Marco. Gavin had even considered sending enough Klatch to capture or kill his old friend. But then another would take his place on the Cunt Council, someone Gavin couldn't read quite as well.

Better the devil you knew than the new Cunt council member you didn't.

When he was sure there were no ambushes waiting for him, Gavin glanced around at the neatly planted rows of cotton, the scents of rich earth filling his nostrils.

Off to his left was a well-used road, and just beyond was a newly built Starbucks. He shook his head. He wouldn't be surprised if Queen Alyssandra soon commissioned one to be franchised on Tador. The thought made him smile.

The new queen brought a breath of fresh air to Tador. She had been raised on Earth by the very Cunts who kidnapped her nearly a quarter of a century ago, and yet she had returned to the Klatch stronger than she might have been if she had been raised in relative luxury on her home planet.

How ironic that the Cunt's treachery had helped shape the very woman who would save the planet they had fought to control.

A truck carrying square hay bales ambled by on squeaky axles, breaking him from his thoughts. Stray pieces of hay filled the air, along with a healthy dose of dust, and Gavin closed his eyes until the debris settled. He trudged up the outer berm of the cotton field and crossed the road to the coffee shop.

Marco sat just inside the large picture window at the front of the lobby in one of the plush armchairs. A large white paper cup emblazoned with the Starbucks logo sat beside him on the round coffee table.

As if he felt the weight of Gavin's perusal, Marco glanced up, and an almost physical blow to the gut stole Gavin's breath as they stared at each other through the glass. For a long moment, Gavin searched the blue gaze for . . . something. Some sign of regret or misgivings over his past actions. But Marco's expression revealed nothing.

Gavin clenched his jaw, broke the contact and walked around the building to the entrance doors.

Once inside, the strong smell of brewed coffee surrounded him, as did the cool blast of air from the air conditioners that ran nearly year-round in every building in the state.

Gavin stretched out his senses to evaluate those around him.

Hunched over their early morning coffee or working behind the counter were a few humans . . . and one extremely powerful Cunt witch.

Something had told Gavin that Marco would come alone, but it never hurt to be cautious.

Not bothering to acknowledge the man, Gavin moved to the counter and ordered a small black coffee, his back turned. Part of him hoped Marco would try an attack, but the part of him that had grown up with the man knew he wouldn't have asked for this meeting if he meant Gavin any harm. So he stood easily at the counter and accepted the steaming cup before he turned to head across the lobby.

The muscles in both his shoulders tightened as he neared his old friend. Marco hadn't changed much over the years, which surprised Gavin.

Those who lived on Tador or visited regularly enjoyed a constant healing and regeneration that those who had been banished would not. But other than some lines around his eyes, Marco looked exactly as he had the last time he had seen him—right before Gavin had spared his life and sealed the portal behind him.

The same portal Gavin had just exited across the street.

He had spent many sleepless nights wondering if he should've killed the man who had been closer than a brother, or if he had done the right thing by letting him live. Gavin bit back a sigh and kept his expression impassive.

"It's been a long time." Marco openly studied him, and Gavin returned the favor.

Marco's long sandy blond hair had been pulled back into a queue behind his neck, and he still looked muscular and fit under the simple black button-down shirt. He didn't appear as sinister as Gavin's memory had etched him all these years. He looked more like the easy-going friend he had grown up with— the same man who reminded him so much of Prince Ryan.

Long-bottled emotions churned inside Gavin's stomach, and he held them in check only with sheer willpower. Unsure if his voice would work, he nodded and sat in the chair across from Marco.

"Still a man of few words, I see." Marco picked up his coffee and took a sip; the only sign of his discomfort at this meeting was the tight grip of his fingers denting in the sides of the stiff paper cup.

Gavin took a swallow of his own coffee and winced as the searing liquid burned the top of his mouth. The physical pain mirrored the discomfort of his emotions, and he bit back a sharp retort. Instead, he made sure when he spoke his words were low and calm. "Why are we here, Marco? I assume after all this time you would contact me only if it was urgent." As his last word trailed off, he raised his gaze and saw pain etched deep in the man's blue eyes before it was quickly hidden behind the mask of nonchalance Gavin remembered well.

Marco nodded as if relieved that things would remain all business between them. "The council has put out a termination order for a woman who has done a lot for both our races, and I hoped she could take sanctuary on Tador."

Gavin pursed his lips. If the Cunt Council had truly marked her for death, her days were numbered on Earth. Inept and radical the council might sometimes be, they were also ruthless, vindictive and annoyingly persistent.

But why did Marco suddenly care what happened to one woman, unless she was someone special to him? Suspicion made Gavin narrow his gaze. "Wife? Girlfriend? Mistress? Spy?" He searched Marco's pale features carefully for any clues to which of his guesses were right, but the man's expression never changed.

"The closest relationship I can claim is friend of the family. She's a doctor who ran a clinic in downtown Phoenix treating both Klatch and Cunts, regardless of circumstances. She's still young, but her efforts have done a lot to keep us off the human radar as a threat."

Gavin's blood ran cold.

Cecily's daughter. The Healer. The daughter that might have been his if the Cunts hadn't been banished from Tador entirely.

What were the odds?

Gavin thought about the petite blond woman who had easily

defeated two Cunt guards and then also escaped from Ryan. She looked so much like Cecily it made his heart ache.

Gavin wondered if Marco held some of the same regrets. After all, Marco had loved Cecily before Gavin had even met her. But it had been Gavin she had wanted, and Gavin whose heart she had held in the palm of her hand until she had been banished.

"She's too much like her mother." Gavin swore under his breath. When he raised his gaze to Marco's, a look of complete agreement and understanding was reflected in the blue depths.

"I didn't realize you'd kept up with Cunt genealogy . . . or with Kiera."

Gavin sighed, suddenly weary. He could've blamed it on his position as head guard of the Klatch, but he knew it was more than that, and so would Marco. "I've never seen her before tonight, but I kept tabs on her. It was the least I could do for Cecily . . . after everything I couldn't do."

Silence fell between them for a long moment, and Gavin suspected Marco was just as lost in memories of the past as he was.

Marco cleared his throat. "Earlier tonight she met with one of the Cunt council members. They were interrupted by a contingent of Klatch, and the council member was injured and left for dead." Marco took another drink and then sat the cup on the table next to him.

I called 911. It was your own people who left him for dead. Gavin kept that observation to himself. Aloud he said, "So now they blame Kiera for an ambush?" Gavin sifted through his thoughts, and more important, his internal gut feelings to judge the situation. He rarely trusted coincidence, but the alternative didn't bear out. He doubted Marco would risk all he was just to lay a trap for Gavin, since there would be little for him to gain by it at this point. Marco might be a traitor, but he was more cunning than that.

Marco nodded. "She's been branded a traitor, and before I

was apprised of the situation, assassins were dispatched to hunt her down."

Gavin started at the use of the term "traitor" when it had just echoed through his own thoughts.

Shit.

He needed to get back to Tador, find Ryan and then find the Healer before the Cunt's assassins found her first. But in order to have any hope of doing just that, he needed information that only his old friend could provide. "What was she meeting with the council for?"

Marco studied his impeccably shined shoes for a moment before meeting Gavin's gaze. "She was lobbying for reunification."

Stunned silence hung between them as Gavin digested the meaning of those words. "Reunification?" He chuckled, but it wasn't a happy sound. "Does she know how unpopular that will make her with both sides?"

Marco's lips curved. "She hasn't yet learned that she can't save the world." He studied his hands in his lap for a long moment, which made Gavin wonder what he wasn't saying. "She reminds me a lot of you and me back when we were young and idealistic."

The obvious affection in his words sparked Gavin's temper. "Just what is this woman to you? She has to be more than just a friend of the family for you to risk Sela's wrath if you're caught even speaking with me. You're not *involved* with Kiera Matthews, are you?" He held his breath as he waited for the answer.

The expressionless mask cracked, and Marco looked twenty years older and jaded, as if he had seen things no one should, and they had left their mark. "I won't rehash old politics with you, Gav. You always knew how I felt about Cecily. I've tried to watch over her daughter. Nothing more."

Gavin exhaled sharply as relief rushed through him. Only then did he let his mind process the rest of the conversation.

The use of his old nickname surprised him, but Gavin made sure his expression didn't show it.

"Suffice it to say, she believes like I used to that our two races won't survive without one another," Marco added. "But I think she's smart enough to not become sucked in by someone so power-hungry as Sela."

Gavin didn't bother to press on that obviously volatile subject. He was surprised at even that small admission. He relaxed back against the chair, resting his elbows on the arms of the chair and steepling his fingers in front of his lips. "How far are you willing to go to help us find her and keep her safe?"

Marco handed Gavin a folded slip of paper. "Here is the address of her clinic and her house, as well as two of the safe houses I know her father kept. Her father is a marine colonel, so she can take care of herself pretty well. Watch out for guns, knives, throwing stars and hand-to-hand maneuvers you wouldn't expect from a petite half-human."

Gavin opened the paper and glanced at the addresses, although he knew as well as Marco did that if he found her at any of these known places, she would most likely already be dead. "You didn't answer my question."

A small bark of a laugh was Marco's immediate response. "If Sela or anyone loyal to her finds out about this meeting, my life is worthless here on Earth. And due to my past choices, my life is worthless on Tador, as well." He sipped his coffee as if he weren't talking about the very limited places in the universe that would allow him to live. "I plan on going back to work as if nothing happened. If you need any help finding Kiera, or anything else, I will do what I can. I owe you a favor for this."

Gavin's temper flared at Marco's trivialization of all that had happened in the past. "You fucking owe me more than a favor after all is said and done." His words came out in a low growl, and he didn't bother to try to calm them. "You betrayed not only your home world, but your best friend, Cecily and, whether you admit it or not, your own race."

Marco's gaze was tired when it met Gavin's. "What's done is done, and I can't go back and see things through wiser eyes, even now when I see that both sides in our war were stubborn and unwilling to bend."

Gavin's fists clenched. "Attacking and killing innocent people and revolting against the rightful king and queen—"

Marco cut him off as if he hadn't spoken. "However, change is better accomplished from the inside, so I will stay until I'm found out and killed, or until a better way to help our people presents itself."

The urge to throttle Marco until he saw reason surged through Gavin. He kept his fists clenched to reduce the danger of carrying out the thought.

The time for arguing was long past. He would help the Healer and then figure out what to do with Marco. "I assume she is a Cunt loyalist if the council member took the meeting, so why would she welcome a visit from us?"

Marco dipped a hand into the pocket of his dress slacks and then flipped something toward Gavin, who caught it as a reflex.

He opened his palm and stared down at a shiny new quarter.

"She is loyal only to the memory of Tador that her mother filled her head with as a child—the old, unified Tador before Sela and all the rest. However, show her this and tell her all her safe houses have been compromised. That's all the help I can offer you in finding her." Marco stood and opened his mouth as if to add something. Several emotions played across his face so fast Gavin had trouble identifying them.

Finally, after a long tense moment, Marco closed his mouth, turned and walked out the door.

4

Kiera bolted upright in bed, the Ruger a comforting weight in her hand as she scanned the room for anything out of place. Her heart pounded, and the sudden rush of adrenaline made her light-headed.

Shiloh stretched beside her and then yawned but didn't bother to stand or even look around.

Wispy dream images floated just beyond her reach, and she scowled as she recalled dreaming about the dark Klatch prince watching her sleep. "Damn, Kiera, you really need to get laid and stop obsessing about the man who got you into this mess in the first place."

She sighed with relief that it had been only a dream that woke her.

Shiloh's head swiveled toward the window, his ears flattened against his head, his eyes narrowed.

Shit.

By the time the cat hissed, Kiera had already stood and slipped out into the hallway, alert for any sounds that would indicate an intruder. Shiloh slid past her ankles, heading straight down the stairs and to the right toward the kitchen. She silently cursed the cat and then remembered if it wasn't for his hissed warning, she wouldn't think anyone had breached her security.

Fine. If she lived through this, she would refrain from shooting him.

Maybe.

She placed each foot precisely on the stairs to ensure she made no noise. She continued forward until she stood on the bottom step. Adrenaline pumped through her body. Her heart pounded, and her temples throbbed.

She swallowed hard, hating the metallic taste of fear on the back of her tongue.

After a deep breath for courage, she placed her finger against the gun trigger and pivoted into the kitchen, the gun leading.

A tall figure loomed before her out of the darkness.

Terror flashed through her in a searing rush, and the scene slowed to a crawl.

She squeezed the trigger.

A loud *crack* filled her ears as the recoil traveled up her arms and into her torso like a shove from a large, unseen hand.

The flash from the muzzle fire illuminated the room, and she blinked hard as her eyes tried to adjust to the sudden burst of light.

An oval of pink sizzling energy surrounded the intruder as the bullet bounced against his energy shield.

Kiera dove to the side to try to avoid the ricochet.

When pain lanced up her side from her abrupt landing instead of a bullet wound, she mouthed a silent thanks to the universe.

She rolled to her left in the small confines of the kitchen, and her head hit the wooden cabinet hard. Silver flashes of light popped just behind her eyelids, and a wave of nausea threatened. She took a deep breath to clear her head and instantly regretted it as a fresh round of throbbing pain reverberated through her head.

Sharp pressure against her wrist made her cry out, and she opened her hand and allowed the gun to slip from her suddenly limp fingers.

Dark boots filled her wavering vision in the weak moonlight filtering in through the curtains. She clenched her jaw and resisted the urge to wince as she waited for the final deathblow to fall.

Oddly, she felt no fear, only anger and a sincere hope she'd be offered the option to haunt the son of a bitch until he threw himself off a building.

Something small and cold landed in her still-open palm, and she frowned as her fingers closed over it. It was round and almost felt like a coin.

She lifted her hand close to her face and held the object between her thumb and first finger, glad her vision had begun to stabilize.

A quarter.

Fresh nausea inched its way up her throat as the implications poured through her.

Who besides she and her father knew about their escape plan and their code? The sour taste of bile filled her mouth along with anger and a protective instinct where her father was concerned.

"All your safe houses have been compromised. I've come to take you to safety."

Kiera started as her brain finally made sense of the words. Her roiling stomach calmed a little as conflicting emotions of relief and fear washed over her as if she were on a strange, undulating rollercoaster.

Only then did she realize she had heard the voice before.

The Klatch prince.

Crap.

She pushed herself up to sit back against the cabinet, surprised when her head didn't protest. It took a moment for her eyes to adjust so she could make out the man's features in the darkened room.

He held out one long-fingered hand, palm open between them, while she decided if she would accept his help or not.

If he'd wanted to kill you, you'd already be dead. Might as well take it.

She huffed at her own indecision and finally reached up to place her hand in his. Warm, strong flesh closed over hers, causing little flutters deep inside her belly as she allowed herself to be pulled to standing.

The world tilted at her sudden change in position.

She closed her eyes and swallowed hard as she swayed on her feet, and her knees threatened to buckle under her.

Damn. Maybe I hit my head harder than I thought.

Irritation warred with mortification as the Klatch prince pulled her tight against his hard chest. The muscular body under her fingertips and against her breasts would've been enough for any woman to appreciate, but it was his warmth and the musky scent of the deep woods which surrounded her that threatened to pull a sigh from her lips. It took a valiant attempt, but she resisted the impulse to bury her nose against his chest and inhale.

Barely.

That urge alone brought her to her senses.

Kiera pushed away from him to stand on her own. She locked her knees and laid a steadying hand on the counter next to her. The cold from the Formica seeped into her fingers, cooling her suddenly feverish skin. It felt so good, she considered laying her forehead against the counter for one long indulgent moment.

"Are you all right?" His rich tenor voice flowed over her in a sensual assault, reminding her of his presence.

Embarrassment at him seeing her during a weak moment quickly morphed into anger, which chased away the last vestiges of dizziness.

"Who the hell are you?" she demanded, not bothering to answer his question. She finally raised her gaze to meet his, which tipped her head back enough to make both her head and stomach swim precariously. She swallowed hard and stared at his Adam's apple.

Dusky skin surrounded his very masculine throat, which also led her to study the hard line of his jaw and the scattered dark chest hairs that peeked out from beneath the collar of the lovingly tight black T-shirt he wore. She bit the inside of her cheek hard, concentrating on the pain instead of the rugged masculinity of the man in front of her.

"Just call me Ryan. We need to get you out of here before the assassins find you."

At the mention of the assassins, heat speared up her neck and into her cheeks. She had been so lost in noticing his fine . . . attributes . . . that she had totally forgotten the situation that brought him here. Her anger burned higher, but at herself this time, and she wrapped it around herself like a shield.

Kiera bent to retrieve her Ruger and then stood to study Ryan for a long moment, careful that her expression was contemptuous rather than inviting. "That's not what I meant. I already gathered from our earlier encounter that you're *Prince* Ryan of the *Klatch*." She glared at him waiting for an answer. When none came, she huffed out a breath and continued. "I'm not going anywhere until I decide if I'm better or worse off with you than the assassins. Who sent you, and why should I trust you? You're the reason the council thinks I betrayed them."

His expression never changed except for his eyes, which danced with amusement.

She resisted the urge to shake him.

"I never meant to cause you trouble." He held his arms out to the side in an "I'm innocent" gesture. "But I don't know if the situation can be rectified at this point."

The fact that he had a point only irritated her further. It wasn't as if he could give her a note or even show up at the Cunt Council headquarters and say, "Hey everyone, just a big misunderstanding. Can you call off your doctor hunt?"

"As for the rest. If I meant you harm, I could've just left you to the assassins."

A blur of orange streaked between them, and then Ryan was holding Shiloh, a shocked look on his face—the prince, not the cat.

"Traitor," she muttered, but Shiloh only cuddled against Ryan and began a loud purr.

Ryan recovered quickly and shifted his grip so he could scratch Shiloh behind the ears. The cat's purring increased exponentially, and Kiera resisted the urge to roll her eyes. Though she was grudging to admit it, the little pain-in-the-ass feline had always been an excellent judge of character. If she weren't so stubborn, that alone would have convinced her that Ryan meant her no harm.

"So, if I agree to go with you, just where do you propose we go where the assassins and half the Cunt race won't find me?" She arched an eyebrow at him in challenge. "Or you for helping me?"

"Tador."

Her mouth dropped open in surprise. Whatever answer she had expected, it wasn't that.

All Cunts had been exiled from Tador almost twenty-five years ago right after the Cunt uprising against the Klatch throne. Even though Kiera carried only half that lineage, her blond hair and blue eyes alone would condemn her with many of the inhabitants of the witch home world.

However, that didn't stop her from being curious. Her mother and several of her patients from both races had told her stories about Tador, and she longed to see it for herself—to walk where her mother had walked and see what she had seen. Not to mention, it would give her a chance to see if the Klatch royals were ready for the reunification of the species that she was convinced was the only way to heal both races.

"Speechless, I see." He flashed a quick smile, nearly a smirk, and then it was gone before she could study it to decide. "I would've thought it would take more than that."

Kiera ignored the jibe and propped her fists on her hips, the Ruger still cupped in her right palm. "Obviously you aren't running for prince of the year, or you wouldn't be considering bringing someone with Cunt blood running through her veins back to sully the sacred soil of Tador."

He laughed and shook his head in mock sadness. "I doubt with the year I've had I'm even in the running." He sat Shiloh gently on the counter and, still watching Kiera, missed the narrowed orange glare of displeasure from the cat. "Regardless, that's the one place the assassins can't get to you." He glanced away and then back as if deciding his next words carefully. "However, Tador is very much in need of a Healer at present, so we could help each other."

Kiera started at the word "Healer." He said it like an office unto itself, not as if he used it as a generic term for a doctor.

A loud hiss sounded from Shiloh, startling them both.

Ryan grabbed Shiloh around the middle and wrapped one large hand around Kiera's wrist, nearly dragging her out of the kitchen. He shoved open the door to the garage and pulled her through into the darkened, chilly room.

"Hey!" she protested when no alarms sounded as the door opened.

How the hell did he disable my alarms?

Another firm yank pulled her toward the passenger side of the Humvee and cut off anything else she would've said.

The sharp spate of gunfire sounded from the back of the house and convinced her to enter the code to open the car door and jump inside the Humvee unasked.

Ryan tossed Shiloh onto her lap and slammed the passenger door. Only then did she realize she sat in the passenger seat and Ryan meant to drive.

More gunfire erased any thought of objecting. She dumped the cat into the back seat, who for once didn't protest, and clicked her seatbelt into the buckle just as Ryan slid into driver's seat.

"Keys." He held out his hand, and she fished inside her front jeans pocket for her keychain. She nearly dropped them on the floor when another round of gunfire sounded from just the other side of the garage door in front of them. Her father had trained her for situations such as these, but tonight was the first time she had ever found herself in a truly life-threatening one.

It was humbling to admit that no matter all her training and knowledge, without her father, she didn't feel ready or prepared.

Ryan plucked the keys from her hand and started the ignition.

"Wait, the garage door—"

Ryan flashed her a grin and then floored the gas pedal.

The Humvee shot forward, and Kiera closed her eyes.

The wrenching sound of metal drowned out the sound of gunfire for a few long moments. The Humvee lurched as it drove over several bumps, so she opened her eyes and craned her neck to look behind them.

Even in the dim moonlight, she could see that the garage door had come off nearly intact, and they had most likely driven right over it, and possibly over some of the men who had come after them.

Me, she corrected herself. *They are after me, not Ryan.*

She was considered the traitor to the Cunts, though she had no doubt that killing a Klatch prince would be a rare treat for the treacherous Cunt Council and their assassins. Ryan would be just a perk—she was the real target.

A quick flash of guilt washed over her, but she quickly shoved it aside to worry about later. After all, if it weren't for his interruption of her meeting with Danen last night, things might not have gotten this out of control.

A car swerved onto the road behind them, the headlights blinding her for a moment while her eyes adjusted. "Shit."

"We need only to get to an existing portal point, and we're home free." The calmness of his voice surprised her and also soothed her for some unknown reason. He sounded as if he were answering her over coffee instead of in the midst of a dangerous car chase.

Kiera glanced over at him, noting that in the excitement of the moment, he had forgotten to drop his chin so his cascade of long dark hair covered his scar. The dappled moonlight that shone through the windows softened the angry pink and red color of the scar. An urge to touch the puckered skin where it met the corner of his lips tingled through her fingers, and she squelched it by clenching her fist.

Unbelievable timing, Kiera! It's not like we are running for our lives or anything here.

As if he felt her intense scrutiny, he turned his head, and their eyes met for a brief moment before he returned his gaze to the road.

In that instant, she had seen deep vulnerability and pain. She felt like she had intruded on something private and wished she could take it back.

A sizzling blue bolt struck the back of the Humvee and shook the windows so hard she thought they would shatter.

"Damn." Ryan turned the wheel hard, steering them off the road and into a patch of trees that lined the road.

Kiera gasped and gripped the dash so hard her fingers hurt. She pictured the Humvee crashing into a thick copse of pine trees and leaving them unconscious and at the mercy of whoever followed them.

However, a moment later when there was no crash, only the high-pitched squealing of branches scratching the sides of the car, she breathed a sigh of relief. Obviously Ryan had seen an opening she hadn't.

Darkness enveloped them now that they were surrounded by thick forest with only a small path to drive through. Weak moonlight filtered in through occasional gaps in the trees, but most of the illumination came from their headlights and the soft glow of the Humvee's dash panel.

Ryan turned the wheel hard to navigate around a fallen tree, and she grabbed the door handle and dash to keep from sliding, even with the restraint of her seatbelt holding her in place. "I don't know how familiar you are with energy blasts, but too much will short out every electrical system in the car."

"Oh," was all she could think to offer as an answer. At least that explained why they were suddenly off-roading through a seemingly impenetrable forest in the murky dark. She stifled a rather girly squeak as they bounced over a large bump and all four tires were airborne for a long moment until they landed hard.

As the tires hit the ground and Kiera's breath whooshed out at the impact, another blue blast encompassed the Humvee but only managed a weak blue glow before it dissipated. Apparently casting through all the trees and brush had its disadvantages.

Kiera had treated plenty of energy burns but hadn't had much experience with the actual beams themselves—until tonight.

"How far to the nearest existing portal point?" She had heard detailed accounts of how horrible it was walking through the *between*, but she couldn't help but feel excited and curious rather than nervous. She was definitely her father's daughter, complete with affection for the unknown—danger be damned.

"The trick will be not only to reach the nearest portal, but also to make it to the other side where there are Klatch guards to discourage our 'friends' from following us." He took one hand off the steering wheel to chuck a thumb over his shoulder toward their "friends."

She craned her neck to look behind them and saw the dim glow of headlights through the thick forest that lay between them. A quick glance down at the backseat showed Shiloh laying flat on his stomach clinging to the leather seats with all four paws, claws extended and dug deep into the material. His expression seemed more irritated than scared, which brought a small smile to her lips. "Hang in there, Shi," she said and was rewarded with the most pitiful hangdog look she had ever seen on the feisty cat's face.

A flicker of blue caught her attention, and she looked up in time to see another energy beam bearing down on them.

"Hold on," Ryan warned, letting her know he had seen it, too.

The Humvee jarred to the side, barely avoiding the blast of energy.

The sudden jolt banged Kiera's temple against the headrest and brought back her earlier bout of dizziness.

She faced front and closed her eyes as she sucked deep breaths into her lungs, hoping to clear her head. "How far?" The Humvee swerved again, and the high-pitched screech of branches scratching the doors screamed through her like nails on a chalkboard.

"I can sense the portal point getting closer, but I'm not sure if this little trail we are attempting to drive on will cooperate." He risked a quick glance in her direction before turning his attention back to the road just in time to steer around a large boulder and into a wider part of a small ravine. "After I emerged from the portal, I used actual roads to find you."

Kiera snorted at his deadpan attempt at humor. She could definitely navigate. The familiar comfort of taking charge surged through her, and her confidence poured back with a vengeance. "Describe the general location of the portal point to me."

"It's just next to a small pond with many ducks. There is a natural clearing near it with ankle high grasses and a natural stream. I had to walk through the forest for about five minutes from there to reach the main road."

A mental map of the area formed inside Kiera's mind, and she knew the "pond" he referred to was Kinnikinick Lake. There were a few possibilities as to the road, depending on which side of the half-mile-wide lake he emerged from. "Was the road you found paved or dirt?"

"Paved."

Crap. That ruled out only two sides of the lake.

"Close to the portal are two pine trees with twined trunks. There were orange strips of cloth tied to them."

Relief and excitement burned through her. She knew those trees and had seen those strips of orange the hunters left to mark the area. Her gaze scanned the moonlight-dappled scenery that bumped and sped by as she tried to get a fix on exactly where they were now and how best to get them to where they needed to go.

The front of the Humvee dipped into a large ravine, and she gripped the door and dash, grateful her seatbelt held her in place. When they reached the bottom of the ravine and started up the other side, gravity pushed her back against the seat just as another blue beam of energy engulfed the Humvee.

Sparks flew from the dash panels, and the smell of burning electrical wires filled the car.

Kiera coughed as the acrid smoke filled her lungs. Icy fingers of panic crawled down her spine.

She shielded her face with her arms as the sparks continued to fly from the dash panels.

Sparks hit her arms like dozens of angry ant bites, and she yelped.

Her fingers groped for the button to roll down the window. When she found it, she jabbed it so hard she was surprised the small lever didn't break off in her hand.

One tense moment later, the window shakily complied with a high-pitched whine. The crisp night air stole the acrid smoke from the cab of the Humvee, and she leaned toward the open window and breathed deep.

Ryan slammed on the gas, and somehow the Humvee made it to the top of the hill and sped forward, leaving their followers to fight their way out of the ravine.

After mouthing a silent thanks to the universe that the Humvee was still running, she spared a quick glance backward and then turned to Ryan. "I should be driving. Switch with me."

"What?" His eyes left the road long enough for them to hit several large bumps that made her nervous.

"Watch the road!" When he complied, she huffed out a breath and restated the obvious, while she held on through the bumps and twists of the road. "I know the surrounding area and can't shoot energy beams. You can, I assume, shoot energy beams and don't know where we're trying to go." She stared at the side of his face, daring him to disagree, although the effect was most likely lost since he was staring straight ahead. "I should be driving, it just makes more sense. If you want some extra firepower to distract any humans in their group, there's a duffel under the hatchback floor. Switch with me."

Not bothering to wait for his approval, she unhooked her seatbelt and laid her seat down into a reclining position to give him room to maneuver his bigger frame when they switched. She gripped the steering wheel with her left hand and slipped her leg over his and onto the gas pedal. When he reluctantly moved his foot from the gas, she lifted her butt off the seat and slid it onto his thigh.

"This would be much more interesting if we weren't being chased by a team of assassins," Ryan said against her ear through gritted teeth.

Gooseflesh from his hot breath against her sensitive skin marched down her neck.

Now was *not* an ideal time to allow herself to become distracted.

He moved out from under her, and she slid into the driver's seat, lifting her butt again so he could retrieve his left leg.

Kiera snapped her seatbelt into place and spared a quick glance for Ryan, who was had already climbed into the backseat. "Hold tight, and try not to land on the cat." She zigzagged through the forest, careful to avoid fallen logs and ravines, while keeping the gas pedal as close to the floorboards as possible without crashing. The Humvee definitely didn't handle like her PT Cruiser, and it took her a several minutes to get used to driving the larger vehicle through forest terrain.

"Bollocks, what *don't* you have in this bag?" Ryan's voice held grudging respect rather than censure.

Apparently he had found her stash of weapons. She heard a thud as he transferred them to the backseat. When no offended feline screech ripped through the car, she knew the bag hadn't landed on Shiloh. If she had any doubts, they were dispelled when the cat jumped into the front passenger seat and then plopped down on his stomach and dug his claws into the leather upholstery.

"I don't see them behind us anymore. Keep an eye out—" Ryan's words were cut off when a large truck careened out of the forest and directly into their path.

A spurt of fear crashed over her like a tidal wave.

She turned the wheel hard.

Twigs and dirt hit the underside of the Humvee like an explosion as the tires spun and then finally caught.

The back quarter panel of the Humvee slammed into the nose of the truck.

Kiera's head smashed against the side window, and she cried out as pain blossomed across her temple.

Sounds of crunching metal filled her ears even as the world swam precariously in front of her.

She stomped on the gas and the Humvee shot forward.

The screech of tree branches scratching metal blended with the loud *crack* of snapping tree limbs and shattering safety glass.

"Kiera!"

She blinked furiously, realizing that she had nearly blacked out. A grouping of trees stood directly in their path, and she couldn't seem to get the message to her arms to turn the wheel.

Ryan reached over the front seat and turned the wheel hard to the right.

The Humvee responded but clipped the trees on the driver's side as they narrowly missed the head-on collision.

"Let up on the gas. Pull over here, and turn off the lights."

Her slow-moving brain didn't argue, which should have told her how injured she was. Instead, she followed his instructions.

When she put the car into park, Ryan reached over her to shut off the lights, his warm hand resting on her shoulder. "Grab the cat and get out." Shiloh's warm body was thrust into her arms.

"Don't forget the gun duffel and my backpack," she said in his general direction before she pushed open the door and stepped out into the chilly night. It was stupid, but those two bags were the last links she had to her father—other than the heavy ball of fur in her arms.

As the cold night closed around her, she shivered, and her nipples tightened into hard nubs against her thin lacy bra as the overwhelming smell of pine filled her senses. The thin material of her T-shirt was little protection against the frigid night breeze swirling through the forest. Shiloh curled tight against her stomach, and she held him closer, enjoying what little pulsing heat he offered.

She glanced up, surprised to find Ryan standing in front of her. "Shit. I'm losing time." The logical part of her brain told her she most likely had a concussion and needed to get to a hospital soon. The rest of her wanted to giggle and then lie down and take a nap.

Ryan captured her chin between his fingers, and the warmth of his skin burned through her, clearing her thoughts and making her frown.

"Arousal should not override the effects of a concussion." Her words sounded a bit slurred, and she wondered if they actually were or if her hearing had been affected.

Ryan laughed as he looked deeply into her eyes. It took her a moment to realize he was probably checking her pupils, not stealing a quick romantic moment. She nearly laughed at her own fragmented thoughts.

"Remind me to explain to you one of the necessary food groups for a witch—Klatch or Cunt—when we aren't in so much danger." He took Shiloh from her and set the cat on the ground with a quick admonishment to stay close.

"I'm a doctor, damn it. I know all about witches needing sexual energy." The severe slurring of her words frustrated her, and she clenched her jaw. A quick shiver ran through her as the warm patch Shiloh had left against her stomach dissipated, leaving her colder than before.

She snorted at Ryan's admonishment to Shiloh. Since when did the stubborn fricking cat ever listen? He had a mind of his own, and it would probably be wiser for her to carry his heavy ass. She tried to say the words, but for some reason, they never made it to her lips.

Ryan slipped her backpack over her arms and settled it between her shoulder blades before he hefted the gun duffel onto his own broad shoulder. "Let me know if this gets too heavy and we'll drop it. Let's go."

She shook her head, which was all she was able to manage. This backpack was everything she needed to survive on the run—money, alternate IDs and more. There was no way she was leaving it.

Ryan didn't stop to acknowledge her denial. He grabbed her hand and started forward just as noises of pursuit reached them from back the way they had come.

Kiera stumbled after him, concentrating on putting one foot in front of the other and not tripping over roots, fallen tree branches, or even worse—her own feet.

Scant slivers of silver moonlight filtered through the canopy of pine branches to dapple the forest floor, which in her current condition, only made it harder to stay upright, since the gently swaying patches of light made her dizzy.

Ryan's warm fingers around hers made her hand the only part of her entire body that wasn't shivering with cold. Even the exertion of jogging through thick underbrush didn't seem to raise her temperature.

When her feet were frozen through and her lips were so numb she could no longer feel them, they stopped, and Ryan raised his free hand in the air.

A shimmering silver oval appeared in front of them and expanded rapidly until it was large enough to step through. Ryan led the way and had just crossed the threshold when the sound of crackling energy slowly filtered through her foggy brain.

A blue beam sizzled past her and hit Ryan in the shoulder. He stiffened and growled through gritted teeth.

Energy tingled through her fingertips where they were joined with his and surged up her arm in a heady rush.

Ryan stumbled and fell back, away from the portal, his hand pulling free from hers. As he fell, he sent a sizzling pink beam back at the assassins.

Kiera whipped her head around just as another beam of energy hit her square in the chest.

She gasped as liquid warmth threaded its way over her skin in a tingling rush.

Every hair on her body stood on end as another blue beam joined the first. A surge of pure power and heat seeped below her skin and spilled through her veins, thawing her extremities and filling her with pure searing energy . . . and lust—there was no other way to describe it.

Her breasts became heavy with need, and her pussy throbbed as her clit swelled until her soft lacy panties were nearly unbearable against the sensitive little nub.

What the hell was happening? Obviously others didn't have the same reaction to an energy beam as she did.

A laugh spilled from her lips at the erotic sensation.

The beams cut off abruptly, and she nearly sagged as the energy left her. When she straightened, she realized her thoughts were clear and all her pain was gone.

Has the world gone crazy?

Her suddenly clear mind registered three black-clad assassins. The man in the middle was a pure human, and the outer two were Cunt warriors.

She didn't stop to question how she knew that information. Especially when they reached over their shoulders to retrieve the rifles slung across their backs.

"Shit!"

Ryan yanked her toward the portal.

But just as she started to step through, it spiraled closed with a fizzing sound and disappeared as if it never existed.

Ryan pulled her down across his lap, his aura merging with hers in a skin-prickling rush just as the sound of gunfire exploded around them.

5

"Tell me what you want, Sela." Aedan, the consort to the Queen of the Cunts grabbed a handful of Sela's white-gold hair and yanked hard. The action caused her to stumble and fall to her knees in front of him.

She glared up at him defiantly, and he couldn't help but smile. Sela looked delicious kneeling before him on the plush burgundy carpet inside her private rooms. His own room inside the large earth house was tiny in comparison, but as he spent considerable time in Sela's, it didn't matter.

He tightened his grip on her hair, and she whimpered deep in her throat—not from fear, but from need.

Aedan had been lucky enough to stumble upon the secret fetish of the normally ball-busting Queen of the Cunts.

She liked to be dominated sexually. And she liked pain—lots of it.

Aedan was more than happy to both oblige her and keep her dangerous secret. After all, he planned to rule at her side, or rather, rule while she lost herself in the sensual depravities she craved so much.

Still gripping her hair in one fist, he backhanded her with his other hand.

His warrior's ring cut her bottom lip and left a slow trickle of blood to drip down her chin. He glanced down at her. "Tell me, Sela. I want to hear you say the words. You know if you don't, I won't give you what you want."

Her tongue darted out to touch her injured lip, and his cock surged to life. He could almost swear the musky scent of her arousal rose around him to torment him. It took all his willpower not to take her right then before she spoke the words he had demanded.

She wore a simple skirt and white silk tank top, which clung to her trim body like a second skin. Her small pert breasts didn't require a bra, and he was grateful, because otherwise he might not be able to see her tiny pink nipples straining against the cloth.

Sela's blue eyes darkened until they resembled a stormy sky at dusk. "I want you to fuck my ass and spank me." Her bottom lip quivered, as if saying the words out loud were difficult.

"And?" he asked, knowing there was more she craved.

A scowl twisted her lovely features, and her searing gaze bored through him, but he only smiled and waited.

Jaw clenched, she said in a low voice, "I want to ride the line between pain and pleasure until I can't take any more."

When he didn't immediately react, her golden brows furrowed, and she huffed out a breath. "I want it now!"

Triumph surged through Aedan. He loved hearing her say what she wanted. It had taken months for him to break through her pride enough so her desire could win out. Since reaching that milestone only a few weeks ago, he had put it into continual practice.

He tightened his grip on her hair and pulled her to her feet.

Sela cried out, the sound of her pain made his sac tighten behind his cock.

He crushed her against him and captured her mouth. The taste of her blood sent his senses into overdrive, and he bit her tongue to keep a moan from escaping, which would let her see his weakness—*his* addiction to dominating *her*.

Sela cried out again as a stronger taste of metallic blood burst over his tongue. But her cry ended in a long moan when he grabbed her tight little ass in both hands and ground his erection against the soft flesh of her belly.

Aedan spun her around and bent her over the end of her large four-poster bed. He pressed her face against the down comforter with an open palm. With his other hand, he pushed up her skirt and pooled it around her waist to reveal her luscious ass to his view.

He pushed her legs farther apart and allowed himself a long moment to look his fill.

Sela wasn't overly fleshed like that bitch Alyssa who now ruled the Klatch. Instead, her perfect ass was rounded but muscular, her skin pale as the full moon and the tight little pucker the pink of the finest rose petals. In this position, he could see the fleshy bottom edge of her labia, a slightly darker pink than her pucker, already glistening with the slick moisture of her arousal.

He resisted the sudden urge to lean down and taste her, knowing that he would lose himself in pleasuring her. Instead, he needed to keep his mind on what she had requested.

She squirmed under his firm hold. "Take me, damn it!"

Aedan slapped her ass hard. The sharp crack of flesh hitting flesh accompanied Sela's squeak of surprise, and he groaned as desire howled through him, weakening his legs and sending hot lava through his veins. His cock ached, and he fought the urge to bury himself inside her tight flesh.

To stave off the nearly overwhelming urge, he slapped her ass again, using all his strength. Sela shrieked, but the sound ended on a long moan, which nearly made him come inside his jeans.

"I don't remember giving you permission to speak, Sela." He pressed her face harder into the mattress and then fumbled with the zipper of his jeans. After a few seconds of frustrated cursing, he slid the zipper open and freed his cock from its confines, which immediately brought some measure of relief.

Not much, but some.

He glanced down at the overlaid red handprints on Sela's flesh and smiled. Her pale skin bruised easily, and he had made her let the marks from their last play session heal naturally over the course of a few days rather than using her energy to heal them.

He enjoyed seeing his marks on her flesh and had intentionally let them totally fade from her body before marking her again, so she was a blank canvas for his possession once again.

"Are you ready for me, Sela?"

"Take me, Aedan," she said through gritted teeth.

He waited, unmoving until she added a reluctant, "Please."

Pleasure burst through him. There was nothing like breaking a strong woman. After Sela, he didn't think he could ever go back to a pliable or biddable woman again. Not that he would have to after he shared Sela's throne.

Aedan dug his fingers into her pale flesh and looked forward to seeing the small dark bruises tomorrow. He smacked her ass once more and then dipped his first two fingers between her glistening labia to gather some of her juices. The strong musk of her filled the air, and he brought his hand to his nose and inhaled, enjoying the earthy scent. He sucked the digits inside his mouth and moaned his appreciation as the sweet tangy taste broke over his tongue. "I love tasting you, Sela. But that's for another time," he said with true regret in his voice.

He dipped his two fingers inside her core again until they were once again coated with her juices.

Sela squirmed, trying to raise her hips to take more of his fingers. But since her legs were spread so far apart, she didn't have enough leverage to do more than tip her luscious ass up to give him a better view of the pink pucker he would soon drive himself inside.

His wet fingers trailed the short distance between her core up to her tight rosebud, and he lingered a moment, tracing the slick circle but not pushing inside her or readying her to take his width in any way.

The pain was part of what made them perfect for one another.

Sela craved receiving it, and Aedan enjoyed inflicting it.

His lips parted in a feral smile as he leaned forward so the length of his cock lay along the crack of Sela's sweet ass. He bent over her back and used his free hand to push up her tank top and capture one of her small breasts in his hand. The rounded globe perfectly fit inside his hand, like a ripe apple. He squeezed the soft flesh and then pinched her nipple hard until she cried out.

"Is this what you want, Sela? This pain?" He pinched her nipple again, and she moaned and wiggled back against him.

"Your cock. Please, Aedan." She whimpered, and he released his hold on her head and straightened just long enough to position the head of his cock against her tight opening.

Without warning, he surged forward, thrusting hard inside her. He felt her body tear and stretch as her scream filled the air around him.

A primal roar tore from his throat as he buried himself deep inside her and ground into her until she whimpered and went still beneath him.

Aedan nearly spilled inside her right then.

Gods, she was so hot and tight. This woman's body was like being surrounded by heaven. He ground against her again, making room for his width while he spanked her ass cheeks with all his strength, the smack of flesh against flesh loud as the tangy scent of sex filled the room.

Her screams of pain mingled with pleasure surged through him, and he nearly laughed out loud with the powerful sensation.

Panting and fighting for control, he stopped with his cock buried deep inside her, his balls resting against her swollen labia lips. He dug his fingers into the sides of her hips, holding her in place. He didn't want her moving around and shattering his hard-won control.

Sela's breath came in harsh gasps, and her entire body shook as if she couldn't control the need coursing through her.

When the tingling inside his balls receded enough where he was sure he wouldn't disgrace himself, he grabbed her around the middle and lifted her feet off the floor.

"Aedan!" she warned.

When he bent her knees and posed her into a kneeling position with her face once again pressed into the comforter and his cock still inside her, she quieted and relaxed into the subservient pose.

This new position opened her wider, and he leaned forward, changing the angle and penetrating her even deeper than before.

A gasp and a long moan were Sela's only responses before he began pistoning into her with long, merciless strokes, again and again, while she thrashed and moaned under his firm grip. Her tight opening milked his cock until he thought he would shatter from the force of the explosion building inside him.

Almost distantly, he felt his balls slap against her flesh in time with his stomach smacking hard against her soft ass as he buried himself deep.

Their harsh breathing quickened as he punished her tight opening, with an occasional slap against one of her ass cheeks just to hear her scream with surprise.

"Come for me, Sela!" he commanded as he grabbed a handful of her hair and yanked back hard.

Sela shattered around him.

She screamed out her release as her body milked his aching cock with an endless wave of contractions.

The pressure inside his balls burst, and he gripped her hips and leaned forward so he didn't fall over as his seed spurted forward to fill Sela's sweet ass.

Sela, Queen of the Cunts, bit back a curse as Marco, the head of the Cunt Council, walked into her personal chambers uninvited.

She and Aedan had just finished another round of hot sex in the shower. However, the fact that she was currently crouched on the floor totally naked with a hard cock between her lips didn't seem to phase Marco, nor did it make him realize she wasn't in the mood for one of his long-winded reports.

Still, her curiosity was piqued. What would make Marco risk her wrath by intruding uninvited? He knew better than most that she didn't like being interrupted—in anything.

Aedan pulled on the silver chain attached to the clamps affixed to her sensitive nipples. The action sent a quick knife of arousal shooting from both nipples straight between her thighs. She winced as her still-sore ass clenched in remembrance of her earlier excursions.

A muffled moan escaped from her throat around the thick cock that filled her mouth.

"Why have you stopped, you lazy slut?" Aedan buried his fingers in her hair and yanked.

Sela bit down on his erection hard enough to make him realize they had company, but not so hard that it would inhibit the resumption of their activities once she got rid of Marco.

She sighed. The work of a queen was never done.

As much as she would like to kill Marco for his bouts of insolence over the years, he actually did a good job keeping the people in check so Sela could live as she pleased. None of her other council members were as competent as Marco—or as good in bed.

Of course, she had tired of him in that capacity years ago, but perhaps this was a good time to renew their acquaintance. The man had always had such iron control of both his body and his mind. She wondered what he would be like if she gave him the chance to dominate her.

Only sexually, of course.

In all other things, Sela liked her men submissive and obedient.

She had only recently discovered the thrill of giving someone else power during sex. And as much as she would love to indulge her newfound fetish freely, if it became common knowledge that the Queen of the Cunts liked to be dominated, her long reign as queen would be threatened.

Cunt society rewarded the strong, not the weak. However, Marco was loyal to her and would keep her secret, as had Aedan.

She gave Aedan's cock one last long lick as she prepared to return to her role as proud Queen of the Cunts.

Aedan's member shrank almost instantly, and she rose to her feet, unclipping the nipple clamps and dropping them to the floor as she started toward Marco.

A low growl sounded from Aedan, raising Sela's ire. She turned a glare on him that she had perfected over her long life. However, rather than sparking fear in his eyes, her consort held her gaze a few seconds longer than was respectful.

"That will be all, Aedan." Her voice dripped with acid. She would have to take some time after her discussion with Marco to ensure Aedan remembered his place in the hierarchy—which right now hovered just above the human who cleaned her toilets every day. He met a necessary need and did it well. But his presence was only required when she wished it.

Aedan scowled but left the room, the small silver chain he still held dragging the nipple clamps until they slithered out the door after him like metallic snakes.

Finally free of distractions, Sela stalked toward Marco like a predator. He had interrupted her play, and she thought she might enjoy having him make it up to her, especially since she would need to punish Aedan.

She took in Marco's chiseled good looks—the clean-shaven jaw, the aristocratic nose, and the sandy-blond hair tamed back into a simple queue behind his neck. His blue button-down shirt stretched over well-muscled shoulders, and his tailored black slacks did little to hide the impressive bulge she knew grew into a thick long cock with very little encouragement.

Marco stood unmoving and watched her with an expression that bordered on boredom.

Sela's temper flashed when she realized he hadn't even bothered to trace her nude form with his gaze. She prided herself on her trim, compact body and had used it to seduce thousands of men and women, both witches and humans.

How dare Marco not even appear to be effected?

There was a time when he would've done anything to spend one hour in her arms. In fact, he had betrayed his best friend for that very same inducement. She couldn't believe that time had changed him that much.

She ran her hands up his hard chest and then twined her arms around his neck as she pressed her naked body against him. The delicious friction from his fully clothed body against her bare skin thrummed power and hot arousal straight to her aching pussy and sensitive breasts. She ground her mound against him and nipped the side of his neck. He smelled like coffee and some type of spicy aftershave.

Marco made no move to embrace her, and no hard ridge of his arousal dug against her stomach like it used to whenever she was close to him. He accepted her attentions tacitly but made no move or expression to say he welcomed them.

Her temper flared, and she resisted the impulse to narrow her eyes, which would only let Marco know he had angered her. "Can't get it up anymore, Marco?" She ran one manicured fingernail along his jaw and over his bottom lip. "Isn't it sad what time can do to a man?"

"No, my queen." He continued to look at the far wall over her shoulder, his body relaxed and unmoving in her embrace. "I am perfectly capable, if you wish it. However, I came on urgent business important to the security of the throne, not pleasure."

She shoved away from him and cursed under her breath. The sudden movement didn't budge Marco from his stance. "I am queen; you'll do as I say." Her anger laced her words like a sharp blade. His statement about the security of the throne reached her, but she chose to salve her pride first.

"Yes, my queen." His voice was calm, as if they were discussing ordering office supplies.

"Prove to me you're still fit to be the head of this council, Marco, or I'll remove you and let the rest of the council decide your fate." Something they both knew would end in a slow painful death, since Marco had ruined many schemes for power in his long tenure as council head. "Look at me, damn it!"

Marco complied, although his blue gaze still held no fire, no anger, no passion—only a calm that grated against Sela's composure.

"Prove your worth *now*." She crossed her arms under her breasts and stared pointedly at Marco's crotch.

To the Cunts, as a society that needed sex not only to thrive, but to survive, a member who could no longer perform was a detriment. She doubted that was the case with Marco. He had always been able to get hard on command or even come or soften when directed. But the fact that he clearly no longer desired her as he once had, and she hadn't even noticed for all this time, grated against her ego.

The already impressive bulge in Marco's pants swelled until it was long and thick. If his dress shirt wasn't tucked in, the swollen head would've poked out the top of his waist band.

Sela licked her lips as memories of Marco's impressive length inside her flooded back to her. A hot surge of moisture rushed between her thighs, and her nipples puckered to hard, tight buds. "Mmm," she purred as she stepped forward to run her fingers over him. "I'd forgotten what a nice cock you have, Marco. Perhaps you would like a bit of pleasure before we discuss work?"

"As you wish, my queen." His voice remained flat and emotionless.

Hot anger rushed through her body, dissipating any fondness she had felt for him. She paced away from him as she ground her teeth.

Power built in Sela's right hand, multiplied from the sex she had shared earlier with Aedan, and she hurled the ball of energy at Marco.

He didn't attempt to evade the blow and didn't even flinch before it hit him full in the chest. Blue energy sizzled against his aura and then quickly dissipated as he absorbed it.

Sela had also forgotten how powerful Marco was. She could crush him, but it would take most of her energy to do it—even with the extra power reserves from her earlier bouts of sex with Aedan.

Aedan and the other lesser Cunts had spoiled her since she could subdue them with a simple ball of power.

Marco stumbled back a few steps but then righted himself and dropped his gaze to the ground at her feet. "My apologies if I have displeased you, my queen."

Insolent bastard! It was a good thing for him that she didn't have time right now to replace him.

"What report do you bring?" she snapped as she snatched up her robe from the foot of her bed and slipped it on. The silk caressed her sensitive bare skin and her tender ass cheeks nearly making her whimper.

Marco's blue gaze never wavered. "I have come to warn you, my queen."

"Warn me?" She turned to glance back at him. "What's happened?" Marco had always been loyal to her. In fact, he had been the one who had led them through the portal behind the castle on Tador the day they had tried to overthrow the throne. She had learned never to ignore his warnings—even when her first impulse was to punish the messenger.

"It has come to my attention that your consort has been making council decisions without my knowledge. He has also tried to portray himself as your political partner rather than your pleasure-giver, my queen." Marco dipped his chin in respect. "I thought you should know. He may be planning to overthrow you and usurp your power."

A laugh nearly bubbled up her throat at the thought of Aedan overthrowing *her*. Her consort was chosen for his sexual resourcefulness, not his power.

Irritation snapped through her veins. She had known from the beginning that Aedan had aspirations beyond his ability, but she had overlooked that since he had pleased her well in other areas. She turned to face Marco. "What decisions?" While she waited to hear the depth of her consort's betrayal, a thousand punishments, each more painful than the last, flitted through her mind. It had been quite a while since she had tortured someone. The thought tightened her nipples and sent a pulsing warmth between her thighs.

Marco glanced toward the door, most likely to ensure they were not overheard. "Do you know of the doctor, Kiera Matthews?"

"Cecily's half-breed daughter?" Sela nodded.

"The doctor met with Danen yesterday night to bring some of the people's concerns to the council, and a group of Klatch found them." When Sela didn't interrupt, he continued. "Danen spoke to two other council members to get approval to mark her for death, and when he could not get approval from a majority of the council needed for such an action, he received it instead from Aedan, who purportedly spoke for you, my queen."

"What?" Her simmering power flashed to a boil and escaped through her skin in all directions to sizzle along the walls and ceiling. A few small beams hit Marco, but they dissipated instantly.

Sela ground her teeth as she paced the length of the room and back. She couldn't care less about the doctor or Danen or whatever internal power struggles currently gripped the council. If Marco couldn't handle them, then he would be weeded out though natural selection.

However, Aedan having the audacity to believe that her submission in their sex play meant anything beyond that was unacceptable. He had been warned after his failures to capture both Alyssa and the Seer, and now he would pay. Worst of all was the knowledge that she had given him the key to her own destruction by entrusting him with her secret sexual desires.

A wistful sigh escaped her lips as she realized she would have to forego her newest domination fetish until she found someone else she could trust.

If she ever did.

She glanced up at Marco, who stood with downcast eyes waiting for her direction. He was a beautiful man, but she wasn't so sure it would be safe to let Marco have dominion over her in anything. Even though the thought made her shiver with anticipation.

Pity.

"Thank you for informing me, Marco." A small nod was all

the thanks she was willing to give beyond her clipped words. After all, it was his duty to inform her, not a favor among friends. "Danen is a fool. You may deal with his attempt to subvert your authority as you see fit." She waved her hand in his direction then stalked to the walk-in closet and threw open the door, allowing her gaze to rest lovingly on all of the sex and torture devices she had collected over the years.

Her banishment to Earth at the hands of the Klatch had taken its toll, but she had done her best to make herself at home on this godforsaken planet. Now she would spend the afternoon finding inventive ways to cause her consort pain and humiliation before he succumbed to death.

She smiled, her mood brightening as excitement lanced through her. "I'll deal with Aedan myself. Please send him in."

"As you wish, my queen."

6
_____

Aedan paced his chambers just down the hall from Sela's, waiting to be summoned back like a common servant.

He ground his teeth until his jaw ached.

How dare Marco interrupt them!

He picked up the lamp off his bedside table, ripping the cord from the wall.

Sparks flew from the socket, and the side of the room dimmed as the overhead light was the only illumination left in his windowless room deep inside Sela's house.

Gripping the lamp like a baseball bat, he smashed the pictures of erotic art that hung over his dresser. He swung again and again, venting his anger with each blow as his muscles tensed and flexed with the exertion.

The sounds of shattering glass soothed his nerves and filled him with an almost after-sex high. He rolled his neck from side to side, working out the muscle tension, and then dropped the ruined lamp at his feet for the servants to deal with later.

When he returned to Sela's chambers, he would punish her for his banishment. He would tie her to the bed and fuck her sweet ass until she screamed his name and begged him for more. Or better yet, he would deny her what she wanted most until she begged and groveled before him.

"Yes . . ." He smiled as the thought took root. A much better approach.

If Marco had business, it could've been discussed with Aedan present. He had proven himself trustworthy again and again, hadn't he?

The inept bastard may be the head of the council, but Aedan held the key to Sela's desires. There was no doubt in his mind that one day, he, Aedan, would rule by Sela's side—allowing her to indulge her whims while he actually ran things, of course. Then he would have Marco killed and fed to the dogs.

Not that he didn't see women as perfectly competent, but they were so easily manipulated, which made them inferior for higher offices, such as ruling as queen without a king to check their fickle emotions.

To prove that point, Aedan had insinuated himself in more and more Cunt business until the council had begun to come to him for approval on matters they were too afraid to approach Sela or Marco for. At that point, he knew his vision would come to pass. It was only a matter of time.

A brisk knock sounded against his door.

"Enter," he said, not bothering to hide the destruction of his quarters.

The door slid open, and Marco stepped through the open doorway.

"What do you want?" Aedan held his chin at a jaunty angle, making sure Marco knew his place.

Marco shook his head, and his lips curved into a grim smile. "Sela wishes you to return to her chambers."

Sweet satisfaction curled inside Aedan's belly. How deliciously ironic that Marco had been sent to him like a common messenger. "You've delivered your message, now be gone."

In the next instant, Aedan found himself slammed back against the wall with an ironlike grip across his throat slowly cutting off his air. It took a few long seconds for the pain to catch up to the realization, but when it did, his head and back throbbed and panic skittered along his spine.

He clawed at Marco's grip, but he might as well have been an ant trying to move a fallen log.

Marco's intense blue gaze burned into his and melted away his confidence like a candle before a flamethrower. "I realize you aren't the smartest man, Aedan. But if you don't learn to hold your tongue, I might have to cut it off."

Marco loosened his hold so fast that Aedan fell ass first on the floor of his room. He gulped in air and rubbed at his throat where Marco's hand had held him. "Your days are numbered," Aedan rasped. "Sela will never trust you with her secrets like she does me."

Marco's expression turned almost to pity. He reached out to pull the door closed before he turned back to stare down at Marco. "I already know her secrets, Aedan. It's my job to know and to keep her safe from others finding out."

Aedan pushed to his feet, confusion and panic pushing back the pain inside his throat. "I don't believe you. You know nothing."

Marco took a menacing step forward, and Aedan stood his ground and locked his knees to keep from taking an involuntary step back. "Sela's sexual habits don't interest me—it's my job to ensure the smooth running of the council and to know everything that goes on. And I do." Marco held Aedan's gaze, and Aedan had no problem reading all the knowledge there.

Aedan's blood ran cold. If Marco knew, how many others did, too? Not to mention, did Marco also know about his recent meddling? If so, Aedan would have to move fast to take Marco out and keep Sela on his side.

Marco turned and placed his hand on the doorknob without looking back. "Sela has asked for you. Don't keep her waiting."

"Something's wrong." Gavin waved his hand in a circular motion in front of him and ground his teeth as nothing happened.

Ryan and the Healer had been about to step through the portal when the shimmery opening had disappeared as if it had never been called.

"We can't wait inside the *between* forever, Gavin. The men are losing energy fast."

Gavin turned a murderous glare on his first lieutenant. "I'm well aware of where we are. I'm also well aware one of the royal family and his future mate are out there at the mercy of Cunt assassins." His deceptively calm voice cut through the stagnant air of the *between* like a whip.

The lieutenant dropped his gaze. "Yes, sir."

Gavin concentrated on the area in front of him and waved his hand over it again, visualizing the portal opening.

A small shower of silver sparks showered him before they fizzled and disappeared.

"Fuck!"

He clenched his jaw and took a deep breath as he prepared to do the unthinkable—create a portal. His gift did allow him to open new portals that had previously never existed, but he had never gambled anyone's life on the reputed instability of his attempts—especially Prince Ryan's.

But he would rather have the prince die in the *between* than by slow torture at the hands of the Cunts.

Gavin closed his eyes and visualized a shimmering silver portal opening just behind Prince Ryan and the Healer. He pictured the star-filled night sky behind them, the dark figures of the looming assassins and even the crisp scent of pine and rich earth.

He waved his hand in front of him again, and only the gasp of his men told him his efforts were successful, since he had kept his eyes closed to ensure his visualization never wavered.

When the loud spate of semi-automatic gunfire filled his senses, he opened his eyes.

Relief flooded through him at the sight of the portal open and shimmering before him.

Twenty feet in front of them, Ryan sat cross-legged on the ground with the Healer and some kind of orange animal pulled across his lap. Ryan's pink energy shield sizzled and popped around the huddled group as the bullets hit and bounced away in several different directions.

Gavin visualized his own internal energy wrapping around his body and the mouth of the portal to ensure no stray bullets caught himself or any of his men.

An explosion of pink energy lit the forest as it surrounded the assassins.

About time the reinforcements arrived.

One of the black-clad assassins screamed as the brightly colored electricity marched through his body, jerking his limbs and singeing all the hair on his body. The burnt hair smell was only an undercurrent within the sulfur and pine that already hung in the crisp night air. Energy traveled through the man's limbs, racing toward the earth, which sucked in the electricity in a greedy rush until the poor human dropped to the ground.

The other two assassins stopped shooting to keep from killing themselves inside their own energy bubble.

Pink merged with the blue energy of the Cunts as the two streams of power fought for dominance. The sharp sounds of electric strikes and sizzling echoed through the forest and drowned out everything else.

With each passing second, the blue energy enveloped by the pink dimmed and shrank until it disappeared completely.

The two Cunts made no sound as the power engulfed them, and they crumpled to the ground.

Five of Gavin's royal guards melted from the darkness to ensure the assassins posed no further threat.

"Clear the area, and recover the vehicle the prince arrived here in. We don't want to leave loose ends for another team of assassins to follow," Gavin said over his shoulder to his lieutenant as he strode toward Ryan. He didn't bother to wait for confirmation. His orders would be carried out exactly, as they always were. His men had been well trained.

Ryan's energy shield faded and then disappeared. The prince groaned and then slumped backward on the ground.

Gavin rushed forward to make sure Ryan hadn't been hurt. He stopped short as the moonlight glinted off a wicked-looking blade. His gaze took in the competently held weapon as well as the long graceful feminine fingers that gripped the hilt.

He resisted the smile of pride that tried to curve his lips. This little spitfire before him reminded him so much of Cecily, it was almost like having her back. No wonder Marco had kept a close watch on the little doctor all these years.

Gavin instinctively held up his hands, palms forward, like he would to calm a spooked animal. "Wait. I'm on your side, Healer. At least let me check on Prince Ryan before you gut me with that harpoon."

Her blue eyes narrowed, but after a quick glance down at Ryan, she slowly lowered the knife. "Sorry. Old habits and all that." She cocked her head to the side. A smudge of dirt swiped across her left cheek, and golden wisps of hair that had come loose from her ponytail fell over her forehead and into her eyes.

The Healer pushed the animal off her lap and then stood to face Gavin. "Ryan's got a mild energy burn on his right shoulder and an abrasion on his left temple from the driver's window. Other than that, he just needs to rest and recover. He's very low on energy."

The muscles in Gavin's shoulders relaxed at her diagnosis. The Healer had an excellent reputation for treating both Klatch and Cunts.

He gave a curt nod as ancient memories rose up to threaten his composure. "Let's get all of you back to Tador so he can rest."

Ryan groaned. "You can all stop talking about me like I'm an invalid. Someone help me up and I'll be fine." His words were stronger than Gavin suspected Ryan felt, but a quick gesture from Gavin, and two guards stepped forward to help the prince up. "Took you guys long enough."

"We couldn't keep the portals open, my lord." Gavin glanced at the other contingents of guards who nodded to confirm they had had the same issue. At least that explained why things had gotten so out of control.

Ryan nodded, his expression showed no surprise. "Gav, you'll have to hold the portal open for us to pass. Kiera has some type of affinity for energy."

The Healer stiffened beside Ryan, her mouth falling open in shock, and Gavin turned an appraising eye toward her.

"She absorbs energy blasts, and her presence interferes with portals." Ryan's steady gaze held confidence and just a touch of "I told you so."

Hot, heavy dread settled in the pit of Gavin's stomach.

Half-breeds didn't have magical gifts. Visions, premonitions and the like, but not true magical gifts. At least none ever had—until now. The significance of that wasn't lost on him or, apparently, anyone here, save the Healer herself.

Granted, Katelyn was a Seer, but she was a full human. Even though it was thought that she had some Klatch blood somewhere in her family line, she was a human with a special gift. And those gifts usually showed up after several generations of dilution. That's why many considered half-breeds to be even more worthless than humans as anything other than a source of gaining sexual energy to thrive and survive.

Cecily's gifts had been to amplify or dampen scents that already existed. She couldn't even create them, so the fact that her daughter had enough power to affect portals surprised Gavin. Perhaps her human father had some unknown Klatch blood somewhere in his distant bloodline? But even given that possibility, the offspring of such a match should not have produced such a powerful energy wielder.

Gavin nodded slowly as thoughts continued to race through his mind. "Yes, my lord. Let's get back to the castle." *And then I can figure out what the hell is going on.*

Kiera jumped as Ryan's fingers closed around hers.

"Let's get you somewhere safe, and then we can discuss this." His quick smile was a weak imitation of the one he'd used back at her safe house, which showed her how exhausted he truly was. She pulled her fingers from his and wrapped her arms around herself, even though with all the energy she'd absorbed, she was no longer cold.

There was nothing to be gained from dwelling on all the surprises she had encountered tonight until she was sure she was assassin free. She would have plenty of time to puzzle everything out later.

Her gaze swept over the dozen or so Klatch guards surrounding them, all dressed in unrelieved black. They were all built like a woman's wet dream, with well-defined muscles that thankfully didn't stray into steroids and muscles-so-big-they-couldn't-cross-their-arms-over-their-chests territory. The combination of the dappled moonlight and the soft silver glow from the still-open portal illuminated them in a fascinating display of alternating shadow and light that made her libido sit up and beg.

All of them had long dark hair either pulled back or spilling free over their shoulders, with varying shades of lavender eyes. They all moved with the same fluid grace Ryan did—contained violence . . . or passion waiting to be unleashed.

A heated shiver flowed over her skin, leaving her tingling and very aware in its wake.

Standing so near all this testosterone was heady and threatened to send her imagination, not to mention her libido, into overdrive—if it wasn't there already purely because of Ryan.

Her gaze settled on the man she'd pulled a knife on a few minutes earlier. He had to be the leader of Ryan's guards. Authority exuded from his every pore except when he spoke to Ryan, and then it changed to respectful deference.

The entire group reminded her of male models who might grace the pages of a calendar, but she had never seen any fireman calendar where all twelve months would be this smoking hot.

Talk about summer all year round!

Of course, Ryan could be the cover model as well as the pullout centerfold, and the leader of the guards could be Mr. December, which would definitely make women everywhere want December to last several months.

The Hot Hunks of Tador or *Once You Go Klatch, You'll Never Go Back.* She smirked at the thought but admitted she would gladly shell out a nice chunk of change to have these hotties to look at all year round.

Damn. Before tonight she had never seen a full-blooded Klatch. Now she was surrounded by them, and her entire body was extremely happy about it. Since when did she waste time drooling over some good-looking men when she was in danger?

"Where's Shiloh?" she asked, as she realized she'd been staring around the circle of men like a starving woman at a buffet line. Her voice sounded hoarse, and she cleared her throat self-consciously.

Maybe they hadn't noticed. She hoped.

One look at Ryan's mischievous expression told her she had been about as subtle as a male flasher in a convent.

Crap! Why can't I keep my hormones under control tonight?

Her cheeks heated, and she glanced around frantically for Shiloh. She wasn't so much worried about the feisty feline, but if he could save her from her own embarrassing actions, she would hand-feed him tuna for a month.

As if summoned by the promise inside her thoughts, Shiloh stepped from behind a copse of trees and picked his way gingerly toward her through the fallen pine needles.

"I'm sure the animal would be more comfortable remaining in the woods—" the leader of the guards began, distaste thick in his voice.

Kiera leaned down to pick up first her backpack, which she slipped over her shoulder, and then Shiloh. She straightened and met the leader's steady gaze with one of her own. "Shiloh stays with me. But I appreciate your . . . concern." Kiera made sure her words dripped with sarcasm. "Lead the way."

A laugh, which wasn't quite successfully disguised as a cough, sounded beside her from Ryan, and she resisted the urge to glance over at him. It was entirely too easy to lose herself in the dark depths of his eyes.

The leader's gaze cut to Ryan and then back to her. He gave a quick nod—something she now realized was his way of indicating acceptance, but not necessarily agreement. "I need to go last to ensure the portal stays open." His voice was cool and polite, with an undertone of something she couldn't quite place. He gestured for her to step through the portal, which still shimmered an ethereal silver.

Kiera glanced back at the guards to make sure one of them carried her gun duffel. When she confirmed that her weapons were safe, she took a deep breath and stepped forward.

The portal disappeared.

She looked around her, noting the concerned expressions from all the guards as well as Ryan and the leader of the guards. Frustration and a healthy dollop of disappointment throbbed through Kiera's temples. She had dreamed about walking through the *between* and seeing her mother's home world her entire life. To be so close and have that chance whisked away cut deep. Not to mention the fact that the entire group was in danger the longer they stood there.

Details . . .

Were the portals always this unstable? The one earlier had closed at a critical point and now this one. What would happen if it closed with them inside? She didn't know if it would wink them out of existence or if all their energy would be slowly sucked out into oblivion. Neither one sounded like something to look forward to.

"Damn. I was afraid of this." Ryan turned to Gavin and gestured toward Kiera. "Gavin, take her hand and maybe you can ensure her energy doesn't counter yours."

Kiera stiffened before she realized it and then purposely relaxed. What did he mean about her energy countering Gavin's? She wished they had time for her to ask more about this "energy affinity," as Ryan had called it. Was she endangering everyone purely by being there?

"I don't see how holding hands with him is going to help keep the portal open." She knew it sounded stupid, but after the night she'd had, she figured she was allowed to be a bit grumpy.

Ryan took her hand and raised it to his lips. He brushed a tender kiss over the sensitive skin on the back of her hand.

Kiera snatched her hand back as a shiver snaked through her—but definitely not from the cold. In fact, an insidious curl of warmth wormed its way through her body and pooled inside her core as she looked into Ryan's dark purple, nearly black eyes.

"Trust me."

She clenched her jaw so hard it hurt. She wasn't good at trusting strangers, but as she had already decided to trust him back at the cabin, she might as well go the full distance. She raised her chin before she offered her hand, palm out, to Gavin.

Ryan tried to take Shiloh with his uninjured arm. When he winced, another guard stepped close and took the cat—surprisingly, without any "mrowrrs" of protest.

Gavin waved his hand in the air, and the portal opened and grew until any of the guards could easily pass through without having to duck—which meant her own five-feet-six frame would fit easily.

Gavin stepped close to her but didn't take her hand. "Breathe deep and hold a picture in your mind of the open portal, just like you see it here. Don't let it waver, and once you take my hand, don't let go, no matter what happens. I'll make sure you're safe."

A nervous laugh escaped from her. She dropped her hand to her side. "Lie back, relax and everything will be fine. Famous last words." How could he truly guarantee her safety? If the portals were failing, that was out of his hands and everyone else's.

"You have my word, Healer." Gavin's gaze was open and genuine as she studied him.

"It's all right, Kiera," Ryan added. "He knows if he lets anything happen to you, I'll kick his ass, and so will the queen and the Seer."

Gavin cast an irritated gaze toward Ryan, but his words did have an effect.

Kiera definitely wanted to meet the queen and the Seer if the mere mention of incurring their wrath could rattle this stubborn guard. Not to mention that maybe the Klatch would be open to her reunification plan, where the Cunt Council was not. She nodded to Ryan and then turned back to Gavin. "Okay, let's do it."

Gavin took her hand in his, and while his fingers were warm, there was no hot spark of attraction like when she touched Ryan. However, she felt some strange sense of familiarity that she couldn't account for. Her brow furrowed as she glanced over at him.

Gavin watched her, but his face was a blank mask. "Whenever you're ready, Healer."

Kiera chided herself for forgetting the task ahead. What was it about these Klatch that rattled her? She shoved the thought aside to study later.

The cool night air stung her nostrils as she inhaled deep and closed her eyes. She pictured the shimmering portal with the individual sprinkles of light that seemed to dance in and out of its surface. A mental image of all of them safely entering the portal played out in her mind, and almost outside herself, she noticed that Gavin tugged her forward.

When a bone-chilling cold closed around her like a greedy hand, she gasped, and Gavin tightened his grip around her fingers. The gasp only served to suck in a lungful of musty air and leave her with the tangy taste of mold on the back of her tongue. Some type of energy sizzled all around her, raising every hair on her body and making her shiver.

"You can open your eyes, Healer. We are inside the *between*," came Gavin's deep voice from beside her.

The *between* was exactly like her mother had described, and yet . . . not. Inky blackness surrounded them as if it were a living entity. This place was both oppressive and barren at the same time. With every second that passed, she felt as if some of her life force leaked out into the void around her. Almost as if it fed on her like a greedy parasite.

A pink ball of throbbing light formed in Gavin's free hand, but its illumination allowed them to see only one step in front of them. The shuffle of the guards' feet ahead of them told her they were still there, but she couldn't see even their shadowy forms.

Her restored vigor from the energy blasts earlier steadily leeched out into the oppressive air around them. Every step was like walking through thick molasses, and after only a few feet, she thought longingly of sitting down to rest. Every limb suddenly weighed a thousand pounds, and she had to concentrate to achieve each small movement.

"It's not much farther," Ryan said beside her. "You can rest all you want when we've made it to the other side."

Kiera didn't bother to spare the energy to answer. Instead, she concentrated on putting one foot in front of the other and moving forward toward Tador.

The thought lent her some measure of energy, and she quickened her pace. For as long as she could remember, she had longed to see Tador. She remembered curling on her mother's lap, safe and warm, while she listened to tales about the magical home world of the Cunts and the Klatch.

In a few more minutes, she would be there.

What if it didn't live up to the fantasy she had built inside her imagination? Reality rarely did, but she was unwilling to give up this last piece of her mother that they shared, so she let her hope continue to blossom.

A sudden blinding light pierced her retinas and shot white-hot pain through her skull.

She groaned as she closed her eyes tight.

When her eyes finally adjusted behind her eyelids, she cracked one eye open. After a few seconds, the light stopped slicing through her skull like a laser, and she opened the other eye and gazed ahead in wonder.

There was still about thirty feet of blackness in front of her, but at least now she could see the guards they followed as the men exited the portal and stepped into what resembled her mental image of the Garden of Eden.

"Amazing." Her voice was filled with reverence and awe she didn't bother to hide.

She rushed forward, nearly dragging Gavin with her.

The portal closed with a snap just before she reached it, and they were plunged into oppressive darkness.

"No!" She stomped her foot in frustration.

Gavin moved beside her, and the portal reappeared and grew once again. "Just like when we came in. Visualize." His deep voice held no rebuke, only a gentle reminder.

Kiera huffed in frustration, but closed her eyes to comply. When tingling warmth bathed her skin, she opened her eyes to a sight that made all her childhood imaginings pale in comparison.

A joyous laugh spilled from her lips.

She stepped forward and then dropped Gavin's hand to turn in a circle as she tried to see everything at once.

Dappled sunshine kissed green rolling hills that reminded her of pictures she'd seen of Ireland and the English countryside. Lush trees and plants of every color imaginable dotted the landscape in blues, greens, lavenders and reds. Birds and wildlife chirped and rustled, giving the impression that she'd stepped into a pristine rainforest. A crisp fresh breeze brushed the escaped strands of her hair against her cheek and carried the sweet scent of flowers.

Emotion welled up thick inside her throat. She wished her mother and father could be here with her right now. A deep breath helped her swallow back her longing and maintain her composure.

"Welcome to Tador."

Ryan's voice spilled over her like an erotic caress against bare skin, and a rush of tingling electricity snaked up through her feet and into her body.

Her nipples pebbled into hard aching nubs and moisture dampened the inside of her thighs as an overwhelming wave of arousal hit her like an open-handed slap, while a loud buzzing noise raged inside her head.

A surprised gasp ripped from her throat, and her knees threatened to buckle.

Strong arms closed around her, steadying her, but the arousal continued to build inside her until even the soft breeze against her skin was torture to her over-sensitized system.

"Kiera?"

"Mrowwr."

"Healer?"

Sounds blurred together with what was happening inside her body until she couldn't distinguish one sensation from the other.

Peaceful blackness called to her, and as Shiloh's fuzzy form curled beside her, she slipped into its calm depths with a contented sigh.

7

Awareness slowly crept through Kiera. Her sleepy mind registered that she was warm, comfortable and not in pain, which was always a plus. She indulged in a small sigh of contentment as she flexed her fingers against fluffy soft sheets.

A woodsy masculine scent surrounded her, and she breathed deep, as if she inhaled pure comfort. Warmth radiated from the roughened male hand cupping her breast, and the hard ridge nestled along the crack of her bare ass thickened as if it sensed she was awake.

A small zing of excitement curled through her, and she cuddled closer, a small "mmm" escaping from her when the thick member hardened further.

Her eyes flew open as she came fully awake and her brain registered the meaning of those sensations.

She scrambled from the bed.

When cool air hit her bare skin, she yanked the comforter from the bed and wrapped it around herself, trying to maintain a fighting stance and her dignity at the same time.

"Morning." Ryan's voice was a low sleepy rumble that turned

her insides to jelly and made her body react instantly, as if she'd entered a second puberty. His dark hair was mussed and frothed around his face and shoulders, looking soft and very touchable.

A sudden picture of all that dark hair skimming over her breasts and arms as he pushed inside her made her clit swell to attention and creamy moisture pool between her thighs. She relaxed her fighting stance and instead curled the comforter tighter around her suddenly aching breasts.

He pushed up on his elbow, his head cradled in his long-fingered hand. The sheet slipped dangerously low on his trim hips, giving her a front-row view of his muscular shoulders and his golden skin stretched tightly over some nicely defined abs. A smattering of dark crisp hairs peppered his chest and made her want to reach out and touch. Faint lines from the sheets still marked his left cheek, and his long scar carved down his right cheek just touching the edge of his lips.

"I'm glad you're awake," he continued, either oblivious or uncaring about the affect his morning voice and everything else about him had on her. "You had me worried there for a while."

Questions flew through her mind too fast for her to choose just one. She held the comforter tighter around her body and glared down at Ryan, who seemed not to notice her displeasure.

"Are you feeling better?" he prompted when she remained silent.

"Better?" she snapped. "I'm naked!"

A slow sensual grin curved his lips and stole her breath from her lungs. "I noticed." His dark gaze traced her body as if he could see through the comforter. "When you didn't wake, we realized the planet had an affinity with you, and the only thing that would heal you was sexual energy."

Her eyes opened wide in surprise and shock—and embarrassingly, just a touch of excitement.

She knew if she was still sane she would be pissed, feel violated and have anger pumping through her veins. Her veins did have lava pumping through them, but it was lust, not anger heating her blood—after all, she *was* part Cunt. "You . . . you had sex with me while I was asleep?" The last word came out in a very girly squeak.

Ryan tossed back the thin sheet that covered him and sat up, baring the rest of his golden skin, defined muscles and the thick, long cock that she had wiggled her ass against mere moments ago. His eyes narrowed, and his gaze turned flat and hard as his dark brow furrowed. "I would never take an unwilling woman, let alone an unconscious one." He tipped his chin and his hair slid into place to hide his scar, almost as if the gesture made him feel less exposed.

Kiera swallowed hard and reminded herself that she had every right to question how she ended up naked in his bed and what had happened since she'd passed out. She raised her chin to chase back a flash of guilt that tried to trickle to the surface from her quick accusation. "Why don't we start over?" Her hair fell into her eyes, and she shoved it away, only then realizing that her hair was no longer pulled back into a ponytail. "I remember blacking out after we stepped through the portal. Then what happened?"

Ryan studied her for a long moment and then relaxed, his posture open and easy as if he sat around naked with a very impressive hard-on every day.

He probably does, she reminded herself.

After all, she had grown up on the fringes of Cunt culture, and the Klatch and Cunts used to live as one race. They couldn't be all that different.

Cunts were extremely sexual people—most honest, hardworking and ethical. However, there were quite a few, including Sela and her followers, who had sexual tastes that went way beyond Kiera's comfort zone. She had seen firsthand in her clinic the aftereffects and pain of the victims of such twisted perversions.

She pulled the comforter tighter around her as she wondered where the Klatch drew the line. Or more specifically, where Ryan did.

"You were immediately brought to the castle, cleaned up and put to bed," he said, breaking her out of her own thoughts. "You slept for an entire day and grew only more pale with each passing hour." He scrubbed his hands over his face as if wiping away the memory. "Your cat wouldn't let anyone near you but me."

A quick glance around the room for Shiloh showed her pristine white walls made of shiny white rock, with pink glittering crystals sprinkled throughout—*balda*, her memory supplied from her mother's stories. There was a chest of drawers, a bookshelf filled with various books and the huge four-poster bed Ryan still sat on. All of them looked to be made out of a combination of cherrywood and the same *balda* stone that made up the walls and floor.

Her gaze took in the maroon and hunter green drapes that billowed at the window and the double French doors that led out to a balcony. A few personal items, such as a brush and a bottle of what looked like cologne, sat on the chest of drawers, but other than that, the room was neat and decidedly masculine. Probably Ryan's.

However, she didn't see Shiloh anywhere.

"He is most likely down in the kitchen again. We don't have any cats on Tador, so he's a definite novelty. He's being spoiled rotten." His voice held a trace of amusement as well as affection for Shiloh, which surprised her.

"So much for him not leaving my side." She shook her head. "So, how did I go from pale and waning to waking up warm and naked with you?" Her voice sounded husky and low, and she swallowed hard and hoped he hadn't noticed.

Ryan shrugged. "The planet sensed you as someone sensitive to its energy. From past experience with the queen and the Seer, we knew the only way to heal you was with sexual energy."

"And?" she prompted, holding her breath for his answer.

"And, since I don't have the benefit of visions like they did, I settled for the next best thing—body-to-body contact and curling next to you with what is probably the universe's longest-running erection." The corners of his mouth curved slightly, but he kept his dark waterfall of hair over his scar.

A flash of heat rushed to every erogenous zone Kiera had as she remembered that large erection nestled against the crack of her ass when she woke. She couldn't help a quick glance down to see the swollen shaft pointing straight at her out of its nest of dark curls. Heat filled her face, and she raised her gaze to his. "Well, apparently it worked." She licked her lips, and his eyes darkened to nearly black. "Thanks."

He stood, which brought his Adam's apple eye level and surrounded her with his woodsy scent. Her nipples hardened into tight pebbles as she remembered his warm hand cupped over her breast as if it belonged there. She swallowed hard.

"Why don't I let you get dressed, and then we can all sit down and talk about what to do next."

"Next?" she asked, feeling as if her brain were drowning in arousal.

Ryan chuckled and cupped her chin, raising it until he captured her gaze.

Her mind screamed at her to pull away, but her body seemed frozen in place.

He stood so close, his warm breath feathered against her lips, and if he didn't still have his hand on her chin, she might have been tempted to close the gap between them and press her lips, along with her body, against him. "Once you understand what's involved in being our Healer, I hope you look at me like that again, Kiera Matthews." He brushed a single kiss across her lips and walked across the room toward the chest of drawers.

Her lips tingled as if he'd applied warm menthol over them, and she couldn't help but brush her fingers over the sensitive skin. "What are you talking about? I know you said you needed a doctor, and I'm more than willing to offer my expertise—"

Ryan's low rumble of a laugh cut through her words. He pulled renaissance-looking trousers, socks and a tunic from the chest of drawers. "I will be glad to partake of any expertise you care to offer. However, I think you had better hear us out before you offer it." He pulled on his trousers, his dark purple eyes studying her with amusement.

She barely heard his response. A shiver ran through her as her gaze drank in every inch of golden skin as it was covered by cloth. When he tucked his still-stiff cock inside the trousers, she swallowed hard against her disappointment.

Damn. Maybe I have more Cunt running through my blood than I thought.

"I don't understand."

Ryan pulled on his tunic and, with his socks still in one hand, stooped to pick up her backpack and toss it on the bed. "You will. As soon as you get dressed, we'll head downstairs for some lunch, and we'll fill you in on everything." He sat on the bed to pull on his socks and a pair of well-worn leather boots she hadn't noticed earlier.

She huffed and chided herself for acting like a child. After all, it wasn't like he hadn't already seen her naked—up close and personal. This was a world where sex was as needed as food or water, and nudity was natural. It wasn't as if her mother hadn't already told her what it was like here on Tador.

Damn it, Kiera. You're a doctor and an adult. Leave the shyness back on Earth.

Kiera squared her shoulders and then tossed the comforter on the bed next to her backpack.

Cool air closed around her and she stepped forward toward the bed and her waiting backpack.

A quick intake of breath from Ryan nearly made her smile. At least she wasn't the only one affected here.

Nothing like a boost to the feminine pride to make something easier.

Without glancing over at him, she unzipped her backpack and leaned over to rifle the contents, well aware that her breasts bobbed just at Ryan's eye level.

Her hand closed around a matching lemon yellow lacy bra and thong. She dug deeper and found a pair of jeans, a soft cotton V-neck T-shirt, some socks and her brush.

She dropped them on the bed and then stepped into the thong, feeling Ryan's heated gaze tracing her every movement as she pulled the wispy scrap of lace into place. She put on her bra next, and as soon as she fastened the front hook and adjusted her breasts inside the lacy cups, she couldn't help but glance over at Ryan.

To his credit, his gaze immediately moved to hers rather than staying on her newly covered anatomy. His small smile held wonder and awe, with no hint of embarrassment. "I think yellow is my new favorite color."

She laughed, the sound breaking through the thick sexual tension coiled inside the room. "I don't know," she said playfully as she reached for her jeans, "I think I preferred the color of your underwear." A sudden mental image of Ryan sitting on the bed in all his naked golden-skinned glory flashed through her mind.

"I'm not wearing any." His gaze danced with amusement, and she turned away to step into her jeans.

"Really?" she asked innocently as she pulled on her shirt. As if every inch of his amazing body wasn't now burned into her mind's eye for later perusal. "I'll have to pay better attention next time."

Ryan waited while Kiera pulled on her socks and tennis shoes and brushed out her long blond hair until it frothed around her shoulders in a golden waterfall.

She had surprised him when she'd dropped the comforter and dressed in front of him. Half Cunt she might be, but she had been raised as a human, and modesty was engrained quite early in that culture.

Not that he hadn't appreciated the view.

He'd had enough time to imagine what her athletic-tight body looked like while she was nestled up against him for a full day and night. And even though Ryan fancied he had quite a good imagination, his had paled in comparison with the real thing.

His hard cock throbbed inside his trousers at the tactile memory of her shapely ass rubbing against him this morning when she woke.

Sasha, the queen's lady's maid, had undressed his Healer and put her to bed. By the time he had been allowed in to see her, her pale arms and shoulders were all that was visible above his thick down comforter. Which had only served to kick his imagination about her attributes into overdrive.

"I don't think I thanked you, by the way," she said as she tossed her brush back inside her backpack and closed the zipper. "I'm sorry about my reaction earlier. I'm not used to waking up naked in a situation I don't remember."

"Or with a man you've just met?"

A smile blossomed across her lips and lit her entire face, making her even more beautiful. "Exactly." She shrugged. "I think it was more waking up *naked* with a *naked* man I've just met that freaked me out a bit."

He nodded and stood to face her. "I want you to know that

if there were any other way to heal you, I wouldn't have placed you in that position without your consent. Although, I must admit, other than my aching erection, it wasn't a great hardship for me."

One corner of her mouth quirked, and she glanced at him from under her golden eyelashes. "I appreciate that. Even if I didn't show it when I woke up." She cleared her throat as if to change the subject and glanced around the room. "So, you mentioned food. I'm starving. And I can't wait to see, well . . . everything."

Her entire body vibrated with curiosity and excitement, which was a large contrast to what he had expected.

"You don't seem very surprised by all of this." He gestured around them. "Most women in your position would be confused, scared or disbelieving." He remembered both Queen Alyssandra's and Katelyn, the Seer's, reactions when they had arrived.

Her quick laugh filled the room and brushed against him like an erotic caress. "I'm not most women."

Talk about an understatement.

She pursed her lips as if choosing her words carefully. "I'll admit, I'm worried about my father, my patients, my clinic and even the house I grew up in. However, dwelling on any of that won't make it different." She shrugged, her clear blue gaze tinged with sadness. "Besides, before my mother died, she told me all about Tador. I've spent my whole life hoping to get to see it, and hoping that both races would come to their senses and see that they need each other." All traces of sadness fled to be replaced by barely concealed excitement.

Her impassioned words surprised Ryan. Gavin had told him about the content of her meeting with the Cunts, but he'd been too busy trying to make sure she was alive and unhurt to give it much thought.

"Gavin told me about your mother." Actually, Ryan had

heard the castle gossip about Gavin and Cecily's torrid affair, but had gotten only a bare bones confirmation from Gavin.

Before a few weeks ago, when Queen Alyssandra had repealed the old law, royal guards were discouraged from having any type of committed relationships except with other guards. So Gavin's open pursuit of the young Cunt had caused a small scandal at the time, but in the wake of the war, it had quickly lost importance. He cleared his throat. "I think they were very close before the civil war."

Kiera's golden brows furrowed, and she rested her fists on her hips, her head cocked to one side as she studied him. "Gavin. The leader of your guards? The overbearing one who wanted me to leave Shiloh in the forest?" She shook her head. "He just doesn't seem my mother's type."

Amusement curved Ryan's lips. "That's him. But I wouldn't judge him too harshly on either count. He hasn't spent as much time on Earth as some of the younger Klatch. Time and events can change people." Ryan reached out to rub a chunk of her golden hair between his thumb and forefinger. The silky texture as well as her sweet musk and cinnamon scent seeped into him as he memorized the sensation for later.

Kiera's brow furrowed, and her eyes darkened as she watched him. With great reluctance, he dropped his hand. "And as I said earlier, domesticated house pets aren't common here, and we have no cats at all, so he thinks all animals are wild beasts unless it's a horse, cow or ox."

Kiera seemed as if she were about to say something else, but instead, she shook her head again and dropped her arms to her sides.

"Shall we?" He gestured toward the door for her to precede him.

Twenty minutes later they had finally made it downstairs to meet the king and queen, Prince Grayson and Katelyn for lunch.

Kiera had asked thousands of questions about everything from the names of every servant they passed to the history of some of the furnishings. Just being near her made Ryan see his world through fresh eyes.

He realized how proud he was of his heritage and how eager he was to show her everything there was to offer if she agreed to become the Healer he knew her already to be.

Her delight with even the smallest things also reminded him how much he took for granted. After all, he had grown up here, while she had been forced to live as an outcast on Earth. Until today, he hadn't realized how truly lucky he was.

"Through here?" she asked as she pointed toward the large wooden double doors that led to the throne room, where they were to meet for lunch.

When he nodded, she eagerly led the way and held out her hand to the majordomo as they approached. "Hi, I'm Kiera."

The aging majordomo, who had held his post for much longer than Ryan had been alive, bowed before her but didn't take her hand. Not that Ryan had ever seen the old man touch anyone—probably not good form for a majordomo, not that Kiera seemed likely to bow to that tradition.

"Welcome to Tador, Healer." The majordomo rose and glanced toward Ryan with a nod of respect. "My lord. I'll announce you."

"Thanks. What's your name?" Kiera asked before he could turn away, which had the effect of making the older man's brows furrow, a genuinely confused expression on his weathered face.

Ryan frowned as he realized he had never thought to ask the man his name. In fact, he had never even wondered if he had one.

The old man had been a fixture at the castle, and just like the walls and the rooms, Ryan had taken him for granted, not realizing or caring that the man had a name and an identity beyond that of a majordomo.

"Silas, my lady."

"It's nice to meet you, Silas." She smiled, and much to Ryan's surprise, the majordomo smiled back like a love-struck schoolboy. Before this instant, Ryan would've bet the man was physically incapable of smiling. "What job do you do here at the castle?" She leaned close as if imparting a confidence. "I'm trying to learn as much as I can while I'm here."

"I'm the majordomo, my lady." The man's chest swelled with pride, and his bright lavender eyes sparkled with obvious delight. "I maintain the privacy of the king and queen and any they choose to meet with. I also maintain their meeting schedules, keep their confidences and manage the downstairs castle staff."

"How long have you been at your post?"

"I was promoted to majordomo one hundred years ago next week, my lady."

Shock traveled through Ryan as Kiera sucked in a quick breath. He knew the man was old, but he had no idea he was quite *that* old. Since Ryan was only in his thirties, he supposed he didn't really have a good perspective on Klatch aging yet.

"Wow. My mother told me some terrific stories about growing up on Tador, but I'll bet you have some even better ones. Would you be willing to share them sometime when you're off duty?"

"Most definitely, my lady." The man practically beamed at Kiera. "I would be more than happy to tell you any you would like to hear, allowing, of course, that I cannot reveal anything about any of the royals' private business. But I've lived through many years of Tador's history and can tell you quite a bit without breaking my trust with the throne."

"It's a deal then." Kiera reached out and grabbed Silas hand, and he didn't pull away. The majordomo's eyes widened in surprise, but he recovered quickly. He bowed and kissed the back of her hand, earning a blush from Kiera and grudging respect from Ryan.

"I look forward to it, my lady. I must say, you remind me very much of your mother. Cecily was a whirlwind of energy." The older man straightened and winked at her.

"You knew her mother?"

"You knew my mother?"

Ryan and Kiera's voices blended together.

"I did," Silas confirmed. "She spent quite a bit of time at the castle until . . ." His words trailed off and an uncomfortable silence followed. Silas cleared his throat.

"Does it bother you that I'm half Cunt and I'm here on Tador?" Kiera asked Silas matter-of-factly.

"No, my lady. I've been around a long time—long enough to know that not all of the Cunts are bad and not all were involved in the rebellion against Queen Annalecia and King Darius." He shook his head sadly. "Unfortunately, it was so difficult to tell friend from foe then, and when the princess was kidnapped . . . lines were drawn that changed all our lives forever."

Kiera brushed a quick kiss across Silas' papery cheek, and the old man blushed like a virgin.

"Well then," he said gruffly. "I'll announce you. I look forward to speaking with you again, Healer."

A sudden thought struck Ryan, and he studied the majordomo for a moment. "Silas." Ryan placed his hand on the door before the older man pulled it open. "Do you know anything about the past implementations of the Triangle?"

The majordomo nodded. "My great grandmother told me stories of it, but I know most of the people have forgotten. A lot of our history is in danger of being lost if we aren't careful, my lord."

The old man's answer couldn't have surprised Ryan any more if he had punched him in the solar plexus. They had been desperate for a solution to save the planet, and if Alyssandra hadn't stumbled upon mention of it in some of the journals in the Queen's archives, they would be facing the eventual destruction of their home planet. "Why didn't you say anything when Queen Alyssandra first suggested it?"

Silas' already stiff posture straightened further, and his mouth thinned into a disapproving line. " 'Twasn't my place to offer, my lord. I'm just a loyal servant. And besides," he sniffed, "no one asked me."

8

Kiera barely heard Silas announce them as she craned her neck to try to see every inch of the throne room at once.

The room was easily as big as her whole house back on Earth, and it was entirely made of the pristine white *balda* stone she had seen everywhere else in the castle. Intricate tapestries adorned the walls, and a strip of plush purple carpet bisected the room, starting at the doors and running all the way up to cover a raised dais against the back wall.

Two high-backed purple velvet thrones sat upon the dais, with a small dark wood table between them. Just at the base of the dais, Shiloh stood eating out of a white porcelain bowl painted with intricate designs. He spared a quick glance for her and then lowered his head to continue eating, his orange tail swishing contentedly behind him.

Kiera rolled her eyes. At least Shiloh was making himself at home.

The sounds of chairs scraping against the stone floor caught her attention, and she glanced toward the right side of the room.

Two couples stood and watched her expectantly, the men's hands protectively resting on their respective women's shoulders.

She and Ryan walked forward, closing the distance and stopping about five feet away.

The first woman had long dark hair down past her ass, which flowed around her almost as if it had a life of its own. She was voluptuous and exotic in a gauzy purple half shirt, which showed the full bottom globes of her generous breasts, and a gauzy skirt that showed more than it hid.

The thing that captured Kiera's attention most was the woman's liquid lavender eyes. She had never seen eyes quite like them—even among the contingent of guards she had met—and she had to resist the urge to stare.

The second woman was a few inches taller than the first and not quite as curvy, with a waterfall of thick red hair, a generous smattering of freckles across her nose and cheeks, and piercing green eyes. She wore a simple V-neck top and jeans. An easy, friendly manner exuded from her like perfume, and Kiera liked her immediately.

Kiera was surprised to notice that the redhead was definitely not Klatch. She had never heard of a full-blooded royal marrying a human, but unless she was mistaken, that was the pairing she saw here.

If that was the case, maybe the Klatch were more open to the reunification than her own people had been. A small spark of hope warmed her.

The men were both well built, with the same golden skin as Ryan and the same long dark hair pulled back and fastened at the base of their necks. However, whereas Ryan's eyes were so dark purple they were almost black, the first man's eyes were a soft lavender similar to the dark-haired woman's, and the second man's reminded her of melted amethysts.

They both stood several inches taller than Ryan, and regardless of their similar coloring and features, would never be mistaken for one another. The first had an unmistakable air of authority, whereas the second exuded the same easy affability as the redhead.

Ryan's warm hand against her lower back startled her out of her perusal, and she stepped forward toward the group. As she neared, she finally noticed the table between them nearly overflowing with food—some familiar and some not.

The scent of cooked meat and rich coffee filled her nostrils, and her stomach growled so loud that everyone smiled. Kiera smothered a laugh and placed her hand over her stomach, silently promising to feed it soon.

The dark-haired woman stepped forward, her hand held out in greeting. Her heart-shaped face curious, she glanced down, since Kiera was several inches shorter, but her gaze was open and friendly. "Welcome to Tador, Kiera," she said as she clasped Kiera's hand in hers. "I'm Queen Alyssandra. But, please, call me Alyssa." She smiled, her kohl-lined eyes sparkling with curiosity. "Come, sit; you're obviously hungry."

A warmth, which felt almost like an instant kinship, spread through Kiera, and she knew she could easily become friends with this woman.

How strange that her people had vilified the Klatch royals so much so that the Cunts had tried to overthrow the throne and had ended up banished from their own home. And yet, this woman seemed nothing but friendly and inviting, and so had Silas. Kiera wondered how many other Klatch were the same way.

Before Kiera could return the greeting, the queen pulled one of the men forward. "This is my husband, King Stone."

The king took Kiera's hand and bowed over it, laying a quick warm kiss on the back of her fingertips before smiling up at her. "Welcome to Tador, Healer. I hope you enjoy it here."

Heat seared Kiera's cheeks, and everyone smiled except for Ryan, who scowled softly beside her.

The redhead extended her hand. "Before the men goad Ryan into a fist-fight and delay our breakfast, I'm Katelyn, the Seer." Her grip was firm and dry, her smile wide and genuine. Kiera wondered briefly what a seer was beyond what she could infer. "And this other testosterone delight is my husband, Prince Grayson."

Grayson bowed over Kiera's hand, brushing a kiss across the back of her knuckles as the king had. "I love it when she calls me that." He winked as he straightened, and at Ryan's warning growl next to her, Katelyn smacked her husband lightly on the shoulder.

"All right," the Seer said. "You guys can screw with Ryan later. God knows he deserves it." She aimed a fond smile toward Ryan, and Kiera wondered what history laid between Ryan and this beautiful redhead.

A small curl of jealousy wound through her, making her gut clench and surprising her. She had just met the man and had no designs on him beyond some steamy sex. So why did the obvious affection and past history between him and the gorgeous redhead bring out her inner defenses?

That was totally out of character for her. Marriage, picket fences and everything that went with it had never been in her life plan.

Her emotions must've shown on her face, because the Seer added, "It's a long story, but Ryan and I were childhood playmates. Then we didn't meet again until several weeks ago when I met Grayson." She arched an eyebrow at Ryan, but her severe look dissolved into a fond grin.

Several weeks? Damn.

Kiera ignored the surge of relief that flowed through her that there had been no romantic connection between Ryan and the Seer. But she could definitely see how easy it would be to get used to having a dark, handsome man around. Something she needed to be on guard against since she wouldn't be here for long—that was, if she could find a way to call off the assassins.

A twinge of regret pinched her insides, and she pressed her hand to her stomach again, silently willing the sensation away.

Out loud, she said, "I'm happy to meet all of you. I appreciate the hospitality, and I'm sorry if I've caused any problems with my sudden arrival." She pointed toward Shiloh, who had finished eating and was making his way toward them. "I hope Shiloh hasn't been a bother. He tends to have a mind of his own."

Katelyn leaned down to ruffle Shiloh's orange fur. "It's been kind of nice having a cat around to spoil. It's one of the things I miss from Earth."

Shiloh rubbed against the Seer's leg before padding over to a pile of fluffy blankets by the wall and curling into a large orange ball to sleep.

Ryan pulled out a chair for Kiera, and she sat as everyone else took their places around the table. Ryan slid into the seat beside her. He was a solid, comforting warmth next to her, and she tried not to enjoy the sensation too much. After all, she reminded herself more forcefully this time, her time here was limited. It wouldn't be good for anyone if she got too attached or too used to Ryan's company.

Everyone reached for food, filling their plates and passing the serving dishes to one another with easy camaraderie that told Kiera they ate together often. Kiera's gaze took in some type of meat pastry that smelled heavenly, fresh strawberries, melons and several fruits she didn't recognize right away but then remembered her mother telling her about, as well as Danishes and pitchers and carafes filled with water, tea and what had to be coffee from the tantalizing scent.

"We're glad to have you here," said the queen, startling her out of her perusal of the food. "We have a lot we would like to discuss with you, if you don't mind us talking over breakfast."

Ryan held up a coffee carafe, and Kiera nodded and inhaled deeply as the aroma of rich vanilla coffee rose around her.

"Thank the Goddess," said Katelyn as she passed Kiera a small plate that held cream and sugar. "I'm glad I'm not the only coffee drinker among us. Everyone else prefers chai tea or water." The Seer wrinkled her nose, which made Kiera smile.

Kiera dumped cream and sugar into her coffee and stirred absently as she turned back to Queen Alyssandra. "Ryan mentioned you needed a doctor. I'm glad to help anyone I can while I'm here. I've never treated a full-blooded Klatch that I know of, but since they are a sister race to the Cunts, which I'm quite familiar with, I'm confident that treatments will be similar."

She dished a healthy helping of the meat pastry onto her plate. "I have treated several half-Klatch, but mostly for energy burns or energy drain from lack of sexual energy. . . ." She trailed off as she realized a charged silence reined around her.

Everyone exchanged glances across the table, and Kiera froze with her fork halfway to her lips. She set the utensil down carefully, her appetite suddenly gone as a heated trickle of suspicion and dread curled through her belly. "Apparently there's quite a bit I'm not understanding about the situation. Why don't we just cut to the chase? What is it exactly that you're hoping I'll do for you?"

Ryan's warm hand settled between her shoulder blades just above the back of the chair.

She stiffened under his touch and turned to face him.

"I mentioned we needed a Healer, not a doctor." Ryan's dark gaze burned into hers as she tried to make sense of his cryptic words. "Although similar, they aren't the same here."

Kiera shrugged off his hand. "Then why don't you explain everything to me so I understand exactly what you're asking."

Ryan wiped his lips on his napkin before he dropped the

white linen in his lap. "Fair enough." He nodded toward her plate. "Why don't you eat while we talk?"

She thought about being stubborn and refusing on principle, but she hadn't eaten in over a day, and her body needed the nourishment. Thanks to Ryan offering her his tacit sexual energy, she was still feeling pretty good considering, but even Cunts and Klatch couldn't live on sexual energy alone. "All right. I'm listening."

Her first bite of the meat pastry burst pure heavenly flavor of spicy roast beef and herbs across her tongue, and she closed her eyes and moaned in pleasure before she realized it.

Soft chuckles from around the table made her snap her eyes open as her cheeks heated.

King Stone set down his fork. "The Royal cook does have a way with meat pies. They've been a favorite of mine since I was a boy."

Kiera forked up another bite and swallowed back her embarrassment as she forced a small smile. "I guess I've been living on my own cooking for far too long." She glanced at Ryan. "Sorry. Please, continue," she said as she took another bite.

"I'm not sure how much about Tador history you know, so I'll give you an overview of what's relevant."

She nodded and sipped coffee that tasted suspiciously like Starbucks. Not that she minded.

"When Sela knew she was losing the civil war, she kidnapped Alyssandra and her nanny and took them to Earth."

Kiera's brow furrowed as she turned her gaze toward Alyssa. Silas had said something similar, but it hadn't sunk in he meant the queen until now. "I remember hearing rumors about a captured royal Klatch from the war, but I never realized they had kidnapped the heir to the throne."

Alyssa nodded. "I grew up as the ugly duckling within Sela's family, knowing nothing of my Klatch heritage or even the Cunt heritage. I was basically raised as a sickly human."

Anger surged through Kiera at a child being treated in such a manner. As a doctor, she had seen how many horrible things humans and even witches did to each other. But she would never be able to get used to it.

Not to mention, Kiera wasn't sure how this woman could ever be considered ugly in any setting. Although Kiera had never actually spoken to Sela, the Cunt queen's cruelty was legendary.

"In the meantime," King Stone added, "Queen Annalecia and King Darius were left with their grief. I'm not sure if you're familiar with the energy symbiosis between the queen and the planet of Tador?"

Kiera shook her head. Her mother had never mentioned anything like that.

"The queen and her chosen king generate sexual energy to heal both themselves and the planet, and the queen heals the planet and ensures there is enough energy flowing at all times." He took Alyssa's hand in his and squeezed it tight, as if he knew his next words would cause her pain. "However, usually the crown princess takes some of the load of that burden when she reaches puberty. And since Alyssa was on Earth, and we were unable to find her, the burden on Queen Annalecia slowly sapped her strength and her health."

Kiera wiped her lips with the napkin. "What effect did that have on the planet?"

"It slowly began to die." Alyssa's quiet words were laced with pain. "By the time I returned and ascended the throne, I was able to save my mother, but the planet was too far gone to bring it back to its former glory. We've been fighting a losing battle ever since."

A hot thread of anger at Sela and all the pain and death she'd caused tightened Kiera's chest. "Surely there's something you can do." Her logical mind drew the obvious parallel between a body and the planet—not enough energy and the organism would slowly begin to die, with the process happening faster as mortality approached.

However, Tador was more than just a case study to her. She had dreamed of visiting her mother's home world her entire life, only to find out it was dying. A sense of loss and helplessness threatened to overwhelm her, and she swallowed it back, allowing her logic to shove aside the uncomfortable emotions.

Alyssa nodded and leaned forward, her forearms resting lightly on the table. "Actually, that's where you come in."

"Me?" Kiera's brow furrowed with confusion. She bit her bottom lip, wishing she could stop the flow of words, which she sensed would change her life forever.

And yet, if there was anything she could do to help save the planet, she knew she would do it—not only for her mother's memory, but also for herself. Regardless that all the Cunts had been banished just before she was born, this planet was her history and her future children's heritage . . . if she ever decided to have any. Thankfully, in this modern age, women could choose to have children on their own.

Alyssa nodded and sat back in her chair, studying Kiera for a long moment, as if the queen sensed Kiera needed time to process this new information. "We discovered mention in the Queen's Archives of something called the Triangle that had been instituted by past queens in this situation."

The Triangle. That's what Ryan had asked Silas about. She dropped her hands into her lap and swallowed hard as a cold wash of dread swept through her. "What's involved in this Triangle?"

Alyssa's intense gaze burned into Kiera's, and Kiera found herself unable to look away. "Two human women with special gifts mate with two full-blooded Klatch princes. At twenty-four years of age, they go through a coming of age ceremony and then a ceremony to institute the Triangle. Then they would help the queen maintain the balance of energy until the planet is fully healed and the Triangle is no longer needed—usually a generation or two later."

Gooseflesh marched over Kiera's skin, making her shudder. "A Seer and a Healer," she said as understanding dawned.

"Yes," Alyssa said, while a charged silence hung around the table.

A fluttering deep inside Kiera's belly made her place her hand over her stomach, a gesture that was becoming very familiar over the last hour. "Let me see if I understand this." A thin thread of anger mixed with panic wound through her. She glanced around the table, meeting everyone's gaze before looking back at Alyssa. "You want me to . . . mate . . . with Ryan and then live here as part of a giant sexual battery cell for the planet until my grandchildren are born and the Triangle is no longer needed?" The whole idea sounded ridiculous, and her last words ended on a small laugh.

"Not exactly," Ryan said. "But close enough." His gaze was guarded, his chin tipped down so his hair covered his scar as if he were bracing against her rejection.

Kiera shook her head, willing herself to wake up from this very strange dream. And yet, she felt the truth of it deep inside her gut. The fluttering was still there inside her belly, but now she recognized it for excitement and anticipation rather than fear.

What the hell? Was she losing her mind?

A half-breed Cunt and a Klatch prince? Talk about a far-fetched version of *West Side Story*. And yet, there was such a strong sense of rightness about everything the queen had said, Kiera couldn't dismiss it out of hand. "Since you aren't looking for my medical skills, what exactly do you need from this Healer?" Signs or not, she was still reluctant to believe she was the healer they were looking for without more proof. "And why are you so sure I'm her?"

"I saw you in a vision," Katelyn said matter-of-factly as she brushed her red hair back over her shoulder. "And we have recently found a statue from the previous Triangle I think you should see before you decide."

Kiera pursed her lips. What about the statue made them seem to think it would sway her decision? "So, as the Seer you have visions. What is the Healer supposed to be able to do? Magically heal people?" Her thoughts flickered to her father, still lying unconscious in the VA hospital back on Earth. She definitely hadn't been able to magically heal him, and she wasn't so sure she could permanently leave Earth while he was still there. "I'm afraid my medical skills are a bit more mundane than that." Her voice sounded bitter, and she swallowed hard, hoping no one but her had noticed.

Ryan cleared his throat beside her. "You already have energy abilities none of us have ever seen. It may just be a matter of figuring out how to use your gift more fully."

"What energy abilities?" she asked and then snapped her mouth shut. The weight of everyone's gazes around the table was nearly overwhelming as Kiera remembered the portals suddenly closing and the few times she had been hit with energy beams. She knew neither of those things were normal, but since she'd been busy running for her life, she hadn't taken the time then to think about it.

Ryan gave her a sympathetic smile, as if he realized where her thoughts had taken her, but then he turned his attention to the rest of the group, effectively shutting her out. "Gavin had to have her help to keep the portals open. Any time she tried to go through, they would close. Also, I've seen her hit point-blank by energy beams twice, and it only seemed to energize her—almost as if she absorbed all the energy."

"If she can absorb energy, she can learn to redirect it." This from Grayson, the Seer's husband, who hadn't yet spoken since their greeting. "It may be only a matter of working with her, Ryan."

Alyssa's eyes sparkled with excitement. "True, and—"

"Hold it." Kiera laid down her fork and sat back, meeting everyone's gaze around the table before continuing. The undertone of muted excitement pricked at her control—especially while they sat discussing her like she wasn't there to hear it. "I appreciate this discussion, but I would very much like to be a part of it rather than an observer while you discuss me."

Heavy silence fell around them until Alyssa slowly nodded. "You're right. I apologize." The queen's lips thinned into a tight line before she slowly blew out a breath. "This situation has been our main concern since I arrived on Tador. We didn't mean to make you feel like a means to an end. Your input as well as your consent will be a very important part of this."

"Thanks," Kiera muttered with a heavy layer of sarcasm. "I'm glad both my consent and my input are important here. I do have a comment and a few questions, if you don't mind."

King Stone dropped his napkin on the table and leaned back in his chair with a glass of juice still in his hand. "Please, ask anything you like. We want you to be able to make a fully informed decision." His voice was cultured and polite, with no sign that he had been offended by her sarcastic remark.

Nods and murmurs of agreement rounded the table.

"Let me preface this by saying that I know the initial reaction to this will be an instinctive denial, but please hear me out. I also realize that I have only been here a few days, and my only knowledge of Tador comes from what my mother told me and from some of her letters I found after her death." She took a fortifying breath before continuing.

"As a doctor, I look at things a little differently than most people. For example, Tador is an ecosystem unto itself, just like Earth. After the war, when all the Cunts were banished, the world lost quite a bit of the natural energy which it used to regenerate itself."

Stone raised one dark eyebrow, his eyes turning cool and remote. "Are you suggesting, in order to fix all our problems we open all the portals and just invite all the Cunts back?" The king's voice was soft, but Kiera heard the thread of steel underneath.

"Not exactly, no. I'm suggesting that part of the imbalance and the reason the previous queen couldn't maintain the planet was because a major source of power was missing from the planet and not just because Alyssa was gone."

Alyssa's lips parted in surprise, and a stunned silence hung around the table.

Kiera continued before they could recover. "You said the king and queen generate sexual energy to heal the planet and its people, but on the other hand, from my mother I know that each individual can tap into the energy of the planet as needed, as well. The entire ecosystem is symbiotic, not just the king and queen. The king and queen just happen to be the piece that ties it all together. The top of the food chain, so to speak."

The Seer pursed her lips and brushed her red hair back over her shoulder again. "I hate to say it, but she might have a point."

When the others at the table began to object, Katelyn held up her hand to stop the outbursts.

"Hear me out." She laid her hand in Grayson's, seeming to gain strength and confidence from the simple physical connection. "From an energy perspective, what she says makes sense. Even though the Klatch are more powerful magic users on average, the Cunts are still a native species of the planet."

Kiera's mother had said the same thing often enough, but Kiera still bristled at hearing the Cunts being described as less powerful—true or not.

Katelyn took a sip of coffee and swallowed before continuing. "Just like on Earth, when you unbalance something in the ecosystem, there are effects—even if they aren't seen right away. The civil war was a social unrest issue. Tador doesn't really care about that. It cares that it has enough energy to thrive and survive."

The Seer glanced around the table, visibly relaxing when no one interrupted. "That could account for the sometimes violent reactions we have when dealing with the planet's power—and even the overwhelming arousal we sometimes experience with each other. And it's been getting worse lately."

Beside her, Ryan whistled long and low. "Half the Klatch on the planet are already trying to figure out a way to murder us all in our sleep for having the gall to introduce humans into the bloodline—not to mention a half-Cunt. Can you imagine the reaction to even the thought of reintroducing full-blooded Cunts? We might just have another civil war over that one."

Kiera sat back and let them process this new information. She hadn't expected excitement and general acceptance from either the Cunts or the Klatch on this issue, just some thought and maybe the beginnings of a long-term plan. But at least she had everyone's attention. "Look, I realize this is a political nightmare, and I'm not suggesting you just open the borders and let chaos and mayhem ensue. In fact, I'm not really sure what I am suggesting, but I think Katelyn explained it very well." She smiled over at the Seer, grateful for the support. "Even if the Triangle is successful, Tador may not recover without reintroducing some of its native species."

Alyssa rubbed at her temples, and Stone immediately laid a gentle hand on her back. "I've already pushed the council further than I thought I could with the Triangle discussion. They are going to start calling me Marie Antoinette if I ask them to consider ways to bring back some of the Cunts."

A small trickle of hope swelled inside Kiera's chest. The queen hadn't totally dismissed her thoughts—that was a definite start. A small plan began to take shape inside her mind, and to her surprise, all her internal alarms were silent and content.

Kiera took a deep breath and plowed on before she could

think better of it. "How about I make at least part of this situation a little easier?"

"By all means," Grayson said as he signaled one of the servants for wine. "I think we can all use some liquid strength while we continue this discussion, don't you?" He accepted a goblet and then muttered under his breath, "I know I could."

As soon as full goblets were set in front of everyone but the queen, who continued to drink water, Kiera took a large gulp for courage and squared her shoulders. "I'm still not totally convinced I'm the Healer you are looking for, but I don't believe in coincidences, and too many of those are piling up for me to ignore."

"Meaning?" Ryan asked, his dark waterfall of hair still covering his scar.

"I'm willing to step in and do what I can to complete the Triangle—with a few conditions."

"Just like that?" Katelyn studied her with a frown, her manner suddenly suspicious. "You're willing to move here, become Ryan's mate, take your place within the Triangle, which means sex in some form with the five of us, and everything else that entails?"

Kiera's stomach roiled at the enormity of what she was proposing, but she swallowed hard and held Katelyn's pointed gaze as she nodded.

The Seer's green eyes narrowed. "What are the conditions?"

"First, that my father is moved here to Tador and taken care of the best he can be."

Alyssa took a sip of wine and studied Kiera over the rim. "He's human, isn't he?"

"Is that a problem?" Kiera shot back.

"Not in and of itself, no. But from what Gavin told us, he's in a coma. Tador has some regenerative powers for Cunts and Klatch, but they might not be enough to revive him."

"I'm familiar with his condition, and I'm willing to take the chance. I just need to be assured he's safe, or I can't commit to staying here."

"Fair enough." The queen raised her glass. "And?"

"Second, Shiloh will be allowed to stay here with me."

"No problem."

Kiera swallowed hard and pressed on. "And I need to get a few things from our house back on Earth. Keepsakes that were my mother's."

"That's it?" the queen asked, her voice wary.

Kiera closed her eyes and gathered her courage. She wasn't sure what spark of inspiration had pushed her down this path, but somehow she knew it was the right one, even if icy claws of terror threatened to rip her insides to shreds. "And if I agree to this"—she slid her gaze toward Ryan before returning her gaze to the queen—"and all it entails, then I want to ensure some sort of plan is in place to slowly reintroduce some of the Cunt population back onto Tador."

9

Aedan strode inside Sela's chambers and stopped short.

Unease snaked through his gut as he took in Sela's imperious glare where she sat on the bed, her shapely legs crossed under a mini skirt, her long fingers wrapped around a tumbler filled with clear fluid—most likely vodka.

A smug glint of anticipation marked the expression of the guards scattered around the room—a sign that did not bode well for him.

He swallowed back the fear that tried to close his throat and made a mental note to follow every protocol to the letter and let Sela reveal her hand as she chose. The Queen of the Cunts liked to play mind games, so he had to tread carefully and not reveal more than she already knew.

Her intense blue gaze burned through him as he dropped his chin, linked his hands behind his back and waited to be acknowledged.

The energy of her displeasure buzzed through the room like a living thing, stinging against his skin in an uncomfortable rush. The only sound was of his own faster-than-normal breathing, which echoed inside his head as his fear sharpened and burned through him.

She knows.

The clarity of the thought stunned him, and, he immediately knew that Marco had told her. Aedan bit back a curse.

If he lived through the next several hours, he would ensure Marco paid for this.

"You have displeased me greatly, Aedan." Sela's voice was conversational and cool.

Aedan resisted the urge to raise his chin and look at her, which would only earn him more of her displeasure.

The sound of rustling told him she stood. "I thought I was quite forgiving last time you expressed interest in rising above your station." Her feet encased in strappy black sandals came into his downcast view as she circled him with slow steps. "And yet, now it has come to my attention you deliberately went behind my back and dared to speak for me."

He stiffened as his worst fears were realized. His ambitions had overridden his patience, and he would pay unless he could cast doubt on Marco's account of events. He knew first-hand how cruel Sela could be in her punishments.

Frustration bubbled up, dark and hot—he knew how much Sela craved sexual domination. He had thought that might override her pride if she found out, but the realization he had miscalculated burned inside his chest.

She leaned in close to his ear and whispered, "How dare you betray me after all the favor I've shown you. For that insult alone, you'll have no mercy in your death." No dark anger laced her voice, which scared him more than any outward sign of Sela's fury.

His cock hardened inside his jeans as scenes of other torturous deaths at Sela's hands played through his mind. He had no desire to die, but if that fact was inevitable, then at least he would enjoy his demise. Sela was nothing if not inventive in devising sexual death sentences.

"Guards. Carry out my instructions to the letter, no magic and no sex. And if he dares utter my name . . . cut out his tongue."

Shock slapped at him as the connotations of Sela's words spilled through him. Not only would she deny him her presence, but he was also to be given the death of a mere human.

His head snapped up in time to show him her unhurried path toward the door. "Sela, please . . ."

She stopped in her tracks and stiffened but didn't turn to face him. Instead, one small gesture from her, and the guards closed in from all sides, anticipation glinting in their eyes.

He barely heard the door click closed behind Sela as the first blows caught him in the stomach and side, crumpling him to the floor at their feet.

Sharp kicks and punches showered him from all sides, and burning pain sliced through him as his nose and ribs broke, cartilage shattered and skin tore.

Time lost all meaning as the pain inside him became one long burning stream of agony.

Finally, the blows slowed and then stopped, and Aedan prayed for a reprieve. He could survive a beating if there was a chance to prove himself and get back into Sela's good graces.

Aedan coughed as he sucked air back into his lungs, accompanied by intense pain and fluid bubbling inside his mouth—blood from the metallic taste. He turned his head to the side and spit out the bulk of it.

He blinked swollen eyes as well as he was able. In a few more minutes, he knew he wouldn't be able to see at all.

One of the guard's boots settled heavily on his chest, while another held his face and pulled his mouth open.

Something cold and hard clamped onto the end of his tongue, and full-blown terror chilled his entire body as his tongue was pulled out as far as it would go, and then a bit farther.

A searing pain sliced through his tongue as the large guard sawed through the thick muscle. Blood spurted in time with the frantic beats of Aedan's heart, and his saliva glands kicked into overdrive.

Icy panic clawed through him, and a high-pitched scream welled from deep inside his throat.

It turned into a gurgle as hot blood filled his mouth, pooling in the back of his throat along with the river of saliva, causing him to cough and sputter.

Maybe I'll drown in my own fluids before they beat me to death . . .

Aedan's vision blurred. Close to unconsciousness from the intense pain, he focused on the overhead lighting as inky blackness closed in from all sides.

The last thing he heard was the deep male laughter from the guards as the beating began again.

"Well, she seems nice in an 'I can kick your ass' kind of way." Katelyn pushed her food around on her plate with a fork, glad Grayson and King Stone had left soon after Ryan and the Healer. She wanted to get Alyssa's take on the Healer.

Not that she thought Alyssa would be less forthcoming around the men, but sometimes female conversation flowed better in a testosterone-free environment.

Katelyn poured herself more coffee and added a healthy dose of cream and sugar before tucking an unruly red wave of hair behind her ear. "From what Gavin said, she grew up a virtual outcast—not quite human and not quite Cunt." She glanced over at Alyssa, noting the way the queen nibbled on the edge of a flaky pastry. "I almost think it's easier to grow up not knowing anything about all this. Sort of like you and I did, and then accepting it after the fact."

Alyssa frowned as if reliving the past, and Katelyn immediately regretted causing her friend pain. They had only met a few scant weeks ago, but Alyssa had already become the sister Katelyn had wished for her entire life. She only hoped the

Healer would blend into their easy bond and not stretch it too badly.

"I'm sorry, Lyssa. I forgot how many miserable years you spent being treated worse than a family pet by Sela and the others who posed as your family."

"Don't apologize. I'll admit I still have some anger when it comes to Sela, but I can't regret all those circumstances since they turned me into the woman I am today. And I'm pretty happy with who I am." She smiled, and Katelyn noted with relief that no trace of hurt marred Alyssa's expression.

"I got the impression our new Healer is an idealist." Katelyn chewed her bottom lip as she turned over everything she had learned about the Healer inside her mind. "Even after being shunned as an outcast, she became a doctor to help both witch races. And Gavin mentioned, she had approached the Cunt Council about the reunification—apparently, that's what Ryan interrupted the night he found her."

Alyssa chuckled. "She's got balls, I'll give her that. Although after all that's happened, I just don't see either race accepting any type of reconciliation easily. There are twenty-five years of pain and mistrust between us." Her soft lavender gaze took on a far-off quality, which made Katelyn assume Alyssa was thinking of her own mistreatment at the hands of the Cunts.

Katelyn sipped her coffee and studied Alyssa over the rim. The queen's dark hair spilled over her shoulders, a few tiny braids adorned with lavender beads sprinkled throughout. "I can't believe I didn't put together that whole energy cause and effect thing earlier. She's right; there has to be some lasting effects from removing one entire race from a planet. I mean, from an energy perspective, every entity in an environment is interrelated. That's one of the first metaphysical things I learned, even before I figured out how to recover from my visions."

A small furrow appeared between the queen's dark brows,

and she met Katelyn's gaze. "Don't beat yourself up too badly; none of us had ever thought about it like that before, either."

"Are you going to agree—about the Cunts, I mean?"

"I don't know. As much as it pains me to admit it, that may be a step we have to take." Alyssa shrugged and leaned back in her chair, which made the gauzy half top ride up, exposing not only the full bottom curve of her breasts, but also the lower edge of her dusky areolas.

Katelyn resisted the urge to reach out and touch. Her body obviously craved sexual energy now that she had sated her hunger for food.

"As much as I would like to deny it, logically, the sudden removal of all the Cunts could have made it that much harder for my mother to maintain the planet. Add to that the grief of losing your child and . . ." She trailed off, her voice clogged with emotion, her eyes glistening with unshed tears.

"And," Katelyn added, "it would also absolve some of the guilt you've been carrying around that your absence was entirely responsible for both your mother's and the planet's declining health."

A watery chuckle sounded from Alyssa. "There is that." She wiped at her eyes with her napkin. "It's a lot to take in in such a short time."

Katelyn nodded as she sipped her coffee. This morning, if someone would've told her that the Healer would agree to take part in the Triangle, she would've bet they would all be ecstatic right now.

However, that last condition threw a very large wrench into their carefully laid plans.

"After Stone cools down a bit more, I'll talk this out with him, but I don't think we have a choice, do you?"

Katelyn had overheard Gavin and the other guards talk about how fast the destruction of the planet progressed. Record crops were wilting and dying, and more and more Klatch were moving from the outlying areas closer to the castle, purely to survive.

"I don't think we have very long before it's all a moot point." She sighed as she glanced over at Alyssa. "If Tador is dead, we won't have to face the unification issue, but if we welcome back the Cunts, we risk another civil war. Sounds like we're a bit screwed either way."

Alyssa's lips curved in a weak smile. "Thanks for that gritty update." She dropped her napkin and pushed back from the table. "Why don't we go calm down our men, and then we can find the Healer and take her out to see the statue. That, at least, we know needs to be done."

Katelyn started to agree, but her field of sight wavered and grayed at the edges bringing with it a sense of vertigo and nausea.

A familiar sign for the onset of a vision.

She hastily sat her cup down and gripped the edge of the table before the vision took her and she found herself with a lap full of hot coffee.

"I suppose we'll have to keep in mind all her conditions as we continue forward with preparations for the Triangle, in case—" Alyssa's words cut off abruptly, and a look of understanding smoothed the furrow from between her brows. "A vision?"

Katelyn tried to nod or even speak, but the gray closed in around her until it swallowed her whole.

Gooseflesh marched over her as she blinked and realized she stood in the courtyard behind the castle.

A light rain fell, making small cool circles on her clothing and skin. The fresh clean scent of rain filled her senses, and she glanced around, noting the withering browned plants and the marked absence of birds and insects.

Panic clawed at her insides as she realized this could very well be Tador's future.

Male voices behind her made her turn.

Gavin, the captain of the guard, stood shaking hands with a tall Cunt man wearing dark slacks and a button-down shirt. The long white-blond ponytail captured at the back of his neck looked out of place on someone attired so professionally.

"I never thought you would willingly open a portal for me and my kind again," said the blonde in a deep resonant voice.

Gavin laughed, and the familiar timbre of his voice made Katelyn's stomach roil.

Was Gavin responsible for the destruction?

The softly whispered stories about the civil war and Gavin's part in it had reached her within days of her arrival on Tador. However, she had assumed along with everyone else that his friend had betrayed him. But what if they were all wrong and Gavin was a traitor?

The blond man turned, and his pale cerulean blue gaze burned into Katelyn with such intensity, she no longer felt chilled by the rain.

How can he see me inside a vision?

One blond eyebrow rose, along with a rogue's smile. A hot spurt of fear wound through her tighter and tighter until her lungs hurt and her throat constricted.

"Katelyn!"

Her cheek stung, and she blinked as Alyssa's face formed in front of her. After a few seconds, she realized Alyssa must've slapped her to bring her back to the present. She swallowed hard before she tried to speak. "I'm okay."

"You don't sound okay, and you look like you just saw a ghost." Alyssa pressed a muffin into Katelyn's hand and ordered her to eat. "I've never seen you look so terrified during a vision. What happened?"

She obeyed without question and swallowed each bite, even though her throat felt raw and her lungs still burned. She, more than anyone, knew that visions could be interpreted in many ways. They often happened as she had seen them, but took on a totally different meaning than she had originally thought.

And yet, her internal alarm systems screamed at her that this vision was an outcome she didn't want to see come to pass.

"Katelyn?" Alyssa prompted.

She raised her gaze to the queen's. "Let's just say, I'm not sure, but I think there are rocky times ahead."

Ryan trailed behind Kiera, noting the stiff set of her shoulders and the regal tilt of her chin. Soon after she had delivered her last condition, she'd excused herself from the table, and Ryan had quickly followed.

"Healer."

She stopped short and turned to face him, and only then did he realize she held Shiloh clutched to her like a shield. Her face remained a calm mask, but her blue eyes were stormy.

He suddenly felt awkward standing in front of her. What did he say to a woman who had just agreed to be his future mate? "Where are you going?"

"I figured it would be easier for all of you to discuss my conditions without me there." Her voice was calm with a sharp edge to it.

He studied her for a long moment, and not for the first time, he wished he could hear her thoughts or see inside her mind. "Why did you really agree to the Triangle?" He hadn't meant to blurt it out like that, but now that it was out, he waited for the answer with equal measures of anticipation and dread.

Her fingers absently stroked Shiloh's fur, and silence fell between them for a long moment, while she seemed to gather her thoughts. "Several reasons. First, my ability to help back on Earth has been severely curtailed by the assassins wanting to kill me. So I might as well be able to do some good here."

She glanced down at the purring feline, as if it was easier not to meet Ryan's gaze while she spoke. "Because of my mother and her heritage, I definitely feel a kinship for the planet. But it's more than that." When her blue gaze rose to meet his, it was clear and thoughtful, and just a little sad. "I've been quietly lobbying for reunification for a long time—a cause I took up when my mother died. Now that has a good chance to become a reality." She shrugged. "As for the rest, I can't explain it, but I think I'm supposed to be here."

A thin thread of anger curled through Ryan, shocking him with its intensity. She hadn't mentioned anything about calmly accepting him as her mate—all her reasoning was about Tador and her own heritage. "So you're willing to share my bed and bear my children as a means to that end?" He recognized the cool undertones in his voice that materialized when he was angry or hurt.

Her chin tilted at a haughty angle, her gaze ice cold. "I knew what I was agreeing to."

"Did you?" he asked as he stepped close, trapping Shiloh between them. "What kind of a woman trades her body and her life away for such an arrangement?"

Her eyes narrowed to slits as his comment hit home, but she stood toe to toe with him and showed no signs of backing down. "I suspect whatever Klatch princess you would've married if the Triangle hadn't become necessary." She watched him long enough for Ryan to feel the fist to the gut that her statement caused before she turned away down the corridor.

"Fuck." He stood staring after her as he calmed his racing thoughts. She was absolutely right, damn her. After all, he had grown up knowing he would marry for duty and not for love.

He had come to terms with that long ago.

Or so he thought.

But her casual acceptance of him as part of the overall "deal" had stung not only his pride, but his heart. He admitted he had held out some small hope that, like Stone and Grayson, he would find more than a broodmare for carrying on the Klatch line. What he wanted was a lover, a partner and a friend. Apparently, that was not to be, and he should be thankful they were all that much closer to saving Tador.

He mentally shook himself. "Get a grip, Ryan. At least bedding her won't be a hardship." He started along the corridor she had disappeared down moments before. When he turned the corner at the end, he just caught sight of her as she set down Shiloh and slipped out the main doors of the castle.

He jogged forward, nodding to the servant who held open the door for him.

She stood halfway down the steps, her expression a mixture of childhood delight and awe.

Ryan glanced around them, trying to see his surroundings as she saw them.

The sun shone brightly, which made the vibrant colors of the many flowers, vines, bushes and birds richer than he remembered. A gentle breeze teased the ends of her golden tresses where they hung around her shoulders, and he thought he could smell her faint aroma of sweet musk and cinnamon even through the rich scents of earth and greenery.

She walked down several more steps and then raised her face to the sun as if drinking in its offered energy. "It's even more beautiful than I had imagined," she said barely loud enough for him to hear. She turned, and her smile faded as she saw him standing behind her.

"Healer." When she stiffened, he stopped and tried again. "Kiera. Look, I'm sorry. Why don't we try that earlier conversation again?"

She said nothing but continued to watch him with a wary gaze.

"Emotions are running high on all sides, and I didn't approach the subject very well." He closed the distance between them and stood on the step below her, facing back up the staircase, happy when she stood her ground.

When her lips parted, he gave in to the impulse to trace her ripe bottom lip with his thumb. Her eyes immediately darkened to a deep navy blue, like the night sky before a storm, and a shiver ran through her body.

At least she wasn't immune to his touch—a fact that pleased him.

And from what he could tell of her reaction to Tador, she really could be happy here. Maybe in time they could build more between them than only duty.

Both for Tador and for himself.

"What are you doing?" She swallowed hard but still didn't move away from him.

Maybe she thought this was part of her "duty" to let him touch her. He hoped not, but he would take that for now, until he could have more.

"Apologizing."

He couldn't remember ever being as drawn to a woman as he was to this one. If she was destined to be his, he trusted in the universe enough to know they would be well suited.

However, if he had learned anything from watching Stone and Grayson with Alyssandra and Katelyn, he needed to give her enough space to open her heart to him as well as her body. Something that definitely wasn't easy for a man used to taking action.

Ryan slowly lowered his face toward hers, enjoying the way her eyes widened, although she still didn't retreat.

She cleared her throat self-consciously. "I'll admit, there's an attraction between us—"

"Attraction, hell," he said with his lips hovering just above hers. "We both know it's nothing as tame as that."

Kiera's eyes slipped close just before he slid his lips gently over hers and prepared to take . . .

"Prince Ryan!"

Ryan's head snapped up to see Gavin and three other guards

hurrying down the steps toward them. He stepped out in front of Gavin, stopping his forward motion. "What's wrong, Gav?"

Gavin nodded toward the other guards, who jogged down the steps and disappeared down the path toward the waterfall. "After nearly twenty-five years of only Klatch on Tador, it might be best if we remained on guard—"

A sizzling pink blast of energy hit Kiera in the stomach.

Her mouth fell open on a gasp, but she didn't crumple or even grasp her middle with her hands. Instead, she spread her arms wide as if welcoming the blast, and a laugh spilled from her throat.

A quick spurt of fear pumped through Ryan, and he started forward to step into the line of the beam.

Before he reached her, Kiera's eyes flew wide, and an expression of panic skittered across her suddenly pale face.

It's too much. I can't take it all in, he heard her voice shout inside his head even as he stared at her unmoving lips.

Surprise froze Ryan for an instant before he spurred himself to action and lunged forward to break the connection, bracing for the accompanying pain even with his energy shield surrounding him.

Instead, a scream sounded from somewhere inside the gardens, and the beam cut off abruptly before it reached him.

Kiera stumbled, and Ryan steadied her against him, the energy still thrumming off her in nearly visible waves. "Please..." she whispered against his shoulder. "Please..."

Damn. He had to help her release some of the energy before the overabundance churning inside her literally tore her apart.

The two guards who had disappeared into the gardens came into view dragging a limp Klatch man between them, the toes of the man's boots tracing two lines behind him in the grass.

"Drop that traitorous bastard," Gavin said to the two guards as he turned to the remaining guard. "Take care of him, and I'll be down to interrogate him after he comes to."

Kiera's knees buckled under her, but she wasn't surprised when Ryan swept her into his arms and jogged back up the steps and into the castle.

A swirling vortex of energy burned inside her like a million stinging bees. Sharp cold fear snaked through her as she realized her body might not be able to handle the churning power.

Had she really agreed to do this full time—even conditionally? What had she been thinking? She clung to Ryan like a lifeline, and with each step he took, the intensity burned higher, and she had to concentrate on the simple act of pulling air inside her lungs.

Ryan's words from this morning came back to her, along with what she had learned at breakfast about the planet and the Triangle. She needed sexual release to get rid of this much energy. Lucky for her, she knew a certain Klatch prince who she had just agreed to "mate" with, who probably wouldn't mind taking the job.

Her skin began to burn and the trembling increased to jerky shakes that threatened to rattle the teeth from her head.

Her gaze met Ryan's, and she read the concern etched into the dark purple depths. *Please . . .* She wasn't sure she said the word aloud, but she must've because she saw the recognition of it in Ryan's surprised expression.

"I'm here, Healer. Don't worry." He gripped her tighter and increased his already fast pace through the castle corridors.

He rounded a corner too fast and scraped his arm and elbow against the hard *balda* stone. The impact left him cursing, but he kept moving.

She laid her head against his shoulder and closed her eyes, praying her body would survive a few minutes longer.

When Ryan reached the room where they'd woken that morning, he kicked the door shut behind him and sat on the bed with Kiera still cradled in his lap.

The heat of his body thrummed against her over-sensitized

skin in endless waves that rippled through her body, nearly making her dizzy. "Healer?" he said softly.

She clenched her jaw and her fists against the onslaught going on inside her body and forced open her eyelids. Through pure stubbornness, she gathered enough energy to speak. "Ryan, help me," she said through gritted teeth.

His entire body stiffened, and he searched her face. "It will take sexual release to rid yourself of this much energy. Do you understand?" His voice sounded strained as he brushed her hair out of her face and gently tucked it behind her ear.

Distantly, she noticed the scraped skin of his forearm and the furrows of blood that had risen to the surface. But soon, sensations overrode her thoughts, and she gave herself up to them. Everywhere his roughened fingers touched, burned and tingled with need.

Damn it! Impatience and frustration snapped through her, and she tightened her fingers in the front of Ryan's tunic. After this was all over, she would applaud his restraint, but for now, she needed him. She'd done everything but sign on the dotted line; why didn't he just give her what she needed?

She gathered the last reserves of her strength and leaned forward to press her lips to Ryan's.

A burst of power exploded between them, and Ryan's loud groan echoed around her. Delicious heat curled along her skin everywhere their bodies met and then sparked out toward the walls and furniture to sizzle along the edges with a sharp buzzing sound.

The faint smell of burnt matches rose around them but couldn't mask the musky deep-woods scent that always clung to Ryan.

Kiera closed her eyes and gave herself up to the sensations of Ryan's mouth exploring hers.

Without warning Ryan rolled them sideways so Kiera lay

underneath him on the soft bed, his hard body molding itself to her softer one like it had the first night she had met him.

The vortex of energy inside her expanded to engulf both of them, which immediately lessened the pain and allowed her to enjoy the rush of pleasure snaking through her.

Instinctively, she wrapped both her legs and arms around him. She welcomed the hard ridge of his cock against her core, which burned with both awareness and energy against her sensitive nerve endings even through her jeans and his pants.

Ryan ground against her, one large hand cupping the back of her head, his fingers speared through her hair, while his other hand kneaded and explored her waist and hip before cupping her ass and locking her tight to him.

At his possessive move, the energy inside her growled, wanting more. *I need you inside me, damn it!* she thought furiously.

Shock slapped at her, and her brow furrowed when Ryan broke their fevered kiss and pulled back far enough to look down at her. "When I take you, you will come to me willingly, Kiera Matthews, not because Tador deems it necessary or you agreed to suffer my attentions for your precious cause." Both anger and arousal laced his terse words.

She opened her mouth to tell him that she was more than willing, and anything else he needed to hear. His pride be damned—she needed him inside her.

The power between them howled in fury at Ryan's words and sliced through her in a painful rush, bowing her body off the bed and ripping a feral scream from her throat, instead.

Almost from outside herself, she noticed cool air hitting her body as Ryan stripped the clothes from her stiff form while she held on to ride the wave of energy careening along her every nerve ending.

Kiera closed her eyes tight and gripped the bedspread in her clenched fists as she gasped in an attempt to bring enough air into her body.

When Ryan's hot mouth closed over one aching breast, she arched against him, offering herself shamelessly.

His tongue swirled over her tightly beaded nipple, sending arrows of burning arousal straight to her pussy. He sucked, nipped and then soothed with open-mouthed kisses until she writhed under him, and her head thrashed back and forth on the pillow as she silently begged for more.

Please . . . make me come!

She gasped and then moaned when Ryan's fingers caressed a path down her stomach to dip between her swollen labia. He traced her slit slowly while he transferred the teasing attentions of his mouth to the other breast.

The swirling energy howled and tightened until Kiera rode the fine edge of pain and pleasure.

Beyond thought, only the sensations of Ryan's hungry mouth at her breast and his skillful fingers between her thighs held her anchored to reality.

When two large fingers pressed inside her, a groan spilled from her throat, and she opened her thighs wider and arched against his hand, hoping for more. Before she could protest, he slid his fingers from her and continued to tease and explore her slit, only pushing inside her enough to tease and frustrate.

As he seemed to do with everything, he slowly explored her, until she thought he would have every inch of her pussy memorized.

He touched, traced and caressed her labia, the sensitive pucker of her ass, the ridged internal walls of her pussy and even the smooth expanse of skin between her pussy and her ass—everywhere but her aching clitoris. All the while, he continued to suckle her breasts and the sensitive skin of her stomach with his hot mouth.

You're killing me, Ryan!

Even inside her head, her thought sounded desperate and pleading, but at this point, she would beg or do whatever else it took to reach her climax.

Almost begrudgingly, the tip of Ryan's finger slid up her slit to caress the silky underside of her clit.

She gasped and bowed off the bed as he applied just the right amount of pressure combined with a soft circling of the tight nub.

The entire world slowed to a crawl and spiraled down to the point where Ryan's roughened fingertips slowly rubbed against the tip of her clitoris. Kiera held her breath, afraid to break the spell of the coming storm.

Finally, the climax she had been waiting for burst somewhere deep inside her gut and slowly blossomed through her body like rich hot chocolate on a cold day. Pleasure coursed through her in a thick wave, and she gave herself up to the euphoric feeling, which reminded her of floating in a warm pool.

Instead of the explosion she thought she needed and wanted, this was more like an implosion that left her weak, limp—and relieved.

"I'll be damned."

The reverent awe in Ryan's voice goaded Kiera to force open her heavy eyelids.

He still leaned over her, his body warm against her hip. He was anchored on one elbow while he held up his other arm, inspecting his forearm where she'd seen the scratches and blood earlier.

His arm was whole and healthy—no scratches at all, just an expanse of golden skin.

A trickle of panic curled inside her stomach, making her queasy.

"The scratches have to be on your other arm," she said, her voice sounding desperate and unsure. She ran her fingers over his other arm, and when she felt only smooth skin under her fingertips, sat up, pushing Ryan off her until he sat on the edge of the bed and held his arm out for her inspection.

"You won't find them there," he said, his voice still husky with wonder. "They were on the other arm, and they are completely healed." He turned to her with a smile blossoming across his handsome face.

She swallowed hard as she inspected both his arms. Her heart beat faster, and bile rose inside her throat as she found no evidence of the wounds she knew she had seen. "How did this happen?" Even as she asked the question, she already knew the answer with a cold certainty that scared her. She could no longer hide behind the last shred of hope she had built into her offer this morning—mistaken identity.

Ryan cupped her chin, and with a tender gesture, ran his thumb over her bottom lip. "You healed me with your energy. You are the Healer we sought."

IO

Kiera sighed as she stepped down the rough-hewn stairs and into the steaming waters of the private hot baths. The gurgling water caressed every inch of her as she relaxed against one of the underwater seats, her head cradled against a thick, fluffy towel strategically placed as a headrest.

Submerged to her neck, she let out another sigh.

It had taken quite a while to convince Ryan she needed some time alone and would be fully safe inside the baths—especially since he'd had guards posted at every entrance after they had done a thorough sweep of the baths, including under water.

At that point, she figured she could finally escape and get some time to herself, but upon entering the baths, she had encountered the queen's lady's maid, Sasha, who had offered to bathe, shave and pleasure her.

Kiera cringed at the memory.

A half-blooded Cunt she was, but after her apparent "healing" orgasm with Ryan this morning, both her mind and her body needed a break while her pride recovered and she sorted through all the ramifications of her agreement to be part of the Triangle.

She twisted her neck from side to side, working out the kinks as the hot water loosened muscles and soothed away tension and stress.

The rhythmic rushing of the waterfall that fell along one wall didn't hurt either.

"This really is a beautiful place," she murmured to herself.

The entire cavern was made of the white and sparkling pink *balda*, with strategic niches for soaps, towels and other accessories. Standing in several places throughout the baths were raised platforms low enough so an inch of the body would still be submerged, but the raised headrest would keep the head and neck well above the water line.

Hundreds of flickering candles placed in small indents in the walls cast alternating shadows and light over everything, giving the place a relaxed, almost romantic ambiance.

Her mother had described the group baths, but as a Cunt who held no office or social position, she was never invited to the private baths.

Kiera frowned at the thought.

The class system had obviously catered to the rich-get-richer mentality—although from her mother's own account, even the lowliest people on Tador were better off than some upper-middle-class families back on Earth.

And now, if they accepted her last condition, she had agreed to pick up and move here permanently. The rightness of the decision still resonated through her, but it didn't neutralize the coiling terror that slept just inside her chest, waiting to burst out.

Thoughts she had been trying to avoid rushed through her mind, and her temples began a dull throb.

"Are you okay?"

Kiera's eyes snapped open at Katelyn's voice, and she sat up straight in her seat, which lowered the churning water to just above her breasts. "Just thinking . . . and trying not to."

Katelyn nodded and waved her back to her relaxed position.

"I did a lot of that when I first arrived." She stood awkwardly at the side of the baths, her red hair piled on top of her head, a few stray wisps curling around her oval face. An emerald green silk robe hit her midthigh and clung to her curves like a lover's caress.

Kiera had a sudden mental image of slowly peeling back the robe and exposing the creamy soft flesh beneath.

Where the fuck did that thought come from?

Katelyn's earlier words about the participants of the Triangle feeling intense attraction for one another returned, and she relaxed. Besides, she did wonder what it would feel like to kiss and caress a woman—and to be caressed in return—free of Earth's societal judgments and restrictions.

The thought sent warm tendrils of arousal curling inside her belly.

"Mrowr."

Kiera jumped at the plaintive sound, feeling like a child caught doing something naughty. She slowly blew out a breath and turned her head to see Shiloh's orange fur glinting in the candlelight.

He padded to the edge of the baths and curled on the stone behind where her head leaned, his purr volume on extra high.

She absently reached up to pet him before remembering that her hands were wet—something she knew Shiloh wouldn't appreciate. In lieu of a greeting, and thankful for the diversion from her own reactions, she didn't complain or pull away when Shiloh nuzzled into her hair.

Katelyn smiled. "He seemed to be roaming the castle looking for you, so I thought I'd bring him down."

"Thanks," Kiera said and meant it. "I wondered where he'd gone off to. He's a pain in the ass, but I think we've grown attached to each other, since . . ." Her words trailed off as the familiar pangs of loss sliced through her like they did whenever she thought about her father. She wondered how he was doing back on Earth.

She pushed the thought aside, pasted a smile on her face and glanced up at Katelyn, hoping her voice wouldn't waver when she spoke. "Do you want to join me?" She was surprised to find that she wanted company, when just a few moments ago, she hadn't.

"Thanks, I'd like that." Katelyn untied the straps holding her robe closed, and Kiera's breath caught inside her throat. "I have to admit, I also thought you might need someone to talk to. And don't worry, I won't offer to bathe, shave or pleasure you. Sasha scolded me that you were to be left alone in all those regards." She waved her hand in a dismissive gesture. "Besides, I remember when I first arrived and she offered me the same thing—I nearly freaked."

The Seer dropped her robe and Kiera's mouth went dry.

"You did?" Kiera asked, her voice so soft she wondered if Katelyn heard it.

Kiera's gaze roamed the newly bared creamy skin, taking in the fiery triangle of closely cropped curls between the Seer's thighs and the light dusting of freckles that seemed to cover her entire body. Full breasts that Kiera knew would overflow her own small hands were tipped in large areolas the color of pink rose petals, with hardened nipples at the centers that Kiera could imagine taking inside her mouth.

She stared transfixed as Katelyn stepped into the water, her creamy skin slowly disappearing below the softly churning surface of the water.

Heat crept up Kiera's cheeks as the familiar ache of arousal weighted her breasts and labia and sent a sheen of slick moisture to her pussy.

Katelyn stopped and cocked her head to one side as she studied Kiera before a tender look of understanding lit her features. She slid into the seat next to Kiera before speaking. "I should have realized you would be affected just like the rest of us. If you don't mind me asking, how uncomfortable are you with having a sexual attraction to other women?"

The Seer's blatant question put Kiera at ease for some reason. She knew she should be embarrassed or shocked, but instead, she was . . . curious. She sat up, dislodging Shiloh from where he had burrowed on top of her hair.

He moved grudgingly and the purrs stopped.

"I'll admit, it's a new experience for me but not one I'm opposed to. It's actually less disconcerting than the pull I feel with Ryan."

Katelyn's impish grin made Kiera bristle.

"Sorry, I know I shouldn't laugh, but you have to remember, I've been through the same thing, and so has Alyssa." The Seer skimmed her fingers absently across the top of the churning water while she spoke. "What I felt for Grayson was immediate and deep—like a building-sized magnet pulling us together, and that eventually turned into a deep and abiding love. But what I felt for Alyssa was attraction, yes, and friendship, but while I love her like a sister or best friend, it's nowhere near the depth of what I feel for Grayson." She shook her head. "I'm afraid I'm not making much sense."

"I think you're making perfect sense," Kiera said and then let a companionable silence fall between them while her thoughts continued to swirl.

Shifting candlelight flickered over Katelyn's features, red hair and skin pale as milk with a light smattering of freckles across her nose and cheeks. She looked like a pagan goddess reclining in the gurgling water. "Katelyn?"

"Hmmm?"

"Did Ryan tell you about the healing?

Katelyn opened her eyes, her green gaze soft. "Yes."

A lead ball settled inside Kiera's stomach. She knew it wouldn't be long before that particular piece of news made its way around.

After all, in their eyes, it was just another piece of evidence that proved she was the Healer they needed.

In your eyes, too, her conscience accused her, and she winced.

Her gut clenched and thoughts spilled through her mind so fast she had trouble following them. She shook her head and sat up again, suddenly agitated. "I know I agreed to the Triangle, and apparently I can act as some type of energy conduit, but what happened with Ryan was a total accident. I'm not even sure how it happened. What if I can't figure out how to harness it, how to be the Healer everyone really needs?"

"Any of us can teach you how to harness and use your energy. The rules are a bit different here on Tador. But you have to be open to it as well as willing to give yourself up to the power—which can be very scary."

Kiera shoved her damp hair away from her face and turned to face Katelyn. "You want to talk scary? Since I've arrived, I've caused portals to close, I've been shot with energy beams and seem to absorb them instead of being hurt by them, I've accidentally healed a few scrapes and now I'm having sexual fantasies about not only a full blooded Klatch prince—the sworn enemy of my mother's people—but also I'm lusting after women." She slowly shook her head, surprised all of that was inside her ready to burst out. But getting it all out felt surprisingly good.

Katelyn smiled, her green eyes twinkling with amusement. "Talk about a busy few days. Just wait until you've been here a few weeks like me."

A smile curved Kiera's lips as the frustration drained out of her, leaving her feeling empty and weak. "I keep forgetting you haven't been here much longer than me."

"Just like I keep forgetting Alyssa hasn't been here much longer than me, even though she looks and acts like a native for the most part." Katelyn leaned back, resting her head on the side of the pool and only smiled when Shiloh immediately curled up just behind her head. "Do you want some advice?"

"Yes, please."

"Relax and wipe all Earth norms from your mind. Look at Tador for what it really is and how you fit into it. We all had to make a choice to accept the role laid out for us or to walk away. I'm a firm believer that everyone has to travel their own path."

The Seer's words resonated inside Kiera's mind and eased her frantic thoughts, bringing her last few concerns to the forefront of her mind. "Does it ever bother you that the pull of the planet is dictating your feelings and emotions?"

Katelyn's red brows bunched as she frowned. "How do you mean?"

"Like a sudden attraction to women that you never felt before." Kiera realized from her own words that she didn't like feeling manipulated and used just so the planet could have energy from her.

Katelyn's frown smoothed away. "I don't think of it like that at all. If I'm very honest with myself, if I would've grown up without Earth's societal restrictions, I probably would've realized I enjoyed women sexually much earlier." Her eyes danced with amusement. "And believe me, I was very shocked to realize that about myself." She cocked her head to one side, a habit Kiera was starting to recognize. "I think we were all raised with the mindset that sex and relationships automatically go together in some form, and that it's sinful or wrong to enjoy sexuality outside of that goal."

"So what you're telling me is that the planet is only freeing me from my own hang-ups and bringing into stark relief my true inclinations?"

At Katelyn's nod, Kiera turned over this new information inside her mind. A tightness deep inside her that she hadn't realized was there loosened and fell away, allowing her to breathe easier and bringing a smile to her lips. "Do you think you could give me some basic energy lessons when you have time?" For some reason she couldn't name, she would rather gain mastery with Katelyn or Alyssa than leaving herself too vulnerable with Ryan.

Katelyn smiled in answer, and Kiera suspected she knew exactly what she had been thinking. "Absolutely. Would you like a small lesson to start, and then you can practice on your own without Ryan knowing?"

Kiera laughed. "That transparent, am I?"

Katelyn shrugged. "I've been there, and not too long ago at that. Besides, Ryan could stand a little humility now and then." A mischievous gleam glinted in the depths of her green eyes.

Now that Katelyn had offered, Kiera found herself suddenly nervous. "What does this small lesson entail?"

"Only a kiss."

The Seer's softly spoken words sent a surge of molten heat humming just under Kiera's skin, making her very aware of her nakedness, her tightly budded nipples and the anticipation tingling deep inside her belly.

Kiera swallowed hard. "Just a kiss." *Only your first-ever kiss with a woman—yeah, nothing to worry about at all. Right.* "What do I do?"

The sexual awareness between them thickened until it became difficult for Kiera to breathe.

"When you feel the energy build inside you, you must learn to control your panic. Your body was made to handle it. As you reminded us all this morning, Cunt blood runs through your veins, and you are a native species of this planet."

Kiera licked her suddenly dry lips. "But I'm half human, too."

"I'm entirely human, remember? If I can handle it, so can you."

Kiera laughed at herself, but the sound came out nervous and jittery. "So all I have to do is let it flow through me?"

"Yes, but like everything, it sounds much easier than it is. Once you're used to it flowing through you, then you can learn how to direct the power where you want it to go." Katelyn stood and moved so she faced Kiera. "Ready?"

"As ready as I'll ever be." Kiera clenched her hands in her lap into fists and took a deep breath for courage.

Katelyn leaned over, bracing her hands on the stone edge of the bath on either side of Kiera's head so they were face to face. The tips of her full breasts trailed into the churning water, and Kiera had to rip her gaze away from the creamy flesh to look into Katelyn's green eyes.

"I won't touch you, except our lips. That should make it easier for you to control the energy—theoretically. If you can help it, try to keep that our only point of contact—especially under water. Water is very conductive to this sort of energy."

"Theoretically?"

Katelyn shrugged, causing her breasts to bob invitingly. "As the planet gets worse, it becomes more unpredictable, but if that happens, we'll deal with it then. Ready?"

Kiera forced herself to relax as she gazed into the vivid green of Katelyn's gaze. "As ready as I'll ever be."

Slowly, Katelyn closed the distance between them, and Kiera allowed her eyes to slip closed.

A sensual jolt of awareness arrowed through Kiera as Katelyn's warm lips brushed over hers in a whisper-soft caress.

Deep inside her, an answering tendril of energy awakened and slowly expanded, tingling through her body as if she had just downed a shot of whiskey.

A soft gasp of surprise spilled from Kiera's throat.

The Seer's lavender scent filled Kiera's awareness and plunged her more deeply into the slowly swirling kaleidoscope of sensations.

She hadn't expected this to be so vastly different from kissing a man. Not only were a woman's lips softer and more giving, but the entire experience was more sensual somehow.

By unspoken mutual consent, they deepened the kiss. Kiera

dipped her tongue inside the soft lushness of Katelyn's mouth, marveling at the warm wash of pleasure curling inside her from just a simple, slow kiss.

She resisted the urge to reach out and touch Katelyn—to pull her body against her own, to feel the warm flesh of those full breasts pressed to her own smaller ones.

The energy curled through her a bit faster now, stretching and twining inside her like a cat receiving attention.

Katelyn explored Kiera's mouth as if time were suspended and she had eternity to memorize every nuance and reaction she pulled from Kiera.

With each passing second, the energy swelled inside Kiera, filling her like warm bubbly liquid pouring into a balloon, and yet, this churning power came nowhere close to what it had been after the energy blast this morning.

"Relax and let it flow," Katelyn whispered against Kiera's lips. "Are you ready for more?"

In answer, Kiera dipped her tongue inside the Seer's lush mouth once more, exploring and tasting, and reveling in the buffet of new feelings surging through her.

When Katelyn pulled back just enough to gently nip Kiera's bottom lip, the energy snarled and surged inside her like a sudden ten-foot wave.

Kiera's loud gasp echoed around them inside the bathing chamber, and she stiffened, fisting her hands at her sides to keep from reaching out to Katelyn as she had with Ryan this morning.

"Relax." Katelyn's voice was soothing and very close. "Breathe deep, and inside your mind, picture the energy flowing easily through you and out your feet, down into the planet."

A maniacal-sounding laugh broke from Kiera as the energy swirling inside her screamed faster and faster. She tried to marshal her thoughts, but they scattered within the vortex spiraling inside her.

"Concentrate." Katelyn's voice was brisk and sobered Kiera enough to gather her strength. "This is nothing compared to this morning after the energy blast. You can handle this."

Kiera gulped in several deep breaths of air and then took Katelyn's advice.

She pictured the energy swirling inside her as silvery particles of glittering light—similar to what made up the portals to the *between*. When that image solidified inside her mind, she sucked in a few more deep breaths and then visualized the glowing particles flowing down through her and out the bottoms of her feet, deep into the planet's core.

Immediately, the pressure inside her body lessened, leaving only a gentle hum of energy traveling through her and harmlessly out into the earth.

Katelyn's lips returned to hers, a gentle slow caress, and Kiera stiffened, expecting the energy to fill her once more.

The flow inside her increased in intensity, but now that the path through her had been created, as new power burst inside her, it followed the flow and funneled harmlessly out.

The kiss ended with one last gentle brush of Katelyn's warm lips across hers, and Kiera sighed as she opened her eyes.

The Seer's lovely face grinned down at her. "You learn quickly."

"Thanks, I guess," she said, not sure if Katelyn referred to the kiss or to controlling the energy. She frowned as she concentrated and realized the energy hadn't left her, she had just become more used to the sensation of it flowing inside her.

Katelyn slipped back into the seat beside Kiera. "What's wrong?"

"That seemed way too easy."

Katelyn's laugh spilled over her like a physical caress. "You just took your first step, but you're a long way from running. The energy Alyssa funnels through her body daily is about ten million times what you experienced this morning after that energy blast."

Fear spiked through her as she remembered the stinging-bees sensation burning every inch of her body for what seemed like endless minutes this morning. Her throat tightened and her stomach roiled as the fear morphed into cold hard terror. "Shit . . ."

11

A strong hand closed around Kiera's upper arm.

Sharp panic snaked through her. Training and instincts kicked into high gear.

She yanked her captured arm forward, pulling her attacker off balance, and then drove her elbow into her attacker's gut.

A satisfying masculine "oof" of surprise didn't stop her from following through. Using all her strength, she brought her fist down to smash into his tender groin area.

As the hand fell away from her arm, she whirled around, automatically assuming her fighting stance—fists up to protect her face, and all her weight balanced on the balls of her feet.

One of the Klatch guards was doubled over in front of her and seemed ready to crumple to the floor at any second.

Gavin jogged down the hallway toward them, a grim expression etched on his rugged features.

"Healer? What happened?"

She swallowed hard as she tried to breathe past all the now-useless adrenaline still flooding her system. "He grabbed my arm. . . . I just reacted."

"I spoke her name several times with no reply," came the strained croak from the injured guard.

Heat burned through Kiera's chest and up into her cheeks.

She had been lost in thought, and probably hadn't heard the guard. "I'm sorry—"

Gavin cut her off with a sharp gesture and then called for two other guards to escort the one she had injured back to his quarters. When the man was out of sight, Gavin turned his attention back toward her. "My apologies, Healer. It was inexcusable for one of my guards to lay hands on you." Whereas his voice had been laced with steel when he addressed the guards, he spoke to her in gentle tones.

"I'm sorry if I hurt him."

The quick smile he flashed changed him from rugged and attractive to devastatingly gorgeous. She could see how her mother could have fallen under the spell of such a smile. "If he can't hold his own against some basic self-defense techniques, he deserved the lesson."

She bristled at his dismissive tone of her abilities. She scowled as she glared at him. The fact that they had been basic techniques was beside the point entirely. "There's no need to waste my more *advanced* skills if those will do just as well. Perhaps you need to train them better."

Amusement played across his features and danced in those lavender eyes. "I meant no insult, Healer. I've seen your technique first-hand when you nearly emasculated a Klatch royal several nights ago."

She fisted her hands at her sides, not willing to admit that smashing her knee into Ryan's groin hadn't been a planned outcome but a panicked attempt to escape from him when he'd flustered her senses.

"Perhaps we can compare fighting techniques sometime," Gavin said conversationally. "I don't use leverage as much as I could because I usually have the size advantage. However, seeing you flip Ryan over when he clearly had the upper hand—or thought he did—made me think perhaps I need to add to my repertoire."

The compliment and request for help made her stop and study him more closely.

His expression and stance held no deception she could see, only an open and easy manner that she'd missed during her first several encounters with the man. "I would love to," she said slowly, carefully watching his reaction. "I've been rather lazy in my workout routine since I've been here; some sparring and practice sounds terrific. As long as you're willing to share some of your own techniques."

She half expected him to brush aside her request to meet her as a peer in abilities, but he only nodded once, a small smile playing at the edge of his lips. "I look forward to it. Prince Ryan knows where to find me when you are ready."

So many years spent fighting against Earth norms and prejudices had made her forget Tador was a matriarchal society where women were respected and revered as much as men, if not more.

"Ready for what?"

Kiera jolted as Ryan's deep voice sounded behind her.

The energy, which she had forgotten still ran inside her from her training session with Katelyn, recognized him and flowed faster and faster, until she had to close her eyes to keep from swaying and falling to the floor.

"Kiera?" Ryan was there in an instant, holding her close to his hard body to keep her from falling.

"The Healer has had a bit of excitement and may need some energy replenishment to make her whole," Gavin supplied and then slipped away after gesturing for a new guard to take the place of the one she had injured.

"Are you all right?"

She inhaled deeply and consciously relaxed her tense muscles, allowing the energy to flow through her as she learned with Katelyn. "I'm okay. No need to get all protective on me." She straightened and stepped away until they were no longer touching. "Do you think we could find somewhere to talk where I won't be hit by energy beams and strangers won't be offering to shave and pleasure me?"

His deep laugh spilled over her, caressing along her skin like a dark promise.

The energy inside her curled like a contented cat but continued to flow as she had directed.

"I take it you met Sasha. She takes her duties to the queen very seriously, but I think that's precisely why Katelyn wanted no lady's maid. . . ." The way he trailed off left her with the impression there was more to the story than he was sharing, but she was more curious about getting to know the man she might be tied to for the rest of her life.

Within minutes, he had whisked her through endless stairways and out to a private courtyard surrounded by high castle walls. Even in the receding light of dusk, Kiera could see blooming trees and riots of different-colored flowers scattered around the square courtyard, all centered around a large tree that reminded her of an umbrella tree, except for the bright blue and purple flowers scattered between its leaves. Wispy branches dripped down almost to the ground on all sides.

Ryan motioned for the guards to stay outside and held aside several branches so Kiera could step inside the darkened shade of a giant tree.

A simple park bench sat inside the shadow of cool shade, a few petals of the tree's blooms sitting on the carved dark wood of the bench.

She brushed away the blooms before she sat and waited for Ryan to join her.

"How's this, Healer?"

"Beautiful, actually." She inhaled, enjoying the subtle lavender scent from the tree. Something her mother had told her as a child tickled her memory, and she smiled. "Is this a *ponga* tree?"

Ryan's deep purple eyes darkened to nearly black as he nodded. "Are you familiar with the *ponga* fruit?" he asked, his voice full of dark promises.

Katelyn remembered her mother's stories of the fleshy purple fruit that felt like whipped cream, smelled of lavender and caused arousal when it came into contact with the skin. "Yes, my mother told me about it." She braced against the sudden swell of sexual tension and energy inside her body. A few deep breaths convinced her she wouldn't be overtaken with power. "That's not what I wanted to talk to you about, so don't try to distract me."

He leaned against the corner of the bench so he could face her, one muscled arm draped over the backrest just behind her shoulders. "Which means I could distract you if I tried?" His tone held warm amusement that sent awareness shooting through her.

She glared at him since his words hit way too close to the truth for comfort. "Can we get back to what I wanted to talk to you about?"

His amused expression sobered, but his lips curved just enough to let her know his amusement hadn't left him entirely. "All right, Healer. Here we are, just you and I. What would you like to discuss?"

"Us."

"Really." When he leaned closer, she placed her fingertips on his chest and pushed him back.

"What I mean is us, as in our relationship." She tucked her hair behind her ear as she searched for the right words. "If my terms are accepted and I stay and participate in the Triangle, then you and I will be . . ." She searched for a word that didn't sound quite so archaic and final, but failed to find one.

"Mated?" he asked with an amused expression.

She swallowed hard. "Yes. Exactly," she continued quickly, ignoring the fluttering deep inside her belly that just the thought of that word caused. "Earlier, emotions were running high, and we never had a chance to discuss what this would mean for both of us. I mean, we don't even really know each other."

His expression sobered, and he leaned back against the bench, dropping his chin so his waterfall of hair hid his scar.

Her fingers itched to reach out and brush the hair away, but she knew it wouldn't be a welcomed gesture.

"What would you like to know, Healer?" His tone was guarded but not cold. "As my possible future mate and mother of my children, I will tell you anything you like." He took her hand in his, ignoring her attempts to tug it back. "I do apologize for my outburst earlier. I hope we can at the very least become friends and hold no secrets between us. After all, if we are to raise children together, we need to build a nurturing home for them."

She swallowed hard and reminded herself and the nervous knots curling inside her stomach that she had willingly signed on for all of this. "I can agree with that," she finally managed.

She thought back to her own childhood. Outside her home, she had been an outcast from both races, but inside her home, her parents had given her love and attention and had instilled in her a belief in herself that she very much wanted for her own children.

Ryan nodded. "Then we are in agreement. Ask me what you will."

"How did you get your scar?" When he stiffened and tried to pull away, she held his hand tight and with her other hand reached out and gently brushed his hair back away from his face. She skimmed her fingertips over the edge of the scar where it met his mouth.

He suffered her touch for a few seconds before he flinched and pulled away, putting distance between them but leaving his hand in hers.

Heavy silence fell between them for a long moment, and she wasn't sure he would answer her.

Darkness that signaled the coming night deepened with each passing second.

When Ryan did finally answer, his voice was soft and far away, as if he relived painful memories with every word. "I've not told anyone of this, not even Stone and Grayson." He inhaled deep as if gathering courage. "I received this the day I turned twenty—from a Cunt." His jaw clenched, and she was surprised at the vehemence and bitter anger laced in his words.

"What happened?" Her stomach clenched at the sudden protective instinct that rose inside her.

His thumb absently caressed the back of her hand as he stared off into the distance, obviously lost inside his memory. "Stone, Grayson and I had been gone on a month-long journey to the outlying areas of the planet. There are Klatch settlements we try to visit at least once a year." With his free hand, he reached up and traced the length of the scar, as if the action helped him remember. "When I returned home, I went to see my mother in her chambers—the same ones we came through to find this courtyard, as a matter of fact. I found her in bed with several Cunt warriors."

Kiera winced and tried to imagine his reaction upon finding them. After all, the Cunts and Klatch had been bitter enemies for over a decade at that point. She could envision betrayal, anger, confusion and hurt.

"At first I thought she was being attacked, but when I realized that wasn't the case, I went crazy. After all, I had been raised to believe—by her—they were our sworn enemies." He abruptly stood and then paced almost to the long hanging branches that shielded them from the rest of the clearing before he turned back.

"I challenged them and attacked." A low, bitter laugh spilled from him. "Even at twenty and in top form, I was no match for the six of them, but I wasn't thinking with anything except the anger and betrayal that burned through me, along with some vague notion that as the eldest of six, I had something to prove in protecting my mother—even from herself."

He shook his head. "In hindsight, I can see they were trying not to harm me for my mother's sake, but through my anger and sense of betrayal, I wanted them dead." He finally raised his gaze to hers. "When my magic wasn't effective, I drew my dagger, and in their attempt to protect themselves, I received this." He pulled his hair away to reveal the entire long scar.

Kiera stood and closed the distance between them. She reached up slowly, in case he flinched away again, and traced the entire scar carefully. Half her mind cataloged the damage inflicted to receive such a scar and the other half ached for the disillusioned young man who would carry the evidence of one mistake for the rest of his life. She knew there were raw emotions still attached to the scar and that he would never seek plastic surgery to remove or lessen it.

"Did you and your mother reconcile after this?" She dropped her hand to her side but didn't step back.

"To an extent. I was angry for a long time, and when not even the planet's regenerative skills lessened the scar, I figured it was mine to carry as a lesson for the future. I moved out of my family's chambers and into the room upstairs, and although I visit, I won't ever return to live here. I have five younger brothers who are all quite close with my mother—especially since I never told them about that day. But she and I have a polite and somewhat reserved relationship."

"So you haven't forgiven her?" Kiera missed her own mother daily and wondered if Ryan ever worried about not making up with his mother before it was too late.

"It's not so much that as we each see the other's position more clearly than we want, and we aren't sure how to bridge the gap of so many years in silence."

"What is she going to think about you mating with a half-breed Cunt when you and she had a falling out over her affair with men of that same race?"

"What indeed." He speared his hand through his hair and sighed. "Ironic, isn't it?"

She swallowed hard before voicing her next question, almost afraid to hear his answer. "With all that painful history with the Cunts, how do you feel about Tador choosing me as your mate?"

A small chuckle sounded from Ryan. "This probably won't come out sounding right, but I did promise no secrets between us." He sighed and shook his head. "When I first saw you, I thought you were human."

She bristled at the notion he hadn't even noticed her Cunt heritage, but he continued before she could think of anything to say.

"You were also fiery and beautiful and sexy as hell the way you fought off the guards." He smiled, which combined with his words, served to salve the sting of his earlier comment. "All my life, I fantasized about dark-haired women with soft lavender eyes and voluptuous curves, but once I met you—all my thoughts were centered around big blue eyes, long blond hair and the compact, athletic body that had pressed against mine on the blacktop in Phoenix." He reached up to trace her bottom lip again with his thumb.

Heat burned into her cheeks and through her body as she

remembered exactly how he felt on top of her. "I am sorry I racked you that night."

Ryan winced, which made her laugh. "I do hope you don't make a habit of it, but I guess I would've reacted badly in your situation as well."

Kiera still couldn't bring herself to admit that it had been an accidental outcome. Everyone was entitled to a few small omissions for pride's sake, after all. She raised her gaze to Ryan's, his dark purple eyes appearing black in the shadows. A deep ache took up residence inside her chest, and she stepped forward to close the small distance between them.

She rested her palms against his warm hard chest and smiled when she felt the gallop of his heart beneath her fingertips. "Mating" with Ryan definitely wouldn't be a hardship if her terms were accepted. And maybe he was right, they might even become friends in the end.

Ryan slowly lowered his lips to hers, his intense gaze burning through her.

Kiera instinctively opened for him, and they came together with a simmering heat that flamed through Kiera's entire body like a blowtorch. She speared her fingers into the thick waterfall of Ryan's hair, enjoying the texture, while the taste of Ryan—spicy and male—burst inside her senses.

The energy inside her howled and churned, but thanks to her lessons with the Seer, she funneled it harmlessly out through her feet.

With a smile of triumph at her accomplishment, she pressed her body against Ryan's, tempting fate. A low "mmm" spilled from her throat as his hard cock dug against her belly.

Ryan captured her tight against him, palming her ass in his large hands and pressing her firmly against his straining erection. The heat from his body and from his palms tingled through her in a sudden rush, and she pulled back to catch her breath.

He released her, his expression wary, and his cascade of hair falling forward to hide his scar.

A quick spurt of surprise burst through her at his sudden insecurity. What could cause such a gorgeous and powerful man to be insecure with her?

She reached between them to cup him, tracing his hard thickness with her fingers as the sudden urge to taste him spilled through her. She remembered the long, thick erection straining toward her this morning, and licked her lips.

Ryan's sharp inhale was all the reaction she needed to spur her on. Her lips curved into a slow smile as she kept her gaze on his and slowly lowered herself to her knees in front of him.

"Healer . . ." he whispered, his voice strained.

With quick fingers, she unfastened the front of his trousers, allowing his hard cock to spring forward into her waiting hands.

Kiera closed her fingers around the hot hardness of him, and Ryan groaned as he widened his stance.

He was thick and long, just like she remembered, his golden skin more of a plum color along the swollen head. She squeezed him and stroked the length of him inside her tightened palm, smiling when a glistening drop of precome pooled inside the slit at the head of his cock.

She gazed into Ryan's dark eyes as she leaned forward and captured the drop with her tongue. Desire and sizzling awareness pulsed between them as the sweet-salty flavor of him burst over her tongue, and the sound of Ryan's labored breathing echoed in the enclosed space around them.

When she slipped her lips over the swollen head of his cock, Ryan buried his fingers in her hair as a long low moan spilled from his throat. But he didn't force her closer or thrust inside her mouth before she was ready—a marked difference from her previous experiences with men.

Ryan seemed ready to let her set the pace, and excitement churned through her along with heady feminine power.

The taste of him still fresh on her tongue, Kiera slowly took him deeper, her gaze still locked with his, until the swollen tip of his cock bumped the back of her throat.

He was long enough that she could take him into her mouth as far as she could and still wrap her hand around him just above the base. His cock was thicker than any she had ever held, so it wasn't difficult to keep her lips tight around him as she reached up to cup and gently knead his sac with her fingers. His balls tightened against the sudden attention, and she gently massaged them until they relaxed while she continued to stroke his hard length with her other hand and her mouth—exploring, teasing, stroking.

Each time the taste of his salty-sweet essence filled her senses, the energy inside her swirled faster and higher, sweeping her along with its intensity and fury. Some still funneled through her, but more swirled inside her like a vortex, bringing a biting-ants sensation just underneath her skin. Yet, where earlier she had been terrified her body couldn't contain the power, Kate-lyn's lesson had given her courage and made her want to test her own limits.

The muscles in Ryan's legs began to shake, and she continued to stroke. A laugh spilled from her throat around the cock still inside her mouth, and small sparks of pink sizzled along her skin and flowed over to Ryan's, pulling another long moan from his throat.

Ryan clenched his teeth, fighting for control as the vibrations from Kiera's laughter traveled through his sensitive cock to send searing tendrils of heat snaking through him. "Please . . ." He tried to pull back, but she continued to stroke, suck and tease him.

The sight of his cock disappearing between her full lips, and then reappearing as she swirled her tongue across his sensitive tip, nearly incinerated him on the spot.

The mischief and desire in her gaze was clearly visible even in the murky darkness. She released his balls and reached around to grab his ass and pull him tight against her each time she took him deep inside her throat.

He gritted his teeth, fighting for control, helpless to stop the tidal wave of pleasure swamping him under with each thrust inside Kiera's hot mouth.

As Ryan's balls tightened against his body and the familiar tingling deep inside his belly told him he was close to exploding, his chains of control snapped, and he thrust inside her mouth, nearly burying himself to the hilt.

A feral shout ripped from his throat a split second before the hot release of his essence spilled inside her mouth.

A sudden shower of pink sparks exploded around him, tickling the exposed skin of his arms and face and leaving an almost charred smell hanging in the evening air.

He opened his eyes to see Kiera still kneeling in front of him, her hand curled around the base of his softening cock.

Remorse at his uncaring treatment of her churned inside his stomach. He'd thrust inside her mouth like she was a common whore, when he already knew she couldn't take all of him. "I'm so sorry, Healer. There is no excuse for my behavior. I—"

She laughed, low and husky, and the sound traveled over him like a sensual caress, which instantly hardened him again, despite the fresh confusion traveling through him.

Kiera gently squeezed his cock, making him gasp. "I think I'm beginning to like this energy thing, and I'm ready for more."

Ryan bit back his surprise at his total misunderstanding of the situation before him, and instead whispered a silent thanks to whatever gods would listen.

Without wasting time to speak, he gently freed his cock from her grip and tucked it inside his trousers before he picked Kiera up and tossed her over his shoulder like a prize he had just fought for and won.

Her laugh spilled around him—a sound he was beginning to love.

He carried her back inside the castle into his family's rooms and stopped short as his mother and all five brothers looked up from their dinner with expressions ranging from surprise to shock to outright hostility.

Damn.

12

A quick flash of movement reminded Kiera the guards still shadowed them. Her face burned at the thought of what those silent guards might have heard of their activities under the *ponga* tree.

Ryan suddenly stopped, jarring her, and she felt him stiffen underneath her, since she was still tossed over his shoulder, her face nearly resting against his broad back.

"Welcome, Ryan. It's good to see you," came a soft feminine voice.

Kiera caught her breath as something Ryan said in the courtyard replayed inside her mind. *When I returned home, I went to see my mother in her chambers—the same ones we came through to find this courtyard, as a matter of fact.*

Shit!

The same mother who Ryan had caught with Cunt warriors would now meet Ryan's possible future "mate"—a half-blood Cunt. Not exactly an Ozzie and Harriet family meeting.

Out in the courtyard, Kiera had been too distracted to wonder about where Ryan's mother and brothers were currently.

Now she wished she would've asked. Not to mention, she hoped they hadn't heard any of the activities going on outside.

Kiera pushed up and twisted so she could see what was going on.

Her action must have reminded Ryan he still held her, because he gently lowered her to the floor and squeezed her hand before releasing her.

Kiera turned and squared her shoulders and raised her chin, ready for anything.

A stunning Klatch woman wearing a soft, flowing white dress and a wary expression stood watching her. Behind the woman ranged five tall men—all different but unmistakably related to Ryan. The men had the same dark features and even physiques; it was enough to make any woman light-headed from all the testosterone permeating the air.

However, unlike Ryan, none of them wore their long hair loose around their shoulders, and all five wore expressions of anger and outrage, their narrowed gazes hard and unyielding, their body language hostile.

Kiera noticed absently that her retinue of Klatch guards had stationed themselves unobtrusively around the edges of the room. Apparently they thought the tension swimming in the room posed little permanent threat to herself or Ryan. She hoped they were right.

"Mother." Ryan's voice was soft but held the unmistakable hint of steel underneath. He nodded to his brothers and received no response. His expression never changed, but he tipped his chin to ensure his hair covered his scar, which told her he felt vulnerable.

"Will you introduce us to your . . . friend?" his mother asked, her voice neutral.

When Ryan remained silent, Kiera smoothed a hand over her hair and then stepped forward toward Ryan's mother. After all, if anyone in the room would be sympathetic to having a half-blood Cunt on Tador, it was this woman. "I'm Kiera Matthews. It's very nice to meet you."

A tentative smile curved his mother's lips. "Welcome, Kiera. I had heard the Healer had been found."

Mutters and angry grumbles sounded from the brothers, but a small hand gesture from their mother silenced them. "I'm Phoebe, Ryan's mother. It's an honor to meet you."

Kiera returned the smile, hoping this was the right path. "I apologize for intruding on your dinner." She spared a glance for the brothers, and when she noted the hostility rolling off them in nearly visible waves, she wished she hadn't.

Ryan took her hand in his. "Things have been a bit overwhelming since the Healer arrived, and I thought she could benefit from the quiet and beauty of the courtyard."

Phoebe laid a tentative hand on Ryan's arm, as if afraid he would flinch away from her touch. "This is still your home, my son. You and any you choose to bring are always welcome here."

The tension churning inside the room suddenly exploded. "Mother, I can't believe you're accepting this!" One of Ryan's brothers pulled Phoebe back away from Ryan, making a definite "our side" and "not welcome" division.

Ryan's jaw clenched, and Kiera tightened her grip on his hand, lending him moral support regardless if he wanted it or not.

Phoebe's eyes narrowed in displeasure, a flash of anger marring the deep purple depths as she stared up at her son, who stood at least a foot and a half taller than her. "Bryan." Her voice held the unmistakable warning that only a mother could wield. "Kiera is a guest in our house and as such will not be insulted by any member of our family."

"The Cunts are our sworn enemies. You can't just expect us to stand aside while our *brother* dilutes the Klatch bloodline and endangers Tador."

Ryan released Kiera's hand, and before her mind could catch up with why, his fist flew and caught Bryan squarely in the jaw.

Bryan's head snapped back, but he swung out blindly catching Ryan in the temple, while the other four brothers surrounded Ryan, fists flying.

Kiera yanked Phoebe out of the path of the fighting and glanced toward the still-stationary guards. Apparently family squabbles didn't fall under their jurisdiction.

Bastards. Fine, she didn't need their help, anyway.

Her anger snapped, and her adrenaline flowed. She started forward, and Phoebe caught her arm. "This is something they need to work through on their own, Healer."

Kiera gritted her teeth, and all sympathy for Phoebe evaporated.

Her heart had gone out to both Ryan and his mother after hearing the story of Ryan's scar. But now she realized Phoebe had *allowed* Ryan to keep the truth from his brothers all these years. And the outcome of that poor decision stood before her in a tangle of swinging arms and legs.

She yanked her arm out of Phoebe's grasp. "They would probably work it out a whole lot quicker if they knew the real reason behind Ryan's scar, don't you think?"

Phoebe winced as if she'd been struck across the face, but she didn't reply.

"You've allowed him to carry this burden on his own for entirely too long. No wonder there is a chasm between you." Kiera turned her back on Phoebe and studied the fight for the best angle of entry.

The guards started forward when they realized her intent, and she glared them back into their places.

Kiera could barely make out Ryan's tall form in the melee that had broken out.

Unable to compete with the larger men's stature, Kiera did what her father had taught her—fought dirty.

She stood behind the back of the closest brother to her, who obligingly stood with a wide stance while he ducked and bobbed and punched Ryan in the stomach.

Kiera planted her left foot and kicked him squarely between the legs with her right. She retracted her foot quickly, and when he crumpled with a loud "oof," she kicked him in the face and ducked a swinging fist from another of the men.

"Cunt bitch!"

The familiar taunt, which had rung inside her ears growing up, only served to pump her adrenaline faster.

A quick jump-kick knocked the speaker back and allowed Ryan enough room to punch Bryan hard enough that the man fell backward like a tall tree cut down in the forest.

Kiera dodged a flying fist, but didn't move in time to avoid the stinging blow that glanced off her cheek and threw her off balance.

She fell to her side, and before she could roll away, one of the brothers was on top of her, pressing her into the hard tiles of the floor.

The hatred in his gaze bored into her, and she took a deep breath as she lunged upward crushing his nose with her forehead.

The hard blow hurt like hell but dazed him enough to allow her to use the same leverage maneuver she had on Ryan that first night.

When the brother landed on his back, his hands cradling his mangled nose, she used another move she learned that first night with Ryan. She settled all her body weight on her knee— directly on his crotch.

A gurgle of pain and surprise bellowed out along with his breath as his body curled up in fetal position, and she scrambled to get out of the way.

She pushed to standing just as a hard beam of power hit the center of her back and tingled through her body in a rush.

Arousal and pure power poured inside her, absorbing into every pore so fast that the small flow escaping through her feet seemed like only a trickle. Every inch of her skin ached, her breasts were suddenly heavy and her clit screamed for release.

Fear pulsed through her in an icy rush as her mind groped for control over the chaotic rush of power swirling inside her.

Katelyn's lessons seemed inadequate in the face of such overwhelming power.

Ryan's face suddenly filled her vision, and she tried to shake her head to tell him not to touch her, but her body had stopped responding to her demands.

As soon as he grabbed her, pink shimmering power exploded outward, sizzling through her veins like a thousand tiny razor blades and out along Ryan's arms like shimmering fireworks.

Gasps and shouts from around the room were her only indication that the energy hadn't gone unnoticed by everyone else.

A sudden after-surge of pink energy exploded between her and Ryan, stealing her breath.

An orgasm slammed into her like a giant wrecking ball, convulsing her entire body in rhythmic waves of pleasure and ripping a raw scream from her throat.

The intensity of power knocked Kiera back away from Ryan and she landed hard on her back.

Pain radiated along her back and through her chest, and she was afraid she might have cracked a rib.

Silence settled around her, and slowly her breath returned and all discomfort abated, leaving her slightly light-headed with a few tiny aftershocks of good sex rocking her system.

Not exactly the way she had hoped she would get to this point tonight, and not nearly as private.

Kiera slowly sat up, super-aware of every muscle that bunched and loosened with her movements. Nothing seemed to be broken or even injured.

A sudden hushed awareness made her glance up.

Every eye in the room was trained on her.

And much to Kiera's surprise, not one of the brothers showed any injuries. No cut lips, no black swollen eyes, and most telling—none of them had a broken nose that she knew she had administered.

"She's the true Healer . . ." one of the unnamed brothers said in awe.

". . . powerful enough to give us all an intense group orgasm . . ." from another.

"Fucking Cunt is the Healer?" from a third.

"Ryan . . ." Bryan sprawled a few feet from Ryan on all fours. Every conversation stopped to center on the two brothers. "Your scar."

Pinpricks of unease raced down Kiera's spine as she turned to look at Ryan. He slowly raised his hand to trace his now perfectly smooth right cheek.

The jagged scar he had carried since that fateful day he found is mother with the Cunts was gone.

His eyes widened, and all color drained from his face as his gaze found hers.

The intensity of the pain and accusation burning in the dark depths surprised her and made her recoil. Heat and shame burned not only into her cheeks, but along every inch of her skin as the air inside the room suddenly became too thick to breathe.

She had to get away. Anywhere but here.

Hot tears burned at the backs of her eyes, and she scrambled to her feet and out the front door of the chambers.

Queen Alyssandra motioned for Silas. "Please station someone outside to keep this an entirely private meeting. No servants, and in fact, no one except those already in attendance."

"My queen?" His already wrinkled face crinkled in confusion.

Alyssa smiled. She wondered if Silas had ever remained on the inside of the throne room during his long reign as major-domo. "I require your unique knowledge of the history of Tador for this meeting, Silas. Would you do me the honor of attending?"

A quick look of surprise ran across his features before he straightened to his full height and nodded once. "Yes, of course, my queen. I'll return shortly."

As good as his word, five minutes later, Silas motioned to his proxy to close the heavy double doors of the throne room while he stood just next to the long table where the five hand-picked members of the Klatch Council sat in tense silence with similar concerned expressions on their faces. King Stone gestured for Silas to take a seat at the table, and after a long, uncomfortable silence, Silas sat, but he refused to accept any refreshments.

Alyssa jumped when the boom of the hard wood door closing against the *balda* doorframe echoed through the large chamber. "I've gathered you here today in a private meeting to discuss several urgent issues."

"Does this involve the half-blood Healer?" asked Raine, the new head of the council. His tone was wary. "The council and I have met on this issue, and I can assure you that the people will not accept this dilution of the Klatch royal bloodline."

Alyssa sighed. Little did they know they would have to accept even more than that before this meeting was finished. Even those loyal to the Klatch throne might question her after they heard Kiera's conditions. "You might want to hear the latest reports before you decree what the people will and won't accept." She tossed a folder with the latest findings on the table in front of them. "As of early this morning, sixty percent of the outlying areas have had to be evacuated and only twenty percent of the crops are usable at this point."

Stunned gasps, murmurs and even some soft cursing were

the various reactions from her council—and from Silas, a sad stoic silence.

Raine rubbed his chin between his fingers—a gesture he always repeated when gathering his thoughts. "My queen, how could the destruction have increased so rapidly? The previous estimates were that we had six more months before we reached this point."

"We have some theories, which I'll discuss in a moment. But I wanted to get the reports out of the way first, so we can discuss our options—which are decidedly few." She flipped open the folder on the table to her most recent report from the royal gardener and steward. "The castle can dispense food to those in need from our own stores, but times are desperate and growing worse by the minute. Several Klatch have even relocated to Earth. At the current rate of the planet's decline, we have less than one month before every inch of Tador matches the desolation of the outlying areas." Her voice wavered as she thought of the first time she stepped through the portal and saw Tador in all its glory. Heavy sadness and loss filled her chest and threatened to drown her.

Alyssandra, she heard her husband's voice inside her mind—one of the many perks of being an ascended queen. *Have faith, my little witch. We will weather this together. Don't upset yourself or our daughter.*

His words helped beat back the overwhelming sensation of panic building inside her. She swallowed hard and placed her hand over her stomach, where her daughter grew inside her. Stone was right. They would find a way to fix this! She refused to be the one who destroyed her daughter's and her people's legacy.

Their daughter would be the next queen, and Tador would thrive and survive for millennia after Alyssa and Stone were nothing more than a story written in a journal somewhere.

If I made it through nearly twenty-four years growing up with Sela, getting through this should be nothing.

Stone's deep chuckle of amusement reverberated inside her mind. *There's the headstrong woman I know and love.*

Alyssa squared her shoulders and turned to face her council. After letting them whisper and mutter among themselves for a long moment more, she broke in. "As I said before, times are desperate. We have to think of what's best for the people and Tador as a whole."

"My queen," Raine began. "Given the most recent reports, I think we can all agree that the Triangle must be implemented immediately—even if the Healer is of half-blood. We would rather stomach that than lose Tador entirely."

Alyssa snorted. "I'm sure the Healer will be overjoyed to hear that hearty acceptance—especially after the attempt on her life yesterday."

Stone rose and picked up the wineskin. "Ladies and gentlemen, I think we all need some wine before we continue with this discussion." He poured each of the council a full goblet of wine before he started to fill Silas' goblet.

"None for me, my king. The majordomo should not drink with the council or the reigning king and queen." His voice was formal and low, a product of a century in his position.

"We asked you here as a consultant, Silas," Stone told him as he filled Silas' goblet despite the man's protests. "And we would be honored if you would drink with us—all of us," he said as he glared at the five council members daring them to disagree.

"This has been your home longer than any of us, Silas," Alyssa reminded him. "And we'll need your expertise to help us through."

The old man nodded regally and took a single sip of the rich wine before replacing it on the table with precise movements.

At least he hadn't outright refused. Alyssa smiled inwardly.

"If there's more bad news than you've already told us, we may need an entire barrel." Raine threaded his fingers in front of him and squarely met Alyssa's gaze. "My queen, you hand-picked us after the council betrayed your mother. We are loyal to you and to Tador. Although I appreciate good wine at any time, please tell us the worst of it so we can deal with whatever situation we're all in."

Alyssa smiled, and some of the tension inside her uncoiled. It was times like these that she remembered why she had chosen Raine as her new council head after she had been forced to kill the last one. She poured herself water in deference to her growing daughter and took a large drink before placing the glass on the table and meeting every expectant gaze in turn.

"The Healer has agreed to participate in the Triangle with some conditions."

"And those would be?" prompted Raine when Alyssa let silence fall for a long moment.

"First, her father is on Earth in a coma from an energy blast. She asks that we retrieve him so he will be safe from Sela and all those who currently hunt the Healer."

The council exchanged glances and a few whispered comments until Raine turned back to Alyssa. "Fair enough. It's the least we can do for a woman willing to give up her entire life to help us save Tador."

"I think there's much more we can do for her, such as find a way to make sure she is safe on Tador, but that's another discussion for another time."

Raine nodded in agreement. "Any other conditions?"

"Two. The second one is her cat, Shiloh, be allowed to stay with her on Tador."

"Done," Raine said with amusement and relief clear in his deep voice. A few of the other council members smiled, relief coloring their expressions until Raine's brow furrowed. "Wait.

My queen, you mentioned two more conditions. What did you save for last?"

Alyssa sighed. "In order for Kiera Matthews to agree to fulfill the role of the Healer and all that implies, we must put into action a plan to begin the reintroduction of the Cunt people to Tador."

The effect of her words was like a sudden explosion. Cursing, angry shouts and raised voices fought for dominance as they echoed through the throne room—all except for King Stone, a comforting presence behind her, and Silas, who sat silently and watched the council's escalating outburst with bored detachment, as if he had expected no less of them.

When she had let them vent, she held up a hand and arched one eyebrow, daring them to disobey her directive for silence.

Slowly, the throne room fell into a tense silence, and the council slumped back into their seats.

"Now that the initial outburst is past, let's discuss this like the leaders we are all supposed to be."

Raine gulped the rest of his wine and then refilled his goblet, his dark brows furrowed with anger.

"As we all know, Tador is a planet that leverages energy and maintains a symbiotic relationship with not only the queen, but with every person on the planet." When a few of the council seemed ready to argue, she held up her hand again. "This is demonstrated every time you need energy and you open yourself to the planet to receive more or you generate healing energy with another person or yourself using sexual energy as the catalyst. However, twenty-five years ago after the civil war, we banished half the inhabitants of Tador, and all their energy along with them."

"The Cunts are not as powerful as the Klatch. Their energy can't have made that much of a difference," Raine muttered just loud enough for everyone to hear.

"They are a native species of this planet, and any time we

take away one entire race, we change the environment irrevocably. We only need to look at Earth to see the truth of that statement."

"The Cunts are entirely different from the spotted owl or the sperm whale of Earth, my queen," Tristan, one of the council, added.

"But the same principles apply. It's just that a faction of the Cunts and not the spotted owls betrayed the Klatch throne a quarter of a century ago. Not all Cunts are like Sela, just as not all Klatch are loyal to the throne, then or now."

"What proof do you have that the entire race isn't depraved and traitorous, just like Sela?" Raine asked archly.

Silas cleared his throat. "My queen, if I may?"

Alyssa smiled, glad this discussion had spurned Silas to add his input, as she'd hoped. "Please, Silas."

"Sela and her faction were but a small movement within the Cunts. Many of them were very loyal to Tador and our entire way of life here. However, it took only a few with an agenda of hate and malice to change things for all. In those dark days after the young princess was taken, it was difficult to know who could be trusted, and there were many Klatch banished along with the Cunts." His gaze swept over every person in turn. "In fact, the Klatch council members who tried to kill Queen Alyssandra just a few short months ago have remained here on Tador, undermining the planet and its people while many loyal Cunts have been banished from their homes to Earth."

13

Sela gazed at each member of the Cunt Council in turn, daring them to speak.

She had called this impromptu meeting when she realized her recent obsession with Aedan and the sexual domination she had come to crave had distracted her more than she liked to admit. Her body still ached for him, which was precisely why Aedan had been killed. A queen couldn't afford to show any weakness.

She supposed she would have to go back to torturing and killing humans during her sexual play—although she doubted it would hold the same appeal as what Aedan had offered. A sad sigh threatened to escape from her throat, and she ruthlessly bit it back.

You are Queen of the Cunts. Strong, capable and in control, she reminded herself.

She spared a glance for the council.

Four council members and one empty chair—Danen's, she suspected—sat behind a long table. She stood in front of them, in a position of power and dominance, and judged that everyone's nerves were stretched tight enough for her purposes. After all, fear was a precise tool to be used, just like any other.

"Marco," she snapped as she poured herself a vodka on the rocks. "Report."

The scraping of the wooden chair across the tile told her Marco stood to give his report, as was traditional. After all, a show of respect went a long way in maintaining discipline and order.

"My queen," he began, his deep voice reminding her of the days when he had wanted to bury himself between her thighs so much he betrayed friends, family and even his own values just for the privilege.

A longing for those simple days of the past flowed through her, and she ruthlessly buried the disturbing emotions.

"I have questioned each of the council members to discover the full extent of Aedan's treachery," Marco said, breaking her out of her thoughts. "Unfortunately, Danen did not survive his interrogation." Marco's dramatic pause made Sela smile. The man knew how to use silence to inspire fear and loyalty, she'd give him that. He cleared his throat before he continued. "Which was just as well since he did not take steps to stop Aedan or to alert you to the danger sooner."

Sela drained half the vodka and then splashed more into the glass before she turned to face the council. "I assume you have a recommendation for a replacement?" She knew Marco well enough to already know the answer, but proprieties must sometimes be maintained for the good of all.

"Of course, my queen. I have a list of candidates with their qualifications for you to consider at your leisure."

She stalked forward, her hand extended, and Marco handed her a single sheet of paper.

The list contained four names—all competent choices, all seasoned and extremely loyal to the cause, and none of them the type of men who had any hope of tempting Sela into asking them into her bed. A hot spurt of annoyance spilled through her, and she glared at Marco.

He did his job and did it very well, which was why she didn't let her temper get the best of her during moments like these, when he was so obviously managing her.

Removing temptations that would distract her was best for the Cunts as a whole, but that didn't mean Sela appreciated the obvious sign that Marco knew exactly what she had let Aedan do to her.

She swallowed back the venomous words that burned on her tongue and nodded at Marco as she tossed the list on the table in front of him. "Any of the four are acceptable. For your continued loyalty, I'll allow you your choice."

Marco dropped his gaze and dipped his chin in a sign of respect. "My thanks for your favor, my queen."

She waved away his too-proper words. "What else?" she demanded as she drained her vodka and slammed the tumbler on the bar, noting the sound of cracking glass with a small surge of satisfaction at destroying something.

"The only other matters Aedan dabbled in were small, and all have been rectified." Marco glanced up, his deep blue eyes distant and formal. "I can give you the full report if you wish, my queen."

A fresh wave of irritation surged inside her, making her heart pound and her fists clench. "Are you afraid you haven't done your job well enough and I need to clean up after you, Marco?"

Her council head didn't even flinch, which ratcheted up her temper and tightened her stomach.

"Everything has been fully taken care of, my queen. However, I would never presume to speak for you. I would, of course, be honored if you chose to look over my work and see if it is to your standards."

All the proper words, along with the proper amount of respect. *Get a handle on your temper!* If she allowed herself to kill Marco in anger, she would only regret her harsh actions later. Regardless of how irritating he could be, he was thorough, competent and, most of all, loyal. "What else is in your report, Marco? I grow tired of listening to you speak."

"Yes, my queen." He straightened and met her gaze. "We may have a lead on the Healer for the Klatch Triangle."

A sharp stab of excitement lanced through Sela.

The throne of Tador would soon be hers. A slow smile spread across her face as the ramifications spilled through her mind.

"Kiera?"

At the sound of her name, she glanced up to see Alyssa peek around the doorframe of Ryan's room—a room Ryan hadn't bothered to return to last night.

Shiloh blinked large orange eyes, his purr suddenly kicked into high gear at the sight of the queen.

Kiera swiped at her drying tears and glanced up to meet Alyssa's concerned gaze, half hoping the entire castle hadn't heard about her group orgasm and healing sideshow down in Ryan's family's rooms.

"Are you okay?" Alyssa stepped inside and pushed the door closed behind her. The queen's expression immediately confirmed her fears.

Kiera laughed, a short, bitter sound, and adjusted the pillow behind her as she sat up straighter, her back against the headboard. "Oh, sure. Let's see, last night I handed out group orgasms to Ryan's entire family—who already hate me for my Cunt heritage—and to top it off, I accidentally heal a scar that is tied to some very deep emotional issues for the man I might '*mate*' with." She used the first two fingers of each hand to make quote marks in the air. "I can never go back to my practice or my patients without being killed by assassins, and I'll never be welcome here because I happened to be born with characteristics passed to me through my mother, whom I adored and miss very deeply. My father is back on Earth still in a coma, and I'm under such heavy guard to keep me 'safe' that I can't even go work through some aggressions by kicking the shit out of something or someone. To top all of that off, I feel like shit because I chased Ryan out of his room last night."

She scrubbed her hands over her face and smiled bitterly at Alyssa. "And now I'm sitting here moping and fucking whining about the entire thing, which is not like me at all. Does that sound like I'm okay to you?"

Alyssa laughed as she took a seat in an overstuffed chair just next to the bed.

Shiloh stalked forward and jumped from the end of the bed onto Alyssa's lap—another damn male deserting her—his eyes half lidded as Alyssa stroked his fur.

Kiera's brow furrowed as anger sliced through her at the queen's reaction. She had just spilled all her frustrations, fears and insecurities, and Alyssa responded by laughing?

Alyssa's sharp gaze held Kiera quiet. "First off, you didn't chase Ryan out of his room. Although I'll admit he's an ass for not coming up to talk to you last night. He spent the entire night talking with his mother and brothers, something that has needed to happen for a very long time."

"Did he tell you . . ."

Alyssa smiled. "About his scar? He told Stone last night when the guards reported the fight." The queen chuckled. "You're good for him, you know? He's bottled that story up for years, and a few scant minutes after telling you about it, it's out in the open and he's finally healing."

Something inside Kiera's chest tightened—a combination of hope and dread. "Have they worked things out?"

Alyssa pushed her heavy mane of hair over her shoulder and tucked her legs up under her, all the while continuing to stroke Shiloh's orange fur. "I think it will take a long time for them to work through everything. Ryan's brothers aren't sure who they are angrier with—Phoebe for doing what she did and then letting Ryan bear the secret alone, or Ryan for not telling them. And as for Phoebe and Ryan, I think they understand each other and their motivations, but there's a lot of history they still need to work through."

Kiera remembered Ryan saying the same thing about his relationship with his mother.

"Second, I don't see you as a whiner. You've had a hell of a few days, and as far as I can see, you're handling things pretty well." Alyssa pursed her lips and studied Kiera. "You stood up to all of us and told us things we would rather not hear but that you knew were right. Then you waded into a fight with six full-grown Klatch warriors to protect Ryan and kicked some serious ass from what I heard."

Kiera winced at the memory and how that must've looked.

"And you nearly emasculated one of them as well as one innocent guard and a royal Klatch prince." The queen laughed, her amusement slowly seeping into Kiera at the absurd picture she had painted. "Come to think of it, I think you'll fit right in here. You should hear Gavin—he tells the story like a proud papa praising his offspring."

The words were like a slap of surprise. Gavin bragged about her performance? For some reason, that pleased her. And as everything else Alyssa told her trickled through her mind, Kiera fought against the lightening of her emotions, as if she didn't deserve to be lighthearted after everything that had happened.

But in the end, a small giggle escaped her, followed by a full-bodied laugh that loosened the knots inside her belly and the tight band of dread around her chest. When she finally caught her breath, she slumped back against the headboard. "Damn. At least I'm giving the Klatch populace something to talk about."

Alyssa rolled her eyes skyward. "That's an understatement." She shook her head. "Anyway, I didn't come up here for any of that, although it's good to see you looking happier."

Shiloh stretched and rolled onto his back to allow Alyssa to rub his tummy.

Kiera sobered and held her breath to await Alyssa's words. She swallowed hard, her throat suddenly dry.

"The Klatch Council has voted to accept your conditions and move forward with the Triangle as soon as possible."

Kiera huffed out a breath of relief, surprised at the realization that she would've been disappointed had the decision been otherwise. Regardless of the strange situation she'd waded into over the past few days, being here on Tador still felt very right. And if the Klatch were willing to talk about reintroducing the Cunts to their native planet, she had achieved more than her mother had on that front.

Excitement and anticipation fluttered inside her belly. "Okay, so what are the next steps?"

"First, we retrieve your things from your old house, then we pick up your father. After that, we must institute the Triangle. The sooner the better." Alyssa closed her eyes for a long moment as if gathering courage for her next words. "And then we can discuss the plan for Cunt reintroduction."

Kiera's throat tightened as hope blossomed inside her that Tador could finally heal her father and one day the Klatch and Cunts could finally live again as a united people.

Memories of Ryan's smooth, freshly healed face spilled through her mind. Realization hit her like a fist to the chest, and she sat up straight. "Shit." She glanced up at Alyssa's knowing smile.

"After we bring my father back here, will you all help me figure out how to control this healing ability?"

"I thought you'd never ask."

* * *

"The perimeter is clear, ma'am."

"Stop fucking calling me, ma'am. Kiera, or even Healer will do, but not ma'am. Got it?" Kiera glared up at the guard who had spoken while Gavin unsuccessfully tried to hide his smile. She had fought long and hard to get them to agree to allow her to even come on this operation. She refused to have the guards continue to think of her as just a woman who needed to be protected.

Ryan stood by stone-faced. An uncomfortable silence still hung between them, since they hadn't had a chance to talk because everyone had assembled in front of the portal to the *between* just after Alyssa had left Kiera's room that morning.

"Yes . . . ma—Healer," said the young guard.

She figured that was the best she could hope for and nodded her thanks, pointedly looking everywhere but at Ryan. "The side door to the garage is our best entry point."

"I agree," Ryan added. "Although a simple energy surge overrode the alarms when I was here before, that entrance will give us the most cover."

Kiera's gaze narrowed. "That was at my safe house where you overrode the alarms. You were never at this house."

Ryan shrugged, still not quite meeting her gaze. "I came here first to make sure I didn't miss you and then started down the list of safe houses. I turned the alarms back on once I was done."

Kiera frowned at the ease in which Ryan had bypassed her father's security systems. Hell, at least he was still speaking to her.

Her mind whirled through possibilities of building a Klatch-and-Cunt-proof alarm. She filed those facts away for later.

Gavin closed his eyes for a long moment, and suddenly impatient, Kiera resisted the urge to shake him. "I don't sense anyone inside the house."

"I wish I could do that." Kiera blew her bangs out of her face and readjusted her grip on her gun and tazer. She was armed and ready for human, Cunt, Klatch or anything else that dared to get in her way. "You'll have to teach me how to do the 'sensing' thing sometime—or is it a specialized talent?"

Gavin cleared his throat before answering. "It's something learned with time and experience. Ryan hasn't mastered it yet."

Ryan's narrowed eyes and dark scowl made a few of the guards take a step back, but Gavin showed no signs of even noticing the prince's wrath from his statement.

"It took me nearly sixty years, but I'll be happy to teach you what I can when we have time."

Kiera met Gavin's lavender gaze for a long moment, surprised at his tender expression, which she wasn't quite sure how to interpret. She glanced away quickly. "Thanks." She turned back to the guard who had called her ma'am. "Let's go."

He signaled to the remaining guards and then stepped forward to slip her key into the deadbolt lock.

The click of the lock disengaging sounded nearly deafening in the quiet night air, and Kiera steeled herself so she wouldn't jump.

However, she did tighten her grip on her weapons and prayed her palms would stop sweating before she dropped her guns.

The guard swung the door inward and then slipped inside the dark doorway.

When all remained silent, Kiera followed him and felt more than saw Gavin, Ryan and several more guards trail behind them.

A soft pink glow emanated from the first guard's palm, which allowed her to see clearly. A small rush of relief flowed through her that both her father's wall safe and her PT Cruiser seemed whole and untouched.

After a quick look around, the guard unlocked the door to the kitchen and stepped inside.

A strong arm grabbed her from behind a split second before two rounds of gunfire split the air in front of her.

She found herself shoved into Ryan's arms, while Gavin rushed forward into the kitchen doorway.

Blue energy sizzled and pulsed from the open doorway, nearly blinding her from the change from sudden darkness. She closed her eyes tight and shielded her face.

"Hold your fire!" Gavin barked and then all fell quiet.

She blinked a few times, squinting to allow her eyes to adjust back to the murky darkness as her heart galloped in time with her surging adrenaline. Ryan's arms were still bracketed around her, his body shielding hers. She glanced up, and their eyes met and held.

His expression softened and turned almost sheepish.

Before she realized she meant to, she raised her hand and touched his now-healed cheek.

Ryan didn't flinch but covered her hand with his and gently released her, his expression unreadable.

She frowned as she realized they were now on Earth, so she couldn't blame the rush of warmth inside her chest on the energy surges of Tador.

"All clear, Healer."

Kiera jumped like a guilty child when Gavin appeared in the doorway. He held out his hand for hers in an odd courtly gesture totally out of place with all of them dressed for stealth and battle. "Come inside; there's someone here to see you."

Ryan stiffened beside her. "Who's in there, Gav?"

"Trust me, my lord. Kiera will be perfectly safe."

Ryan studied Gavin for a long moment before he relaxed and released Kiera.

Kiera frowned. "I thought you said you didn't sense anyone inside?"

"The bas—" Gavin closed his mouth before finishing the word. "He came through a portal, and I sensed him a split second before you heard the gunshots. That's why I grabbed you from behind and shoved you behind me and into Ryan's arms."

She opened her mouth to demand to know what the hell was going on, but the calm expression on Gavin's face stopped her for some reason she couldn't name. Instead, she holstered her weapons and placed her hand in Gavin's, allowing herself to be led inside her own kitchen and through the archway into the living room.

Two guards held glowing pink energy orbs above their palms, illuminating the room and casting everything into a surreal rose-colored glow.

A striking, full-blooded Cunt warrior stood with his back to her in the middle of the living room. His easy commanding presence filled the entire room and reminded her oddly of Gavin.

His body was lean and athletic in the way of the Cunts, his long blond hair pulled back into a simple tail at his nape that hung nearly to his waist. He wore expensive gray dress slacks that showed off his muscular ass and thighs, and a white dress shirt that looked like it would cost more than everything she currently wore, including her weapons.

He turned, and his familiar deep blue gaze raked over her, reminding her of a parent making sure their child was whole and healthy.

"Marco." Alternating streams of fear and hope surged through her, sending her stomach roiling. "What are you doing here?"

Relief colored his features, and he stepped forward to pull her into a nearly bone-crushing embrace. "Kiera, I'm so glad you're all right. What are you doing back here? It's dangerous. I would've brought you anything you wished."

Kiera buried her face against his chest, inhaling the scents of coffee and some type of spicy aftershave that always clung to him.

When several guards took menacing steps forward, and Ryan's face darkened with anger, Marco loosened his grip.

Kiera stepped away and waved the guards back.

Marco had been a long-time friend of her mother's and had

often paved her way through the fringes of Cunt society—even though he still thought her ignorant of all he had done for her. She had only kind memories of this man, and his presence somehow comforted her.

"Gav," Ryan began, his tone holding an unmistakable warning. "What the hell is going on?"

Gavin squared his shoulders and met Ryan's gaze. "Marco was the one who advised me the assassins had been sent after Kiera."

Ryan's gaze narrowed, and his eyes blazed with anger. "He's the head of the fucking Cunt Council, Gavin."

"Yes, my lord, he is." Gavin didn't even flinch under Ryan's heated gaze. "He also risked his life to alert me, which makes his life worthless if he is found out. And since his life is already worthless on Tador, I judged his motives to be worthy."

"Thank you," Marco said and nodded toward Gavin. "I realize the risk you took in trusting me."

Gavin scowled. "I didn't do it for you," he said barely loud enough to be heard.

Kiera frowned as suspicion burned inside her chest. She looked back and forth between the two men, their carefully blank expressions confirming her thoughts. "Would one or both of you like to tell me what the hell is going on that you obviously didn't feel was important enough to share with me?" She crossed her arms and glared at them both.

Marco smiled the same charming smile she remembered throughout her childhood, and she steeled herself against its calming effect. "Why don't we sit? I've ensured this house will have no Cunt surveillance for the next several hours, so we have a few moments to talk."

Ryan wrapped his arm around Kiera's shoulders in a protective gesture. "Why don't you just tell us what's going on right now?" His tone was laced with protective anger and hard steel.

"Very well." Marco took a seat on the soft leather couch and adjusted his cerulean blue necktie, which was the same color as his eyes. "For the sake of time, let me give you the quick version. Some treachery on the Cunt Council allowed a hit to be placed on Kiera after her meeting with former Council Member Danen."

"Treachery on the Cunt Council? Isn't that common practice?" Sarcasm melded with the anger in Ryan's voice.

Marco only smiled. "It is unfortunately quite common these days. However, I've ensured Danen and those who conspired with him behind my back will no longer be a problem."

Kiera stiffened as she realized the cultured man sitting in front of her had just casually mentioned the murder of more than one of his own people.

"I hope you don't judge me too harshly, Kiera." Marco's gaze found hers. "After all, if the choice was between you and them, I'm glad you're still here and they are not."

Kiera swallowed hard, grateful for the very same thing. After all, her father had killed in the military, and she was no naive young girl. Unfortunately, in her clinic and in her place on the fringes of Cunt society, she had seen murder, death, torture and quite a few other things she tried not to think about too often. She shrugged. "I suppose it's difficult for me to reconcile my childhood memories of you with the things you obviously have to do to maintain your place on the council."

A small crease appeared between his sandy blond brows, and he looked suddenly weary. "The council no longer stands for the things I fought for long ago—if they ever did." He scrubbed a hand over his face and sighed.

"You still haven't told us why you're here." Gavin's face remained an impassive mask, and Kiera wished she could see beneath and understand the underlying currents of the situation.

Marco nodded. "I've called off the assassins and placed Kiera under my personal guarantee of protection." His intense gaze captured hers. "You should be able to return to your life."

A hard knot uncoiled inside Kiera's belly as relief rushed through her. Her house, her patients, her father and even her PT Cruiser were all waiting for her.

She could slip back into her life like the past several days hadn't even happened.

A vice squeezed her chest, constricting her heart and making her throat tight and dry. "Should?" She glanced at Ryan's grim features and realized that she had already come to terms with all she was giving up, and even more than that, she was happy with the change.

Tador and Ryan were her life now, and all of this—she glanced around her at the furnishings that held a million memories—was from her past, not her future.

"Thanks for that Hallmark card's worth of reassurance, Marco, but I'll be staying on Tador."

If Marco was surprised, he never let it show. Although shock quickly flowed across Ryan's features before he tipped his chin to let his hair fall over his now-perfect cheek.

Marco glanced at Gavin and Ryan before returning his gaze to Kiera's. "What kind of life will you have on Tador? The Klatch will never accept you, and you'll have to be under constant guard. I'm grateful they kept you safe, but you would be a virtual prisoner."

"Like I would be here?" She smiled. "The Klatch have already accepted me . . . as their Healer."

She expected shock or even confusion from Marco, but he merely nodded as if he'd already known.

"Take the Healer to retrieve her things," Gavin barked at the guards, who immediately surrounded her and led her away from the growing tension inside the living room.

She thought about resisting but then thought better of it. No matter what Marco said, she couldn't wait to get back to Tador, so the sooner she had her things and her father, the sooner she could get back home and complete the Triangle.

She nearly laughed as she realized how right it felt to think of Tador as home.

Besides, if the men were going to have a pissing contest, she wasn't in the mood to watch them make asses of themselves.

Damn, I'm glad I'm a woman!

14

"What are you really doing here?" Ryan stalked forward until he stood directly in front of the head of the Cunt Council. If it wasn't for Kiera's affection for the man, he would have incinerated him on the spot—even though power rolled off the man in almost-visible waves.

Marco casually draped his arm across the back of the couch. "I've already gone over that. I wanted Kiera to know she could return to her life."

"Then why did you have to call off Cunt surveillance teams for the next few hours?" Gavin asked softly from behind Ryan.

Ryan stiffened. He hadn't even thought of that.

Marco sighed. "Per normal procedure, she would be watched for the next several months to ensure she wasn't a threat, but before any action was taken, such action would be cleared through me."

"Unless Sela intervened or went behind your back," Gavin added more sharply. "You lied to her. She wasn't offered a free pass back to her old life. She would be in more danger here at the whims of Sela and the winners of whatever power struggle is currently in play among the council members."

Marco sat forward, piercing Gavin with a sharp glare. "She has lived in the very same environment you speak of her entire life. You never worried about her before I came to you, so you have no right to judge my level of protection now." He stood so he faced Gavin toe to toe. "I've sacrificed my existence if Sela finds out what I've done. What have you done for her, or for Cecily's memory, Gavin?"

Ryan frowned as he glanced between the two men. If he wasn't mistaken, there had been a love triangle, with Cecily as the third point. So, if he'd deduced correctly, not only had Marco betrayed Gavin all those years ago, but he had also competed with Gavin for Cecily. Although in the end, Cecily had married a human and spurned them both.

Damn. That was harsh.

Gavin's eyes narrowed. "If you hadn't betrayed your planet, the throne you pledged loyalty to and even your own people all those years ago, both Cecily and Kiera would've lived safely on Tador, or at least had a home there. And Cecily might never have married the human."

Marco's eyes widened as if he'd been slapped, but he didn't step back. "You could've chosen Cecily and gone to Earth with her instead of cloaking yourself in martyrdom. She waited for you, you know." His tone dripped with bitterness. "She stayed with me for a time, but she kept waiting for you."

Pain flashed across Gavin's features, and he took a step back, as if just proximity to Marco had burned him.

"When she finally accepted you wouldn't come, she married the human." Marco closed his eyes and shook his head. "Only then."

As heavy silence fell, Ryan glanced at Gavin's dark features and then at Marco's. So much pain and self-loathing on both sides, and over the same woman.

If Cecily was anything like her daughter, Ryan didn't blame either man for falling under her spell.

Even though Kiera had agreed to stay on Tador, Ryan still

wasn't so sure his heart wouldn't end up broken in the end. He already cared far too much for his future mate. "Kiera will be down soon, and while I think she has every right to know the history of her mother, now isn't the time."

Both men nodded, and Gavin recovered first. "Kiera wants her father to be taken to Tador. Can we enlist your cooperation to ensure we don't run into problems retrieving him?"

Marco cleared his throat and then nodded. "I'll meet you there." He started toward the back of the house and then stopped. "Please tell, Kiera . . . it was good to see her." He stood still for a long moment before adding, "She reminds me so much of her mother, it hurts."

Ryan noticed the single nod of agreement from Gavin before Marco walked away.

Kiera stepped out of the portal behind Gavin. She opened her eyes and dropped his hand as the hot Phoenix night closed around her, prickling her skin after the bone-chilling cold of the *between.*

A few guards had returned to Tador with the things she had collected from her house. The rest of the guards surrounded her, Gavin and Ryan in the shadowy courtyard just behind the Phoenix Veteran's Hospital.

"Stand down," Gavin murmured, and the guards relaxed their stances. "Marco is near, and he's alone. There are only humans and a few non-powerful half-breeds inside the hospital."

Kiera winced at the mention of half-breeds but wished for the second time tonight she could do that sensing thing. She vowed to herself to hold Gavin to his promise of teaching her—as soon as she made it through the next few days.

Marco calmly stepped out of the shadows like he'd been out for an evening stroll rather than walking into a circle of highly trained Klatch warriors who were itching to kill him.

He had balls and a cultured style that made him an interesting dichotomy. In fact, as a child, she'd even harbored something of a crush on the powerful Cunt warrior.

As the circle of Klatch closed around Marco, a sudden wave of heavy sadness and tension crackled between Gavin and Marco, which made the hair on Kiera's arms prickle. She glanced between the two men and bit back a sigh.

Damn. Guess I should've stayed for the pissing contest back at the house. I wonder if Ryan will tell me what I missed.

She shoved her curiosity aside and concentrated on the task ahead. "So, how are we going to sneak Dad out of there?"

Marco smiled. "I took the liberty of calling in a few favors. According to hospital records, you, as the next of kin, are moving him to a private facility, and an ambulance has already loaded him and is ready for transport."

As if on cue, an ambulance pulled around the corner, the headlights blinding them all briefly before it pulled to a stop.

"That's it?" Kiera couldn't believe there wasn't more to the entire process. She glanced toward Gavin to see if he sensed anything out of place. When he gave her a curt nod, the bunched muscles across her shoulders relaxed slightly.

"That's it," Marco confirmed.

Gavin motioned four guards forward toward the ambulance, and Kiera watched them go. "They'll know it was you."

Kiera frowned as she tried to figure out who Gavin had meant those words for.

Marco smiled. "Yes."

A curl of dread wound inside her stomach. "What are you two talking about?"

Marco cupped her cheek in his hand and panic clawed at her insides.

"What's going on?" she demanded, suddenly desperate to understand what was happening.

"Don't come back to Earth, Kiera. It won't be safe here for

you." He caressed her cheek with his thumb, and she placed her hand over his.

Ryan's anger churned beside her in a heated prickling sensation, but he remained silent.

"Come with us," she blurted out.

Marco shook his head, his charming smile on full beam. "Unfortunately, I can never return to Tador." He held up a bundle of letters tied with a purple ribbon and placed them in her hand. "Be happy, Kiera, and don't look back." He turned and walked past the ambulance and on through the parking lot.

Her fingers closed around the letters, and she started forward.

Ryan gently caught her arm. "Let him go, Kiera."

Tears burned at the backs of her eyes, and her throat closed with churning emotions, but she only nodded.

Marco melted into the night, and she watched him go until she realized two Klatch guards carried her father's limp body toward the portal.

"Let's go," Ryan said softly from beside her.

Gavin held out his hand, and she swallowed hard as she threaded her fingers with his and closed her eyes to hold the picture of the portal inside her mind.

For her father's sake, she would go along for now. But Gavin and Ryan owed her some answers once they were back on Tador. And if either of them thought to do the Neanderthal act and *protect* her from the past—they were going to be in for a very rude awakening.

"Let's go," she murmured.

Kiera studied the still form of her father. He lay on one of the overstuffed bed in the room next door to Ryan's. His catheter and feeding tubes had all been brought with him, which gave the room the air of a private hospital. And even though as a doctor, Kiera was comfortable in such environs, it still pained her to see her formerly robust father in them.

Shiloh jumped up on the bed Kiera had shooed him off of while she had gotten her father comfortably settled. The feline curled next to her father's hip, his orange eyes wide and alert, like a tiny sentinel.

Suddenly weary, Kiera pulled one of the overstuffed chairs close to the side of the bed so she could sit and still hold her father's hand.

His gray hair had been kept close-cropped, the military style he had always favored, and his rugged face had softened a bit with all the years of inactivity and muscle atrophy. Even his hand in hers felt weak and soft—nothing like the hard muscular hands she remembered him to have.

Familiar emotions of loss and helplessness swelled inside her chest until they formed a throbbing ache. She rubbed at the spot but knew from past experience the action wouldn't lessen the sensation.

With a sigh, she reached out and ran a gentle hand over her father's cheek as she wished he would open his eyes and look at her like he used to.

"Healer?"

Kiera glanced over her shoulder to see Alyssa and Katelyn standing in the doorway.

"Are we intruding?" The Seer's voice was soft, as if she was afraid to speak too loudly in front of the still man lying on the bed.

Kiera nearly laughed as she thought of her father's probable response to two beautiful women visiting him at his sickbed. *Is it time for my sponge bath already? I'm all yours, ladies. Please be gentle.* She could almost hear the underlying laughter his voice would hold.

The thought lightened the pressure on her chest and made

her feel closer to her father than she had since that long ago day she'd found him injured on the living room floor.

"Please come on in. I just got him settled."

Dark smudges rode just underneath the queen's lovely eyes, and her normally olive skin seemed pale and drawn.

A quick glance toward the Seer showed no change in the redhead's appearance. And something told Kiera that it was stress, not any type of sickness, that marred Alyssa's features. Otherwise, the obviously close relationship between Alyssa and Katelyn would drive the Seer to take action.

Kiera decided to respect the queen's privacy and remained silent on the issue.

"You had asked us to teach you how to control your energy once your father was here on Tador." The queen smiled with warmth. "We thought now might be a good time to try to heal him."

Kiera's head snapped up, and she straightened as an electric current of excitement twined with hope fired through her. Her previous healings had all been accidents; she wasn't so sure she could achieve the same effect at will. "Do you think we can really do this?"

Katelyn pulled another chair up to the end of the bed while Alyssa sat in one on the opposite side of the bed from Kiera.

Alyssa settled back into the chair with a sigh. "To be honest, I'm not sure. I accidentally healed my mother right before I ascended, but the alternative was to watch her die. So I had nothing to lose."

Kiera smiled at the diplomatic answer. "What you're trying so gently to tell me is that by attempting to heal him, we may end up killing him?" She nodded, answering her own question. "I'm well aware of the risks. But I also know he wouldn't have wanted to live like this." She gestured toward the bed as memories of the robust and full-of-life man she had known all her life cycled through her mind like a slide show on fast forward.

Katelyn motioned toward the door, and one of the servants entered carrying a trayful of food, with Gavin close behind her. "We figured you would say that, so we came ready to give it our best shot."

A low thrum of excitement took up residence inside Kiera's belly. "What's all that for?"

As soon as the tray was arranged on the nearby table, Gavin waved the servant away and stood silently nearby.

Katelyn leaned back and stole a few grapes from the nearest plate. "We are going to need energy once this is done, so we came prepared." She gestured toward Gavin. "And in case you need a jump start, Gavin is powerful enough and has enough control that he can hit you with a blast of energy in varying degrees so you aren't overloaded."

Kiera swallowed hard. True, the energy blasts she'd been hit with hadn't been unpleasant, anything but—however, they always left her horny as hell, something that didn't feel quite right with her father in the room.

But if that's what it took to wake him up and restore him to the man he had been, she would gladly dance naked in Times Square. "Okay, what do we do?"

Gavin stepped forward. "Do you remember how I taught you to picture the portal inside your mind?"

She nodded.

Gavin's expression never changed, but she could've sworn she detected a hint of approval in his gaze. "We're going to try that same thing, except you picture your father inside and out. We need you to visualize the burn scars on his chest, the calluses on his fingertips, an old battle scar—anything and everything. Once you have that map inside your mind of what needs to be healed, you'll give me a signal, and I'll provide you the energy to funnel through you into him to heal the affected areas."

"That's the theory, anyway," the Seer added. "Alyssa and I are afraid to link with you for this first attempt because our power is still too volatile. That, and we don't have medical training enough to know what needs healing and what doesn't. We could do more harm than good, so we don't even want to risk it."

The fact that they had said "first attempt" put Kiera at ease. She could try this, and if it didn't work, there would be another chance to try again—as long as her own fumbling attempts didn't kill him.

She didn't have to wonder what her father would think of the situation. A man of action, he would rather be dead than live like this.

She took a deep breath and let it out slowly. "How do we begin?"

Gavin crossed the room, so he stood just behind her with his hand on her shoulder. "Hold his hand, then close your eyes and visualize just like we talked about. Signal me when you are ready for the energy flow—and don't use your own, you're already weaker than I would like before we begin."

Alyssa smiled from the other side of the bed. "Katelyn and I will be right here in case you need help."

Kiera ran her free hand over Shiloh's soft fur as if gathering strength and then closed her eyes. The warmth emanating from Gavin's soft touch on her shoulder was a marked contrast to the lukewarm fleshy feel of her father's hand against her fingers. Icy tendrils of panic clawed through her until her stomach roiled and tangy bile stung the back of her tongue.

You're not doing him any good by losing it! she reminded herself sternly.

As she often did, she pictured pouring all her panic and fear into a large shoebox and then closing the lid before stacking it on top of the growing pile of closed boxes inside her mind. God help her when she ran out of room for more shoeboxes!

Now that her emotions were carefully closed away, she turned on her clinical mind that she used in her medical practice. She visualized a male body with energy burns on the torso, atrophied muscles from lack of use and the set of four bullet wounds her father had received to his right shoulder in combat.

In her mind's eye, the man formed before her—faceless. Just a body to be studied and healed. Dark shadows marred the chest and right shoulder, while a general gray dullness covered all the muscles and even shadowed part of the brain.

She turned the figure in her mind to note the dark shadows along the back—most probably due to bedsores and . . .

Her study broke off as she saw the heart was so black she couldn't make out the individual ventricles. Kiera frowned. Just a week before she'd found him, her father had insisted he had gone to his doctor for a full physical and had received a perfect bill of health. Apparently, he hadn't wanted to worry her with the truth.

If her vision was accurate—and her gut told her it was—if the energy burn hadn't incapacitated him, his heart would have. The only mystery that remained was why his heart hadn't killed him during the stress of receiving the energy burns or even during his long stretch in a coma.

She shook her head. Now wasn't the time to wonder; now was the time to act.

A gentle squeeze on her shoulder reminded her of Gavin's presence, and she nodded that she was ready.

Kiera took a deep breath and braced for the sudden explosion of energy.

So it took her a long moment to recognize the slow curl of tingling warmth that entered through her shoulder and filled each cell of her body like water into a dry sponge. Once her body had absorbed all she needed, she breathed a mental sigh of relief that Gavin was powerful enough to regulate what he gave her.

Inside her mind's eye, she pictured Gavin's energy entering

through his connection with her shoulder and then taking a straight line down to her hand and out into her father.

The neon pink energy responded, and she mentally funneled it first to the blackened heart.

Pink pulses sparkled around the heart muscle as it beat in its slow and steady rhythm. Kiera pictured the heart as it should be—pristine and healthy—and she watched in awe as each beat brought the organ that much closer to the picture inside her mind until it was textbook perfect.

As if reading her mind, Gavin's energy contribution increased, the electricity flowing faster and faster, until she felt her hair crackle with static.

A curl of excitement quickened her breath, and she chided herself to stay on task. She gripped her father's hand harder as she directed the energy next to the shadows on his brain.

Kiera softened the flow of pink current until it was diffuse and very light. She used it almost like a gentle massage against the tender tissue of the brain. Slowly, as if she had polished away tarnish on silver, the dark smudges disappeared, leaving only healthy tissue behind.

A sigh of relief escaped through her lips, and she increased the intensity of the borrowed energy once more. This time she funneled it toward the atrophied muscles, then the energy burns and last to the internal scarring left by the bullet wounds.

The external scars she left as she'd found them since she knew her father bore those scars proudly as evidence of a duty fulfilled.

When she was finished, she sighed and studied the picture in front of her. The only shadows that remained were four small scars on the back of the right shoulder.

Satisfaction warmed her, and she blinked her eyes open and winced against the light as if awaking from a very long sleep.

Gavin staggered behind her, and Katelyn and Alyssa steadied him and helped him into one of the chairs. His face was pale, his eyes dull.

Kiera tried to stand to check on him, but her unsteady legs refused to hold her.

"Whoa." Alyssa pushed Kiera back into her chair and handed her a piece of bread liberally spread with honey-butter. "Eat. You need to regain your strength and so does Gavin. It's our turn to take care of you now."

Kiera glanced toward the bed and sat forward despite Alyssa's protests. Her father's skin glowed with health, and the hand still clutched in hers was strong and warm under her fingers. "It worked?"

"We think so," Katelyn answered. "He looks better at least."

Deep inside her gut, Kiera knew she had healed him. But she didn't know if his body would respond and wake or not—especially with the work she'd done on his brain. There was still so much not understood about the brain and the healing abilities of the human body.

Now only time would tell.

"Healer?"

Kiera woke from the light doze she'd fallen into several hours ago when Katelyn and Alyssa had taken Gavin to replenish his energy with some willing Klatch women.

She glanced up from her father's bedside to see Ryan standing awkwardly in the doorway. His expression wary, he slowly approached her and stood on the opposite side of her father's bed.

"How is he?" Ryan's voice was soft, almost as if he was afraid of waking the still man lying on the bed between them. He reached down to absently pet Shiloh, who hadn't budged from his master's side since settling there.

Kiera shook her head. "He has more color, and he seems

stronger, but I'm not sure if that's just what I hope for, or if it's actually what's true. Either way, it's nice to have him here."

"It's only been twelve hours," Ryan reminded her. "Katie-cat told me you healed him."

Sadness and hope warred inside her, and she closed her eyes before they morphed into darker emotions she had battled since she had opened her eyes from her trancelike healing state. "Only time will tell if he wakes or not, though." She hoped the words would convince the hope starting to blossom deep inside her belly to be cautious before believing too much in miracles.

She squeezed her father's limp hand before she pulled away and stood. Her back and legs ached from sitting in the same position for so long, and she stretched and winced as a few vertebrae popped back into place between her shoulder blades. "Okay, I've already spoken with the queen, and I trust that my last condition will still be met, so I'm ready for the coming of age ceremony, the Triangle ceremony and whatever else this entails."

Ryan walked around the bed and took her hand in his.

As his warm skin closed around hers, she shuddered, and the energy flow inside her expanded—growling out its hunger but not overwhelming her. She let out a deep breath, grateful she had at least some control over the power now.

Ryan led her outside, and she was surprised to find darkness had fallen.

Time had lost all meaning as she'd sat with her father. Katelyn had mentioned that the healing session alone had taken six hours, but Kiera still had issues wrapping her mind around that. And Ryan had just mentioned another twelve hours had passed since the healing session.

No wonder her back hurt as she'd sat vigil for nearly an entire day.

Ryan waved the two guards back inside the room, and they closed the patio doors behind them.

He led her onto the wide stone patio and pulled her down onto an overstuffed couch, her hand still captured in his.

"Healer . . . Kiera," he began, and then paused, caressing the back of her hand with soft strokes from the pad of his thumb. "I wanted to speak with you about what happened with my family."

Kiera immediately stiffened and pulled her hand away. In all the events of the past day, she had nearly forgotten about the fight and healing Ryan's scar—and especially about the group orgasm.

Embarrassment churned inside her belly and heated her neck and cheeks. "I'm not sure what to say." She stared down at her hands, which lay limply in her lap.

"I do, if you'll give me a chance."

She slowly raised her chin to meet his deep purple gaze as exhaustion settled over her like a heavy weight.

"I apologize first of all for putting you in that situation. I should've realized my family would be back soon and also how my brothers would react to you."

"Alyssa said you spoke with them, and with your mother." Her voice came out in nearly a whisper, and she braced to hear the rest.

He nodded. "And I apologize for the way I looked at you when you healed my scar." He traced the smooth skin of his cheek, and frowned. "I've had it for so long, my face just doesn't feel like mine without it." He reached out for her hand, and this time she didn't pull away. "My mother and I, and my brothers and I, still have much healing to do, but you started us on the right path."

She shook her head in denial. "Some right path. I beat up a few of your brothers and then . . ." Kiera faltered. She just couldn't bring herself to say it again.

"First of all, sharing energy with a roomful of people is a sign of a powerful witch and nothing to be ashamed of. My entire family was impressed by the display as well as the healing that came with it." He smiled and tipped his chin, allowing his hair to fall over his cheek in an old habit.

Kiera's brow furrowed as Ryan's words sank in. "But how will they ever accept me after everything that's happened?"

The edges of Ryan's lips curved. "After my mother told my brothers what truly happened all those years ago, I think my brothers have started to rethink the beliefs they have been raised with. Although it will be a while before they get past their anger with my mother." He reached out to trace her bottom lip with his thumb, which sent a sudden spike of shivers straight through her.

"They were very impressed that I found a woman who showed no fear in confronting five powerful Klatch warriors to protect me. Not only that, but you were able to heal all their injuries once you were done kicking their asses." He smiled. "In fact, I think they are jealous I found you first."

A knot of stress inside her chest loosened a little with Ryan's words, and she reached up to brush his hair out of his face and tuck it behind his ear. "With or without the scar, you're an amazing man." She reached up and pulled the band out of her own hair, allowing the long strands to cascade over her shoulders. Then she stood and gathered Ryan's thick hair in her hands and captured it behind his neck with the band.

When she sat next to him again and studied his chiseled features, she smiled at his confusion. "There's no longer any need to tip your chin and hide your scar. From the outside, you can't tell it was ever there, and from what you've told me, you've started healing the internal scars as well." She placed her palm over his hard chest, enjoying the feel of his heartbeat under her fingers.

Ryan placed his hand over hers, trapping it against him. A slow smile curved his lips, and his dark eyes pinned her in place as he slowly leaned forward until his lips hovered just above hers. "By the way, Healer, happy birthday."

She frowned and cocked her head to one side as she mentally counted the days she had been on Tador and compared it to the last known date when she had been concerned with a calendar. "My birthday isn't until tomorrow," she whispered against his lips.

"Technically, it is already tomorrow," he said as he searched her gaze. "Your coming of age ceremony can take place any time during your birthday since you're not ascending the throne."

His warm breath feathered against her lips, making her tremble with need as her bones melted and thick arousal churned through her veins. "What's involved with this ceremony?" She swallowed hard as she realized she wanted this man more than she had ever wanted anyone in her life. "Katelyn told me about hers, and I'm not sure I'm ready for the altars and the twenty hot naked Klatch warriors."

His low laugh spilled over her, hardening her nipples into tight buds and sending a rush of creamy moisture to dampen her slit.

"Katelyn's had to be done that way because she wasn't physically here on Tador to mate with Grayson. Yours can be as simple as you and . . . whomever you choose, exchanging energy."

"Whomever I choose, huh?" She playfully mocked his proper verbiage. "So you would just step aside and let me choose someone else?" She tried unsuccessfully to hide her smile. "One of the guards or one of your brothers maybe?"

Ryan's eyes narrowed fractionally, and he brushed his lips across hers so softly, she thought she might have imagined it, other than the surge of energy that shot through her like a cannon. "You would choose a guard or a younger prince rather than the first prince of the Tenth House of Klatch?"

She exhaled a shaky breath. "I suppose as the official Healer of Tador, I should have only the best. You're probably right."

Before he could return her banter, she leaned forward and pressed her lips against Ryan's.

He instantly opened for her, and they came together as if made purely to fit each other.

His musky deep-woods scent filled her senses along with the taste of wine and the spicy taste that was purely Ryan.

He growled and pulled her tight against him, crushing her achy breasts against his hard chest.

Kiera plunged her fingers into his hair, stripping away the hair band, and threading her fingers through the heavy warm waterfall of hair. She crawled onto his lap, straddling him. His erection was a hard rope against the soft skin of her belly, and she ground her body against him.

Ryan stripped off her shirt, and she pulled at his tunic until he whisked it off over his head and tossed it away.

When they came together again, mouth to mouth, Kiera gasped at the intense sensations churning through her.

The heat of Ryan's body burned through the thin lacy cups of her bra as he skimmed his hands over her back and shoulders as if memorizing every inch of her.

Her skin felt suddenly hot and achy like she had a fever. She whimpered as her clit throbbed and her core ached to be filled.

She clawed at Ryan's breeches as her entire body screamed for skin-to-skin contact.

Ryan gently set her off his lap and stood to shuck off the rest of his clothes, while she wriggled out of her own, tossing them aside until she sat naked in front of him.

The moonlight spilled over his olive skin, making him an erotic study of hard lines, light and shadows. His thick cock jutted out from his body, and she reached out to touch him.

Before she could, he stepped forward, gently pushing her hand aside, and laying her flat on the couch. He followed her down, his hard body capturing her softer one under its weight.

Everywhere their skin touched, Kiera burned with need.

The crisp hairs on his chest and thighs scraped exquisitely against her sensitive skin and sent both her arousal and the energy inside her howling.

She wrapped her legs around his waist and arched her hips until his cock sat poised at her entrance.

He braced himself on his forearms and looked down at her, his entire body vibrating against her as if he strained against the chains of his control. "Look at me, Kiera." His soft demand made her heart gallop and her throat constrict. "I want to see your face when we join."

She smiled. So many men would've taken that opportunity to say things like, "when I claim you," "when I enter you" or something else that smacked of ownership and invasion. But not Ryan.

She cupped his face in her hands, and pinned him with her gaze. "I want to see you, too."

Ryan let out a shaky breath and nudged her opening with the tip of his cock.

She bit back a groan and tightened her legs around his hips, urging him inside her.

A muscle in his jaw jumped as he slowly slid inside her, inch by exquisite inch.

All the while, she watched his face. As a myriad of sensations exploded inside her, the entire universe spiraled down to center around the fullness that was Ryan sliding inside her, filling her more with each second that slowly ticked by.

An expression of awe and wonder slowly chased across his features, softening the harsh lines of his face as he continued to push forward.

When the swollen tip of his cock bumped the deep insides of her core, and his hips sat flush against the cradle of her open thighs, Kiera let out a shaky breath as she gazed at the man whose face hovered just above hers.

"I feel like I've finally come home." The softly whispered

words registered inside her mind a split second before Ryan began to move inside her.

The muscles of her pussy tightened around him, aching with the loss of him filling her, but when she opened her mouth to object, he was already sliding back inside her.

He captured her lips in a slow but thorough exploration of her mouth while he thrust inside her in a steady slow rhythm that she thought might drive her insane. The friction between them sparked the energy that always sat just inside her, and it churned to life, growing with each slow plunge and release of his body inside hers.

Kiera gave herself up to the slow rhythm, floating inside the ocean of sensations building between them. She tightened her legs each time Ryan thrust inside her to pull him as far inside as he could go and then loosened her grip to allow him room to slide out before filling her again.

Her orgasm slowly built inside her, layer by layer and second by second.

The tingling deep inside her core began slowly, almost like watching a flower bloom in slow motion.

Rather than the hard quick release she was used to with other lovers, this one started in her core and traveled out through her body in all directions like hot molasses through her veins. A low moan escaped her as a hot rush of pure pleasure spilled through her—Ryan's warm body her only anchor to reality.

Her core rhythmically milked Ryan until he cried out and stiffened over her, his cock buried deep inside her.

The hot rush of his come as he emptied himself inside her channel surprised her, and she gasped.

The sounds of crackling energy made her jump, and she opened her eyes to see pink and silver sparks traveling across every available surface around them.

The smell of burning electrical wires filled her senses.

Ryan brushed the hair off her forehead and glanced down at her with an expression of such tenderness that a giant unseen hand squeezed her heart until she thought it would explode. "Happy birthday, Healer."

A low smoky chuckle was all she could manage in response before she pulled his face down for another long kiss.

15

An almost druglike euphoria surged through Sela, making her laugh out loud, the sound echoing around the shower chamber as she raised the whip again. "Tell me again, so I believe you."

The Cunt warrior strung up on his tiptoes in front of her whimpered, earning nothing but her contempt.

Using all her strength, she snapped the whip forward.

A loud *crack* filled the room as the leather struck the man's pale back, leaving a raw welt behind.

He cried out as he stiffened against the blow and then sagged against the bonds that held his arms over his head and suspended his entire body off the floor until only the tips of his toes scraped the bathroom tiles.

"I'm waiting," Sela snapped as she eyed the pulley system she'd had installed on the ceiling for just such occasions. Perhaps she would install a few more things in the shower chamber. After all, clean up was much easier in here than in her bedroom with the plush carpet.

"The Healer that Marco sent us to find." His voice was a gravelly rumble. He swallowed hard, his head lolling forward onto his chest.

"Yes?"

"She has moved again; we haven't caught up with her yet."

"That's what I thought you said the first time." She adjusted her grip on the whip and sent it in a graceful arc forward, the momentum flicking the long tendril of its end against the warrior's back once more. Sela widened her stance and settled into a steady rhythm—arm back, swing forward, arm back again even as the reverberations from the blows still tingled along her forearm.

Long raw strips appeared in increasing number on the warrior's back as she continued her assault. His involuntary shouts of pain merged with the musky scent of his fear. Precious energy poured off the man in waves, and Sela breathed it in like expensive perfume.

She might have lost her favorite vice with Aedan's passing, but violence would always sustain her. Not to mention, it couldn't hurt to instill a regular dose of fear into the ranks.

"My queen?" Marco's low voice broke through her euphoric haze, and she paused halfway through her windup stroke.

The guard sagged against his bonds, and Sela exhaled slowly as if recovering from an intense orgasm. "I'm in a good mood, Marco, or I would punish you for your interruption."

"If it pleases you, my queen, I will submit to any punishment you see fit." As usual, his words were all the correct ones but totally devoid of the emotion and even devotion they used to hold.

She ground her teeth and turned to face the council head.

His chin was tipped down in the proper show of respect, his gaze trained on the floor just in front of his feet. "Some days I wish you would forego proper etiquette, Marco, and give me a reason to punish you just for irritating me."

"Yes, my queen."

She took a deep breath to cool her sudden spark of temper. Marco was too valuable to her to allow her anger to weaken him. Men like Marco were few and far between and needed to be tolerated, she reminded herself. "What do you want, Marco. And make it fast. I'm busy."

He raised his deep blue gaze to hers. "My queen. I have found more treachery among our ranks I thought you should be aware of."

Her brow furrowed. It wasn't an immediate threat or Marco would've already taken care of it and told her after the fact. She stepped around the still-slumped form of the beaten guard and motioned for Marco to follow her out into her bedroom. "Tell me." She picked up a bar towel and wiped the small spatters of the guard's blood off her fingers before reaching for the ice bucket. The ice cubes clinked against the sides of the cut crystal tumbler. She poured vodka over them, enjoying the small pops the ice made as it cracked from the introduction of the room-temperature liquid.

"Cecily's human mate has been moved from the VA hospital."

The glass was halfway to Sela's lips when a sharp stab of foreboding sliced through her. She turned to face Marco, the glass still suspended in her hand. "Why, and by whom?"

"According to hospital records, Kiera Matthews signed him out to move him to a private facility. However, the signatures match councilman Danen's handwriting." His face remained the calm mask he always presented. "Both the human and the doctor have vanished."

Sela's gut tightened. "Why? What would Danen gain from either of those actions?"

"Unknown, my queen, but I will keep you informed. I took the liberty of visiting the doctor's house. Everything appears undisturbed."

"So Danen's reasons may have died with him." She pursed her lips as she studied Marco. The man had always been loyal, but something about this situation didn't feel right. Sela didn't follow her women's intuition often, since it often limited her enjoyment of the fruits of being queen, but in this instance, she might have to do some checking. "How . . . inconvenient."

Marco stepped inside the dark, crowded bar. Smells of sweat and whiskey permeated the thick air and blended well with the thumping bass beat of the unrecognizable song that played through ancient speakers.

He pushed past the group of tough-as-nails women huddled at the front entrance and stepped into the main room, raking his gaze over the sea of unwashed humanity who huddled in close-knit clumps or played pool or darts along the far wall.

Glad I changed out of my suit.

When he'd received the odd summons, along with the address for the meeting, he'd immediately pulled on worn, faded jeans and a simple button-down shirt. This wasn't exactly a great part of town in which to appear very affluent.

Not that he was afraid for his safety. He could decimate every human in the bar and still have enough energy to fight off some Klatch or Cunt warriors, but staying off human radar entirely was always his first choice.

"It's seat yourself, hun," drawled a squat waitress in between pops of her gum. Her face was lined and rough like well-used leather, and Marco guessed her age to be somewhere in the mid to late forties. She raked her watery gaze over him with obvious suspicion. "What can I get you? And before you ask, we don't serve martinis or spritzers here."

He smiled, using his most menacing expression, which didn't seem to impress the waitress one bit. "I'm here to meet Silas."

As if the sun had come out from behind a bank of clouds, the woman's entire countenance changed. She smiled and brightened, which took at least ten years off her age. "Well, then that makes a world of difference." She looped her arm through his and half dragged him through the sea of leather-clad bodies and bawdy laughter toward the dark rear wall of the bar.

Amused, but still alert for any treachery, Marco followed while he stretched out his senses. Dozens of drunk or high humans, a few weak-blooded half-breeds . . . and one very strong Klatch presence. Not a warrior, and certainly not a powerful magic-wielder, but a full-blooded Klatch just the same.

The waitress led Marco to a dark set of stairs that were nearly invisible in the inky blackness. "You head on up; he's expectin' you. What can I bring you to drink?"

"Whatever Silas is having is fine. Thank you." Marco pressed a fifty-dollar bill into her open palm and after her eyes widened slightly, she glanced up at him and gave him a saucy wink.

"I'll be back with that drink. You let me know if you need . . . anything else." She leaned forward, displaying over-tanned cleavage that had seen better days—a very blatant invitation of just what else she had for sale—before she turned and threaded her way toward the bar.

Marco ascended the stairs and pushed open the door at the top.

A soft blue glow lit the room, and it took his eyes a minute to adjust to the weak light. When his vision sharpened, he realized he stood in some sort of an enclosed loft. A large glass panel dominated one wall and allowed a full view down to the main floor of the bar that he'd just come through.

Whereas the room downstairs had definitely seen better days, this room was comfortable, with plush carpeting and overstuffed couches that faced the glass wall. The blue illumination came from soft blue recessed lighting tucked discretely at even intervals along the side walls.

Across the room, a man stood and walked forward. He was thin and slightly stooped and stood just a few inches shorter than Marco. "Welcome, Marco. It's been a long time." The man might have looked frail and wizened, but his voice was strong and proper, just like always.

Marco smiled as bittersweet memories of his days on Tador

came back in a sudden flood. He held out his hand, glad when Silas's firm grip closed around his, showing him the man was still strong behind his nearly frail appearance. "Silas. It's good to see you." Marco was surprised at just how good.

Silas nodded with a small smile just before he released Marco's hand. "Please, do come in. I'm sure Kit will be back with a beverage for you very soon, and then we can discuss why I asked you here."

Marco walked forward, close to the glass, where he saw the waitress—Kit, he supposed—headed toward the stairs with two Coronas. He turned toward Silas with a raised brow. "Coronas?"

A hint of pink flooded Silas's weathered face, and he shrugged. "It's nothing like the ale on Tador, but it's crisp and refreshing without being overpowering. That, and after wiping the rim, I can usually trust what's inside the bottle."

In spite of the odd circumstances, Marco found himself laughing. An even bigger surprise was the light, almost airy feeling of happiness that spread through his chest. "I would've pegged you for a martini or spritzer man, just the kind that Kit wouldn't appreciate."

Kit chose that moment to burst through the door, a whirlwind of energy as she gave them both their Coronas and then stared at Marco as if deciding the best way to eat him like a dessert.

Silas cleared his throat. "Thank you, my dear. Do tell your mother we appreciate the use of the facilities, and let her know I'll drop by for dinner soon."

Kit brushed a kiss across the old man's papery cheek. "You got it, Gramps." She tossed another wink accompanied by a leer toward Marco before she whisked back out of the room.

"Is she . . ." Marco trailed off as he searched for the right words that wouldn't offend the older man.

Silas chuckled and wiped the open tip of the bottle with his handkerchief before tucking the cloth back into his pocket and taking a long drink. "Goodness, no. Kit's grandmother and I spent quite a bit of time together back when I was a younger man. When I showed no interest in settling down, she married a human. I've known both Kit and her mother since they were born." He raised his bright lavender gaze, and suddenly Marco was struck with how youthful and intelligent Silas's eyes were. The man might be stuck inside an aging body, but his mind and his spirit were still intact.

"My apologies. I didn't mean to pry."

"Nonsense." Silas sat on one end of the overstuffed couch and motioned for Marco to sit as well. "You have been nosey as a fish wife since you were old enough to crawl. Just because you've grown up doesn't make that any different."

Marco barked out a short laugh that he tried to disguise as a cough. "Well, you're just as blunt as I remember you, Silas. I never did understand why you didn't have a seat on the council. You were offered one, if memory serves, and you turned them down flat. If things were different, I would've welcomed you onto my council in a second."

Silas took a drink before answering. "Let's not rehash politics, my boy. I come from a long line of majordomos, and I'm proud of that tradition." He took another drink before piercing Marco with intense scrutiny. "I'm sure you're wise enough now to see that I was right. Sela was never after equality for the Cunts. She was only after power and the freedom to be cruel and use others in any way she saw fit."

Marco dropped his gaze to study his beer bottle since he couldn't bring himself to look into those too-discerning lavender eyes. Instead, he only nodded and let silence fall between them.

What would've been different all those years ago if I would've listened to Silas?

Silas's dry chuckle filled the room. "You were young and full of life and still smarting from Cecily choosing Gavin over you. Sela is a master manipulator, and she took full advantage of all those circumstances."

Marco leaned back as he finally raised his gaze. "You're giving me too much credit, Silas. I knew what I was doing." He sighed as his regrets weighed heavy, making it difficult for him to breathe. "I betrayed friends, family and the throne all in a wild bid for power that has still left a lasting scar today."

Silas slapped Marco's knee once before he leaned back in his chair. "What if I were to offer you a way to redeem yourself, my boy? Would you take it?"

"It's too late for me, Silas."

"It's never too late for a man to make new choices. Don't make me prove you a liar." Silas's voice was gentle yet firm, and made Marco's brow furrow as he studied the man's lined face. "I heard how you sacrificed yourself and your security among the Cunts to save your daughter."

A hard punch to the kidney couldn't have grabbed Marco's attention any better than Silas's softly spoken words. He understood Silas referred to Kiera Matthews, but Cecily had assured him he wasn't the father and neither was Gavin.

However, Marco also knew Silas well enough to know the older man wouldn't say something just for effect. "What do you mean, 'daughter'?"

Silas's thin lips curved up into a small smile. "Well, that got your attention, now, didn't it?" He studied Marco for a long moment and then nodded, as if in approval. "That will be something for a bit later, but don't worry; all will be known in time. 'Twasn't a whim that I called to meet with you. I'm here on official business for her majesty, Queen Alyssandra de Klatch, and her mate, King Stone."

"What would the reigning queen and king want with me?"

"Will you give me your word that this discussion is private and that you'll not betray my confidence in you?" Silas pinned Marco with a hard stare that reminded him of when he was ten and the majordomo had caught him sneaking into the female bathing chambers.

He shrugged as if he could put aside the sensation with a simple movement. "Why would you trust the word of a traitor to Tador, Silas?"

"While I'll admit you've made some poor decisions in the past, your current ones have shown me you've gained wisdom and compassion in your exile." Silas straightened in his chair, his kind gaze bathing Marco in warmth. "Besides, I'll not have you tell me where I can and cannot put my trust. A wise man must trust his own knowledge, and I believe you to be a man of honor. Will you dare to prove me wrong?"

Something thick and warm filled Marco's chest and tightened his throat. After all he'd done, it surprised him that the majordomo was the one person who hadn't written him off.

Growing up as a Cunt even on prewar Tador, Marco hadn't paid much attention to Silas, since he was merely another servant inside the castle. But he did like the soft-spoken man with the impeccable manners and droll proverbs for behavior. Marco had considered Silas a fixture of the castle just like the turrets or the large *balda* front doors.

It was humbling to find an ally in someone Marco had always taken for granted.

He swallowed hard before answering. "You have my solemn word, Silas. I will not betray your confidence in any way." The air seemed to hum around Marco, but instead of an energy shift, he thought it might be a shift deep inside him. A step back from the brink of apathy, where he'd resigned himself to after helping Kiera and her father escape to Tador.

Silas beamed like a proud father and nodded once. "Good." He leaned forward, shrewd anticipation sparking inside his lavender eyes. "Now, before I catch you up on what our feisty Kiera has been up to since she's come to Tador, I have a warning for you."

Marco instantly bristled as a dagger of hurt sliced into him. "Silas, I gave you my word—"

Silas waved the words away. "And I've already accepted it, so let's speak no more about that. This is about Sela."

Marco's thoughts instantly sharpened. He kept close tabs on the Queen of the Cunts, so if there was something he didn't know about, he was leaving himself wide open for treachery or worse.

"She's suspicious of your recent activities and has found a new playmate in hopes of finding some incriminating information about you. And I think we may be able to use that to our advantage." He pointed toward Marco with the neck of the bottle. "Lucky for you, that playmate's grandmother was also a great friend of mine."

Marco's eyes widened as he tried to imagine Silas in the role of a playboy.

The older man's chest swelled, and he lifted his chin. "I may be nearly one hundred and thirty years old, but I am a Klatch, am I not?"

Marco smiled and nodded. "Yes, sir. That, you most definitely are."

Kiera stepped out of the castle, surrounded on all sides by tall muscular guards, Ryan and Katelyn.

She understood the necessity of the oppressive security, but she didn't have to like it.

The warm rays of the sun played over her skin, and she breathed deep, enjoying the scents of gardenias, roses and several others that filled the air around her. She glanced over at Ryan and smiled as memories of their "birthday celebration" last night came back to her in vivid detail.

Her entire body felt energized and achy in all the right places, and it had been only this morning when they had woken still tangled together on the couch on the balcony that she realized the guards and half the planet had probably heard them last night.

But in light of how good she felt, she pushed aside her embarrassment and basked in the afterglow of a night of mind-blowing sex.

A twinge of unease sliced through her at the word "sex," but she pushed it aside. She just wasn't ready to consider what else to term it at this point.

She tried to glance through the gaps between the wall of guards that surrounded her but had very little success seeing the overall scenery from her protected view. "I hate being short."

Katelyn laughed. "I understand, but I think you hate being shot with energy beams even more than that."

"I don't know," countered Ryan. "I sort of enjoyed helping her recover the other day."

Kiera shot him a mock glare as heat seared into her cheeks. Now that she knew exactly what it felt like to be the center of Ryan's attention, her body craved him, which was extremely unsettling for her.

"Besides," Katelyn cut in, "once we get Tador back to its former glory, I'll bet you won't have to worry about getting shot anymore. The people will be so happy to have the planet restored, they might even overlook you being half Cunt."

The familiar sting of her half-breed parentage made her bristle, but then she glanced up at Katelyn's amused expression and realized the Seer had only been teasing. After all, in the eyes of the Klatch, introducing a human into the revered Klatch royal bloodline was nearly as bad as introducing Cunt blood.

"So how far is it to this statue, anyway?" Kiera walked on her tiptoes, craning her neck to try to see through the wall of hunky guards, but saw only tantalizing glimpses of color. She huffed out a breath, fluttering her bangs, and sank down to walk flat-footed.

"Just past the maze and by the waterfall." Katelyn smiled over at her.

As if on cue, a large green wall of manicured leaves and vines rose up in front of them a few feet higher than the tallest guard. As a unit, they all turned left, edging along the large wall.

Kiera's mother had told her stories of playing inside the maze and all the beauty hidden inside the twists and turns. Now that she knew more about the planet, she knew without a doubt that the maze was also used as a rendezvous place for lovers or even groups to meet. But she was glad her mother had left out those details at the time.

Kiera itched to dart away from everyone and explore, to walk where her mother had walked and see the sites she had seen.

Ryan's hand closed over hers, and she jumped like she'd been caught doing something wrong.

His low chuckle brushed over her, caressing deep inside her core like he had with his body last night.

Kiera squeezed his hand as a quick shiver ran through her entire body.

"Once the Triangle is completed, we'll figure out a safe way for you to explore every inch of Tador, including the maze." He raised their joined hands to his lips and placed a warm kiss on the back of her hand, along with a quick hot swipe of his tongue.

She bit back a moan that nearly escaped to embarrass her and then shot Ryan a glare, which only made him smile. But his words had touched something deep inside her, softening her resolve and sending a surge of warmth through her. Her glare slowly fell away until she grinned at him in return.

"Hey, now," Katelyn said with a laugh. "We are at the statue, so don't you two get too distracted."

The guards in front of her parted to reveal a four-foot gap in the foliage that looked as if the opening had been made recently from the raw cuts on the vines and branches.

She followed Katelyn and stepped through the gap to find

herself inside a small clearing with a large white *balda* three-sided statue that dominated the entire space. Tangled vines obscured the sides of the bottom platform, but the persistent foliage had been trimmed back to reveal the statues.

All three figures on the statue were naked and stood back to back. The one currently facing her was a perfect replica of Katelyn, the Seer. And if her memory served, it was an exact replica down to the close-cropped hair that covered the Seer's mons. Long hair frothed around the statue Seer's shoulders, ending just above the nipples of the generous breasts.

Kiera looked down at her own smaller breasts before returning her gaze to the statue. Her own breasts were very proportional with her trim athletic figure, and she had never felt like she was lacking in any area, even now. However, studying the Seer's lush curves caused a flutter of arousal deep inside her core she hadn't expected.

Apparently, like Katelyn, she might have found an enjoyment for sex with women that probably wouldn't have been revealed to her in the more conservative environment she lived in on Earth. She was too much a doctor to be embarrassed by a physiological response that she didn't directly control, and besides, most likely her mother had enjoyed the attentions of women as well as men. From what Kiera could tell, there was no stigma at all for homosexuality on Tador among the Klatch or Cunt culture.

A few steps took her around the statue until she stood in front of the likeness of Queen Alyssa. The queen had a heart-shaped face, with sensual lips curved with the hint of a smile. Her voluptuous figure rivaled the Seer's, and her hair frothed around her body and down to her shapely hips.

Kiera trailed her fingers over the statue's full breasts and the gently rounded stomach while she tried to imagine the queen's cascade of hair spilling over her bare skin. The sudden vivid mental image sent a shiver of awareness shooting through Kiera.

Her nipples pebbled, and slick moisture formed between her thighs.

"Katelyn, please tell me my stomach doesn't really look like that."

At the sound of Alyssa's voice, Kiera nearly stumbled as she jumped away from the queen's statue as if it had burned her fingertips.

Alyssa laughed and walked forward to join them. "Sorry, didn't mean to scare you." The queen fisted her hands on her hips and stared up at her doppelganger. "You two look great, but I'm seriously not happy with that tummy of mine up there for all the world to see."

Katelyn laughed, the sound slicing through the gentle background noises of the wildlife and waterfall off in the distance. "You've done how many ceremonies entirely naked for everyone to see, and you're worried about how the statue looks?"

Alyssa shrugged, a sheepish expression on her face. "Hey, a woman has her pride, right? Besides, Stone keeps me distracted during the ceremonies, so I don't think about it."

"I think you both have beautiful bodies." Kiera started as she realized she's said her thoughts aloud.

"I personally think all three of you have wonderful nude bodies, and I'd be happy to inspect them to see how accurate the statue is."

All three women glared at Ryan until he held up his hands in front of him, laughing. He took a quick step back. "Just a joke to lighten the mood."

Alyssa shook her head with a smile, and Katelyn stepped forward to envelop Kiera in a quick hug. "We'll need those compliments more often with you around, you skinny bitch." The Seer pulled back far enough to let Kiera see her smile.

Amusement spiked through Kiera, and a laugh spilled from her lips. "I think that's the first time I've heard 'skinny bitch' used as an actual compliment."

Katelyn linked her arm through Kiera's. "It definitely is. I know curvy here is more the norm for all the Klatch, but all that Earth conditioning about being thin has been engrained deep."

Kiera shook her head as she thought about the Seer's words. "You know, I guess you're right. I've always had this body type, and I've taken it for granted. But to tell you the truth, I'm a little afraid to see what my side of the statue looks like."

Alyssa linked her arm through Kiera's free arm so both women flanked her. "Let's check it out."

Kiera swallowed hard and deliberately took a few more steps until she was even with her own likeness. Her own straight hair hung to just past her shoulders and seemed to accentuate the trim femininity of her form. She may not be as rounded as the other two women, but she could admit as she stared up at her likeness, she was happy with her body and confident that Ryan found her desirable.

"More than desirable," Ryan said from behind her.

She jumped, her heart kicking into a fast pounding. Katelyn and Alyssa released her arms. "I didn't realize I'd said that out loud." She laughed and laid her flattened palm over her beating heart.

Katelyn and Alyssa exchanged a quick glance, and something passed between them that Kiera didn't understand, but she didn't feel comfortable pressing them on it just yet.

Kiera glanced up at her nude body depicted in the crystal-white *balda* with soft seams of pink crystals scattered throughout and smiled. "Wow. The likenesses are uncanny." She slipped her hands into her back pockets as she stood beside the queen and stared up at her own nude form.

Alyssa cocked her head to one side as if considering. "It makes me wonder if this was built after the last Triangle just for us or if every time there is a Triangle, the three women have our same likenesses." The queen's dark brow furrowed as she glanced at each of them in turn. "It's kind of spooky to imagine doppelgangers of the three of us walking around at various points in history."

Kiera laughed and glanced over at the queen. "I hadn't thought about it like that. But I guess it would save time and energy to use the same statue." She gestured toward the statue with her chin. "Either way, I wonder how they knew we would look like this."

Alyssa chewed her bottom lip for a moment as she circled the statue, studying it from every angle. "You've got me there. Sometimes this entire magic and energy thing just fries my brain."

Surprise made Kiera's brow furrow.

"Don't forget, I didn't grow up knowing about Tador and Klatch and Cunts like you did." Alyssa pushed her dark hair back over her shoulder, causing the few beaded braids scattered throughout her hair to tinkle softly as they struck each other. "I grew up thinking magic only happened in the movies and that I would die a frumpy old virgin." She grinned, which had the effect of turning her features from just pretty to ravishing.

"I'll have to remember that for both you and Katelyn." Kiera glanced down toward the base of the statue and knelt to pull some of the tightly tangled vines away from the surface.

Just behind the vines, several ragged scratches marred the otherwise smooth expanse of the rounded sides of the base. "Look at these."

Kiera ripped away more of the vines and then used her fingertips to trace the roughened marks as if the tactile input would help her process more information than purely the visual. The grooves seemed too uniform to be accidental damage from the overgrowth of greenery against the *balda* that had engulfed its sides.

Kiera knelt so close that heat from the queen's body radiated against her. Sudden awareness flared between them and hit Kiera with a flash of molten heat deep inside her core.

"They're pretty deep just to be damage from the vines." Alyssa's voice, which echoed Kiera's previous thoughts, was husky and low, as if she hadn't meant to say the words aloud. The queen traced the deep grooves, and her arm brushed Kiera's thigh.

A starburst of energy careened through Kiera and stole her breath.

She bit back a small gasp at the electric sensations coursing through her entire body, and she steadied herself against the base of the statue.

Seemingly unaware of Kiera's reaction, Alyssa stood.

Immediately, Kiera's breathing became easier, and the sudden awareness eased but didn't disappear.

Damn planet. She gritted her teeth and sucked air into her lungs.

The queen stepped away and then knelt in front of the statue of the Seer. "The markings are similar over here." Alyssa glanced over her shoulder toward the guards. "Can one of you send someone for some paper and some chalk or crayons?"

Five minutes later, the Seer appeared with large pieces of rolled white paper and several thick sticks of blue chalk.

Now that Kiera had seen the naked statues, she took in Alyssa's full figure clad in a simple gauzy skirt and half top with the knowledge of someone who knew what lay under the other woman's clothes.

Ryan's warm hand closed over her shoulder, and she swayed until he pulled her tight against him. "You okay?"

She placed her hand over his and squeezed. "I'm fine, just the damn planet messing with me again."

He laid a hot open-mouthed kiss on the side of her neck and released her.

She nearly stumbled from the jolt of energy that pierced her from that simple gesture, but she steeled her resolve and faced the Seer.

Katelyn handed both Kiera and Alyssa some paper and chalk before taking her own supplies to the third side of the statue. "I spent hours carefully trimming brush, vines and branches away from the statues without hurting them. I take a break, and you two spend five minutes and find something cool." Her green eyes sparked with amusement, which belied her words.

"It wasn't me." Alyssa knelt in front of the statue of herself. "Kiera noticed them first. I'm just along for the ride."

Kiera finished clearing away the heavy vines that wrapped the base of her side of the statue in a stranglehold and then brushed her hand across the smooth polished rock face, only the deep grooves adding texture under her questing fingers. "It certainly doesn't look like letters or numbers or even Japanese or Chinese characters." She definitely wasn't an expert, but she was well read and had seen many written languages, such as Hebrew, Sanskrit and others. And even though she couldn't read them, she could tell these grooves weren't even close to similar.

The Seer crouched next to Kiera, her fingers tracing the lowest gouges at the bottom of the statue where it sat flush against the ground. "I agree. They are long and flowing and look like they continue off the face of the statue like there wasn't room for them."

They all returned to their appropriate corners and, laying the paper flat against the base, ran the side of the colored chalk over the paper, capturing the pattern of the grooves for later study.

Kiera finished capturing the markings and stood, holding her scroll of paper at arm's length as she tried to make sense of the markings. When the paper still wasn't far enough away to give her perspective, she laid it on the grass and stepped away, slowly circling as her eyes tried to find a pattern.

Katelyn and then Alyssa placed their papers on the ground

next to Kiera's, and all four of them stared at the papers until Kiera's eyes began to blur.

Ryan knelt just in front of the scrolls of paper. "Wait a minute . . ." His words trailed off as he reached for the papers, rearranging them on the ground until they overlapped.

Katelyn's sound of surprise startled Kiera and she stepped forward.

The overlapping pictures had created a Triangle with a crown above the top apex, an eye next to the bottom left and a symbol she hadn't seen since medical school next to the bottom right corner. It was a symbol for a healer and looked like a teardrop, except that at the top where the lines would normally meet in a point, they continued outward so they resembled outstretched arms. A small dot sat above the symbol.

Katelyn knelt and ran her hand over the drawings as if that would make them more real. "This is almost identical to the drawing in my journals, and the one the Cunts tried to use in the false coming of age ceremony."

Kiera rubbed her temples as she tried to fit all the puzzle pieces together. "Okay, so it's obviously got something to do with the Triangle, so why is it so cryptically etched around the base of the statues?"

Kiera turned back to the statues and knelt below her likeness to run her fingers along the base. She leaned closer and blew a long breath across the markings, hoping to see them more clearly.

A small dark line at the bottom corner of the base caught her attention, and she traced it with her fingers, brushing more dirt away. She wet her finger and ran it along the line, surprised to find it an indented seam in the base rather than just another etched marking.

The hair on the back of her neck prickled and excitement curled inside her gut. "I think I found something."

Ryan crouched next to her. "Hey, this looks like a seam in

the base, like it might open here." He glanced back at Alyssa and Katelyn. "Is there one on the other sides as well?"

Kiera continued to clean off the small straight crack along her side of the base.

"I've got one here, too," Katelyn called out.

"Me too." This from the queen.

"Clean them off, and maybe there's a trigger or switch or something." Kiera frowned in concentration as she continued to explore the line.

Bright pink light glowed from the crack, nearly blinding her.

Kiera jumped back, shielding her eyes and landing hard on her ass.

Muffled feminine curses of surprise told her that the queen and the Seer had seen the same thing on their sides.

"What the hell?" Ryan's voice sounded loud just behind her, and she risked a quick glance over her shoulder in time to see his dark brow furrowed and his mouth open as he stared at the statue.

She turned back toward the statue and stared.

A long thin drawer at the base of the statue had slid forward, and several yellowed scrolls were clearly visible inside.

"Look up," Ryan whispered from behind her.

Her gaze traveled up her likeness's nude form to the flat stomach, which now showed the same shiny pink healing symbol they had seen on the tracing paper.

Kiera shook her head to make sure she wasn't seeing things and then crawled forward to look down into the open drawer at the scrolls. She reached forward to touch one when the queen's voice startled her.

"They are genealogies . . . of us." Something in the queen's voice sent dread curling inside Kiera's stomach like a bucking ship on the high seas.

Kiera glanced up as Alyssa came into view from around the side of the statue. Ryan and Katelyn flanked the queen and studied the open scroll before turning their surprised gazes on Kiera.

Kiera tried to will herself to stand, but her legs refused to cooperate. The blood in her veins had suddenly turned to ice, and she swallowed hard. "What is it?"

When no one spoke, she gathered her strength and pushed to her feet. After a fortifying breath, she squared her shoulders and held out a hand for the scroll.

Silently, Alyssa handed it to her.

Kiera opened it and scanned down the treelike depiction of marriages and births until she found her mother, Cecily.

A single line drawn from the right of Cecily's name showed not one, but two names: Gavin and Marco. Kiera's own name was listed as the single offspring of this odd entry. A small healer's symbol was etched in glowing pink next to her name.

Bile threatened to inch its way up her throat as the implications churned through her mind.

Her thoughts flashed back to her father—the only father she had ever known—lying upstairs in the castle. She shook her head in denial as icy claws of panic shredded her insides and left her shaking. "This isn't right. They must not have wanted to include a human in their precious genealogy." Even as the words left her lips, she didn't believe them but still hoped they could be true.

She would rather believe anything except the cold hard realities facing her.

Ryan laid a gentle hand on her shoulder, and she shrugged it off. "There are two other full humans on that page alone."

Panic surged inside her, and her logical mind grasped for anything to prove she hadn't grown up with lies. "This is impossible. This can't be accurate; after all, there are two men listed as my . . ." She trailed off and swallowed hard. She could not bring herself to say the word "father" out loud.

"I hate to say this, but I think they are magically updated instead of manually." Katelyn's soft voice held a note of apology. She held out another scroll that showed Queen Alyssandra de Klatch and King Stone de Klatch listed along with their full titles. A child line snaked downward from their marriage line to the name "Tess."

Alyssa's hand covered her stomach in a protective gesture as she gasped. "I haven't even suggested that name to Stone yet. How did it know?"

Anger surged inside Kiera, bright and hot, as the evidence mounted for her own parents' lies and betrayal.

The energy inside her answered, howling with fury like a sudden tsunami called forth to do her bidding.

She turned toward the statue that stood like an accusation in front of her. Her own familiar face stared down as if mocking her.

Hot anger exploded, and her vision tinged white hot and then red. With a feral scream, she took a few running steps and pushed off the ground with her right foot, twisted in midair and delivered a hard jump-kick to the chin of her own image.

As soon as her foot connected, power exploded outward, sending her flying backward.

Kiera landed hard—flat on her back, her breath pushed out of her lungs in a painful rush, as a loud grinding noise took up residence inside her brain.

She slapped her hands over her ears in an effort to drown out the noise, but that made her only more aware of the ground shaking beneath her as a cloud of dust choked her with each labored breath.

Icy dread snaked through her. *What the hell have I done?*

When the rumbling inside her head and beneath her body finally stopped, she relaxed back against the hard ground with one arm flung over her eyes. How many times had her father told her to think before she reacted? And how many times had she ignored his advice and reacted first and regretted the consequences later. She hoped no one was hurt.

Several seconds later, her logical mind reminded her that the man she knew as her father might not be any relation to her at all.

Now that her anger was spent, her eyes burned with unshed tears, and her entire body felt hollow and aching.

"Kiera?" Ryan's voice sounded from somewhere off to her left, and she couldn't bring herself to move or speak just yet.

"Kiera?" he said again, from just beside her. He gently lifted her arm away from her face and brushed her hair back off her forehead, a gesture that nearly made the dam of tears break free.

His face was streaked with dirt, his hair dusty and tangled, but he looked unhurt. "Are you all right?"

When she nodded, his face broke into a relieved smile.

"The queen and the Seer?"

He gently helped her sit up. "They're fine. You're the one who was thrown like a rag doll and landed next to the door. We were all worried about you."

"Door. What door?" Surprise and confusion whirled inside her as she turned her head to see a large gaping doorway into the side of the mountain that hadn't been there before.

"The rumbling sound in my head . . ." She gently touched her temple and realized that there was no pain now—at least no physical pain. "And the miniearthquake under me—that was all the door?"

Ryan nodded and gathered her into his arms despite her protests. "The guards are going to explore the cave before they let Alyssandra and Katelyn go inside. But in the meantime, you and I are going to take a break."

She squirmed in his arms, not ready for the intimacy he offered or the pity she was sure she would see in her eyes. "I don't need a break. Ryan, put me down."

He stood and turned so their faces were only inches apart.

"After the scrolls, you need some time to recover. Otherwise, you wouldn't have tried to decapitate your own statue."

Shame at her impetuous action returned, and she dropped her gaze.

Damn it. Why did Ryan have to be right?

She pulled the tattered shreds of her dignity around her like a cloak. "Fine, but you might not have found the cave or the scrolls if it wasn't for me."

"Very true."

The fact that he was so clearly mollifying her made her want to jump-kick something else this time.

16

Sela stalked forward into the dark interior of the seedy strip club. The rhythmic thump of the loud music sent a surge of anticipation through her in time with the beat of the music. Her eyes adjusted quickly as the scent of sweat, alcohol and stale sex surrounded her in a familiar combination.

Four hundred pounds of black-clad badass, complete with tattoos, piercings and scars that criss-crossed the weathered skin of his face appeared before her, sweat dripping down over his shiny bald head.

Sela smiled and shook her head. It had to be seventy degrees in the club, but no matter the temperature, the fearsome bouncer always looked like he was standing in the middle of the tropics. But the fact that he looked a lot like something spit from the bowels of the human's version of hell made her like him all the more.

"Little Jon," she shouted near his ear as she slid four hundred-dollar bills into the man's open palm. "How's business?"

"Hopping, as usual, mistress." He pulled a hand towel from his back pocket and wiped at his sweaty pate.

"I'll bet." Her gaze swept the room, taking in the sea of human filth along with a smattering of Cunts—most of whom were the "dancers," both male and female. Although for a price, much more was available on the menu here.

Soon after the Cunts had been banished to Earth, Sela had purchased several establishments that would allow her people to gather the sexual energy they needed without alerting the humans. This club had been one of her earliest purchases, and due to the seedy nature of the clientele—along with some very extensive blackmail information employed against local law enforcement—one of the most successful.

She didn't often come here in person, trusting Little Jon to watch after her business interests for her. But since she needed to find information outside of Marco's usual contacts, this had been the first place she'd thought of. "Has my guest arrived?"

"Private room four." Little Jon extended one beefy hand toward the dark interior of the club.

Sela nodded and threaded her way through the dark, smoky interior, dodging couples and even groups of writhing bodies in various stages of copulation. With the heavy rock music pouring into the room, the movements of the masses almost seemed like some macabre dance—one that spoke to something deep inside Sela and made her wish she had time to stop and join in.

The pungent scent of sex assaulted her, making her think of Aedan. Damn the man for betraying her!

She had toyed with the idea of chaining him up at one of her clubs and using him whenever she pleased. But she had also known he was a weakness she couldn't afford to keep.

Along the back wall of the club were four doors with security touch pads next to each. She chose the fourth door and punched her personal code into the touch pad as she laid her other palm against the hard wood.

The vibration of the sharp click under her fingertips told her the lock had disengaged.

She slipped inside, and the door closed behind her, shutting out the loud music and even the smells of the club.

Even in the soft lighting, Sela saw her.

The woman would never be called beautiful, but she was definitely stunning—someone who would have every eye in every room following her every movement.

Long light brown hair the color of deep rich honey spilled over her smooth shoulders as she sat with her legs crossed on the king-sized bed that dominated the small room. She was entirely naked, the expanse of her tanned golden skin showing off her gentle curves and her long shapely legs. Her small rounded breasts were high and proud and tipped with large round dusky pink areolas with tightly budded nipples.

Sela's mouth watered and slick moisture pooled between her labia.

"Sela, I presume?" The woman slowly licked her lips and raked her gaze over Sela as if evaluating her.

In answer, Sela pulled the tight tank top off over her head. The silky material grazed her sensitive nipples, hardening them instantly. She tossed it on the floor beside her and pushed her capri pants and thong down over her hips and then kicked them off so she stood in only her stilettos.

The woman's hazel eyes darkened with lust, and Sela smiled. She propped her fist on her hip, enjoying the way the woman's gaze tracked over every inch of her exposed flesh. A swift tug of regret reminded her that Marco used to look at her just like this, but she shoved the unwelcome thought away. "Do you have my information?"

"I do, but you know my terms." The woman pushed back so she leaned back against the wooden headboard. One long leg dangled off the side of the bed, and she spread her legs, propping one foot up on the bed to give Sela a full view of her smooth-shaven, glistening slit. "Payment first." The woman traced her own fingers down between her breasts, over her gently rounded stomach and on down to her dusky pink pussy.

The musk of the woman's arousal called to Sela like a siren, but she stood her ground, knowing the woman wasn't finished.

"The extent of my information will depend on how satisfied I am with the payment."

A slow smile curved Sela's lips. "I have no doubt, I can offer payment that will surpass the worth of all the information you have. What's your name, by the way?"

"Samantha."

The softly spoken name set off small explosions of heat inside Sela's body, and her core clenched in anticipation. It had been many years since she'd had sex with only a woman. Usually women were involved in her group play, but this one had specifically wanted sex with Sela as payment, so who was she to argue?

Sela stalked forward until she could slide her left knee onto the bed in between Samantha's open legs, her knee resting against the woman's hot core. She threaded her right hand into Samantha's hair, the silky strands spilling over her fingers.

Desire swam in Samantha's hazel gaze, and her full lips parted.

Sela tightened her grip on Samantha's hair and lowered her lips until her warm breath mingled with Samantha's. "Just so we are clear on your request. You wanted to know what it was like to receive the full sexual attention of the Queen of the Cunts, correct?"

Samantha lifted her chin in defiance, even though it tightened Sela's grip against her hair. "I have human as well as Cunt and Klatch blood running through my veins, but I'm not welcome in any of their worlds." Her voice was flat and hard. "However, I've always felt like more of a Cunt than the other two, so my information is for sale only if you make me feel like I belong totally and utterly to you."

The wording struck Sela as odd, but she ignored it. As long as this woman had the information she hoped, it would be no hardship to give her a night of unforgettable sex.

Sela leaned forward, closing the distance between their lips—warm soft flesh against warm soft flesh. Using her grip on the woman's hair for leverage, she held her in place while she plundered her mouth, thrusting her tongue between her hot lush lips and meeting Samantha's tongue stroke for stroke.

The woman tasted sweet like honey with an aftertaste of the rum she must've drunk beforehand.

The energy inside Sela swirled and churned until every inch of her skin was achy with need.

A swift spurt of surprise made her pull away from Samantha. She sat back on the bed, her breath ragged, her body screaming for more as she raked her gaze over Samantha.

The woman's lips were swollen from Sela's hard kiss, her hair on one side tousled from Sela's fingers. The first stirrings of unease fluttered deep inside Sela's belly. A quick image of meeting this woman as a sexual equal made heat flare through her body—which was ridiculous. Samantha was a half-breed, someone to be used, conquered, fed from.

"I asked Little Jon to stock the room so we wouldn't be disturbed." Samantha gestured to the far wall of the little room, where black inset shelves were crammed with all types of lubes, creams, dildos, strap-ons, silk scarves and even some small velvet floggers.

Sela's usual tastes ran to much more violent toys, but the heat pumping through her body told her that nothing Samantha proposed would be a hardship. She reached forward to cup Samantha's firm breast in her palm. The flesh was soft, warm and smooth, and Sela's core clenched as a low "mmm" spilled from Samantha's throat.

Samantha leaned forward and pressed her lips against Sela's, the woman's warm fingers finding Sela's breasts and aching nipples.

A low growl spilled from Sela's throat as Samantha rolled the sensitive tips between her fingers with just the right amount of pressure. A zing of hot arousal speared Sela, and she yanked Samantha lower on the bed until the woman lay flat beneath her.

Sela kicked off her stilettos and settled her weight onto Samantha, enjoying the way their breasts pressed together between them as her lips closed over Samantha's again. She pressed her body into the open vee of Samantha's thighs, enjoying the wet heat of Samantha's core against her mons.

When Samantha's long legs closed around Sela's hips, Sela bucked against her, her tongue plunging inside her mouth, mimicking what she wished she could do with her body.

Sela marveled as she did each time she touched a woman at how soft they were and yet how resilient and strong. A marked difference from the hard, muscular planes of a man. Even the movements between them were more fluid and graceful rather than hard and forceful.

Samantha skimmed her short nails down the skin of Sela's back, sending a hard shudder through her as they bucked against each other.

Samantha's breasts heaved against Sela's with every panted breath, and the sudden urge to taste every inch of Samantha's soft flesh spilled across Sela's tongue, until she kissed a path from the side of Samantha's full lips over to the soft skin of her throat.

Samantha moaned as her head relaxed back against the pillow, giving Sela better access—although the woman's busy fingers still stroked and kneaded Sela's body wherever she could reach.

The taste of Samantha's skin was clean and light like crisp

champagne on a summer day, and Sela couldn't resist sucking her skin inside her mouth and nipping hard.

Samantha moaned and bucked under her, and Sela traced a path down the woman's chest with her mouth until she could suck one hardened nipple into her mouth.

It was Sela's turn to moan. The tight nub tasted almost sweet, and Samantha was so damned responsive that everything Sela did caused a moan, a gasp or an answering flush to the tanned skin. Not to mention that the pungent smell of Samantha's arousal filled Sela's senses, making her almost light-headed as she craved the taste of this woman inside her mouth.

Not bothering to take time to give the other breast the same treatment, Sela scooted down until she could bury her face against Samantha's hot pussy.

The dusky pink skin of her labia was soft and smooth against Sela's lips as she sucked first one and then the other inside her mouth before she plunged her tongue into Samantha's slit to taste her.

Samantha's rich taste burst inside Sela's senses, sending her entire body into overdrive as the energy swirled inside her faster and faster. A slow tingling began deep inside Sela's core, and she mentally frowned.

Dear god, I'm going to come just from tasting this little half-breed.

Sela drove her tongue deep, and Samantha screamed and bucked against the sudden invasion, but Sela wrapped her arms under Samantha's thighs, holding her open and still so Sela could feast on her.

Long slow licks of the glistening slit weren't enough, so Sela sucked, nipped and licked until Samantha's fingers were fisted into the sheets and her head thrashed back and forth.

Unintelligible words spilled from the woman's lips, and Sela finally traced a slow path with her tongue up toward the hard nub of Samantha's clit. She flicked her tongue over the tight nub and enjoyed the scream of surprise that wrenched from Samantha's throat. Then she slowly sucked the tiny bud into her mouth.

Samantha stiffened and screamed again as her orgasm claimed her, and a fresh rush of silky moisture coated Sela's tongue. Sela continued to suck on the tight clit until the flavor died away and Samantha relaxed back against the bed, panting.

Sela raised her head, her entire body screaming for release, but she was not quite ready to give in. She eyed the collection of toys on the wall and pushed off the bed to stalk toward them.

A purple strap-on sporting a large purple dildo caught her eye, and she fitted the straps around her thighs, making sure the back panel was correctly positioned over her own clit.

She stalked toward the bed. Samantha's answering smile as she widened her legs in welcome made Sela's core throb.

"I've never used a strap-on before," Sela said, remembering how Samantha's legs had felt clamped around her hips. "But I want to fuck you until you scream my name and beg for more."

Samantha welcomed Sela back into the cradle of her thighs. "I've been dying to try out the strap-on, too. In fact, I've fantasized about bending you over the bed and plunging inside your ass. . . ."

Sela swallowed hard as she remembered Aedan doing that very same thing. Instead of speaking and betraying how much Samantha's words had affected her, she positioned the head of the dildo at Samantha's core and slid deep.

She couldn't feel the dildo as it parted Samantha's hot flesh, but she pushed inside until her mons pressed tight against Samantha's clit and the intense vibrations hummed to life against her own clit.

Sela froze and Samantha widened her thighs. She grabbed Sela's ass, pulled her in tight, making the vibrations faster and harder against Sela's own sensitive clit.

A low moan broke from Sela's throat, and she eased out a little until the exquisite vibrations stopped.

Her breasts were pressed against the softness of Samantha's, her face buried against the side of the woman's neck.

"When the tip of the dildo hits the back of my core, it triggers the vibrator on your harness." Samantha's hot breath feathered against the side of Sela's neck, sending thousands of tiny shockwaves through the queen's body. "So, fuck me hard, and we'll both get off. Then it's your turn."

Sela shuddered again, but this time from Samantha's words.

Before she could think too much about her reaction to the idea of letting Samantha dominate her, she began to piston her hips inside Samantha hard and fast.

As promised, each time she pounded deep, the vibrator shocked her clit until she felt like the dildo was an actual extension of her body.

She fucked Samantha harder, pistoning her hips and not bothering to slow down when the woman came repeatedly and each stroke made a wet slapping sound between them.

A fine sheen of sweat broke out along Sela's skin, and the entire world narrowed until her energy mingled with Samantha's, their two bodies slapping against each other as Sela fucked the other woman mercilessly.

Sela's orgasm slammed into her like a solid punch to the gut. Her core convulsed so hard she thought she would double over. She thrust hard one last time inside Samantha, jamming the tip of the dildo hard inside the woman, so the vibrating sensations were at their peak as Sela rode the hard waves of her climax.

When the sensations finally died away, she pulled the dildo out of Samantha and slumped across the woman's body in a boneless heap.

After what could have been minutes or hours, Samantha

slipped out from under Sela and gently unhooked the strap-on from Sela.

Samantha pulled Sela toward the side of the bed until her feet met the floor and she was in the right position for bending over the bed like Samantha had described earlier.

Sela thought about objecting, but her body flared to life, and excitement poured through her.

Samantha positioned Sela's arms straight over her head, lying flat on the bed, her breasts crushed flat against the soft bedspread, her cheek laying flat.

A cool tickle against her ass made Sela jump, and she widened her stance to give Samantha better access.

Samantha's finger traced the tight pucker of Sela's ass with something cool and slippery. "Don't move your arms, and stay flat against the bed."

Sela didn't nod, she only remained still as the pressure of the head of the dildo slowly stretched her wide.

The sensation of the invasion was so markedly different from Aedan's that she wanted to pay attention to every nuance.

Whereas with Aedan's cock, there was ripping and hard pain, with Samantha and the lubed dildo, there was only a stretching sensation and then fullness . . . until the tip of the dildo hit her insides.

The vibrations she had assumed only the wearer of the strap-on could feel burned through her, ratcheting her arousal until a raspy moan ripped from her throat.

Samantha grabbed the back of Sela's hair and leaned down close to her ear as she ground the dildo deep inside the queen, making the vibrations harder until Sela felt like she might come again. "How do you like being on the bottom, Sela?"

A ragged gasp was all she could manage, and Samantha's throaty laughter was all she heard before Samantha began to pound inside her ass just as Sela had done inside the other woman's pussy.

Time stretched out and lost all meaning between one overwhelming orgasm and the next. Her throat was raw and scratchy from screaming, and her lungs ached as she dragged air into them to scream again. The only sounds other than her own throaty cries were the slap of flesh against flesh and Samantha's throaty laugh and cry of triumph each time Sela came or begged for more.

When Sela and Samantha were both too limp to move, they curled on the bed together in a panting heap.

Sela's mind slowly resurfaced from the sensual haze, and she cleared her throat, hoping she could still speak. When she did, her voice came out in a painful croak, but she could still understand the words. "Did I earn my information?"

Samantha laughed, the sound dry and brittle from her own screaming. "I think so." She pushed up so she leaned back against her elbows. "And I think I could be persuaded to keep my ears open for more, for the right . . . payment."

A sensual shudder ran through Sela's body at the thought of more sessions like this. She cradled her head in her open palm. She smiled at Samantha, very glad she had decided to go searching for information today.

With her free hand, she traced her fingertips around one of Samantha's dusky pink areolas, smiling as the nipple hardened to a tight peak from the attention. "So, tell me everything you know about Marco and a contingent of Cunts being allowed back onto Tador. . . ."

17

Kiera slipped out from under Ryan's arm and rolled off the edge of his bed.

After her meltdown with the statue, he'd spent several hours valiantly distracting her from everything else but him. However, now that her body had recovered from the sensual haze and Ryan snored softly beside her, she wanted some alone time to think.

She pulled on her clothes and slipped down the corridor to the room where the man she had grown up calling "Dad" lay.

Two guards stood just outside, and heat burned her cheeks as she realized one of them was the man she had nearly emasculated.

"Hi," she said awkwardly.

They both dipped their chins and then eyed her with something that she could've sworn was respect. "Good evening, Healer," they both murmured as one opened the door and motioned her through.

Wow. That's total man logic for you. Kick their asses and earn their respect.

The room was dark except for the small spill of moonlight that filtered through the open French doors, which led to the patio. Memories of she and Ryan celebrating her birthday out on that patio surged back to her, reminding her of the pleasant ache between her thighs and throughout her body.

Rustling from the bed caught her attention, and she stepped forward in time to see Shiloh stretch and yawn. His large orange eyes blinked owlishly before he stepped over her father's legs to head butt her hand until she ruffled his soft fur and scratched behind his ears.

"Still taking care of him, are you?"

"Mrowr."

Kiera smiled. "Well, I'm here if you'd like to take a break."

As if Shiloh understood her, he jumped off the bed and disappeared through the open French doors.

Kiera pulled the overstuffed chair closer to the bed, so she could hold her father's hand and still sit without disturbing him. The skin of his hand was still warm and strong like it had been since his healing, and as was her habit, she rose to check the IV fluid that fed him and ensured his catheter bag didn't need changing.

When she was sure all was as it should be, she sat again and threaded her fingers with his.

A thousand happy memories involving the man before her spilled through her mind, but then a perfect picture of the genealogy chart Alyssa had shown her scattered the memories, and her chest constricted as if there were a giant hand squeezing her.

"You knew," she said softly to her father's still form. "You had to know." She swallowed hard. "But you never told me, and you never let me even suspect."

A hot tear dropped onto their joined hands, and she blinked hard, only then realizing that she'd begun to cry.

Emotions flowed through her too fast for her to identify, and she laid her forehead against their joined hands and just let them flow. Gradually, they slowed until she could distinguish some of the stronger ones—fear, anger, betrayal, longing, sadness . . . and hope.

She raised her head surprised to find hope hiding among the others.

"Kiera?"

Ryan's low voice came from the doorway.

"Come on in." She didn't turn around, but when his hand closed over her shoulder, she welcomed the warmth and the comfort he offered.

Silence fell between them, and she breathed deep, realizing that even though Ryan had offered no words, none had been needed.

"Do you think he'll wake up?" She winced as her voice sounded too hopeful, like a child asking to go to the amusement park.

"I don't know. You are the Healer, so I have no doubt you've healed him to the best of your abilities."

She let out a shaky laugh. "You just aren't sure how far gone my father is." It wasn't a question, and Ryan didn't bother to answer her.

An orange blur of fur streaked through the French doors and jumped onto the bed in front of her. Shiloh pranced and circled, his eyes wild.

"Shiloh?" Kiera tried to pick him up, and he nipped at her until she pulled her hands away.

He jumped off the bed and walked halfway to the French doors before turning to stare back at them, a plaintive "mrowrr" spilling from his throat.

Ryan started forward, and Shiloh took a few more steps toward the patio doors before turning back. "I think he wants us to go out onto the balcony."

Kiera rose and followed Shiloh and Ryan outside.

The moonlight was stronger out here and allowed her to see the crowd advancing on the castle. She couldn't make out specifics, but from what she could tell, there were thousands of Klatch as well as some animals headed toward the castle at a steady pace.

The doors burst open behind them, and she and Ryan turned to see Gavin, his face darkened with concern.

A sudden awkwardness rose between her and Gavin, and heavy silence fell for a long moment. She hadn't seen him since discovering his name on the genealogy chart in one of her father slots. The entire scene was made more uncomfortable by the fact that the father she had known her entire life laid just in the next room.

"Gavin," Ryan said, breaking the tension. "What's happening?"

"You both must come immediately. The destruction of the planet has accelerated, and most of the outlying areas died earlier in the night. The people have congregated in the few thriving areas, and one of those is the castle." He gestured toward the oncoming crowd. "The Triangle Ceremony must be performed. Now."

Sharp metallic fear sat like a lead weight inside Kiera's belly and stung the back of her tongue as she silently followed Gavin and Ryan through the castle and out into the chilly night.

"Thank the Goddess." Katelyn grabbed Kiera's arm and pulled her forward into the cave Kiera had inadvertently opened with her "behead the statue" stunt.

The mouth of the cave was massive and reminded her of a giant maw that would consume them all without a second thought. A shudder ran through her, and a heavy sense of dread tightened her chest as she stepped through the opening.

A long, darkened passageway closed around her, and only the soft pink glow at the very end beckoned her forward.

"Wait until you see this," Katelyn said from beside Kiera, startling her with the intensity of the words. "You won't believe it."

Kiera opened her mouth to tell Katelyn there wasn't anything she wouldn't believe after the past few days, but then she reached the end of the passageway and stepped through the opening.

Her words died inside her throat as she whipped around to try and see everything at once.

They stood inside a huge chamber so large it seemed like the entire mountain had been hollowed out just to make the place. Everything was bathed in a soft rose-colored light.

The backside of the waterfall she had heard so much about but not yet seen fell in a gentle stream to a pool big enough to hold twenty people. The floor, walls, ceiling—everything—was entirely made of smooth *balda*, the pink crystals that ran throughout glowing from within.

A triangle made entirely of the pink crystals dominated the middle of the floor, and cushions were piled inside the diagram. Next to each corner in pink crystals were the three symbols that Kiera had seen on the tracing paper at the edges of the triangle. She mentally measured the triangle and figured she could park at least six of her father's Humvees inside the area without touching any of the sides.

She glanced up and realized that just above the point of each corner of the triangle, a huge stalactite of the pink *balda* crystals hung from the ceiling like giant razor-sharp fingers.

She dropped her gaze and noticed a small ledge protruded from the walls at seat level and ran the entire circumference of the cavern, except for the doorway that led to the passageway she had just come through. Hell, the seat even ran along the back wall of the pool behind the flow of water from the back of the waterfall.

"Wow," was all she could think of to say as she turned in a circle.

Katelyn grabbed her hand and pulled her toward the side of the cavern where Alyssa, Stone and a few other Klatch Kiera didn't recognize stood talking. The Seer leaned close to her ear. "The rest of the scrolls had directions for performing the Triangle, directions for how to close everything up until another Triangle is needed, and tons more genealogies that would just blow your mind."

Kiera's stomach felt like she'd swallowed a thousand squirming lizards that were all trying to slither their way back up her throat. "We're really doing this, aren't we?"

Katelyn stopped short, and Ryan and Gavin ran into Kiera from behind. "You're one of us, Kiera." Katelyn squeezed the hand she still held and pinned Kiera with a glittering green gaze. "And you can do this." Katelyn smiled and held her free hand over her stomach. "Besides, you're not the only one who's scared shitless of what's going to happen."

Kiera couldn't help the smile or the sudden rush of relief that flowed through her like a welcome spring breeze. "I'm not the only one?"

Warm hands settled over her shoulders from behind, and Ryan kissed her gently on the side of the neck. "I'd have to say, no. I have a feeling that every single one of us is terrified beyond belief but just too worried that if we admit it, we'll be the only ones. We're just *more* terrified to lose Tador."

Kiera lifted her free hand to lay it over Ryan's and gave it a gentle squeeze as the squirming inside her stomach quieted and firmed into a much more familiar sensation: determination. She raised her chin and smiled at Katelyn. "Let's do this."

An hour later, Kiera stood barefoot on the point of the giant pink Triangle with the healer symbol next to it. She wore only a see-through gauzy robe that barely covered her ass cheeks. On the other two points of the Triangle stood Alyssa and Katelyn with Grayson and Stone just behind them.

Ryan's comforting presence loomed behind Kiera, and she envied him the black robe he and the other two men wore that covered them enough that the entire room didn't know what they looked like naked.

Katelyn arched a brow over her shoulder at her mate, Grayson. "How come you guys get black and we get see-through robes that leave nothing to the imagination?" She turned her attention toward Queen Alyssa. "I thought this was a matriarchal society. What's up with this sexist crap?"

Alyssa shrugged. "You're asking me? I've only been here a few months." The queen rubbed her arms as if she were cold. "If it was up to me, the men would all be oiled up wearing skimpy loin cloths and giving us foot massages, but maybe we can look at rewriting the Triangle dress code for the next generation who needs it."

Heavy tension filled the room making the air thick. "So what happens now?" Kiera's soft words echoed around them despite the soft *shushing* of the water falling into the pool.

Ryan wrapped an arm around her middle and pulled her back against the heat of his body. She instantly softened against him, melting into the comfort he offered. "We could always pass the time while we're waiting," he whispered against the side of her neck, sending a line of goose bumps marching across her skin, along with an answering ache of arousal deep inside her belly.

"Prince Ryan." The gravelly sound of a woman's voice rang through the chamber. "You must save your strength for the Triangle and for caring for your mate afterward." An elderly woman dressed in the normal Klatch gauzy clothes, braids sprinkled throughout her long gray hair, stood just next to them as if she'd materialized out of thin air. Her thin lips were curved into a small smile, and her ancient eyes sparked with amusement.

"It is an honor to meet you, Healer." The woman dipped her chin in the normal Klatch sign of respect before raising her gaze to Kiera's. "I am Annara, and as the eldest princess of the second house of Klatch, it falls to me to officiate the ceremony."

Kiera's brain finally caught up with this newest turn of events, and she frowned at something Annara had said. "Ryan and I aren't mated, unless my coming-of-age counts. Will that affect the Triangle?"

Annara's lavender eyes pinned her in place as if seeing inside her soul.

Kiera tried not to squirm under the scrutiny.

"Unknown," came Annara's gravelly voice. "But doubtful it will have any adverse effect. The planet cares not about social agreements such as matings, but it does care about the energy generated between individuals, or in the case of the Triangle, between you six."

"Annara." King Stone's voice was respectful as he addressed the woman. "Since you have had time to study the scrolls while we have prepared for the ceremony, can you tell us what to expect?"

"The instructions were vague. This ceremony is similar to the Ascension, but all six must share sexual energy with the help of the warriors in order to build enough power to fuel the Triangle." She held her arms wide, palms up. "The scrolls say only that the planet will guide us toward what it needs to thrive, and we must follow. We are all servants to the survival of Tador."

Several concerned gazes were exchanged, leaving Kiera feeling left out. When a cold wave of foreboding swept over her, she swallowed hard. "What's going on? Please don't tell me we have to have sex with a bunch of warriors, too?"

Alyssa straightened and addressed Annara. "Assemble the warriors. We will need every one we can find. The six of us will take a few moments to prepare."

"All but Gavin will be assembled, my queen. Due to the information revealed about the family lines, his attendance would be—awkward." She glanced meaningfully at Kiera, whose blood ran cold inside her veins. "He will guard the exterior of the cavern during the ceremony."

Yes, definitely awkward to have your possible father witness your induction orgy into a new world order. Kiera swallowed hard against the sudden urge to laugh. She was glad someone had thought about that little wrinkle *before* the ceremony.

"Of course. Thanks for thinking of that, Annara," the queen said quietly and then turned her attention away from the woman, effectively dismissing her.

Annara placed her hands together in what reminded Kiera of a prayer position and bowed to the queen before she backed away, presumably to gather the warriors.

The queen motioned them all forward to kneel on the cushions piled high in the center of the crystal Triangle. Kiera settled cross-legged and leaned back against Ryan.

"Okay, troops," Alyssa said with a small smile. "Apparently Tador will show us the way, but I think I should warn both Katelyn and Kiera exactly what was involved in my ascension so they aren't surprised. And no, we don't actually have sex with the warriors."

Kiera's audible sigh of relief brought smiles to everyone's faces. "Am I the only one relieved by that nugget of information?"

Alyssa chuckled. "I asked the same thing before my ascension, and I was relieved, too." The queen glanced over her shoulder at Stone before facing forward again. "And also, if the planet will show us the way, I think we all need to define clear boundaries of what is and isn't acceptable as far as the men."

Kiera stiffened, and Ryan immediately began to rub comforting circles over her back. "Why do I get the feeling I'm not going to like this?" Her whispered words sounded loud in the close quarters of the group, and one look at the Seer's eyes showed Kiera she wasn't the only one who was worried.

"My ascension was basically in five parts." Alyssa studied her fingers as she spoke, as if it would be harder to get the words out if she looked Kiera and Katelyn in the eye. "Anyway, Sasha helped prepare me, then . . ." She trailed off and swallowed hard.

Ryan reached around Kiera to squeeze Alyssa's hand. "Alyssandra is afraid she will scare the two of you." When Alyssa nodded, he continued. "After Sasha, then it was basically a blow job, anal sex and then Stone took her virginity and the warriors lent their essence to give her enough power to ascend the throne."

Damn! Alyssa lost her virginity in front of a roomful of strangers?

Katelyn whistled long and low, the sudden noise breaking the quiet tension. "Okaaay. If you can give up your virginity in a roomful of people, then I think Kiera and I can do this." She glanced at Kiera for confirmation.

Kiera nodded, not so sure she was up for the anal sex since she'd never tried it before, but willing to do whatever it took to save Tador.

Stone cleared his throat. "Before Alyssandra and I mated, we promised I would enter no other woman's pussy or ass, and no other man would enter Alyssandra's pussy. And if memory serves, we agreed that as long as she could watch, another woman could suck my cock and I could give my essence where needed."

Alyssa's face burned bright red, but she nodded with a small smile while she looked up at them from under her lashes.

Katelyn huffed out a laugh. "Well, that's pretty detailed."

She pulled Grayson's hand into her lap as she studied him. "I don't think we've put such an agreement in place yet, but I suppose now is the time." She shoved her waterfall of red hair over her shoulder. "If I'm being totally honest, the thought of watching Grayson doing anything except vaginal penetration with either Alyssa or Kiera turns me on like crazy. But no others."

A sudden vision of the six of them entwined on the pillows in various and sundry forms of copulation flashed across Kiera's mind like a blockbuster movie in high-definition surround sound.

Hot molten arousal slammed into her body, and she gasped.

Moans sounded all around her, merging with her own.

Then . . . nothing. As if a switch had suddenly been flipped, the vision along with the sensations receded, leaving her bereft and achy.

"Sorry," Katelyn murmured as Grayson muttered his agreement with her terms.

Sharp cold shock slapped at Kiera, and she stared at the Seer as if seeing her for the first time. "That was from you?"

Everyone still looked just as shaken as Kiera felt, and Katelyn shrugged. "Sometimes if I visualize something and concentrate on it, the vision broadcasts out to others." The Seer's pale freckled skin glowed pink with embarrassment.

Grayson grinned, his dark hair falling over his shoulders as his eyes glinted with a combination of lust and amusement. "The stories we can tell you about some of those visions she has shared will have to wait, but you'll definitely have to remind us to fill you in."

Kiera blew out a shaky breath and ran her hand through her hair for lack of anything better to do. "Katelyn, don't apologize. I think that little flash just helped me understand what I'm really comfortable with and what I'm not." She closed her eyes and shook her head, unable to believe what she was about to admit. "I think I totally agree with Katelyn's take. Ryan doesn't enter anyone else's pussy, but everything else—"

Tingling awareness hummed under her skin and threatened to turn into a full-blown inferno of need. "Everything else sounds erotic as hell."

18

_____

Kiera jumped as Annara clapped her wrinkled hands and signaled to Gavin.

Gavin stepped away from the mouth of the long dark hallway that led outside, and a line of Klatch warriors walked single file along the wall of the large chamber, following the path of the inset seat that circled the entire room.

Even in the soft pinkish glow that emanated from inside the pink crystals, Kiera could tell all of the men had the same golden dusky skin as Ryan, with varying shades of purple eyes running the gamut from a lavender so light it could have been almost white to deep dark purple that appeared almost black.

When those nearly black eyes reminded her of Ryan's, she glanced back at his encouraging smile and then found the five warriors with identical eyes who now stepped down into the pool to continue to follow the wall around.

Ryan's brothers . . .

Shit! I'm going to do kinky things I haven't even imagined yet in my lifetime—all of it in front of Ryan's brothers?

Ryan's warm hand closed over her shoulder. "They respect

you. Not only for protecting me, but also for kicking their asses and participating in the Triangle for the good of Tador. There's nothing we will do here to be ashamed of."

"I thought they didn't like the fact that I'm half Cunt?"

Ryan pressed a kiss to one of Kiera's shoulders. "I think the fact that you don't fit the stereotypes of Cunts that they were raised with makes them more willing to give you a chance."

Kiera nodded, but then ice-cold dread pooled inside her stomach as similar instances in the past where Ryan had "known" her thoughts flowed through her mind.

She whirled around to face him, dislodging his hand on her shoulder. "How did you know that I was freaking out about doing these things in front of your brothers? I *know* I didn't say that out loud."

His entire expression softened, and he cupped her cheeks in his large palms, the warmth chasing back the cold inside her belly. "On Tador, sometimes mated pairs can hear each other's thoughts."

Her brow furrowed as she processed his words.

She reached up to lay her palms over Ryan's and locked her gaze with his, drinking in the joy she saw there, but not quite sure how she felt about Ryan seeing inside her head.

"It has always been so for the king and queen, but then Grayson and Katelyn surprised everyone by enjoying a similar ability. It's not consistent with us yet, but when you have a particularly strong thought or something attached to strong emotion, I can hear it."

The cold dread was long gone, but a slight twinge of unease still remained. "Well, at least I like the idea of getting to hear yours."

Ryan laughed and leaned forward, closing the distance between them. Just before their lips met Annara cleared her throat loudly just beside them, and they broke apart like guilty children.

"Soon enough you will have free reign with each other. But the time is not yet right." Annara's gravelly voice managed to chide and sound amused at the same time, which made Kiera smile. She shrugged at Ryan and then turned around to face the pile of soft cushions and pillows stacked inside the pink crystal Triangle design on the *balda* floor.

Her gaze swept the room, and she realized the long line of warriors now ringed the entire chamber. She didn't bother to count them but guessed about five hundred men stood around the perimeter ready to watch her have sex with five other people.

Yeah, no pressure there.

The men varied in height and build, but all of them were impressive specimens of the male form, and the energy inside her chose that moment to wake and start a slow churn, tightening her nipples and rushing over her skin with the warm rush of arousal.

Kiera swallowed hard and hoped her stomach lizards didn't return, or she might throw up right now and ruin the entire ceremony. But Lord help her, the thought of being watched—even en masse—was erotic as hell.

The weight of someone's intense scrutiny prickled along her skin, and Kiera glanced over to find Gavin watching her. His lavender gaze captured hers, locking her in place while emotions thick and rich and too numerous to name sped back and forth between them.

In light of everything else that had happened, Kiera hadn't spoken to Gavin since she found out he was . . . well . . . one of her three fathers. But she knew once this ceremony was over and the planet was safe, she would have to make time for all three men who held that role.

She took a deep breath and shoved those thoughts from her mind. There was enough to worry about in the here and now; she didn't need to add more.

Gavin nodded to her, a kind smile on his lips, before he dropped his gaze.

Her throat tightened as she watched him turn and disappear down the long dark hallway. The strange thought popped into her mind that she wished she would've found time to spar with Gavin before she found the genealogies.

For some reason, she wanted to earn his respect on that front before either of them knew about a possible family tie.

The ground underneath her feet shook, breaking her out of her thoughts as an echoed rumbling filled the air of the cavern.

Ryan caught her as she stumbled off the corner of the smooth pink crystal Triangle she stood on. A quick glance at Katelyn, Grayson, Alyssa and Stone showed her they were all experiencing the same problems staying upright. Only Annara stood serenely as if it were a calm spring day and the ground wasn't doing the cha-cha beneath their feet.

Dimly, through her case of nerves on a caffeine binge, Kiera realized Gavin had found the mechanism to close the door to the cave. She just hoped he also knew how to reopen the damned thing. Getting stuck inside even this huge cave for any longer than necessary gave her the heebie-jeebies.

As the rumbling quieted and the floor stilled beneath her feet, she placed her hand on her stomach, hoping to calm the lizards that were back in full force doing somersaults and figure eights inside her belly.

Two more staccato hand claps from Annara drew Kiera's attention as the elderly woman opened her mouth to speak. "It is time." The woman's gravelly voice echoed around them, sending a wave of gooseflesh marching across Kiera's skin and making her shudder even inside the warmth of the cavern.

Across from her, the queen and the Seer stood on the remaining two corners of the Triangle, and as they unbelted their nearly translucent robes and dropped them to the ground, Kiera took a deep breath and followed suit.

The silky cloth slithered over her body and down her legs until it pooled at her feet.

Instantly, the energy level in the room skyrocketed, the air heavy and thick with buzzing awareness and power from so many magical beings in one concentrated location.

Cool air hit Kiera's bare skin along with hundreds of pairs of hungry eyes, which felt like a blatant caress.

Her body responded with a deep ache that nearly doubled her over with need.

She gasped, and the sound merged with two others—Alyssa's and Katelyn's.

Kiera kept her gaze focused on the two women, afraid if she looked around at all the other people filling the chamber, she would lose her nerve and run screaming.

Alyssa squared her shoulders and raised her chin, looking every inch the regal queen, regardless of the fact she stood entirely naked.

Kiera's gaze raked over the queen's generous curves—the full rounded breasts, the lush hips and the smooth mound at the apex of lush thighs. The statue was a perfect representation of her, but this full-color, live version of Alyssa fired Kiera's blood and sent a slick pool of moisture to form between her labia.

Alyssa stepped forward onto the lush pile of cushions and pillows and then motioned for Katelyn and Kiera to join her.

Kiera glanced toward Katelyn, trying and failing to keep her gaze only on the green eyes now darkened with the same arousal Kiera had seen when she and Katelyn had kissed inside the baths. That all seemed so long ago now that she stood ready to complete the Triangle ceremony.

Katelyn raised one shapely leg and stepped up onto the expanse of cushions, her full breasts bouncing with the movement, making Kiera's mouth water and the energy inside her howl for more.

Alyssa took Katelyn's hand in hers, and then they both extended their free hands toward Kiera.

As if an invisible force pulled her forward, Kiera stepped up onto the platform of cushions and took each of their hands in hers.

A tingling rush of energy surged through each of them, locking them together and screaming with fury as the power built in intensity inside their bodies.

Kiera felt like a blade of grass in a hurricane as she battled against the sudden onslaught.

She tightened her grip on Alyssa and Katelyn as her legs turned to rubber. She collapsed onto her knees just as the queen and Seer dropped to their knees as well. Luckily, the impact against the overstuffed cushions kept Kiera's teeth from clacking together as she landed hard.

An aching arousal smoldered and burned through Kiera's body like nothing she had ever known. Even the soft silky cushions under her knees scratched against her over-sensitized skin like coarse sandpaper.

She opened her mouth to gasp for breath, but her lungs seemed to be filled with molasses and wouldn't accept any air.

Icy curls of panic licked at her as she began to shake uncontrollably with the need to breathe. Kiera thrashed her head from side to side in an attempt to escape the vise around her throat, clamping her eyes shut in a futile attempt to keep any air she may already have inside her.

"Relax, don't fight."

Kiera heard the words distantly, but her mind refused to register if the female voice had been Alyssa or Katelyn. Her brain felt as if it were on fire, and light-headedness made her thoughts fuzzy as blackness teased at the edges of her awareness.

We're here. Let go.

The softly spoken words were like a command that rang out inside her head, echoing over and over until she obeyed.

Kiera forced her body to relax as she gave herself up to the power rushing through her.

The pain and the panic instantly receded, allowing her to draw in a miserly dose of air. She sagged against the cushions, opening herself to whatever may come.

For what seemed like days, she allowed the surging energy to flow through her, buffeting through her until she thought her body would rip apart and disperse across the universe in tiny pieces. The inside of her skin and even her bones felt raw and sore—definitely in danger of disintegrating at any moment.

But, slowly, Kiera became aware of her fingers caught in a vise grip on either side of her.

Katelyn . . . Alyssa . . .

We're here. Breathe, came the soft reassurance inside her mind.

Those simple words spread a warming glow of confidence inside her, salving her sore insides and returning her thoughts along with her resolve.

"I can do this." The whispered vow slipped from her lips as she forced open her heavy eyelids.

Katelyn and Alyssa still knelt in front of her, their hands still linked, their expressions weary as if they had just fought an epic battle and won.

At least I wasn't the only one!

Kiera gingerly tipped her head from side to side, working the kinks from the tightened muscles in her neck and shoulders. She sucked in a deep breath and let it out slowly.

The soft flow of energy that had lived inside of her since she first stepped onto Tador still rushed through her, but now instead of a steady stream, it resembled Niagara Falls. What had nearly ripped her apart mere minutes ago now remained in the background—almost unnoticed until she concentrated. "Damn.

It's still there." Her words sounded loud in the tense silence that filled the cavern. She couldn't believe she was starting to get used to the overpowering invasion.

Surprise and awe filled Kiera as she took in Alyssa and Katelyn's reassuring smiles.

Annara smiled, her lavender eyes sparkling. "Your body was made to handle the energy needed for the Triangle, Healer. You are truly one of us."

The sting of tears burned at the backs of Kiera's eyes, and she blinked them away. She had long ago come to terms with the fact that she would never fit in fully to either of her parents' worlds. But now . . . now she had, and she wasn't sure what emotions she should be experiencing. Although relief and joy were definitely at the top of her list.

Alyssa squeezed Kiera's fingers, pulling her attention back to the present. "Right now, the three of us are controlling all the energy shared with Tador."

"Shit." Katelyn shook her head. "That's all? It feels more like the energy from an entire solar system."

Kiera silently agreed. She tried to wrap her mind around the concept of what Alyssa described, but before she could, the queen continued.

"If one queen can take a hundred times that when the planet is at full strength, then the three of us can easily handle all of this between us." Alyssa's confident lavender gaze met Kiera's and then Katelyn's. "The three of us together are invincible. And with the hunky studs we have ready to help us build up some energy, we should be able to generate enough to power the entire universe as well as create a few new suns."

One queen is supposed to handle one hundred times the energy that nearly ripped me to shreds?

Damn.

"I'm in. Let's do this before I chicken out." Katelyn blew out a slow breath as if bracing for the next onslaught.

Kiera swallowed hard but smiled and nodded. "Okay. Now that the initial shock has passed, I'm back in the game. How much worse is this going to get?"

Alyssa nodded, all business now that she had full buy-in from them both. "When we drop hands, all hell is going to break loose, and the planet will guide us to generate the energy it needs to restore itself. I'm not sure how hard it's going to get, but whatever you do, don't panic and don't fight."

"Easy for you two to say. I like to fight." Kiera grinned as the familiar thread of adrenaline replaced the uneasiness and the fear that had trickled just below the surface. "And right now, I'm ready to fight to get Tador back to full strength. Let's do it."

"On three," Alyssa said as she squeezed both of their hands. "One . . . two . . . three."

The warmth of Katelyn and Alyssa's hands fell away and the power that had flowed through the connection rebounded and slammed into Kiera's chest like a jackhammer.

Kiera braced her legs, refusing to be thrown backward out of the triangle. She tried to relax as the razor-sharp power felt like it carved eddies and curlicues in the soft insides of her body.

Around the chamber, a high wailing scream rose around them, which Kiera instantly recognized as the swirling energy. The volume increased exponentially until she longed for the good old days of standing in front of the floor speakers at a rock concert instead of the painful pressure of noise that beat against her eardrums now.

A punishing wind whipped around the chamber, thrashing Kiera's hair against her face in painful slaps and buffeting against her naked skin like hard crystals of sand.

Unable to keep her balance against the barrage, she crumpled forward and landed against something soft and fleshy. The familiar scent of the Seer filled Kiera's senses, and she reached out until her hand landed on smooth skin—a stomach, if Kiera had to make a guess.

Sudden silence rang out, and for a long moment Kiera was afraid she'd gone entirely deaf until she heard her own sigh of relief from the respite.

Kiera raised her head with shaky muscles and realized she was staring up the length of the Seer's naked body, with Katelyn's green gaze glittering back at her.

"I've pulled us into a vision so we can do this without the loud howling and can at least sense each other over the onslaught of power." Katelyn's voice sounded strained and gravelly, and Kiera instinctively knew that the Seer had sacrificed a large dose of energy to bring all of them this relief.

As if Kiera's body suddenly realized she was sprawled between the spread legs of a very naked woman, heat pulsed along her skin, and hot deep arousal spilled through her in a breathless rush.

Alyssa crawled toward Katelyn and brushed a kiss across the Seer's lips before the queen pushed up on her knees and straddled Katelyn's face, leaving Kiera a full frontal view of the queen's lush body.

Kiera watched in fascination as Katelyn's arms threaded around the queen's thighs, bringing Alyssa's core close enough for Katelyn to lick and suck.

At Alyssa's first throaty moan, Kiera's body demanded inclusion in the erotic scene in front of her. She suddenly noticed the hot wet warmth of Katelyn's pussy pressed against her chest and shimmied down the Seer's body until she could see the glistening, dusky-pink lips of the Seer's pussy laid out before her like a banquet.

The urge to taste and take burned through Kiera, and she leaned forward to slowly swipe her tongue the length of Katelyn's slit.

Kiera jumped as she felt the swipe of a tentative tongue between her own thighs even as the sweet musk of the Seer's arousal burst over her tongue and filled her body with longing.

She glanced back over her shoulder but saw no one, not even Ryan, behind her. In fact, a hazy white curtain of fog obscured everything beyond the perimeter of the triangle.

The vision.

Of course.

Katelyn had shut them off from seeing outside the triangle with her vision.

Kiera turned back to the beautiful sight of Katelyn's spread thighs, curiosity overriding any reluctance she had about tasting a woman's pussy for the first time—especially in front of an invisible audience.

She traced her fingers through the short-cropped red curls on the Seer's mons and jumped again as she felt the sensation against her own mons—even though she was smoothly shaved.

Kiera smiled. *At least I won't have to worry that I'm not doing this correctly since I've never gone down on a woman before. Talk about instant feedback.*

She leaned forward and licked Katelyn's pussy once again, and this time she was ready for the sensation against her own body. Even so, a long low moan broke from her lips as well as Katelyn's.

Kiera widened her thighs as her own clit and labia swelled with the phantom attention as she returned to Katelyn, sucking, licking and nipping in earnest. She loved the feel of the slick juices on her tongue and the musky, sweet taste of Katelyn's warm arousal inside her mouth.

She couldn't help returning to the silky-smooth underside of the Seer's clit again and again as Kiera's own orgasm built inside her body in time with Katelyn's.

Her breath came in short choppy pants as she pulled the Seer's clit inside her mouth and sucked hard as she swirled the tip of her tongue over the sensitive tip again and again. The vortex of energy swirled tighter and tighter inside Kiera as her core began the slow pulse that signaled impending orgasm.

When a hard cock slammed into her, filling her, her orgasm broke over her like a sudden storm. Her scream of pleasure merged with Katelyn's and Alyssa's inside the enclosed space of the vision.

A strong arm around her middle lifted her up onto her knees and another pressed down on her upper back, keeping her face tight against Katelyn's core, her breasts pressed into the soft cushions below her.

The welcome sensation of Ryan's large cock pistoning inside her, his deep, woodsy scent mixing with the musky scent of Katelyn's arousal nearly plunged her over the edge into another orgasm.

Kiera panted with need as she traced the Seer's hot core with her fingers as well as her tongue and lips.

Warm hands closed over her breasts, kneading the sensitive nipples between strong fingers and wrenching a cry from her throat.

Confusion warred with reality as she realized her breasts were still planted flush against the soft cushions. She glanced up to see King Stone behind Alyssa, his large hands closed over the queen's full breasts, his fingers plucking and pulling her large dusky nipples as the queen arched back against him.

The phantom touch burned through her, and she returned her face to Katelyn's slit. The multiple sensations merged inside her, feeding the energy and churning it faster and faster. The taste of the spicy arousal inside her mouth, Ryan filling her again and again as the tip of his cock slammed against the sensitive core seated deep inside her, and the large demanding hands kneading her nipples and breasts all came together to careen her toward a climax so large she wasn't sure she would survive.

She nipped Katelyn's clit with her teeth and shoved them all over the precipice.

Ryan's hot come spilled inside her as her body spasmed around him, milking him, even as Katelyn's clit pulsed between Kiera's lips and Alyssa cried out her own orgasm.

Before the euphoric haze had a chance to clear from her mind, Ryan withdrew from her, and she felt her body being lifted and then settled again.

She tried to open her heavy eyelids, but too much arousal still warred with the lethargy from the world's biggest orgasm to date. Dimly, she realized she straddled someone's face—a man from the stubble that exquisitely abraded the sensitive skin of her nether lips. A long swipe of a tongue delved deep before tracing a path up to tease her clit.

A gasp ripped from Kiera's raw throat, and she reached up to cup her aching breasts as her nipples throbbed for attention.

She kneaded and pulled at the tight points, enjoying the hot pulls of arousal that shot straight to her clit with every touch, and every swipe of the man's tongue beneath her.

Something soft brushed against her lips, and she opened her mouth, allowing a hard cock to slip between them. Hunger and arousal made her lean forward and take as much of the thick length as she could before it bumped the back of her throat.

She raised one hand to wrap around the base of the cock that she wasn't able to take in and began to stroke, suck and swirl her tongue around the tip until the spicy taste of precome burst inside her mouth.

"Mmm." Kiera reveled in the taste as a slap of pure power plowed through her, making every hair on her body stand on end. A bubbling laugh escaped from her mouth around the thick cock.

She felt powerful and feminine and never wanted the sensations to stop.

A small voice in the back of her mind pointed out that she couldn't be sure if either man was Ryan, but her body, and lord help her, even her rational mind, no longer cared. She felt like she was part of the planet, coexisting and sharing its mountains and plants and even the very air surrounding it.

She wanted the energy that Alyssa, Katelyn and the men could provide. She wanted to build the power up inside them and then take it inside her body until they lay panting and she could move on to the next man.

The urgency of the tongue against her clit increased just as the man in front of her began to fuck her mouth in earnest, thrusting inside her with long hard strokes until he bumped the back of her throat with the swollen tip. Kiera kept her lips and hand tight around the invading cock, coaxing the man's essence forward until she could swallow each drop.

All at once, the man underneath her stiffened and nipped her clit, while the cock inside her mouth pulsed and hot come spilled inside her mouth—the tangy, spicy taste filling her with power until her skin sparked with little aftershocks of electricity.

The hot fluid seemed to trigger her own orgasm, and her body convulsed as her shout joined others, both male and female, all around her.

When her mind cleared, she realized her skin was slicked with sweat, and she was being lifted again and turned.

Need more . . . Not enough . . .

She forced open her eyes, the need for more energy a desperate survival instinct that drove her onward. She smiled, glad to see Ryan's lust-darkened eyes come into view as he lifted her so she faced him and could wrap her legs around his waist.

In one smooth motion, he impaled her on his cock, and she groaned as he filled her. Her sensitive breasts rasped against the crispy hairs on Ryan's chest, and she hissed as the sensation arrowed through her and straight to her over-sensitized clit.

She braced her arms around Ryan's neck and captured his lips. The tangy tastes of both male and female arousal and essence inside their joined mouths made her groan and gyrate faster against Ryan's cock.

However, Ryan didn't piston inside her as she wanted; instead, he reached around and grabbed her ass in both hands, spreading her wide and holding her up.

She stiffened and pulled back from Ryan as something soft and cool spread over the sensitive pucker of her ass.

"Relax," Ryan murmured as an intense tingling started at her ass and traveled outward to every part of her body.

Ponga fruit, her mind identified distantly as the intense sensations burned through her like lava.

More was spread forward over the soft skin where Ryan's cock joined with her pussy and then up farther to cover her clit and labia.

Then two large male hands reached between her and Ryan and smoothed more *ponga* over her breasts and belly.

Kiera gasped as the tingling spread like wildfire until she thought small electrodes had been implanted just underneath her skin, making her entire body a hair-trigger erogenous zone.

She reached down and grabbed the hand that had lathered her breasts with *ponga* and sucked each finger inside her mouth, cleaning them and welcoming the intense tingling onto her tongue and inside her mouth. The sweet nutty flavor burst inside her mouth even as her body roared to be filled with more and more energy.

The male groan from behind her blended with her own as well as Ryan's, and the pounding energy inside her took over.

She leaned forward to capture Ryan's lips and share the sweet, nutty *ponga* that still coated her tongue.

As their mouths met and she plunged inside, tasting him and exploring him with nips and licks, a cock nudged against her ass, making her gasp.

Ryan kissed her gently, his large hands still holding her spread while the man behind her slowly pushed inside her, stretching her wide and startling a long moan from her lips. A hard chest leaned flush against her back, bracketing her between the two men and wrapping her in a cocoon of warmth and hot arousal.

She relaxed into the sensation of being filled from both sides, allowing her body a moment to adjust to the new invasion while her clit throbbed, pushing her perilously close to her next orgasm.

Distantly, she noticed the sounds of flesh slapping against flesh nearby as well as moans and gasps, and her body wanted to be part of that cacophony, part of that energy generation.

"Fuck me." The words slipped through her lips like a plea, and instantly, both Ryan and whoever filled her from behind obliged.

Between them, as Ryan thrust deep, the cock in her ass would recede and then plunge forward as Ryan pulled out, so there was an alternating rhythm between them.

Never too much, but always pushing her higher and higher, that much closer to the energy that she needed . . . craved.

"Please . . ." The fevered plea sounded hoarse and scratchy in the humid air that surrounded them.

Kiera closed her eyes and relied on the two men to hold her up as they fucked her—faster and harder.

The entire world spiraled down to the sensations of her body being filled and refilled, the hard male bodies sandwiching her between them, the smell of sweat and sex and the strong hands that held her and the sounds of moans, grunts and gasps that surrounded her.

Tiny staticky sparks popped and sizzled along every inch of her skin and made her hair crackle and stand on end from the sudden charge in the air.

A feeling of anticipation built around them as all Kiera's muscles tightened, and she rushed headlong toward her impending climax.

Time slowed as the intense pleasure flowed through her body like thick sweet wine.

The intensity of the thrusts inside her and the frantic breathing that surrounded her told her the men were close as well.

She licked her lips, craving the hot taste of power and vigor that they could give her.

With a smile of anticipation, she opened her eyes to look at Ryan.

His eyes appeared entirely black with need swirling inside the dark depths. He opened his mouth, and she took it as an invitation.

She leaned forward and bit Ryan's bottom lip just hard enough to draw blood.

And then the world exploded in a shower of pink. . . .

As twin bursts of hot come spurted inside of her, power erupted upward as if geysered from a high-pressured torpedo.

Kiera's entire body convulsed as every inch of her experienced the most exquisite orgasm she could ever imagine. Her toes curled as spasms rocked her from the tip of her scalp down to her toes, each wave drowning her in lava-hot pleasure.

Her head was thrown back, and she cracked her skull against the man who still held her from behind, but the pain was no match for the sensations pouring through her and being sucked upward into the pink crystal that loomed on the cavern roof.

When energy continued to flow out of her in a steady stream, and her vision began to waver, with black spots forming in front of her like burn scars on a movie film, the wave of energy lessened but didn't stop.

Two staccato bursts of sound registered distantly, but her brain refused to process them further.

Both men pulled out of her, leaving her feeling empty, lonely and bereft.

Almost from outside herself, she noticed she was settled gently on her knees on the soft cushions, her hands closed around someone else's on either side.

She opened her eyes to see Alyssa and Katelyn kneeling

across from her, their hands joined in a circle just as they had started.

Movement from beyond the circle caught Kiera's attention and punched through the haze of sexual miasma she was still caught inside. She blinked hard to clear her vision and realized that a wall of very naked Klatch men surrounded them on all sides.

They were all erect and thick and stroking themselves while they stared at the three women kneeling in front of them.

"Close your eyes. Give yourself up to the vision," Katelyn mumbled, her words slightly slurred.

Kiera gave up fighting and allowed her eyes to slip closed as the meaning of "the warriors donating their essence" finally caught up with her.

But strangely, the thought of all these men coming against her naked skin broke a moan from her lips as she visualized all the power and energy the essence of these warriors could generate and how much healing could be spread.

The sound of flesh slapping against flesh increased around Kiera until it became just a dull roar of background noise underscoring the anticipation.

The first several cries startled Kiera, and she jumped as seconds later, hot essence hit the bare skin of her back and shoulders.

She stiffened as an electrical charge snaked through her as if she'd plugged herself into a high-voltage outlet back on Earth.

More and more jolts hit her in quick succession until her entire body stood straight and stiff on her knees, her teeth locked and her eyes shut tight against the current surging through her body.

The only thing that grounded her was the solid feel of Katelyn's and Alyssa's hands in hers.

A thousand flashes of pink light exploded inside her field of vision until she thought she was stuck in a room with a million flashing strobe lights. Dizziness threatened, and she swallowed hard as nausea churned inside her stomach.

Deep inside her core, she felt a light tug. She frowned as she realized the light tug was some type of invisible tether linking her with not only Tador, but with Katelyn and Alyssa.

The sudden warmth of belonging enveloped her like the gentle rays of sunshine after a long winter, and emotions choked her throat closed.

A sudden pink flash behind her eyelids nearly blinded her, then she was flying.

She, the queen and the Seer were still joined, but by more than just their hands. Their minds were merged. A sudden jarring vertigo sensation flashed through Kiera as three minds overlapped and joined like puzzle pieces that had finally found each other.

Their shouts of joy merged with her own as a dark marble of a planet with a tiny circle of blue and white formed below them as if they floated in outer space, examining it from above.

As one, they pointed toward the planet, and a thick surge of pink energy shot forward, engulfing the entire planet—nourishing, restoring and feeding.

The gentle, persistent tug of the planet absorbing the energy made Kiera feel like a mother breastfeeding her newborn—an exquisite pleasure totally unlike anything she'd ever known. The two minds joined with hers agreed with her analogy, and they shared the intimate sensations while the planet fed.

Slowly, the darkness of the surface bled away to be replaced by a brightening blue and white.

It's working!

Kiera wasn't sure if the words that echoed inside her mind were hers or one of the others, but she agreed with them, and her chest tightened as she watched Tador slowly recover.

A trickle of excitement curled through her as the darkness

inued to bleed away until the entire planet glowed with the ...gile blue of health and vitality.

Her joy slowly faded as she realized the progression of healing had stopped.

The orb turned slowly in front of them as if acceding to their will to see the entire surface.

No patches of inky blackness remained, but the planet was far from healthy.

Dread curled inside Kiera's stomach as she was plunged back inside her body with a sudden drop.

She blinked open her eyes and realized that every inch of her body ached with exhaustion.

She lay on her back, her fingers loosely linked with Kiera's and Alyssa's, but she'd given all her energy to the planet and had none left even to move.

"Summon Silas while we see to the women." King Stone's deep voice was colored with exhaustion, but it rang around the cavern with a force that said he expected to be obeyed.

It's time to bring back the Cunts, was the last thing she heard inside her mind before a comforting blackness engulfed her.

19

A spill of warm sunlight in combination with a purring weight on Kiera's chest woke her from her deep sleep.

She forced open her eyelids and blinked in an attempt to clear some of the orange haze from her vision. But then the orange haze shifted and her entire field of sight was filled with two orange unblinking eyes.

Still too tired to jump even though she was startled, she sighed. "Morning, Shiloh." A slow surge of relief swept through her, waking her further. If her father had worsened during the night, Shiloh wouldn't be happily purring on top of her chest.

She reached up and gently scratched behind one fuzzy orange ear, smiling as Shiloh's eyes closed in cat ecstasy and his purr volume jumped up to high.

"You're awake." The obvious relief in Ryan's voice made her frown.

She pushed up so she could lean against the headboard, which forced Shiloh to move. "Was there some reason you thought I wouldn't?"

Wispy memories of the Triangle Ceremony flashed through

mind like a slide show stuck on fast forward. Heat seared her cheeks as she was reminded of not only everything she had done, but also how much she had enjoyed it.

Hell, even thinking about it started a slow throbbing ache between her legs.

After that, she had vague recollections about Ryan carrying her to the baths, cleaning her up and then bringing her up to his bedroom and tucking her in, his comforting warmth curled beside her.

The bed dipped under Ryan's weight as he perched next to her. He brushed her hair away from her face as if he needed to reassure himself she was healthy and whole. The relief shining in his deep purple gaze was a sharp contrast to the dark circles riding just under his eyes. "All three of you have been out for the past three days. We were starting to wor—"

"Three days?" Kiera stiffened and internally took stock of her body. She felt surprisingly good for taking a three-day nap, and now that she thought about it, she wasn't sore—anywhere.

But something was definitely different. She closed her eyes and concentrated inward. The small stream of energy that had taken up residence inside her since she'd arrived had now turned into the Colorado River rapids. In fact, she felt as if there were enough energy inside her to provide orgasms to the entire planet and not just one family, as she'd done with Ryan's.

Her eyes snapped open as a slow breeze kicked up outside the open French doors that led to the patio. The trees began a soft *shushing*, and the wind brought the gentle rushing of the waterfall. "Did it work? Is the planet saved?"

Ryan took her hands in his, and her throat dropped into her stomach as she imagined the worst. "All the dead areas of the planet have been revived but not to full health, and we're not even sure that can be maintained." He squeezed her hands. "Before Alyssa left the ceremony, she called for some of the Cunt population to be reintroduced."

Kiera blew out a slow breath as her mind sifted through all that had happened. She knew she should be ecstatic, shouting from the rooftops that reunification would soon be a reality—even on a small scale. But after spending time here, she realized just how resistant the two races were and knew the most likely outcomes were more violence and mistrust on both sides.

She wasn't sure what made her look up, but when she did, she noticed Ryan watching her intently. Her gut clenched, and she braced for what came next. "What aren't you telling me?"

"Your father is awake."

Heat bloomed across her skin as she remembered Shiloh happily purring on her chest when she woke. She waited for the joy, the excitement or even the impulse to jump up and run to the man who had raised her even after her mother was killed.

After a few long moments, she realized those emotions weren't coming.

If only this would've happened before she'd seen those damned genealogy scrolls.

Her chest constricted as though someone had suddenly dropped a thousand-pound weight on top of her. Anger, hot and thick, percolated through her, making her adrenaline surge even as a howling wind suddenly beat against the windows and whipped the curtains into stinging lashes against the open French doors. The room suddenly plunged into near-darkness as if someone had blotted out the sun.

She glanced out toward the patio at the sudden changes that predicted a harsh storm.

Where the hell did that come from?

Ryan took Kiera's hand in his and raised her gaze to his. "I know this has to be difficult for you. We haven't really had time to talk much about the genealogy scrolls. But you need to calm down; your moods will now affect Tador." He glanced meaningfully out the window at the gathering storm.

Shock slapped at her like a large, open hand to the face,

ı instantly drained much of her anger away. A long few ᵤₑₓ ₙds later, the wind calmed, and the sun brightened some but not all the way.

Kiera blinked up at Ryan. "You mean—I did that?" She pointed out toward the hair-trigger weather just past the patio doors.

Ryan's gentle smile was all the answer she needed. "You, Alyssa and Katelyn now have a full symbiotic relationship with Tador. Alyssa woke up a few hours ago, sad at our lack of success, and it rained for forty-five minutes."

Kiera knew in other circumstances, she would laugh at the absurdity of the situation. But right now, there was too much on her mind to see any of this objectively. She huffed out a breath. "Well, then Tador had better get ready for a tornado, because it's time I went to see my dad." She pushed the covers down to free her feet, the cool air hitting her naked skin like a refreshing drink after a long drought.

"All three of them."

Gavin took a deep breath, concentrated and waved the portal behind the castle into existence in front of him.

Memories of the long ago destruction on this very spot tried to assault him, and he shoved them away to deal with later. For now he had work to do.

He turned to the line of guards and waiting Klatch. He was surprised at the general air of excitement that permeated the group. In his own grief, he had never stopped to consider that friends, lovers and even family members would've been torn apart by the mass deportation of the Cunts.

He sighed. Leave it to Cecily's daughter to have a broader view of the situation than he did. It was always so with Cecily, too. An unmistakable surge of pride swelled inside his chest. He was still coming to grips with the fact that she was his child—even with the strange situation of him being one of two fathers of record.

Not that he doubted the veracity of the scrolls—especially not after he had seen Alyssandra's daughter's name listed—a name that Alyssandra hadn't even shared with King Stone before that day. He accepted stranger things every day in the guise of magic, so this was no different. However, that brought the additional problem that he wasn't sure what to say to Kiera, or to Marco, about any of it, so he had steered clear, hoping something profound would come to him.

He shook his head. *Stop woolgathering and get to work!* he scolded himself. This entire plan had so many possible risks that it made his head throb. But Alyssandra was the reigning queen, and he trusted her judgment. He just wished he would've been allowed to approve the list of Cunts coming through the portal rather than leaving that choice purely up to Silas.

He took a deep breath and said a silent prayer to the universe that this plan would work and Tador would be saved. "Marco will come through first as agreed. And then the invited Cunt families accompanied by Silas." He paused and met as many gazes as he could within the crowd before continuing. "The survival of Tador depends on the success of the queen's plan. So if anyone of either race makes a hostile action—the guards will kill them before they compromise us all."

The guards nodded, and the crowd grew silent at his dire words.

Gavin stood at the mouth of the portal peering inside the *between*, searching for any sign of Marco. An unfamiliar sensation curling inside him made him examine it closer—anticipation.

He shook his head. If everything worked as they'd planned, Marco would live on Tador permanently. Gavin was surprised to admit that he'd missed the man. Even after the betrayals and the hurts, he and Marco had grown up with the friendship and closeness of brothers, and something inside Gavin recognized his

ng to have that back. And now with both of them having a
p̤ ̤ntal tie to Kiera, they would have to work out the past so it
didn't affect their daughter's future.

A flash of white caught Gavin's attention, and he held up his
hand to signal the guards that all was well.

A few long moments later, Marco stepped through the portal and onto Tador wearing dark slacks and a button-down
shirt. The long white-blond ponytail captured at the back of his
neck looked out of place on someone attired so professionally.

The blue eyes that Gavin remembered well glistened with
moisture, and Marco held out his hand to Gavin.

After a long moment, where Gavin debated propriety against
a show of acceptance, he shook Marco's hand.

Marco smiled, his features reserved but unable to hide the
awe in his expression. "I never thought you would willingly
open a portal for me and my kind again." He dropped to his
knees in front of Gavin and pressed their joined hands to his
forehead. "I swear on my life I will never abuse the trust that
you and the queen have so freely given."

Thick emotions threatened to close Gavin's throat, and he
breathed deep to clear them. He glanced around self-consciously,
noting Katelyn, the Seer, standing just at the edge of the assembled group, her eyes wide, her brow furrowed.

He turned his attention back to the man in front of him.
"Stand up and give me back my hand, you daft bastard. We
have work to do." He was glad his voice came out gruff instead
of shaky and emotional.

Marco stood and faced him, a smile of relief on his chiseled
features.

Gavin pinned Marco with an intense stare. "Besides, if you
ever betray us again, I'll let the queen, the Seer and the Healer
have your hide, and I won't pity you the fate in store for you."

Marco turned his head and locked gazes with the Seer, and
Gavin could've sworn something passed between them. One of

Marco's blond eyebrows rose and a rogue's smile curved his lips.

Katelyn's gaze narrowed, and she raised her chin—a defiant gesture.

Before Gavin could examine the ramifications more closely, Marco turned back to face him. "As I said, I will never give you cause again. But first, let's make sure this plan of Alyssandra's works, shall we?"

Several long moments later, fuzzy shapes appeared inside the *between* off in the distance. As they neared, Gavin was surprised to note that he knew them—or nearly all of them. These were men and women he'd grown up with, laughed with and some he had even dallied with upon occasion.

Silas came first, and after shaking both Gavin's and Marco's hands, he stepped off to the side and allowed those behind him to come through.

As each Cunt stepped through the portal and onto the grassy ground of the back castle courtyard, tears filled their eyes, and they either shook hands with Gavin or threw their arms around his neck to capture him in a tight embrace, which threatened his composure each and every time.

Marco and Silas weren't exempt from this treatment where they stood next to Gavin, and only when the newcomers had paid their respects did they rush forward to greet their waiting friends and extended families.

The stream of Cunts seemed endless as Gavin saw people he hadn't seen since that fateful day when he closed the portal behind them. The general plan might be to reintroduce native beings onto Tador, but it also had the happy effect of peeling away scarred pieces of Gavin's emotions and salving them with healing happiness.

"It's okay to cry, Gavin. I wouldn't blame you a bit."

The queen's voice from just beside him startled him. He

turned to see Alyssa peeking through the gap between his elbow and Marco's.

Icy panic filled him thick and bright. The queen had agreed to stay out of sight. "Alyssandra! What the hell are you doing out here?" As soon as the words left his lips, he cursed. Who was he to speak to the queen in such a way?

Marco stepped aside and let Alyssandra through; King Stone ranged just behind her.

The crowd instantly stilled, and in recognition of the queen and king, dropped to their knees, Klatch and Cunt alike—all except for Gavin, Marco and Stone.

Alyssa waved his reaction away. "This is my plan, and I refuse to be shut away upstairs like some porcelain doll in a tower." She turned her imperious gaze toward King Stone, who still stood stone-faced behind her. Which clearly told Gavin, Stone had already lost the battle—barely—and Gavin could only make the best of it.

Alyssandra smiled at the kneeling crowd. "Please, rise. There will be plenty of time for all of that later. Right now, let's get everyone back home where they belong, so we can move on to the next phase."

The unspoken words, "Before the Klatch who are totally against us realize what we are up to and make trouble," hung in the air between them. Ninety-nine percent of the Klatch decided they would rather have Tador back at full strength than nurse their grudge over the Cunt rebellion—especially since Alyssandra's plan would offer them some form of retribution for those who had caused it. But as in any group, there were also those who refused to give up their hatred and waited only for their chance to cause mischief.

Slowly, everyone rose to their feet as Alyssa motioned those still inside the *between* to continue to move forward. She took her place among the small receiving line as did Stone, and despite all the tearful reunions, the line continued to snake forward at a brisk pace.

Gavin cast a sideways glance at Stone, and they shared a long-suffering look of men who had to deal with headstrong women. Gavin was the first to offer a grudging smile, which Stone and even Marco returned.

Gavin already respected Alyssandra as a leader and a fearless advocate for her people. But placing herself at risk by welcoming back the Cunts raised her even higher in his esteem.

He sent another silent prayer to the universe that phase two of the plan would go as smoothly as phase one.

Kiera steeled herself as her fingers closed around the doorknob to the room where her father stayed.

Ryan's comforting presence loomed just behind her, but even with that, it was difficult to make her wrist turn on the knob and push open the door.

Why couldn't he have woken before I saw that genealogy?

When she finally forced herself to open the door through pure willpower, familiar, booming laughter was the first sound that reached her. The door swung inward, and she stared, frozen in place.

Her father sat up on the bed, wearing a tunic and trousers much like those worn by Ryan. Except for the clothing and the location, he looked just as she remembered him the last time she had seen him before finding him on the floor injured.

How was this possible? Even after the healing session with the queen and the Seer, he hadn't looked this recovered. Maybe the healing of the planet after the Triangle ceremony had given her father an extra healing boost as well.

Shiloh was busy chin marking his knees and head butting her father's hand for more attention, and Kiera took a moment to drink in the sight of both of them.

She inhaled on a shaky sigh as thick emotions welled up, filling her chest and throat until she thought she might explode from the pressure.

He turned, and she knew the minute he caught sight of her by the way his entire face lit as a smile curved his lips and his brown eyes danced with joy. "Kiera!"

She only had time to blink before he was up off the bed, across the room and had pulled her into his familiar embrace.

The male scent uniquely her father's filled her senses, relaxing her tight muscles and loosing the tears she hadn't realized were there to shed. The only thing missing was the chocolate-cherry smell that always clung to him after he'd smoked his favorite cigars.

She promised herself she would find some for him soon.

Kiera inhaled a watery breath and wrapped her arms around him, clutching him tight to her as an endless stream of different emotions flowed through her—each more confusing than the last.

"Damn, it's good to be awake and back among the living again." He stroked his large palm over her hair like he'd done when she was a child, and she buried her face against his tunic as large sobs wracked her body.

He held her, with Shiloh twining around her ankles, his hands stroking her hair and telling her that everything was fine.

With each tear that escaped, a little of the bitter sadness and fear inside her escaped as well.

When she had finally cried herself out, her insides felt empty and hollow. She squeezed his large muscular frame one last time before she pulled back to look up at him. "Dad. I missed you."

He laughed and led her over to the bed to sit down.

"You must be Ryan."

Kiera startled as she realized she had forgotten all about Ryan following her into the room.

"Please call me David." Her father stood and shook Ryan's

hand. "I've heard you've taken good care of my Kiera. It's appreciated."

Ryan nodded, his hair streaming over his shoulders instead of covering his previously scarred cheek. "Yes, sir. It's been my pleasure." He dropped his hand to his side and sent a reassuring smile toward Kiera before returning his attention to her father. "We'll have time to talk later. I'll get some food and drink sent up so you and your daughter can catch up. I'll be next door if either of you need me."

The door clicking shut behind Ryan sounded loud in the still quiet of the room.

Kiera took a deep breath and let it out slowly. "So . . ." The word "dad" died inside her throat. "How do you feel? Any muscle weakness, dizziness, disorientation?"

He sat beside her, the bed dipping under his weight, and Shiloh jumped up to curl between them. "I'm fine, so let's cut all the bullshit, shall we?" His wide smile and the concern filling his hazel eyes told her he already knew about the scrolls and was worried about her reaction.

"How long have you known?" Her voice was steady, and she wondered why she had ever worried about talking to the man she still thought of as her father about anything.

He cupped her cheek in his large hand—something he had done as long as she could remember. "I knew your mother was pregnant with you when we met." He dropped his hand and started to absently scratch Shiloh's fuzzy head.

Surprise was like a sucker punch to the gut. "Did you also know about Marco and Gavin?"

He nodded. "The military has known we coexist with several other species for years—and that means many more beyond even the Klatch and Cunts. So when I met your mother, her heritage wasn't a big shock, but falling for her hard and fast was."

Kiera frowned at the knowledge that there were even more

species on Earth besides the humans, Klatch and Cunts. She would have to mull that piece of information over later. "Why didn't you ever tell me? About my true parentage, not the species."

A long sigh escaped him, and his gaze wandered as if he was reliving the past inside his mind. "Things were too dangerous for you to be too closely allied with either side. On one hand, as the daughter of the head of the Cunt Council, you could be used as a bargaining chip. On the other hand, as the daughter of the head of the Klatch guard but a woman who looked like a full-blood Cunt, you wouldn't be welcomed on Tador." He captured her hand in his and squeezed. "Ironic, isn't it? As the daughter of a simple human, you were relatively safe on the fringes of all three societies, regardless if you knew it or not."

A low chuckle sounded from his throat. "And besides, I still love you as if you were mine alone." His gaze remained on Shiloh as if he were afraid to look at her after such a statement. "I'm grateful to both of those men and your mother for allowing me to have you for all those years, and I hope to have the chance to meet Marco and Gavin while I'm here."

Kiera leaned over and brushed a kiss across her dad's cheek before resting her forehead against his shoulder. "I'm so glad you're back."

He gently took her chin between his fingers and raised her head so she faced him. "And that's it? No more questions?"

She smiled as he dropped his hand from her chin. "I'm sure more will come, but for now, I'm just happy you're awake and well and that there's a chance of reunifying Tador."

"Your mom would've liked knowing that," he agreed. "In fact, I'm surprised you're not down there right now."

She stiffened, her brow furrowing as she frowned. "Down where?"

"From what that pretty little lady's maid told me, there are a bunch of the friendly Cunts coming through the portals right now, and then later today is when the real battle begins."

"I just woke up. I—" She broke off, warring between the desire to sprint downstairs and the need to be here with her father.

He smiled and kissed her on the cheek. "Go. I'll be here when you get back."

Excitement and anticipation swirled inside her chest and stomach as she threw her arms around her father's thick neck and squeezed. "You always did know me well. I'll be back. Love you!"

She ran across the room, nearly running down Sasha who had brought a tray of food up for them.

Her father's booming laugh followed her out of the room.

She whipped to the right toward the stairs and ran face-first into a hard, unforgiving surface that made an "oof" noise as she impacted.

Strong hands grabbed her shoulders and steadied her.

Ryan's dark gaze burned into hers. "I thought we had more time, but we need to move now. Get your fighting gear on and meet me on the back steps of the castle."

20

Kiera burst out the back doors of the castle, down the steps and into the middle of what seemed like an endless sea of Klatch and Cunts—many who she recognized from both Earth and her time on Tador.

"Get her out of the way and bring her up to speed—fast." This from Ryan to Alyssa and Katelyn.

The queen and Seer grabbed Kiera's arms and pulled her back toward the castle steps.

"Hey," she managed while she stumbled backward in their grip. "Does someone want to tell me what the hell is going on?

Alyssa glanced at Katelyn. "I'll concentrate on shielding while you fill her in." The queen closed her eyes, and Kiera turned her attention to Katelyn.

"Well?"

"Okay." Katelyn pinned Kiera with an intense green gaze. "We thought we had more time—like another day or so, but the information must've been leaked to Sela early." She blew out a long breath. "All three of us just woke up this morning, so we aren't even sure what we can do with our Triangle powers yet—other than the whole effect on the weather thing. But the general plan is that Silas handpicked Cunt families loyal to Tador and brought them back through the *between*. That's been going on for the past six hours and just now finished." Katelyn gestured around her, and Kiera finally realized that the milling crowd of thousands were busy forming a dense circle around the still-open portal.

"And?" Kiera prompted.

"And we let Sela find the information that we were opening the borders of Tador to certain Cunt families, in hopes that she and her army of guards would come through and attack."

"Are you insane?" Shock and outrage warred inside Kiera, causing her stomach to roil as fear churned through her. "You're inviting another war? What—"

"Listen," Katelyn interrupted. "Alyssa can shield the group here now—apparently she's done something similar even before the Triangle. And then we let Sela's group attack with their energy bolts while the guards protect everyone from hand-to-hand assault."

"But—" Kiera trailed off once again as understanding crystallized. "And since the new Healer—aka, me—is something of a battery cell when hit with energy bursts, I attack Sela and her group and get them to hit me with their best shot. . . ." The idea took root as she rolled it around inside her mind.

"Exactly. And the extra energy you collect, Alyssa and I help you funnel back into Tador."

Kiera's dread morphed into determination, and adrenaline surged as she readied for the fight of her life. "Damn, I'm glad Ryan told me to suit up." She ran her hands over her black vest, which housed throwing stars, daggers and anything else she had in her gun duffel besides guns.

In light of her enemy's resistance to bullets—especially since they wanted to invite energy exchanges, not discourage them by killing the source—she had left those out of her arsenal.

Movement at the top of the stairs caught Kiera's attention, and she glanced up to see her father jogging down the stairs, his tunic bulkier than it had been when she met with him upstairs. Without even checking, she knew he was armed—most likely with enough equipment to infiltrate a small terrorist cell single-handedly.

A thin thread of fear surged through her. Her father was highly trained in hand-to-hand combat, but he'd just recovered from a coma—miraculous Cunt and Klatch healing or not. "Where do you think you're going? You just woke up. I don't want to lose you all over again."

He winked at her as he tucked the leg of his trousers inside his boot to give him ready access to the wicked-looking Bowie knife that rested there. "I think I'm going to fight, my girl." He held up a hand, which succeeded in cutting off her outburst of denial. "This fight needs winning, and thanks to you and these two lovely ladies"—he gestured to the Seer and the queen, who still stood with her eyes closed—"I'm able to fight again." He straightened and reached out to cup her cheek. "I love you more than my own life, Kiera, but not enough to turn my back on what's right and sit on my ass up in the room when I know I can help down here."

Kiera read the determination in his eyes and sighed in defeat.

"Incoming!" Gavin's voice boomed across the clearing as he made a beeline toward them, with Marco close behind him. The guard approached Kiera's father but then stopped short. "David." He nodded. "It's been a long time."

Her father nodded in return. "It has. But there will be time for catching up later. Let's kick some ass."

"Are you at full strength?" Gavin stood his ground as Kiera's father scowled down at him from his perch behind Kiera on the steps.

"You don't worry about me. I may not be able to cast, but I

can handle anything hand to hand or even longer range with some daggers or throwing stars."

Alyssa's eyes snapped open, her lavender gaze intense. "The shields are in place, the best I can make them."

Ryan squeezed Kiera's shoulder as he addressed the others. "David, you and Grayson cover the Seer. She has no magical defensive abilities, but we need her to help with—"

The sky darkened suddenly, and a bolt of lightning hit just outside the circle of gathered Klatch and Cunts. The metallic stench of burning ozone filled the air, tickling Kiera's nose and nearly making her sneeze.

One look at Katelyn, and Kiera knew their new ability to affect the weather was in full force.

The Seer's eyes narrowed and anger poured off her in nearly visible waves. "I'm not some helpless little girl to stand in the background while all of you—"

"Katelyn," Kiera interrupted. "Stay pissed off."

The Seer's mouth opened, most likely to object, and Kiera cut her off by gesturing around them at the churning weather. "The weather can only help us at this stage."

Katelyn's green eyes sparked with anger and understanding. She nodded, her eyes narrowed with determination. "No problem at all. I still owe those bastards for kidnapping me and trashing my store."

Kiera's father cleared his throat and pierced Ryan with a laser-intense gaze. "No offense to the Seer, but I'm not sure I want to trust my daughter's safety to others."

Gavin stepped forward. "My place is beside the queen along with King Stone. But I trained Ryan myself and know exactly what Marco is capable of, as do you. I would never knowingly endanger her."

The two men held each other's gaze for a long moment—measuring and evaluating—as the tension around them mounted. Finally, David smiled and turned to Marco and Ryan. "You two better give me your word you'll protect her from everything except energy blasts." He pointed one beefy finger at each of the men in turn. "Got it? I don't want to see so much as a broken fingernail on her when this is done."

Kiera's anger flashed hot and bright, and a sudden howling wind surged around them, whipping clothes against bodies and hair against faces with stinging slaps. A few sizzling bolts of lightning accompanied the building storm. "All of you can stand down from your pissing contest. I appreciate the backup, but I'm perfectly capable of taking care of myself." She turned her glare on her father, then Ryan, Marco and Gavin. "As all of you well know."

She fisted her hands on her hips. "So, watch my ass, and stay out of the path of my blades, and we'll come out of this just fine."

Sela's gaze roamed over her gathered warriors—a shadowy sea of bodies in the stingy moonlight. A slow smile spread across her face as anticipation grew inside her gut.

Finally, Tador would be hers to rule.

A throaty laugh spilled from her lips as she motioned her new second in command forward. "You." She wouldn't bother to learn his name until he proved himself worthy. He was tall and muscular, with his white-blond hair spilling over a set of very impressive shoulders. However, Sela had learned her lesson about becoming distracted by the eye candy around her. "Let's go."

The man stepped forward and waved his hand in front of him.

A shimmering portal formed, at first only the size of a baseball, but the sparkling silver particles rapidly grew wider until even the tallest of her warriors could enter without stooping.

Her second in command pointed to five warriors near the

front to precede Sela into the *between*, and once they had entered, motioned for Sela that it was safe for her to enter as well.

As instructed, the guards in front of her, as well as those behind her, jogged their way across the icy barren stretch of the *between*. The less time spent in the energy-sucking void, the more vigor they would have to fight with on the other side.

When they reached the end of the portal, Sela expected to see the bright sunlight of Tador, since that planet was on an opposite schedule from Earth. However, the muted light of dusk and bad weather met her instead.

"What the hell have they done to my planet?" She ground her teeth. Her source had advised the Triangle Ceremony was complete. Apparently, that wasn't enough to restore the planet.

Win control first, then a solution can be found.

"Go," she shouted, giving the signal for the warriors in front of her to spill out onto Tador, taking down anyone in their path.

She followed them out into the churning, wind-whipped landscape of Tador.

Quick flashes of lightning illuminated a sea of milling Klatch and Cunts, but the storm wouldn't allow her to make out any details. Her palms itched as power built inside her, waiting to burst forth.

She jogged forward and opened her palms. Bright electric blue current spilled from her fingertips and sizzled along an invisible wall in front of her targets.

"What the hell?"

Sela's anger ratcheted her power higher, and she allowed the pure power to flow through her body and erupt from her fingertips once more.

The invisible wall sparked and crackled as her energy hit, but not one of her targets screamed or fell.

She whipped around to see her guards either having the same results or engaged in hand-to-hand combat with several Klatch guards—and two Cunts she immediately recognized.

Sela's eyes narrowed as she saw Marco and Kiera Matthews—Cecily's daughter.

The doctor was dressed in black ops military fatigues and was busy downing Cunt guards as if they were made of tissue paper instead of flesh and bone. Marco fought back to back with her, not only holding his own, but easily defeating any of Sela's Cunt warriors who came forward to threaten him or Kiera.

Anger spilled through Sela in a fiery rush. "Fucking traitor!" With her murderous gaze intent on Marco, she started forward.

A quick flash of a fist was the only warning Sela received before pain sliced through her jaw, forcing her teeth to clack together and her head to snap back.

The hot metallic taste of her own blood burst over her tongue, and she whipped around, ready to defend herself from attack.

Katelyn, the Seer who had escaped her, stood before her, with Prince Grayson and Cecily's damned human protecting her back.

"Welcome to Tador, Sela." Katelyn's smile could only be described as predatory as she stood calmly while Grayson and the human fought at her back.

In an instant, Sela's anticipation of victory was back. She raised her hands and unleashed the full dose of fury into her energy beam aimed directly at Katelyn's chest. The tingling blue beam engulfed the Seer but never dampened the taunting smile that still curved the bitch's lips.

All around Sela, the sounds of battle raged, interspersed with the sizzling crack of thunder, lightning strikes and the howling wind.

A slow trickle of unease wormed its way through Sela's anger. Something was wrong here.

This was no surprise attack as she had envisioned. Instead, this felt more like an ambush.

Her beam of energy cut off abruptly, and she kicked forward suddenly, hitting the Seer squarely in the stomach and doubling her over onto the ground.

Sela dodged to the side, away from Marco and Kiera and directly toward her second in command. "Retreat! It's a trap."

Without waiting to see if the man carried out her orders, self-preservation had Sela fighting her way toward the shimmering oval of the still-open portal.

Just as she fought her way nearly to the silver opening, it fizzled and seemed to float away toward the other side of the clearing.

Sela cursed as her brow furrowed. "What the fuck? That's not possible."

Kiera ducked under a sucker punch and shot a quick kick forward to connect squarely with the Cunt warrior's crotch.

The man crumpled, and she jumped to the side so she wasn't caught under his large body. Then she stepped over him toward the next.

A flash of silver shimmer moving around the clearing sporadically made her smile. Apparently, Katelyn was having fun with another group vision, making the portal appear to move before anyone could reach it, when in reality, Gavin had closed it as soon as the small contingent of Klatch guards had ensured all of Sela's resistance force had exited onto Tador. After all, they needed to keep the energy here, not let it all escape back toward Earth.

As the "portal" streaked by again, Kiera caught sight of Sela. She pointed toward the Cunt queen, and both Marco and Ryan nodded.

She made her way toward Sela, dodging fights and allowing Marco and Ryan to protect her back.

Just as she stepped behind Sela, the queen whipped around, blue energy already sizzling from her fingertips.

The beam of energy hit Kiera in a rush and ripped a surprised gasp from her throat.

Sela was extremely powerful, and the energy beam was so concentrated that it was like filling a water balloon with a fire hose.

Kiera opened her arms wide even as she opened her senses. The ropelike bonds that now existed inside her, tethering her to Alyssa and Katelyn, quivered as the energy poured along them and into the other two women.

Now! Kiera sent out the thought, knowing that at least the queen, the Seer and Ryan would hear it and signal everyone else.

In the next instant, thousands of energy beams hit her body like splashes of bracing cold water against her skin.

Her hair crackled around her body as a laugh bubbled up from deep inside her and spilled around her into the raging storm.

Kiera pictured her body sucking the blue energy out of Sela and the combined energy from all the other beams working like a giant straw to funnel energy out into the queen and the Seer and ultimately down into the planet below her feet.

Distantly, she noticed the storm around them lessening and the warm rays of sunlight spilling over her, warming her.

A sudden wrenching sensation tipped her stomach until she thought she might throw up. She swallowed hard as vertigo gripped her. Kiera sucked in a breath against the onslaught of sensations, but just as she thought she might black out, her vision steadied, and she hovered above the shining marble that was Tador. She felt more than saw Alyssa and Katelyn beside her—their comforting thoughts easily fitting with hers.

As one mind, they poured their newfound energy into the planet. They aimed their focus deep inside the core of the planet, healing from the inside out.

Slowly the planet began to brighten and glow with warmth

and health, and still Kiera continued to suck energy from the powerful source which offered it.

A long shriek of terror and pain registered in the back of her mind, but Kiera kept her attention firmly on the planet.

Finally, the draw on the offered energy lessened and then stopped, as if Tador had enough and was now happily sated.

Triumph and elation flowed through the three minds, which overlapped inside Kiera's consciousness.

Another sharp tug of vertigo, and then Kiera felt as if someone had tossed her mind back inside her body like a fast-pitched baseball into a net. She groaned as her eyes fluttered open, and she winced away from the bright sunlight that nearly blinded her.

Silence reigned around her as if the entire planet held its breath to see the effect of their efforts.

Kiera pushed herself up to sit and glance around her as her eyes adjusted.

Sela lay a few feet away from her, dazed but not dead. Several Cunt warriors lay on the ground, no doubt brought down in the battle, but while wounds had been incurred, Kiera was sure the mega dose of healing for Tador had probably healed them as well.

A quick glance around her showed the milling wall of Cunts and Klatch glancing in awe, slowly dispersing until she could see the lush greenery of trees and plants as far as the eye could see.

Ryan and Marco sat behind her. Both men still looked a bit dazed, but they smiled at her. She opened her mouth to ask them if they had seen her father when their expressions hardened, and Kiera whipped around in time to see Sela lunge at her throat with a knife.

A feral screech filled the air as an orange blur hit the side of Sela's neck hard, knocking her to the ground and loosening the knife from her fingers.

Before Kiera could dart forward to help Shiloh, her father loomed large in front of her, his movements a blur.

When he slowly stood and moved aside, Sela's motionless form remained on the grass—her eyes open and staring, her neck tipped at an odd angle and nothing but a mass of bloody furrows from Shiloh's claws.

21

———

Kiera jogged through the maze just ahead of Ryan with a grin on her face. In the month since Tador's return to its former glory, Ryan had been true to his word and allowed her to explore every part of the planet.

The maze and its outlets of pools and offshoots had become a favorite hideaway for both of them. Granted, it had taken weeks for them to find homes for the newly replanted Cunts and to weed out those who would have continued to cause unrest.

However, with Sela's death and Marco's strong leadership, most of the remaining Cunts were more than happy to be welcomed back to the paradise that Tador had returned to.

Strong arms snaked around Kiera's waist, yanking her backward. "Got you."

Kiera laughed even as she squirmed in his hold.

Ryan lowered her so her feet touched the ground.

She immediately turned to face him, captured his face in her palms, and his lips with hers.

Ryan's warm hands cupped her ass, pulling her close against the hard length of his cock, which strained inside his breeches.

Kiera nipped his bottom lip and pulled back to look up into his dark purple gaze. A now-familiar warmth filled her chest for the man in front of her, daring her to deny its existence. She blew out a slow breath before speaking. "So are you going to mate or marry me, or whatever the hell you call it here on Tador?"

A flash of surprise chased across Ryan's features, and then a throaty laugh spilled from his lips. "I was only waiting for you to be ready, my little Healer."

She smirked. "I can't believe I'm saying this. In fact, I'm surprised I would want it at all, but I'm damned well past ready."

The thick emotion swelled into her throat as if in accusation. "Well, it seems I've gone and fallen in love with a pain-in-the-ass Klatch prince, so I might as well go all the way, right?"

All humor drained from Ryan's face, and for once, he seemed too shocked to remember to tip his hair forward to hide his now-healed scar.

Kiera's stomach clenched as she suddenly wished she could call the words back. She had thought—well, at least hoped—that Ryan felt the same way.

"Could you say that again?" The deep vulnerability in Ryan's soft voice sent a wash of relief through her. Apparently, his reaction was shock and not discomfort.

Kiera lifted her chin and met his guarded gaze. "I love you, Ryan." She blinked hard as tears stung the backs of her eyes. "I'm not sure how or when it happened, I just—"

A slow smile spread across Ryan's chiseled features as he closed the distance between them, his arms enveloping her and holding her close as his lips captured hers. He kissed her gently—almost reverently.

She had her answer—even if he never said it; she knew, and that was enough.

Kiera buried her fingers in the warmth of his long dark hair as she melted against him, the thick emotion spilled through every inch of her, warming her and filling her with happiness. As she'd started to tell Ryan, she wasn't sure how or when it happened, but she loved this man with an intensity she never thought possible. She loved him enough to crave marriage, children and all that went with it—as soon as possible.

Ryan gently broke their kiss with a reluctant slide of his lips across hers. He leaned his forehead against hers, their noses brushing against each other. "I'd convinced myself that knowing how you felt was enough, that I didn't need to hear you say it. But hearing those words makes it so much sweeter." A shaky laugh escaped him. "I love you with all my heart, Kiera Matthews, and I'll marry you right now if you'll have me."

Love swelled inside Kiera until she thought she wouldn't be able to contain it all. When the warmth spilled over, heating her face and swelling her chest, tears spilled down her cheeks, and she gave him a watery smile. "I think I might need you to say that again, too."

He brushed her hair away from her face and cupped her cheeks in his large palms. "I love you." He laughed as she closed her eyes to savor his words. "You do realize the mating ceremony is done entirely naked and will be witnessed by all the people of Tador?"

Kiera's brow furrowed as she imagined standing naked for everyone to see. She shrugged as the idea took shape inside her mind. "None of my three fathers can watch me get married naked." She wrinkled her nose. "Way too awkward."

As strange as it had all seemed at first, the letters Marco had given her from her mother had shed only partial light on the situation of her three fathers. Both Marco and Gavin had been with Cecily repeatedly around the date of conception, so no one could be sure who gave the deciding sperm—except that the magical genealogy scrolls they found still insisted both men contributed.

Kiera had come to terms with having three fathers regardless of the part each of them played in her biology, and she looked forward to building a relationship with each of them based on her new understanding.

"Totally understandable." Ryan picked her up, and she wrapped her legs around his waist, rubbing her aching core shamelessly against his thick cock. "I don't think I'll want to watch any daughter of ours marry naked either."

"Understandable," she murmured against his lips. "In that case, we'd better get married soon since those daughters may have a head start on us."

Ryan pulled back enough to look into her face. "Are you trying to tell me something?"

The blatant note of hope in his voice made her laugh. "No. Not yet. But it can't hurt to be prepared, right?" She leaned forward and ran a line of open-mouthed kisses down the side of his neck, enjoying the way his cock swelled even further between them as Ryan gasped.

"Temptress. We are supposed to meet with the others at the waterfall, and you're distracting me—again."

Kiera sighed. She supposed four times in the last two hours was pushing things when they were already an hour late meeting everyone. But her throbbing pussy and aching breasts disagreed with her logic. Ryan was right, but she didn't have to like it.

Kiera sighed as she unwrapped her legs from his waist, stood and grabbed his hand. "Then let's hurry and get this meeting over with so we can come back here and finish what we started—just before our mating ceremony."

He laughed but nodded his consent to her plan. "Let's go."

When they spilled out of the edge of the maze still giggling like guilty children, they discovered a picnic already spread out in front of the large waterfall.

Kiera stopped short, and Ryan nearly ran into her.

All her life she had convinced herself that she didn't mind being on the fringes and never quite fitting in with either the Cunts or the humans. But now, as she glanced around at the scene in front of her, she knew she was part of something even more close-knit than a family—and even better yet, she belonged.

She smiled as her gaze raked over the scene in front of her.

Alyssa's head lay on Stone's lap, her ever-expanding stomach showing the future queen was closer to being born with each passing day. Katelyn sat nearby, laughing as Shiloh chased butterflies that flew just above his reach.

Grayson, Marco, Gavin and David—as she'd begun to call her father, now that she had three—all sat talking, laughing and eating. Silas and the five council members milled around the water's edge, along with a mixture of Klatch and Cunts. A warm breeze rustled the trees and grasses and blended with the soft *whooshing* of the waterfall to make a utopian scene right out of a Norman Rockwell painting.

Thick emotions welled, nearly closing Kiera's throat and making her swallow hard against them. This was her mother's vision. A united Tador. Cunts and Klatch living together as one.

"I wish you could see this, Mom," she whispered. Tears stung the backs of her eyes, and she blinked them away.

Ryan wrapped his arms around her, his chin resting on her shoulder. "You had a hand in this, my little Healer. Your mother would be proud." He chuckled, his warm breath feathering against her neck and sending a wash of gooseflesh marching over her. "As are your three fathers."

Kiera swallowed hard before speaking, hoping her voice wouldn't tremble. "Let's go enjoy our success, shall we?"

Shiloh streaked between Kiera's feet into the maze, nearly toppling her over.

Her muffled curse must've caught the group's attention, because all three of her fathers smiled at her and motioned her forward.

"Damn cat." She smiled with affection at the orange feline before she started toward the happily ever after she'd always hoped for.